06/08 JBD

Jem (and Sam)

Jem (and Sam)

a novel

Ferdinand Mount

Carroll & Graf Publishers, Inc.
New York

First Carroll & Graf edition 1999

Caroll & Graf Publishers, Inc.
19 West 21st Street
New York, NY 10010-6805

Library of Congress Cataloging-in-Publication Data is available.
ISBN: 0-7867-0649-X

Manufactured in the United States of America

Everyone born in Kent is born free.

Statutes of the Realm of Edward I

God taketh no notice of our prayers.

The Acts of the Witness of the Spirit of Lodowick Muggleton

Copperas or Green Vitriol is a mineral substance, formed by the decomposition of pyrites. Its colour is bright green, and its taste very astringent.

The British Cyclopedia

Introduction

When a clerk working for the Great Western Railway dropped a half-finished cigarette in the waste-paper basket in my uncle's study (his house being requisitioned 'for the duration' as the railway's regional office), among the things that were badly scorched in the consequent inferno were all the records of the family, the various houses they had occupied, built or knocked down, and the business which they had sustained with ever slackening attention for more than two centuries: Mount & Page of Tower Hill, stationers, marine map-makers, booksellers and, with whatever cash they had managed to squeeze out of these lines, investors in anything going from soap to — well, in this age of openness let us have it out — slaves. Even before they were so singed, these plump bundles of paper had long since ceased to tickle our failing curiosity (I speak collectively, I was five and a half at the time) and they were shipped off to the County Record Office, where they lay undisturbed giving off that dismal odour of half-burnt things for fifty years or so.

It was not until a cold spring day in 1994 — I was watching one of the Cup semi-finals — that the telephone rang and an eager voice announced himself as the Assistant Archivist at the Kent Record Office and he had some exciting information for me if he was speaking to the right person. I didn't catch his name because of the football commentary. When I switched it off, the commentary went on at the other end, and I could not help remarking that the information couldn't be that exciting if he was watching the match at the same time.

He laughed and said that he always had to do two things at the same time, it was the only way he could keep out of mischief. This was the beginning of my friendship with Derek Olaf Dupree ('Doddy'), my fellow editor and archivist *extraordinaire*, to whom this present volume is dedicated.

Somehow he persuaded me over the phone that it would be worth making the pilgrimage to Canterbury to view his discovery. When I came into his frowsty cubby-hole somewhere below the main reading-room, he had it there waiting for me: a dumpy box, of oak he said, about twenty inches in each of its dimensions.

'Key?'

'No need, the fire burnt the wood off the hinges. I've left it all just as I found it, in the reserve store where I do a bit of fossicking about at weekends. It was too big to fit in the ordinary files so they just shoved it down there. There was a lot of chaos after the war and the bombing.'

He stood back to allow me to open the box, his bustling figure stilled into a kind of reverence which he could not resist breaking into with:

'There now – the memoirs of your forebear Jeremiah Mount. Or memorials, they would have said then.'

I took out one of the large brown leather ledgers which were piled in pairs and almost square. It was burnt at the edges, but the writing on the pages was mostly undamaged: a neat hand but so small as to be nearly illegible, the 'a's looking just like the 'o's, the 'i's like the 'l's.

'I asked around,' I said, 'and none of us has ever heard of Jeremiah Mount. How exactly is he, was he, related?'

'You'll be amazed you ever asked that,' he said.

'And you think all this is worth deciphering?'

'You'll be amazed you ever asked that, too.'

'Will you help me?'

'I'm halfway through the first ledger already.'

Even after we had got the hang of Jeremiah's handwriting, we were frequently puzzled not merely by the language of the late seventeenth century but also by the gaps and non-sequiturs in the text (we were to discover that much of it had been written late at night and after a couple of drinks). We have filled in the gaps where we could make a reasonable guess at the meaning. We have also modernised the spelling, and the punctuation, and replaced the occasional archaism and obscure word or phrase with their modern equivalents. For the reader's further convenience, we have also included the relevant page from the Diary of Samuel Pepys wherever that immortal work covers the same day or incident as Jem's memoirs.

But that is just the trouble. For to begin with, I found there was something distasteful about the task Doddy had pressed me into. Perhaps disappointing would be a better word. The 'Mr Mount' who pops up now and then in Pepys's pages may not be a very alluring character. But he is sweetness and dignity compared to the character who emerges from Jem's own account. Time and again I have muttered under my breath, Come on, endear yourself, but he wouldn't. I began to wish for a kinsman of some moral substance, a personality whose life and opinions would bring alive the challenges and disappointments of his age, and so speak across the centuries, whispering a sort of solace to us in our own perplexities. But there it is, the past is a cussed place.

Yet as I ploughed on through the minuscule acres of Jem's script, I found to my surprise, even to my shame, that I was starting to feel differently about my subject. His later years were certainly peculiar enough (though they did him little more credit than his youth), but I had fallen into the habit of making allowances for him. Why? Hard to say. I was somehow more passionately concerned for him, or on his side anyway, which is not quite the same thing.

And even when he was young, there was something about him, something kindred, I suppose.

Here they are then, the Memorials of Jeremiah Mount. My fellow editor wanted a fine title-page with an engraving, but I thought better not.

I

The Marsh

I remember first the blossom.

It was apple blossom for the most part, but on the slope down towards the marshes there was a pear orchard as well. At first it appeared all white but then pink when I came close and ducked down under the boughs to escape from my schoolfellows, Tommy Court, Lob Loader and Bare-arse Jack Scott. I was always the one they chased, not because I was the runt of the litter but because I could show them the best sport. Jem for our hare, they would cluck, and off I went, running bent like an old man for miles under the apple boughs, until my hair was full of the blossom and my head was as hoary as my grandfather Ralph's. But by then I would have lost the hounds and I could amble along the bank of the Drain – it has a learned name too, the River Reculver, but we all called it the Drain, for that was its usage – and I would draw aside the rushes and look down into the foul water in the hope of seeing a drowned maid or at least a water-rat. My mother was always telling stories about girls who had thrown themselves into the Drain because they'd been got with child. But I never saw anything there but a few sticklebacks. Then I would lie down in the grass to recover my breath and look back at the white blossom covering the hill. The day was so bright that I could not see where the hill ended and the sky began.

They were but low hills in our country, for the land was all marsh down to the sea five miles away. On a clear day, if there was no sun, you could descry (but barely) the ships roving out at anchor in Herne Bay and count their masts, the country was that flat. Our own church at Churn was itself as a ship with a queer spire like a mast and a hipped roof which had the aspect of sails. You could climb into the little gallery below the spire and fancy you were a cabin boy in the crow's-nest, giving warning of land on the Spanish Main.

That gallery served also as a refuge from my mother. She was the one I took after, being tall and black. Even then I was nearly two yards tall like the late King and as dark as he, or black-avized, as our ponderous rector Mr Hignell would have said. My mother was not much shorter, but my father was a little fluffy man with red cheeks, and my sisters took after him, so that when my mother and I quarrelled we were as two ravens croaking at one another while a flock of fieldmice fled and hid themselves.

My father was seldom indoors and scarcely sat down to eat as he came in muttering some foolishness about the cows must be moved from one field to the other when he had only put them there the day before, and he would be out the back door again with his bread and cheese still in his hand. He was a futile restless man who always sold his calves too early or cut his hay too late. We did not bandy words for he could not abide prolonged discourse, except to his cows whom he would coax and reproach with all the speech he dared not use to us.

But my mother – ah my mother. Her voice was as resonant as a bell, but one that is cracked. I have heard Welshwomen with such voices, so that when they are talking to their husbands in bed, it is as though they were whispering fond nothings in your own ear. Not that my mother's nothings were fond. Her perceptual powers belonged to the supernatural order. She could tell when I had failed to construe my Latin even before Mr Hignell our rector and schoolmaster had remarked on my errors, she knew when my underlinen was dirty though she had not seen it, when I had teased the neighbour's cat before it mewed. Then would come that harsh low call – Jeremi*ah*, Jeremi*ah* – and the indictment exact to the last particular. When I complained that I was the universal scapegoat, my sisters would say that I was unkind and that she persecuted me because she loved me the best and expected the most of me. Did I not remember how she would tickle me and call me Jemmy Junket? But I could not explain how even these sunny interludes alarmed me for they were so precarious, the sun so easily turning to storms, the tickling to pinches and slaps. When I was almost grown, I must yet stand like St Sebastian while she supplemented her verbal injuries with her fists which struck as sharp as flints. So when I saw the storm brewing, I would slip out of the back door past my father singing lullabys to his flyblown herd and pelt up the spiral steps to the gallery.

It was an ancient church, and the parish was yet more ancient, founded by St Augustine himself, and second only to St Martin's in Canterbury. Mr Hignell was much possessed with such matters and spent his hours of leisure (which were numerous, for he was an idle greasy man who never visited the sick and who paid a clerk to conduct his services) in useless study of the old charters and registers that were kept in the vestry.

The church possessed a mill upon the Drain and Mr Hignell had title to the revenues of it. But the water was so low and the current was so sluggish that except in times of flood it would not turn the mill wheel. In a dry summer the farmers took off their corn to the great mill at Stourmarsh and so Mrs Scott, a widow woman who kept the mill, had scarce a penny to feed her son and none to pay Mr Hignell.

One day we were lying on the bank by the race (though to call it a race is a melancholy irony, for it had barely strength enough to shift the water-daisies) and I saw Mr Hignell go into the mill with his broad black hat on, and the door shut behind him. The sun beat hot on our backs. We tickled Mary Court (Tommy's sister) with straws and her face grew red and Tommy told us to stop and Bare-arse Jack (his mother was so poor he had once come to school with breeches that were torn at the back) said he would push Tommy into the stream but in pushing Tommy he pushed me too and I was the one who fell in, but even in the race the water came up no higher than my knees and I stood there wreathed in daisies like Ophelia swearing mock vengeance on Jack Scott. He towered there above me on the coping stone, tall and black as I was, his ragged breeches falling off him, shouting insults at me. Then behind him I saw the door of the mill opening and Mr Hignell clapping on his hat and Mrs Scott coming out and she was weeping.

Mr Hignell had them out of the mill before the week was done and we heard they left the country before the year was out. We knew no more of them which I was sorry at, for Bare-arse Jack made me laugh. It was not the last I knew of Mr Hignell, or of his lessons that were both tedious and painful. As is common in that profession, at least among schoolmasters who are bachelors, beating boys was his great diversion. If you misbehaved in church or were idle in lessons, he would have you held down by his poor creature, Voules the beadle, and waddle half a dozen yards back and then come at you with his birch, grunting like a pig as he came. I perceived that he took an unwholesome pleasure in this chastisement and after he had beaten me once for whistling in the graveyard and then for forgetting the theorem of Pythagoras (which has been of no value to me in my life) I resolved to take revenge upon him and to do it by striking at that which was dearest to him of all things in life, viz. his old charts.

He kept the key to the muniment chest behind the door to his scullery and I could have taken it without being seen, but I thought it more cunning to break open the chest with the old ploughshare which had been left in the farmyard, such as a robber might light upon and take to his use. One night towards the end of Lent when there was no moon, I stole down to the church, knowing that the lock on the vestry door had rusted, slipped in and smashed the lock on the chest, gathered up the oldest scrolls and books that I could see and ran with them down to the Drain, but I stumbled as I ran and dropped the scrolls into the ditch. The next morning I heard Mr Hignell crying from the lychgate of the church: Robbers, robbers, we are undone. I have never heard sweeter music. We ran in all directions to apprehend the monster who had done this deed. I ran towards the Drain. There they were, the silly scrolls, perched on the tops of the rushes, dripping with dew and mud and blossom. Oh Mr Hignell, look here, look here, I cried. I do believe these be, etc., etc. And the greasy fellow galloped panting down the path. Oh Jem, you're an excellent fellow, yes here's the so-and-so charter, and this is the register. And he picked up these old papers, with the blossom and the mud on them, and clasped them to his bosom as though they were his children, which they were, since no woman had been lunatic enough to permit Mr Hignell up her petticoats, and he had breath like a badger.

But then as he was chattering there with these stinking old rolls in his arms, all of a sudden he stops and looks at me. Jeremiah, he says, you were quick on the scent, very quick. Sir, I am a quick lad, anyone will tell you that. Yes, he says, so you are indeed. But he goes on looking at me, and although he said nothing more – for what more could he say? – I perceived at that moment the awful power of reputation and determined to acquire a reputation which should help rather than hinder my progress on this earth.

The rest of my family resembled my father and my sisters. They had curly hair and faces as red as the apples they grew for a living. There were plenty of us Mounts. The family had so many branches and they all grew apples (as they do to this day) except my father and thus prospered as he did not. All but me were named Ralph or Richard. The only way to tell one Mount from another was by the names of our villages. My father was Ralph Churn, his younger brother Richard Elmstead, his son my cousin Ralph was Ralph Elmstead, etc., etc. My cousin did not much care for his nickname which was Fluffy Ralph or Fluff. His curly hair was so thick and unruly that birds could have nested on it. That was the only unruly thing about Ralph. He was a neat boy. His breeches were always clean and his face shining. He was an excellent penman. The rector of Elmstead had declared his Latin verses to be the finest in Kent for his age. Sometimes Ralph would walk over from Elmstead which lay up in the Downs beyond Canterbury, ten miles off, for the pleasure of showing off his verses to Mr Hignell. In return, Mr Hignell would show him the old charters. I would skulk behind them squashing flies against the window pane. I stayed only because Mr Hignell would then invite us to dinner and he kept a magnifico's table. He would give us a fine piece of roast beef or a rich mutton pie or a barrel of oysters or a jowl of salmon. He would drink a deal of sack and would put on a good humour, but I never saw my cousin Ralph merry. Fluff would drink but little, pleading that his head ached or that he had a pain in his cods (he was hypochondriac even as a youth). And when Mr Hignell cracked a feeble jest, he would smile as much as to say: 'Ah, that's a jest, I salute it, now may we pass on to more serious matters', and he would begin to talk of the old charters and the other ancient rubbish that Mr Hignell kept in the vestry. In truth, it was as much to pique my cousin Ralph as to vex Mr Hignell that I stole the scrolls. And the day after they were found, I hit upon a droll device.

I knocked upon the vestry door and there as I surmised was Mr Hignell brushing and rubbing the mud off the books and scrolls. Mr

Hignell, I said, don't you think that Fluffy Ralph – I mean Ralph – will be much distressed to hear of all this? Why, you are right, boy, he says, you must go tell him, he loves these old things. But perhaps he knows already, I said. Why, what do you mean? How should he know? Oh I meant nothing, I said, with seeming innocence, nothing at all, news travels fast across the marsh. Why so it does, he said, and then fell to cleaning books again.

Five minutes later I asked: Who do you think stole these articles, Mr Hignell? I do not know, he said. It's a strange thing, I said, an ordinary thief would not guess their value, it must have been a fanatic for books, some person who has an incurable passion for old papers, don't you think so? That's possible, he said pretending to be engrossed in his work, but I could see he was beginning to ponder. The thief must have been a young man, I said (the sport was coming a little near home here), an old man would not have the strength or the audacity for such a game. A young man ... yes, you are probably right. And someone who is learned? Yes perhaps, he said. Perhaps Ralph would know of such a person, he goes to school in Canterbury and is hugger-mugger with scholars and booksellers. Perhaps, Mr Hignell replied.

I could see coursing through his brain as plainly as if it had been written in letters of fire on his forehead the thought: Ralph is the villain, I have been gulled, my trust has been betrayed. The jest was all the finer because he had no evidence to support his suspicion. He could only boil with impotent rancour, while Fluff would be much offended that his old patron was now so cold to him.

But that estrangement did not last long, for soon Ralph was to go up to London to be apprenticed to a bookseller on Tower Hill and Mr Hignell was mighty sorry, for who would listen to his tedious discourses now? Certainly not Jeremiah. I had other fish to fry. There was Mary Court, Tommy's sister, who was tall as a lily, but she was too young and cried out when I tried to kiss her, and Tabitha, who was unwilling also but smelled of pickled herring so that I did not mind, and then there was Emma, darling Emm who had great bubbies and threw her skirts up as cheerfully as if she was hanging out her washing and laughed and groaned and had her pleasure so freely that I thought paradise had come. There was nobody to match Emm. She was the *nonpareille*. My mother called her a slut and said she would lead me to perdition, but she led me to Heaven – or Heaven's gate. We would go down the path to the Drain and a little way along, where there was a field hidden by the hawthorns, she would plump herself down and say come on slow-worm and I would be down upon her and feeling her soft velvet and calling her chuck while she lay back shielding her eyes from the sun with her hand. And away beyond the fair forest of her hair across the marshes I saw the ships joggling at anchor in the bay. Or was it me joggling? Oh Jemmy, Jemmy, she would say so that it sounded like a catch such as dull morris men might dance to, but she would not admit me to the ultimate delight for fear of being got with child.

As we were thus engaged, two old men came along the path beside the field. We could see their heads above the cow parsley stalks but they could not see us. 'Tis the Dutch, says one. 'Taint, says the other. I warrant you those are Dutch bottoms, says the first. That's good English oak, says the other. And so they went on, and we smothered our laughter, for we cared not at all whether the enemy was in the Thames or not.

When I see ships at anchor in a swell, when they rise and fall, and their masts clash and clink, I think of Emma, although she is long dead.

By the autumn, for all her protestations to me, she was with child and I was disgraced, for everyone loved Emm and blamed me for seducing her. It turned out the true criminal was Jack Scott, but he was already gone to New England to seek his fortune, and everyone knew that I had been walking with Emm. My reputation was sliding. I have forgot to say that when I pirated the papers from the muniment chest, a glint of gold caught my eye. Mr Hignell kept in the chest a gold seal with which he liked to seal his own papers and make believe he was Lord High Chancellor of Churn. This little bauble I snatched up and put in my pocket. I found it a pleasant sport to roll it around secretly in my fingers while playing the innocent in front of Mr Hignell.

Unfortunately, my mother made search of my pockets before my breeches were washed and she found the seal which she hastened to return to the greasy old parson. This is a serious matter, he grunted, you've brought shame upon your family, Jeremiah, you have betrayed

my trust, the crime is too heinous to be atoned for by corporal chastisement (well, there was that much to be said for it, then), there is
nothing for it but to take you before the magistrate and yet – he raised
his hand to his heart with a grand gesture as though he were Burbage
himself – ties of friendship may bind the strong arm of justice, I am a
man of compassion, I am not blind to your mother's tears. There had
been no such tears, my mother repeating in much the same words how
I had brought shame upon her family and how she ought never to have
married my father, for he had bad blood which had issued in me – a
gross untruth, there being no more respectable family in Kent than his,
while her brother was a sot and her uncle had been transported for false
coinage.

The upshot: Jem is to be sent apprentice to uncle John Elmstead,
the fair village of Churn is to know him no more, and the Man of
Compassion, the Rev. Mr Hignell, is to dine with my parents once a
week, a barrel of oysters and a fine piece of beef to be of the party. I
did not then know that our farm was half-mortgaged to Mr Hignell,
and the other half was to go the same way within the year. Nor would
I have cared to know. My father's failing was a theme that I shut my
ears to, for it made sour music. Besides, I was impatient to quit Churn
and seek the horizon, having resolved to be a voyager in life, though to
be bound to my uncle John were but a dull beginning for a Meteor.

Thus in my ignorance I was very merry my last night in Churn.
When the stars came out, I went up Beggars Lane to Emm's house
and threw small stones at her window. She put her head out and bade
me hush, but I kissed her before she could put her head back in. Let me
in, I asked. I daren't and besides you know my condition. You wouldn't
want me to go away without a last embrace. She opened the window a
little wider, and I slithered through it like an eel as I had done so often
before and my stockings snagged on the roses as they always did. She
was already plump but was as much to my liking as ever. We must be
very careful, she said, for I would not lose the baby. Even though he's
to be a bastard? You're too round, Jem, and besides it's in your power
to make him honest. Or her, I said. It will be a boy, I'm sure of it, she
said, wouldn't you like him to be yours? Not Jack Scott's boy, I said,
besides I'm too young to marry. My uncle Potter was but seventeen
when he wed, she said. And wasn't he a fool to marry your aunt, I'd

rather marry a hedgehog, Emm you're a goddess, let me in, let me in. Very well, but we must make shift like this, so, and very gently.

On the morrow I was off on the road to Canterbury and then beyond on the high road over the downs which the Romans built. It was a vile morning, rain and wind, and my coat too thin for the weather. As I came up on to the crest, I perceived a band of men ahead of me. They were marching in step and when I came up abreast of them I realised that they were soldiers, but a more bedraggled bunch of knaves I never saw in my life. Where are you bound? I asked. We are off to Dover to beat the Dutch, they said. When I heard this, I laughed and one of the men swore oaths at me. Will the Dutch step ashore for the privilege of getting a beating from you? Get off, you impudent little shit, we're trained men, at Dover we'll go aboard the *Daring*, which is a first-rater. Oh, sir, I'm a little simple and I've been walking this road since dawn.

And in truth I looked so like a whipped dog in my wet coat and my hair filled with rain that they took pity on me and gave me a crust of bread and a mouthful of ale and invited me to march on with them to the next tavern, the Crooked Billet at Halfway Street. As we were shaking the wet off ourselves in the tavern, a dismal hovel in the trees with moss growing in the tiles, the wench came up to inquire our pleasure and I saw that it was my old acquaintance, Tabitha who had been unwilling. She was grown tall and amazing handsome, a veritable *bella figura*, and when I approached she no longer smelled of pickled herring but of beer. She knew me at once. Why, Jem, you're as wet as a minnow. Didn't you know, Tabby, I'm a soldier now, we're off to beat the Dutch at Dover, but first I need a quart of ale. My fellow *milites* laughed heartily at this, but they did not peach against me. Tabby installed me in the seat of honour next the fire, and brought me ale in her best tankard and permitted me all manner of familiarities which had been forbidden at Churn.

When the soldiers gathered their baggage and made off, I stayed in the ingle to finish my ale. Tabby who had been busy in the back room came forth to bid them farewell. As she shut the door behind them, she saw that I was still at my tankard. Jem, why didn't you go with the others? You've been gulling me, you're no soldier, you're a cheat. Madame, I said rising from my chair and drawing myself

up to my full two yards, you do me an injustice, I am the rearguard.

Why aren't you dressed as a soldier? (My clothes had dried and
she could see that I wore country garb.) If you reflected, I riposted,
you would see that it were folly to advertise my presence. So long as
I am the rearguard, I must travel *incognito*. Incog what, she said.

Let's not talk of war and these unpleasant matters, I said, you're
grown too beautiful for such talk. Oh, Jem, I was quite in the right, you
are a cheat! You mustn't be so distrustful, Tabby, distrust turns the best
wine to vinegar. A maid in my position must protect herself. A maid? I
whispered. What do you mean, she said, but she was smiling, and I was
already caressing her thigh and looking forward to the contest. Will
you show me your bedchamber? I asked. But she said the landlord was
ill in bed upstairs and his chamber was next to hers, and so we embraced
where we stood by the fire. But before embarking on the voyage, I had
not stopped to think whether I was fully armed, and as we came close
to the harbour, I realised that my pen had no more ink in it since my
joust with Emm the night before. I was entirely downcast and began
buttoning my breeches. I wonder you trouble to button up, she said,
for there is so little to hide.

She made a sucking noise with her lips which I ignored. Injured
dignity had best make itself scarce, and my clothes were dry, so I
shut the door of the Crooked Billet behind me and took off for Dover,
observing to my displeasure that the storm and wind had not abated.
After half an hour I wearied of the trudging and turned aside to shelter
under the broad oaks. I sat down beside a little weedy pond which was
full of marsh-mallows, or blobgoblins as we call them in Kent. The rain
poured down upon the pond, breaking up my reflection in its weedy
mirror. I was a shattered man. This was my first great reverse in an
engagement with the fair sex, and the humiliation was sore. But then
a wanton thought came upon me and I began to avail myself of that
faculty which Dame Nature in her bounty has provided for the solitary.
To my surprise and delight I observed that the infirmity which had
afflicted me in the tavern had gone and I was once again in possession
of the full vigour of my youth. It is not often that I am moved to
pray but on this occasion the moment of ecstasy brought from me an
exclamation of gratitude to my Redeemer.

Ah 'tis thee, Jem, I thought I knew the voice.

I was greatly alarmed to see the plump figure of my uncle John Elmstead coming through the trees in his plain brown coat and broad hat.

'Tis a pleasure to hear thee give thanks to Our Lord, your father had not told me thou wast so pious. We've stood in much need of the rain in these parts and this downpour indeed deserves our utmost gratitude to the boundless generosity of Divine Providence.

He shuffled on in this vein whilst I ordered my clothing. The old fool meant no harm. He was as garrulous as a magpie and he had brought his cart to meet me with a sailor's tarpaulin to cover us. He was a country stationer who sold sermons and law-books and charts to all the nobility and gentry and as he geed on the old nag that was taking us along the straight road, he instructed me in his trade and its mysteries. Never sell books in the lump, Jem, when you can sell them singly, for no one will believe that a book is scarce if you sell it in the lump. And always let them off the packing penny, for then they will think they have a bargain though the books may cost five shillings. And set great store by personal acquaintance. Madam, thou must say, I can vouch personally for this book, for the binder is well known to me, an honest man, and pious too, and adept with calf leather and sheep leathers alike. Never keep open shop, Jem, thou mayst starve behind thy shop-board for want of custom. There is no certainty in a dropping trade. Thou needst only a convenient warehouse and a good acquaintance among the booksellers and thy fortune will rise as surely as the sun doth in the morning.

I quickly saw that I could not endure this patter as a *continuo* to my life. Our connection must be brief if it was not to end in tears. I resolved that it should also be profitable to myself. Patience must be my motto.

Uncle John showed me my quarters, a miserable attic only lately vacated of books and with mouldy book odours in every corner of the chamber. The smell infected even my bed – as though it had been lavender or some delicate herb put there a-purpose. The attic had one little window, *duodecimo*, such as a sparrow might look out of. The window gave upon a miserable alley which was so narrow I doubt my uncle could have got along it, for he was a portly fellow. We dined early upon stale bread and old mutton with small beer. These be good Kentish hops in this beer, my uncle would say, the finest beer in all England, sayst thou not so, Nephew? Yes, Uncle, I never drank beer like it. This was the truth, for the beer was so sour nobody but Uncle would have drunk it. It was good only for pouring upon runner beans to make them grow.

Dover is a fine town, my uncle said, there's no place to match it for the marine trade. I have had sea-captains from the seven seas vying for my charts.

But this was a phantasm. I never once saw a sea-captain knock upon his door, and I soon discovered that, when we called upon them at the harbour, we received but dusty answers. I wheeled the handcart behind him over the cobbles and up the gangway whilst he raised his hat to the ships' officers who gave him dull looks as much as to say we would rather be flogged or hanged at the yardarm than read one of your books. When we went down into the captain's cabin for a glass of canary, my uncle tried to sell him one of the fine new charts he had had sent from St Paul's Churchyard, but the captain slapped his rusty chart-box and said I've sailed the world with these old shipmates, I need no fresh instructions. I looked at the chart on his table, all greasy, foxed and torn as it was, and wondered how he navigated beyond the Needles let alone in the South Seas. Then my master pressed upon him some edifying book of sermons or some obscure law-book and the captain went harrumph, Archbishop Duguid's Discourses, well here's one shilling and ninepence, 'twill do to prop up a table-leg. And I wheeled the handcart back to my master's lodgings with the sweat running down inside my shirt. Yet I own I was much pleased to step aboard these barques (though they were but shabby coastal craft for the most part) and smell the ropes and the tar and feel the tide shift the deck beneath my feet.

And while he was talking to the captains – this is excellent Madeira, sir, upon my word it is – I observed these master mariners with a prospective eye. They were rough men of ruddy complexion. I could see from the manner in which they dispatched the canary that they were no flinchers from the glass. I hazarded therefore that they might not be immune from other pleasures of the flesh. Throughout the long months at sea, they would pine for female company (for these old tarpaulins of the Dover patrol did not take their wives with them as would a Lord High Admiral) and so I formed an ingenious design.

Uncle, I said, you wish me to learn the trade thoroughly, do you not? Indeed, that is my dearest wish, Jeremiah, thorough is my motto, just as it was that of the late accursed traitor Strafford, though my diligence is directed towards the Lord's work and not that of the Antichrist. Quite so, I said, wouldn't it be useful for me then to save your legs (he suffered much from the gout) and fetch the goods from Canterbury? Mr Billingsley is an honest man and you say yourself a rare judge of books, and Mr Coggan ditto of charts. They will send you only fair parcels which shall prove to your taste, and as for the price, I have heard you say of each gentleman that should a child be sent to his shop he would not take a farthing more than his due.

True, Nephew. I perceive thou art a brisk industrious lad, and not the wild spark thy cousin Ralph painted thee (I treasured up this intelligence for future revenge). And I am resolved to try thee, and if the experiment should fail, then we must put the bill down to Experience, for Experience worketh Hope, as St Paul teacheth us. I would not send thee to a pirate like Mr Dancer, he is a Cormorant among booksellers, and a trader in lewd books moreover. But Mr Coggan is a paragon and so is Mr Billingsley.

So I set off in my uncle's cart with his blessing and a multitude of instructions and a loaf of bread and a mutton pie and, a true blessing among so many godly words, £25 sterling for the purchase of the merchandise. Three shillings I spent straightaway in the Crooked Billet, in the hope that I might return the blow Tabby had dealt my pride, but she was absent, being gone back to her friends at Churn, and I sat alone in the inn.

Nevertheless I was in good heart as I came down the hill into the fair city of Canterbury. For who would not be of good cheer at the age of seventeen with £24 17s in his pocket? I lodged in fine style at the Mitre with a chamber overlooking the Market. Since I was hungry, I bought a pound of cherries of a fruit seller and retired to my chamber where I had great sport throwing the cherry stones down upon the heads of the citizens.

But now it was time to drop upon Mr Coggan and Mr Billingsley. I put on my clean linen and my black coat and assumed an earnest mien which might sort with the sober character my uncle had given me. For he had forewarned the honest booksellers of his great Experiment and they were ready of their charity to extend me every courtesy.

With each wheezing (for he was Asthmatic) Mr Coggan docked another shilling off the price of his chart of the West Indies. This is a sheet direct from the *Waggoners Pilot Book* giving true and particular details of the shoals plumbed by HMS *Jason* during her late voyage. To you, young Jem, I shall sell it for but seventy per cent of my strangers' price. My hearty thanks, Mr Coggan, sir, I know how grateful my uncle will be.

And so it proceeded with Mr Billingsley who was a tall pale man with a nodding head like a bird pecking at a bush. Before the day was out, I had a full load of sermons and law-books and marine charts and I had laid out but £9 13*s*.

I bade farewell to Mr Billingsley who was putting up his shutters. When the shutters were secure and he could no longer see me, I darted next door, to the infamous Mr Dancer's. The proprietor was a low, grubby sort with a smile upon his face. I could see at once that he was a man of quick intelligence. I explained my requirements and he understood them perfectly. Never was an actor less in need of a prompter. My dear sir, you shall have exactly what you need, you have come to the right man to accommodate you, sea-captains you say, I'm acquainted with the taste of sea-captains if ever a bookseller was.

And so I came away with a fine parcel well wrapped by Mr Dancer's boy — we believe in discretion, sir, a discreet trade is a thriving trade, I always say — and I was well pleased with the contents, viz.:

1.* 1 doz. copies: *The Night-Walker*; or, *Evening Rambles in search after lewd women, with the various Conferences held with them.*
2.* six copies: *The Raven Fleece*: *wherein a Dark Lady discovers her adventures among Men of Quality.*
3.* five copies (very rare): *The Anatomy of Venus,* a learned treatise upon the amorous science by a Doctor of Medicine in the University of Padua translated from the Italian.
4.* *Aretine's Postures*, translated from the Italian full and entire with the original illustrations.

5.* *Captain Cuttle's Decameron*, a collection of curious tales comical, romantic, astrological and fantastical, by the Author of *The Strange Fate of Sebastian Shortbreech*.
6.* six copies: *Jokes, Jests and Jollities* by Portia Plackett, a woman of parts.

Certain other works were also made up into the parcel, but I do not like to set their names down here.

After these purchases, I still jingled £3 10*s* in my pocket and took a fine dinner at the Crooked Billet on my way home. Tabby waited on me and seeing my gentleman's clothes and my bulging purse (I mean the money) spoke me very fair. But I would not forgive her. I had resolved to apply myself to trade and there was work to do besides. After dinner, I copied out the receipts which Messrs Billingsley and Coggan had given me, but in place of the moneys which I had paid I set down the price I would have paid had I been a stranger. I took great pains with this task, for although my uncle was dull, he was not blind. Thorough was to be my motto, too, though I had no intention of ending up on the scaffold like my Lord Strafford, nor of ending up like my uncle a pious country bookseller.

Well, said my uncle, thou hast done well, Jem. These are first-rate charts, Waggoner is a Michael Angelo of the art, Archbishop Duguid a favourite of mine and the sheepskin bindings excellent on the *Ars Clericalis*. Thou will make a bookseller yet if only thou learnst to bargain like a man. I confess that I had thought Mr Billingsley would favour thee with a somewhat larger discount, Mr Coggan ditto.

I tried as best I could, Uncle, but they swore prices had increased greatly since your previous visit because of the Dutch and the embargo.

The Dutch, said my uncle as though he were spitting out a fishbone, I hate not any man or any race, my religion forbids it, but I hate the Dutch. These mynheers are desperadoes, they will ruin our trade before we are in our graves, etc., etc.

On the morrow I made haste with my handcart down to the harbour and boarded the first ship I came to, a dirty old collier, the *Cherub*. The master was as black as his ship. Charts, bellowed this sack of coals in human shape, what do I want with charts, I know this coast as well as I know my own arse. These are new charts, sir, which portray the currents, shoals and winds as discovered by the last Admiralty survey. I want nothing to do with the Admiralty, Coalsack returned, they're a gaggle of old women who make an honest seaman's life a misery with their regulations and their caterwauling. Sir, I shall not detain you further, said I, perceiving that no time was to be lost in moving to the *primum agendum,* I can see you are a gentleman of taste, I should be failing in my duty if I departed without show-ing you one of the rare and curious volumes which I have also for sale. They come direct from Mr L'Estrange in Warwick Lane who draws the custom of the most elegant young rakes of the town. Any gentleman with a lively faculty for pleasure would desire such works for his private library. Hum, hum, says Coalsack pretending not to be listening, books, books, I've no time for such things, but his eye has lighted upon *The Raven Fleece* and, heaven be praised, the book has fallen open at the frontispiece which depicts the first encounter between Rosalinda and the Chevalier de Grosseprong, and he is hooked. He desires the book with all his heart, he foresees many a pleasant evening in his cabin, while storm and wind make roar outside, tucked up snug with the adorable Rosalinda and her insatiable Chevalier. In a trice, I have sold him *The Night-Walker,* and *Captain Cuttle's Decameron* into the bargain, but a furrow crosses his grimy brow, a serpent creeps into his Eden. Where is he to stow these lewd volumes that the seamen may not catch sight of him and make mock of his solitary tastes? They will call him Captain Toss-Off and other such low names.

I come to his rescue. Sir, I have here the very thing – a portable library for the seafaring man, made of fine polished Norway firwood. The charts fit into this upper compartment that they may be ready at hand on any pressing engagement and, below, safe from prying eyes, you may stow your books. Whether they be maritime, legal, religious, or consecrated to the delight of the senses, 'tis all one, they lie there together hugger-mugger.

Hum, hum, goes the gallant captain, pretending now to be a fanatic for charts, I shall have need of the Strait of Dover, and the Estuary, and the Dogger Bank if you have it, oh yes and this little thing will fill up a corner (picking up *Aretine's Postures*).

You may find it convenient, sir, if I parcel the lot up into one bill which you may post to your navigation accounts, for I am sure your proprietors would wish their ship to be well furnished.

Why, so they would, to be sure, says Coalsack, it is a most necessary expense that a ship should be well stocked, a modern chart may be a Life-preserver.

Very true, sir, so it may. Shall we say nine guineas *in toto?*
Done.

An ineffable joy seizes me as the contract is concluded, and I settle the books into the lower compartment, replace the ingenious flap and roll the charts tight that they may fit into the upper storey of the box. Coalsack counts out the £9 9s, takes the box, cuddles it as though it were a baby. I take my leave and dance for joy down the gangway. Oh the beauties of commerce! I wish I were a poet that I might hymn the delights of that trade into which it hath pleased Dame Fortune to plump me.

By noon, I have sold a similar parcel to Captain Proudfoot of the *Ceres*, for £11 10s. In celebration, I take a barrel of oysters and a pint of canary at the Eagle, to refresh my voice which is strained by the *recitativos* of the morning. Then in the afternoon, I board what shall be my greatest prize, the *Firecat*, a second-rater newly come from Chatham, and Captain Quiney, a languid gentleman reputed learned (though, I fancy, seafaring men are but poor judges of erudition). This captain is at the other extreme of the gamut from Coalsack. He sprawls upon his chair as though he were half asleep and affects to be well acquainted with all my wares. I have seen such charts many times on Tower Hill, I doubt these are much improvement – and – oh these volumes are but poor trash, in my father's library, etc., etc. Yet in the end he too cometh to heel, choosing *The Raven Fleece*, the *Anatomy of Venus* and two other volumes which I do not care to name. To Captain Quiney, HMS *Firecat* at Dover, *One Chart box and set of Charts and other maritime necessities: thirteen guineas.*

But after one more customer I, too, must put into port, for my cabinet-maker had fashioned but four boxes and they are all gone. I say 'cabinet-maker', though he is old Hedges, the coffin-maker in

Herring Street, who makes up these boxes from off-cuts of his coffins for 2*s* the finished article. Don't worry, young Jem, I'm quick even if my customers aren't, you may have half a dozen more by the morning.

Thus passed my first day as a Man of Business on my own account and it was a Jubilee. Total takings: £53 11*s*. Total outgoings: £28. Profit, that glorious invention of our modern age, £25 11*s*.

But my labours were not yet concluded, for if I presented the account to my uncle in raw state, he would collect all the proceeds. I needs must continue that Double-keeping which I had first practised in my traffic with the booksellers of Canterbury.

Thus in my chamber at the Eagle, after dining on a stewed carp, I hastened to draw up a fresh set of accounts for my uncle's eyes, viz. total takings £38 3*s*, total outgoings £28, profit £10 3*s* – which latter sum I proudly presented to my uncle on my return to his house.

Heaven be praised, Jeremiah, thou art an honest apprentice and heaven hath rewarded thy honesty, etc., etc. But I could see in his little blinking eyes that my success had nonplussed him. He would not cease from worrying me with his questions. Tell me now, Jem, how didst thou shift the charts? What was the trick? Uncle, I said looking at the portly old hypocrite with due severity, I would not stoop to jargon. I merely pointed out to them the advantages of sailing with first-rate maps. Oh, he said, somewhat downcast, that was all, was it? Yes, I said, as thou knowest, Uncle (what sport it was to return him a thou), goods of quality will always find a buyer. So they will, Jem, so they will.

But I could see that he could not abide my success, for though he was lazy he was a proud little man and it was not fitting that the apprentice should outshine his master.

For my part, I had hauled into my nets several great principles of commerce:

primo, that a shopkeeper must impart to his wares a Property that will make them indispensable. Thus, this is the only article of its kind in our hemisphere.

secondo, that Novelty is a powerful engine of purchase. Thus, this item is but lately imported from Amsterdam, there is none like it in London, for the design is entirely new.

tertio, that a bargain smiles all the more warmly upon the purchaser, if you throw into the balance some extra article. It matters not that the article be trumpery, so long as it be unexpected.

quarto, that accounts cannot be digested raw. Books are all the better for a little cooking so that they may answer the purpose more exactly than in their natural state.

quinto, that a cheerful demeanour and an open countenance will put the customer in a buying vein. He will reject the fairest bargain if he suspects the tradesman be a rogue or a cormorant.

A Man of Business who bases his enterprise upon these five principles cannot fail to prosper.

But in this wicked world merit provokes envy and I saw that my uncle was growing suspicious. Meanwhile, Mr Hedges turned out my portable Libraries as fast as he turned out coffins during the late plague.

II

The Shop

Did you ever hear the like
Or ever hear the same
Of five women-barbers
That lived in Drury Lane?

I imitated my horny captains, for in my attic I too kept a chest with
an ingenious flap which Mr Hedges had constructed for me, but mine
was of fine oak (the leavings from some gentleman's coffin) and cost
me 5s. In the secret compartment, my winnings mounted gloriously. I
wrapped them in a cloth of red genoa velvet that they might not chink,
for the floorboards in my uncle's attic clucked like young magpies. And
on the Lord's Day I went to my private devotions, that is – counted
my money. I vowed that when my purse was worth £100 I would go
to London and preen my feathers in sight of the world, for young as
I was I itched for a wider stage and a more discriminating audience
than my uncle.

The old hypocrite visited the Metropole but twice a year to
replenish his stock, though I fancy he also had some naughty business
to despatch, for on his return he would smile to himself as much as
to say this old dog is not done yet. But his gout was so grievous at
Michaelmas that he could not contemplate the journey and I offered
to go as his proxy. Thou art a bold volunteer, Jem, my uncle said,
London is a city of vile temptations and wicked merchants who are
on the look-out to gull poor country tradesmen. Uncle, I said, didn't

you see me withstand the temptations of Canterbury and outwit the booksellers of that great city when I was but a lad? Now that I am full-grown, etc., etc.

Well, well, he said, time marches on, and youth must have its day. I can't afford to defray thy travel, but heaven knowst thy wages are commodious enough and it will be a rare privilege for thee to travel as my agent. I gave effusive thanks for this privilege while resolving that the old hypocrite would be defraying my odyssey in ways he should know not of.

How pleasant was that journey along the old Roman roads with the orchards filled with women climbing the ladders after the apples. I still think of their round rumps straining this way and that as they reached for the rosy fruit. I whistled or shouted some low jest and they turned and riposted with words I should blush to set down here. I reflected that if I could thus skirmish with the apple women of Kent then London should not be beyond the sweep of my rapier.

But I must confess that the sharp wits in London discomposed me at first. When I inquired the way, they spoke quickly and with a twang that I was slow to master. Here's another Kentish cunt, one man said to his fellow. What did you say, sir? A Kentish gent, sir, you are such, are you not? That was not what you said, sir. Why, sir, it was, wasn't it, Toby? It was, John, and a fine young gentleman if I may say so. You may say so, Toby, I never saw a cunt like it. Don't make game of me, or I'll knock your block off. Oh he's going to knock my block off, Toby, whatever shall I do? Run for your life, John, and call the constable.

I perceived that there was no profit in bandying words with such trash. A gentleman ought to preserve a dignified, sombre mien, and a warm man should show a cold exterior. I resolved to buy a black suit and some fine white linen to bolster my new character. A bookseller of my uncle's acquaintance recommended Mr Radford the mercer, at the sign of the Three Spanish Gypsies by the Exchange.

This was a shop for magnificoes. First there were the gloves, silk and leather and kid in grey and scarlet and canary, as soft and supple as though the living animal still inhabited them. Then there were the perfumery wares with wash-balls from Castile and French pomanders and bottles of every fragrance from China and the Indies and our own English hedgerows: lavender and lily and honeysuckle and oil of bergamot and camomile and carnation and a hundred others. But I was bound for the Mercery where behind the pile of silks and cottons I espied half a dozen young seamstresses at their work, their bright eyes lowered as their needles flew in and out. There never was such a pretty sight as these fair Penelopes in their lace caps so diligent and unconscious of being looked at.

Well, sir, you may stare for free, I suppose, but my young ladies are not to be disturbed or distracted.

She that spoke to me thus was a woman somewhat older than those she spoke of: a tall, well-set woman not handsome but with an air of command, dark with proud lips (she might have been one of the Spanish gypsies on the painted sign outside). I could not help noticing that she was also somewhat negligent in her dress. Her bodice-strings had come loose, and the curls of her frizzled hair had escaped the hairnet. Her fragrance too was not one of those being dispensed from the perfumery, being composed of two parts honest London sweat to one part Virginia tobacco.

Madam, I apologise, I said in my new man-of-quality's manner.

Accepted, I'm sure, she said. I'm Mrs Radford, how may I be of assistance?

She spoke so warmly and with such friendly smiles that I dropped my dignity, gave my name and explained that I was newly arrived from Dover, my clothes had not yet come after me, I needed rigging out from head to toe.

Come into the back shop and we'll have you fitted out like a galleon or my name's not Nan Clarges.

But I thought you said you were Mrs Radford?

And so I am and very grateful to Radford for the honour he did me, but everyone in the parish knows me as Nan Clarges, for Clarges is a celebrated name in these parts. My father is the farrier in the Savoy and my mother, well, everyone knows my mother. Take off your coat and we'll see what you're made of.

Why does everyone know your mother? I asked as I stood there behind a green curtain in the little back room in my shirt and stockings while Nan Clarges *alias* Mrs Radford darted round me taking measure.

Oh you are a bumpkin. She chuckled like a jay in the springtime. Have you never heard of the five women-barbers of Drury Lane?

I fear not, madam, I said, reverting to my man-of-quality frigidity of manner.

You don't know the ballad? Then I will sing it to you. And she sang it in a merry sort of whisper that the other customers might not hear her singing. I have set down the first verse at the head of this chapter. The other verses are too obscene to be printed here but I will give the explanation.

There was a married woman in Drury Lane that had given the clap to another woman's husband, a neighbour of hers. Well, this neighbour complained to *her* neighbours and they decided to take their revenge, viz. to give her a good whipping and shave all the hair off her you-know-what, well, the offending part as you might say. And Mrs Radford's mother was one of the five women-barbers and proud of it.

You're a firm young man, very firm, Jeremiah, that's too much of a mouthful for me, what do they call you for short?

Jem, I said spitting the word through my teeth, for her ministrations had begun to work their effect upon me, and it was a severe discipline to control my unruly part.

That's strange, she said, Jem is mostly short for James, is it not?

I know, I gasped.

Her fingers were dextrous and her odours prepotent. Then she gently, as though by chance, touched me in that region and gave a little start like a partridge flushed. Yet I suspected this start to be feigned, for she must have already seen the evidence of my agitation.

I'm sorry for this.

Upon my faith, there is nothing there for which you should be sorry, she said. In fact, I think you are standing somewhat proud.

That was the most glorious half-hour of my life. As we set to amid the bales of cloth with all the perfumes of the Orient assaulting my nostrils from the other side of the curtain, I wondered that none of her assistants interrupted us, for though we tried as best we could to conceal our movements she did not prevent a gasp of delight when our duet reached its excelsitude. She kissed me on the face and on the nape of my neck as she clung about me and clucked: Oh Jem, you're well suited now, aren't you? And I freely gave my assent to this proposition, for I had to own myself a satisfied customer.

Do you give credit, madam?

Oh no, sir, I must be paid on the nail.

And so you shall be, madam, as often as I can manage it.

Thank you, sir.

She plumped her skirts and made shift to tidy her hair, which had the aspect of last year's bird's-nest. When I looked at her now that our passion was spent, I perceived once more that she was no beauty such as a Dutch master might yearn to paint, but a full-hearted woman worthy of any honest man's love and her lips had a cherry colour of rare quality. Moreover, she was expert in the *ars amatoria*. How she clipped me. Poor Emm seemed but a beginner by retrospect.

Mr Radford is very often away at this season, he has much business to conduct with the Turkey merchants.

May I wait upon you then and keep you company? I'm a bookseller by trade, but anxious to broaden my experience of commerce.

That you shall, Jem, I promise you. Here, take this pomander as a keepsake. I like every gentleman to leave my shop sweetly scented.

I took the perfumed ball from her and carried it off in my pocket. All day long my fingers felt the rough cloves which studded it and remembered the pleasures of her body.

It was autumn by the calendar but the sun was still shining and it was my own springtime. I would stroll and take my wine with the map-makers of Tower Hill or the wits of Covent Garden before proceeding to my rendez-vous with Nan. At the back of the Three Spanish Gypsies there was a door with a gold Turk's-head knocker. I was to knock four times upon the Turk, and she would appear at the upper window and throw down the key. But she did not always hear at once if she was busy, and so I would wait and repeat the knocking. But it was a pleasant trysting place. She had planted the court with red and yellow flowers on either side of the path, for she loved fragrances of all kinds, albeit she was disorderly in her person (her enemies called her Dirty Nan). And it was pleasant to stand there and shuffle my shoes upon the gravel and think of the pleasures that were to come in the narrow bedchamber (for we had graduated from the fitting-room where we had made havoc among the bales of silk and calico).

But the time was fast approaching when I must return to Dover. I had purchased sufficient stock to last my uncle through the winter and my own supplies were depleted, for I had determined to live like a young dog and not to stint myself. My purpose was to avoid enrolment in the militia and I kept my eye open for some grizzled agent of the Parliament faction, so that if one should say: You seem a fair young fellow, I wonder you are not enrolled, I would reply *instanter* how greatly I regretted my absence from the battlefield but I was engaged on work of supreme military import, I was not at liberty to describe its exact nature, but if he wished I might confide a clue to him, and as the grizzled sergeant bent lower, I would whisper Charts – Admiralty Business into his hairy ear, and he would nod as much as to say I know the game and offer me a pint of ale to seal our alliance.

But before I took ship for Dover (for I had resolved to travel leisurely), I had to take my leave of Nan. It was a sad parting for me, but I had not reckoned how sad it would be for her. She threw her arms about my neck and wailed Oh, Jemmy, Jemmy, it's the end of life, I'll be an old woman when you come back, you will come back won't you, you'll come back to your Nan, even if she is an ancient hag, I can't live with Radford, that can't be my destiny, I was made for you, Jemmy, my Jem, etc., etc.

I was caught betwixt tears and tedium. In truth I was heartily sorry to leave her, but, as the poet says, methinks she did protest too much. I could not have been the first customer she had served so and I would not be the last. But this is the bravado of retrospect. For the most part I was very sorrowful and heavy.

I was still more sorrowful when I was returned to my uncle's, for he was old and gouty and yet more parsimonious than before. There was no merry company to be had, not for one such as I, who had tasted the superior delights of the Metropole. The sea-captains were coarse and the shopkeepers low Dissenters of my uncle's sort. When I had disposed of my charts, I wandered on the hills behind Dover and became a veritable melancholy Jaques. There is many an oak and ash tree in those sylvan glades that still bears the name of Nan cut by her solitary lover. I wrote her letters in which I poured out my heart but answer came there none. I formed the unworthy thought that she could not write, but then I remembered that I had seen her hand upon a mercer's bill. Perhaps she was ill of the plague. I put this thought out of my mind, for it was intolerable to me. All I had to comfort me was a dry pomander.

And as my solitude bore harder upon me, so my impatience mounted and the gloom of my uncle's house more damnably inspissated. He had become sleepy in his dotage. The floorboards in his house were so ill joined that from my attic I could hear his stertor in the afternoon. This was hell in Kent.

My captain's chest was so heavy now that I could scarce lift it. The secret compartment contained the grand sum of £176. I did not wish to depart without having established a headquarters for my manoeuvres, for I had experience already of how quickly London could swallow up a fool's gold. I must display my talents in a greater arena, but first I needed friends and connections to further my business.

I soon saw that my uncle was equally resolved to be rid of *me*. For there is no gratitude in this wicked world, and he was envious of my trade and could not understand how I had sailed through where his rickety barque had been dashed upon the rocks. He also suspected that I was cheating him, though he knew not how, for he was making more money per annum than he had before my advent. He did not like me. I do not know why. When he was forced to congratulate me – Jeremiah, thou art an honest lad – he had to force the words through his cracked lips.

The opportunity came for both of us when Fluffy Ralph paid a visit to Dover. Lord! how gingerly he greeted me. Did he know that I had thrown suspicion upon him in the matter of Mr Hignell's scrolls? Perhaps he misliked my reputation with the fair sex, he being timid in that respect.

But our uncle was determined that we should be friends, for he hoped that Ralph would take me away up to London where he was bound apprentice to a bookseller on Tower Hill. Ralph knew nothing of this and began a tale of woe, how he was overworked beyond endurance, for his fellow apprentice had taken a skinful of liquor and fallen into a ditch and drowned, yet his master would not take on a new apprentice because he was close-fisted, and how Ralph did not care for London and wished only to return to Kent and step into his father's shoes.

My uncle saw his chance: Take Jem, he is an honest lad and will work hard and he is cheap.

Fluffy Ralph hummed and hawed, but I melted him with flattery and sweetened him with honeyed phrases, so that, before the day was out, he was explaining how we could share out the work printing and selling and where I would lodge in the house.

Never did two persons take their leave of each other more cheerfully than Uncle and I. We had sucked one another dry and it was time to try another stall.

London ho! I said to Fluffy Ralph as we set off. He gave me a wan smile such as you might give to greet a stranger at a funeral.

This chest is very heavy, he said, as he helped me put my sea-chest upon the cart.

Oh it's our books, I said, greatly hoping that the velvet would keep the money from chinking.

Books? said Fluff, much impressed.

Thus I came to the Metropole for the second time but upon this latter journey I was vexed by Fluffy Ralph's chatter. He was that sort of preacher who delights to tell you either what you know already or what you do not care to know, and interrupts his discourse with exclamations at his own ingenuity. Thus: Maidstone is the second city in Kent, yet it hath fewer booksellers than Dover, is not that extraordinary? Or they do not grow the old pippins in these parts now, a sad thing for I am fond of them, but they do not keep so well as the French apples, at this rate there will be no English apples left in the Garden of England, is that not an astonishing thought? Astonishing, I answered, but my thoughts were upon my projected reunion with Nan. Would she love me still? I was bold enough to think she would, for I had an ample estimate of my worth and my youth would supply any deficiencies. Would I still love her? There was the rub. Youth and age were fickle allies and she had a dozen years' start of me. Yet I was in a fever of impatience. As we rode over the North Downs (for Fluffy Ralph had insisted that we take horse), in my mind's eye I saw myself knocking on the Turk, and her face at the window with her cap skewed by the window frame, crying: Wait a minute, Jem, and I'll be down.

When we came to Mr Fisher's house on Tower Hill, I was already thinking of the route I should follow on the morrow to the Exchange: should I go via the Minories and Cornhill or along Eastcheap? My mind was so set upon this campaign that I greeted Mr Fisher in an absent manner that must have made a disagreeable impression. When I realised this, I sought to repair the damage by waxing fulsome at supper: Mr Fisher's house was a fine mansion, Mr Fisher's hangings were worthy of the Grand Duke of Florence, Miss Fisher's gown – there were no words to describe its elegance, and so on. *Simul* Fluffy Ralph was regaling the company with his astonishing observations upon the relative sizes of London and other cities of his acquaintance, upon the ups and downs of the book trade in these troublous times, upon the expense of paper, leather, ink and all other commodities necessary to the said trade, upon the vicissitudes of finance in the said troublous times. Between us we made such a noise that Mr Fisher and his daughter looked like hares startled by the threshers. When Mr Fisher proposed that we retire to bed, being fatigued with our journey, we renewed our *duetto fortissimo.* Is it not remarkable, said Fluffy Ralph, that in Kent we retire at such-and-such o'clock, whereas I have heard that in Cornwall – upon which I broke in: I had but snatched a glimpse of our bedchamber but I was most exquisitely satisfied, never had I seen such a bed, nor such a prospect from a bed-window, for though it was dark I could see the masts of the ships at anchor and it was a noble sight, etc. At length they got us up the stairs and I fancied I heard Mr Fisher exhale a sigh of relief after he closed the door behind us.

Fluffy Ralph snored.

The next day was the Lord's Day and we must attend at Mr Fisher's church of St Katharine by the Tower and listen to the longest sermon that ever was preached and then go walking with my master while he discoursed at length upon the sights of the City, at such length indeed that Ralph began to seem a miracle of brevity. And on the Monday, we were introduced to the mysteries of the bookseller's art, the dealings with the printers and binders and the wholesale merchants for ink and paper and glue and the like. It was near evening before I was released and trotted up Eastcheap on Cupid's errand.

The door of the Three Spanish Gypsies was open, and through it

I could see a small dull man walking to and fro. I recognised him as Mr Radford, for though I had not seen him before, a portrait of him by a Dutch limner hung in their parlour. Behind him the sewing-girls were still at work. But of my Nan there was no sign.

I did not like to go in and inquire for her, for to make myself conspicuous were the tactics of a novice. So I skulked in the shadow of the shop. It was raining and after an hour of vigil I was as wet as a water-rat. But finally a girl came out and I caught her arm.

Oh, sir, let me go. Please, I said, can you tell me where is your mistress, Nan, Mrs Radford, is she away, is she ill? Why, 'tis Long Charlie, I never thought we should see you again. Why do you call me Charlie? My name is Jeremiah. Oh, sir, we called you thus because you look the image of the Prince and we called you long because ... And then she collapsed and began to giggle. No matter, I said, not displeased, but where is your mistress?

Oh sir, haven't you heard? She is gone to the Tower. To the Tower, oh calamity, by whose order? I hadn't thought she was one to meddle in politics. No, sir, nor does she, she's not imprisoned. Well then, what does she there? Oh sir, she sews and ... performs other services upon request. The girl laughed again and then took on a serious mien. But, sir, we are strictly advised that she does not wish for any visitors whatever. So it is no use to go there, for you will not be admitted.

Not admitted? No, they won't let you in. Are you sure of this? Quite sure, sir. Not even Mr Radford? Mr Radford is dead, sir, dead this past year. He went away and then he died, Mr Clarges told us.

But then who was that gentleman walking the shop floor but an hour ago? That was Mr Clarges, sir, Dirty Nan's brother – beg your pardon, Mrs Radford's brother – he is an apothecary and he has the management of the shop while she is away.

Here was a strange pickle, and one that was sour to the taste. Nan imprisoned in the Tower, and yet not imprisoned. Seeing no one and yet seeing someone, for there must be some corporeal being to fill the clothes she sewed. And performing services – oh what services – for this *Nemo*, yet performing none such for me. And widowed, having lost this Radford who was not the Radford I had thought, though surely she had told me that the man in the portrait was her husband. These were mysteries which I could not fathom and, having thought myself a strong swimmer in the currents of the world, I was now beyond my depth.

And Dame Fortune had dealt me yet another cruel trick, for when I went to the little window of the attic I shared with Ralph, it was not the masts of the ships at anchor that I saw. In the distance I had mistook the spires and pinnacles of the Tower of London for a fleet of ships, just as that poor Spanish knight Don Quixote tilted at windmills mistaking them for giants. Now I must stand at the window shivering in the cold of a morning and wonder in which tower my Nan was immured (or had immured herself), whose buttons she was sewing and what other services she might at that moment be performing for him. I was not well pleased when Fluffy Ralph, already dressed and washed, came to my side and began to point out the monuments and curiosities of the Tower together with choice details of who had been imprisoned in which tower and for how long, when released or beheaded and other such superfluity of information. I thought only of my Nan. Surely she could not be there by her own free will, some vile fellow must have compelled her to it, for I had warned her by letter that I was to come to London again. And yet I had to admit even to my lover's heart that she was not an easy woman to compel. She lived as she pleased, and would not be bridled without resistance.

You may be sure that I lost no time in knocking upon the door of the Tower, the door that is beyond the causeway over the moat, near the Lion Tower where they keep the wild animals which roar at night (it is a strange fancy to imprison wild animals alongside wild men, as though all Nature wanted penning up). I inquired of one of the warders of the Guard whether Mrs Radford was within. He knew no one by that name. Mrs Clarges then? He knew no one by that name neither, and he had other fish to fry than to call the register of all the women of London. A handsome woman, tall and with a fine head of reddish hair? At which the impudent Beefeater laughed in my face and told me if I had a woman like that I should take better care of her. Yet I suspected that even he knew more than he would admit, just as the sewing-girl seemed to have some ulterior particulars which she would not confide to me.

But mixed in with their laughter, there was fear, for these were times of doubt and strife, when a man might sit upon a throne one day and sit in a prison cell the next, when pros and cons were all jumbled up and *sauve qui peut* and devil take the hindmost were the wise man's mottoes. Therefore I began to train myself in that most excellent art, viz. that of keeping my head below the parapet.

I reasoned thus: that if Nan did not come looking for me, then she did not wish to see me. And if she did not wish to see me, she must have good cause. Had she perhaps murdered Radford and taken refuge in the Tower with some protector that she might escape justice? It would be an odd course to hide from the executioner in the executioner's lair, but therein might lie the very cunning of the ruse. Such weird fancies filled my head and made my brain ache. But I was young and without influence or friends. It was not three years earlier that the giddy multitude had stood in Whitehall and cheered to see the traitor's head topple from its perch (I mean that of King Charles the Martyr, for I write this retrospect in kinder times when the earlier passions are quite forgot). And from that misfortune I deduced a supplementary lesson: that he who thrusts himself forward will make a fine neck for the axe, a maxim which is as true for a bookseller's apprentice as for a king.

> Also thus it came to pass in the same year that one Jeremiah Mount, a young gentleman, hearing that God had spoke to John Reeve, and that he had damned several of his acquaintance, he came to us to discourse about those things.

The Acts of the Witness of the Spirit of Lodowick Muggleton

There is a tavern on the south side of the Minories towards the Tower end, the Five Bells, which was also a victualling house, and kept by a most ferocious Ranter whose name was George Quill. And there I became acquainted with one Captain Clark, a young man who had fought for the Parliament and lost an eye and who was thereby esteemed to be the author of the Ranters' tract *A Single Eye*, though it was in truth written by Mr Clarkson, no kin of his but also to be found at the Five Bells, for he said that a tavern was the House of God. This Clarkson had a wife in Suffolk with a quiverful of children but he gave his body to other women, having told us that there was no sin but as man esteemed it sin and therefore none can be free from sin till in purity it be acted as no sin, which I esteemed a convenient doctrine.

Today if these Ranter folk are at all remembered it is as severe preachers calling down hellfire upon the rich and proud, but in truth they were a merry crew and I was happy to hear them tell of the end of the world which was to come next Tuesday, or if not, the Tuesday following. We were free-born Englishmen and we might think as we pleased and do as we pleased too, which was another convenient doctrine.

I was taking a glass at the Five Bells when there was a commotion at the door and a huge man with red hair flaming like the archangel's came in and behind him a little man with long black hair who, though so much smaller than the other, yet bore an air of authority.

We are come to bear witness, said the red-haired man, for this is John Reeve whom the Lord hath appointed his Last Messenger, and I am chosen as his Mouth. Thus he and I are the two witnesses and there is no other true witness that the Lord hath chosen. My name is Lodowick Muggleton.

At first I thought that the company would laugh at the two men, for we had much experience of travelling preachers and some of our number were of a cynical humour. But the man's voice was so strong and melodious and had so little of the Ranter in it that we were quietened and listened closely as the smaller man explained how God had chosen him John Reeve his Last Messenger for a great work unto this bloody and unbelieving world, and in his First Message had given him understanding of the Scriptures above all men in the world.

For fourteen centuries, he told us, there hath not been one true prophet nor minister sent with a commission from the Lord. All the ministry in this world with all the worship taught by them is a lie and an abomination unto the Lord. There will be no more commission but ours until the end of the world, then God will appear suddenly after we have delivered this dreadful message and Christ will make it evident that he hath sent us.

On that first visit to the Five Bells, even the most disputatious Ranters were silenced, for they were curious. One of them said to the two men that he wanted them to come and discourse every week, and Muggleton said:

If you will hear the message, then it is our commission to deliver it. If you will each club twelve pence a week, then we shall come.

But when the Two Witnesses came next week, the most disputatious of the topers came there also, prepared to mock them and call their teaching Blasphemy, the voice of the Devil and such like.

At this John Reeve stood upon a chair, for he was a little man, and stretched out his hand upon them and said:

For that you deny God's Messenger and his Mouth, you deny Christ himself and seeing God hath sent me in his place here upon earth to give judgment upon those froward spirits who rebel against his word, and do blaspheme against the Holy Ghost, therefore I do pronounce you – and here he took the nearest man by the shoulders, for he did not know his name – cursed and damned, soul and body, from the presence of God, elect men and angels to eternity.

Then he took the man next to him by the shoulders and damned him too, and so on with half a dozen more.

But one of the men he damned, a pustulent man of a choleric temper, said he would be truly damned if he allowed this little usurper to curse him and he would wring his neck, and ran at John Reeve so violently that five or six men could hardly keep him off, his fury was so hot.

Then John Reeve said to the people standing by: Friends, I pray you stand still on both sides of the room, and let there be a space in the middle. And I will lay down my head upon the ground and let this furious man tread upon my head.

So the people stood still and made a space. Then John Reeve pulled off his hat and laid his face flat to the ground and said, do what you will. And the man came running at him full tilt and lifted up his foot to tread upon John Reeve's neck, but then he turned back as though some force were pulling him and said, no, I will not, I scorn to tread upon a man lying down, and began scratching his head like a man waking up from a dream.

John Reeve got up and continued his preaching.

From that moment I believed and accepted the Two Witnesses as true Messengers of God's word, and they became very friendly to me, for I was one of the first of our crew to see the light as they saw it. And I was flattered by their friendship and was glad to bear the expense of printing some of their epistles and pamphlets, addressing the Lord Mayor (who had put them in Newgate), and other high personages (who disapproved their preaching). But the expense was not great, for they knew printers who were of their faith and would take no payment for their labour but only for the paper and ink. And they were most grateful to me not only for my generosity but, I fancy, because they thought I was a gentleman and their other disciples were mostly common folk.

How could I have believed such stuff, I who am no man's gull, and was before that day in the Five Bells of a strict sceptical temper, though the Mouth took me for a Ranter? I can but plead that I was young and lonely and lacked a rudder to guide me through life's storms.

You are a good servant of the Lord, Jeremiah, one or other of them would say, the printer wants but five shillings to bring out another hundred copies of my Remonstrance to the Quakers, which is much called for.

And I would give the money with a gladsome heart. So it went on for some months until I was brought to see the error of my faith. It was during a disputation in another tavern, between John Reeve and a pale little fellow I did not know, that doubt began to assail my soul.

How far off is Heaven? asked the pale little fellow.

It is some six miles up, John Reeve answered.

And are the sun and the stars very big?

No, they are not much larger than they appear to the eye.

And God, how big is God?

Oh he is of the dimension of a middle-statured man with all parts as a man hath.

Taller than Your Worship, is he?

He is much of my height (John Reeve was not much above five feet tall).

Of mine too then? said the pale little fellow, pleased by this intelligence.

An inch or so taller perhaps, Reeve replied. Jeremiah, my throat grows dry from this discourse.

I fetched him a glass of ale, but the worm of doubt had begun to eat at my faith. A five-foot tall God? Heaven no further away than Hounslow?

At first I thought that John Reeve was jesting as preachers may do to show the folly of those who question them. But then I heard him say the same to others of his following, and I could see that he believed these things to be true.

Thus, but only by slow steps, I came to be cured of my delusions and it was Astronomy that cured me, for I had always been curious about such things and had read one or two of Mr Hignell's books upon the matter although he thought me a poor scholar.

Yet I still lacked the courage of my disbelief and durst not challenge the Two Witnesses, for I feared their cursing which had made stronger men than me faint and tremble. My strategy was rather to absent myself from these taverns and other meeting-places which they frequented.

You are diligent of late, Jeremiah, Mr Fisher said, clapping me upon the back as I carried a dozen reams of fresh sheets into the back store.

Thank you, sir, I returned prettily from beyond the door.

At that instant, I heard the noise of customers. My master was so garrulous that it was often five minutes before any purchaser had space to tell him of his wishes: A fine day is it not, though the wind is keen, you must excuse the condition of the shop, we have been taking in a new edition all day and we have not an inch left to spare, etc., etc.

Yet some instinct warned me that I must pay heed. It was not the words the customer said – Good-day to you sir – but the sonorous manner of his delivery, like the music from a bass-viol that is afar off, that told me that the Prophet Muggleton had come to call, with or without the Other Witness.

You have, I believe, a young gentleman in your shop, a Jer— But by then I was out of the back door and running on tiptoe down the lane.

It may seem ungrateful that I should have made such stir to escape those who had been kind to me and done me honour, but the truth was that I feared they wanted only money out of me and I did not see why the earnings that had come to me by the sweat of my brow should vanish down the Prophet's throat, for being a Materialist in philosophy he did not shrink from those delights which the Lord has rained down upon us, viz. food and drink.

Thus I commenced to lead an economical life, knowing not which tavern the Two Witnesses might choose to visit and so I avoided them all and drank small beer in the back store.

But there was other entertainment to be had that was closer to home and cost not a farthing.

Here is Mary Court. You remember Mary, don't you? She said she knew you a little at home in Kent. She is from Elmstead too and we Elmsteadites must stick together like burrs.

Oh yes indeed, I remember Mary.

And so I did, for I had tried in vain to kiss her and, as I have said, though she was tall as a lily she was scarcely fifteen years old then and she had cried out, but now . . . I kissed her hand like a Frenchman and gazed into her pale eyes like an astronomer at the stars.

London has made you silly, I see, she said, and to Ralph: I hope you have not been so corrupted.

I fear I have too little time for diversion, Mary. The bookseller's trade is a deep study.

So it must be, Ralph. She looked at him gravely and I could see him thinking, here is a serious girl who will be well suited to be my life's partner, for he was a thinker-ahead and never paused on the way to pick the flowers. He wearied her already with his endless recitals of tonnages and longitudes and latitudes and octavos and duodecimos. It was not for such discourse that she had come to London, and I resolved to suit her fancy as best I could. Fluff might have her in the end but I was resolved she should see something of the great world first.

Do you care for ballads, Mary? Wiggins and Ponder have given me some of Garland's latest airs. I remember you have a voice like a nightingale.

More like a jay. She laughed but was touched by my offer.

And if you should need lace or pomanders or any such trifles, the girls at the Three Spanish Gypsies will gladly let me have any article at half the price.

I have very little money, alas, she said. I'm in service with my aunt in Islington and she can't afford to pay me, except my board and lodging.

Well then for nothing, to you.

I could not accept such gifts.

Oh it will be but Kentish kindness, I said airily. There is no time like the present, let us go now – for I knew that Ralph was needed back at our master's and could not go with us in the afternoon.

So we walked through the City, the two of us, and the pavements being narrow I had to hold her to keep her from being splashed by the carriages or falling into the mire, and she was happy to take my arm in a simple country fashion. At the Gypsies I loaded her down with ribbons and silk which were in truth trumpery stuff but gaudy.

We must celebrate your finery. There is a tavern nearby where they serve only beer from Kentish hops.

Oh I couldn't go to a tavern, besides I'm unused to liquor.

Well then, he has the best canary too and that's a true ladies' drink, I don't know a lady of fashion that does not drink canary (I did not tell her it was stronger than beer – there are some things we must discover for ourselves).

She trembled upon the step of the Three Tuns. I shall not forget how she trembled and turned her pale face to me as though I were her confessor and she was asking absolution for the sin that I hoped she was about to commit.

It is a worthy inn, I said, a superior establishment, Sir Edward Hyde himself lodged here when he was parleying with the Lord Mayor.

Is that true, Jem?

You may ask the Lord Mayor, for he is often to be found here too. The Guildhall is but next door.

Oh Jem, she said and tapped me on the shoulder as though to knight me for my wit.

And so we went on into the Three Tuns which was in truth a dark and smoky place as all such taverns are, but she did not care and sat down on the bench by the fire as though she had been frequenting taverns all her life. And I took her hand and told her fortune: You shall meet a tall dark man, etc., and then I kissed her hand, then kissed her lightly upon the neck.

Oh this canary is strong, I do not think I –

It is but lemonade, Mary, everyone drinks it by the gallon.

And she tossed it back bravely and I kissed her on the neck again, on her long white neck, and a strange fierceness overcame me.

Jem, do not hold me so, don't, oh –

She pushed me off and jumped to her feet.

I am very sorry, I said, and began to shower down repentances on her, yet there was no repentance in my heart but a savage longing that had no love in it. I wanted to be revenged – upon Ralph, upon Nan who had left me, upon the whole world, and long pale Mary was to be the scapegoat for them all.

It was kind of you to give me all these things – she began to sob – but we are strangers to each other and I am –

Oh, Mary, I would not for a fortune have you weep. You're so beautiful that my passion got the better of me, it won't happen again, I wouldn't for all the world distress you. Please take another glass, as a sign that you forgive me? You must not return to your aunt's so distressed.

Thus in the end she took another glass and we discoursed long (and it must be said tediously) of her family and her aunt, and her desire to learn Italian and the flageolet and her mother's hope that she might eventually marry Ralph. So I walked her back to her aunt's and we were friends again but the kiss I gave when we parted at the door (a mean dwelling next the Angel) was a lover's kiss, full and long, not a friend's kiss. And I knew I had planted the seed of passion, one that Ralph would never in a millennium plant.

The next day I took her on a boat, a blue wherry with red oars, and I rowed her down to a quiet place under the willows below Greenwich and after a bottle of wine and two beef pasties I pulled up her skirts and had her with as little feeling as though I were plucking a chicken. When I went in, she cried out twice but not loud, as though she were calling for aid but feared to rouse the enemy, and then was quiet and I could not tell what she thought. Afterwards, she wept but not much and there was not much blood either.

Will you always love me, Jem?

Yes, I said, I will, but not meaning it, nor did she in her heart think I did.

Yet though I did it out of lust and revenge, that savagery did have something of love in it after all, though perverted, and I think of it often now, more often than other, kinder scenes: Mary lying against the headboard with her skirts still disarranged and spilling over the side, and the path of the tear still wet on her cheek and the sweet soreness I had and the red oars slapping the water *piano*. And summoning up this recollection, I come to wondering whether I would have fared better if I had been truly in love with her or had at any rate made some simulation of love such that she would have married me and we would have made an honest pair keeping pigs and sheep in Elmstead – but it was only a dream, for even in the thinking of it the serpent Tedium would creep into the image and I knew I could never have borne such a life. Meanwhile, to draw up the account: I had done her, Ralph could have her. There was other business to be carried forward.

I forgot to say that I had carried on my former trade with the ingenious chests and found twice as many acceptances as I had in Dover, so that I was the most prosperous prentice on Tower Hill and much respected by my fellows who dubbed me Gorgeous Jem. Yet I knew full well that I was yet but in a small way of business, for I lacked connections with those great sluice-engines which pump wealth into the pockets of their operators, viz. the Admiralty and the Treasury. Mr Fisher had no notion of how to get on in the world, being but a simple tradesman resolved to buy cheap and sell dear. He was full of honest saws: quality will always tell, a bad workman blames his tools, penny wise pound foolish and the like. There was no great future to be had in his shop, and I was determined to leave after I had served my articles.

It was in the spring at the time of the Dutch wars and the Pool of London was crammed with men-o'-war like herrings in a barrel. It was harvest time for us, for many of the tarpaulins newly promoted to captain had no knowledge of the North Sea and the French waters beyond Portland, while we had an unrivalled collection of Dutch maps. In fact, all our maps were copies of the finest Amsterdam charts with our own crest and legend superinscribed upon them, for though Mr Fisher was a pious man and went to church twice upon the Lord's Day, in matters of trade he was a veritable pirate and quite unashamed. Imitation is the sincerest form of flattery was another of his saws.

Thus one morning I called upon the *Vanguard* lying at St Katharine's and begged to wait upon the captain with a bundle of the latest charts of supreme quality (no ingenious boxes on this visit, for I fancied there would be no time for such diversion when the cannon were roaring). While I stood upon the deck, I heard a seaman speak to his fellow upon the land: He's a rare commander though he's but a landlubber. Not a sailor then? the fellow inquired. Lord bless you, never been to sea in his life before this trip except as a passenger, knows no seamen's terms. When we'd say tack about, he cries wheel to the left, or the right. The quartermaster says that when he asks for instructions – larboard or starboard as you might say – the Admiral just shouts aye, aye, boys, let's board them. You never saw such a thing in your life, but he knows how to fight, and fighting's fighting.

I wanted to hear more of this strange Land-Admiral, but just then I was called for downstairs and brought into the presence of a low dull stocky man, more like a butcher than an admiral. He looked at me with a black choleric sort of suspicion. Charts, you say? Charts of Dutch waters?

Yes, sir, and I began to expatiate upon my wares – their exactitude, their originality, their hydographical science, etc., etc.

Do you have a chart of Sheerness and the Medway? he broke in impatiently.

Yes indeed I do, sir.

He snatched it from me and took it over to his chart-table where he laid it beside an old chart, much cracked, brown and stained with sea-water. There was a dead silence in the cabin, I could hear the Admiral's heavy breathing as he bent over the charts that he might compare them.

Yes, he said, it is a passable copy, the printing is not so fine as de Blauw's but it will do; I'll take a dozen for my flag officers. Mr Fido will examine the rest of your stock and choose what else we might want. And, Fido, take his name, the boy's a likely rogue and we may have need of him back on land.

I thanked the Admiral warmly, being willing to overlook his accusations of knavery since I had a higher object in view. Mr Fido took three dozen more of my maps and congratulated me: General – I mean Admiral – Monck is likely to prove a powerful friend, you would do well to cling to his coat-tails. I thanked the fellow for his advice, which as you may imagine I had no need of.

This proceeding was on the eve of that great battle in which the Dutch Admiral, that pirate Tromp, was killed and the sea ran red with blood. We English lost a thousand men but our landlubber Admiral came back home without a scratch on him to a hero's welcome. A gold chain to the value of £300 was put upon his neck and a medal struck to commemorate the victory and there was a public thanksgiving ordered.

He had indeed proved to be a powerful friend and I was resolved to be as faithful as Fido, losing no time in writing to remind the Admiral of our former acquaintance and trusting that I might wait upon him and serve him in whatever capacity he might, etc., etc. I wrote this letter in a fair hand, gave out that it came from my master's shop, and sent it by the hand of my master's boy.

Imagine my rapture, my ecstasy, when a letter came back the next day, in the Admiral's own hand, in truth, a scurvy hand with much misspelling and far out in its grammar. But the message was clear enough, viz. he well remembered your obedient servant and had much to thank me for, for he had beaten the Dutch off their own shore *and with their own charts* (this phrase he underlined with a thick nib). He was an enemy of pirates, but he would readily grant a pardon to those who pirated charts, for they had their uses. And the upshot of all was, he would see what he could do for me.

This was glorious, but I had to keep my jubilation private, for I fancied that my master would not have approved. I had kept secret the exact number of charts I had sold to the Admiralty (some half of them I had not written down in the books) and had represented myself as the head and principal of the house. Indeed, Mr Fido had remarked that I was remarkably young to have acquired the dignity of a Stationer (though I am sure I was younger still than he thought me, for my stature and my black complexion aged me).

At last the great day dawned. By luck I was looking out through the shop window and saw Mr Fido coming down the lane and had time to take off my printer's apron and put on my fine blue coat that I might greet him at the door in my character of proprietor (though what was I to do if he asked to be shown the shop and I had to take him to my master's room?). But I was in luck again. Mr Fido was in haste and he had scarcely breath to tell me that I was to be Under-Clerk to the Council and have £100 a year, and that I was to wait upon the

General in the afternoon, for he was off to Scotland on the morrow to hunt down the last of the King's men.

I much looked forward to this reunion with my personal Protector, but when I came up the steps to his lodgings in Whitehall, I met only Fido again who told me that, alas, the General was much cumbered with business and begged me to accept his apologies (he said with an insolent expression, as though to say: what, apologies to a tradesman), but the appointment would be confirmed within the week.

And so it was. Thus at the age of twenty-one, Jeremiah the yeoman's son was made Under-Clerk to the Great Council and a gentleman. I had my foot upon the first step of that great staircase which leads to the topmost thrones and citadels of our kingdom, or rather, for we had no king at that juncture, of our glorious State and government. True it was, as Lord Bacon wrote in his Essays, that all rising to great place is by a winding stair, but I fancied that I was pretty well acquainted with the twists and turns of the business.

At the Clerks' chamber I met with Symons and Llewelyn and went with them to Mr Mount's chamber at the Cockpit where we had some rare pot venison and ale to abundance till almost 12 at night; and after a song round, we went home.

Diary of Samuel Pepys, 23 January 1660

III

The Palace

Then began the days of my greatness, but to confess the truth I was
in a whirl six days out of seven for fear that I should do the wrong
thing and stumble back down that slippery staircase.

The offices of the Clerks to the Council lay in that rabbit warren
of rooms below the great Council Chamber which was named the
Cockpit, for there was still a cockpit in the north-west quarter of it
(though it had been closed by order of the Commonwealth). It was
said the Palace had two thousand rooms, some were ancient already
when Cardinal Wolsey had the Palace, some were modern-built, but
all tacked on higgledy-piggledy in brick or stone or plaster without
any arrangement as might suit the convenience of the fancy of the
builder. In all my years there I never mastered the plan and knew but
half a dozen rat-runs, viz. from my chamber to my master's, from my
master's to the Council Chamber via the Privy Chamber (for I had the
run of that route, unlike the *vulgus* who must come at it via the stairs
from the Pebble Court). And if I had but imperfect knowledge of the
topography, I also had much to learn about the business. When I began,
I scarce knew the difference between a warrant and a patent, a writ and
an instrument, and a hundred other such terms. All I knew was buying
and selling. But I soon perceived that I was still in that same business,
and if I struck a sharp bargain in the service of the State my share of
the fee would be commensurate. In this delicate art my first tutor was
one Will Symons, a lovely man and no flincher from the bottle, for his
greatest legacy to me was: he taught me how to drink.

There was not a tavern within two miles of Whitehall we had not desiccated. When we were pressed for time, we drank sack at the Leg in New Palace Yard or at the Dog in that same yard – both large and commodious taverns which were also suppliers of venison, carp and other delicacies to us Clerks when we entertained in our chambers. But if we had time to spare, we would go for a frisk down Fleet Street to the Devil, where Mr Ben Jonson the poet was formerly wont to keep the table on a roar, or to Hercules' Pillars on the south side, where you might meet with a sot or a lord or a philosopher or a whore. Or if we had a taste for Hock or Mosel, we might go to the Rhenish winehouses in Wise's Alley, or to Mr Prior's in Common Row; his cousin the poet I heard it said, later lived on tick at his cousin's tavern, and I can well believe it, for poets are powerful drinkers but generally lack the means to gratify their thirst.

In bawdy talk Will Symons was a veritable *virtuoso*. And his anecdotes were not those second-hand tales which the timid tell who will report with much sniggering how such-and-such a gentleman did this or that to such-and-such a lady and what were the consequences. Will spoke always of his own trials with the softer sex, and he reported failure and success alike with the same grave and reverend demeanour as though he had been rehearsing a sermon he had just heard. Thus: Jem, you know that fair girl Paulina at the Leg, the one who serves at table? I had no luck in that siege until I discovered she was Scottish, and when I put my hand up her skirts I began to talk of Arthur's Seat and the Tolbooth and the fine society that was to be had up there and her resistance began to weaken, and she took my other hand, etc., etc. But he was no tedious braggart, for he was just as content to describe how his engine had failed him when he and Mrs Bracewell had been in a rowing-boat at Chelsea Stairs, a full moon and she willing. His impotence had made her angry and she compelled him to row her up to Hammersmith against the tide. He had attempted a song to lighten her, but she interrupted him: You can't row, Will Symons, now I know you can't sing, so I'm not surprised that you can't do the other thing. But it was the gloomy parson's voice he had that made me laugh, all on one solemn note, not like a wag who overcooks his jests.

Will's other art was he knew how to survive. He told me later that he had made shift to keep in employment in eight governments in one year and was only turned out along with Peter Llewelyn (who had formerly had my apartment at the Cockpit) and the other clerks when the King came in. He was a master at his craft which was to be at the head of the regiment when places were given out for the service of a new committee.

And those years of O.C. (amongst ourselves we never called him Lord Protector or any such highflown title, for he was but a Huntingdonshire squire and a heavy man) were also the great years of committee. The Palace of Whitehall stood as deep in committees as corn in August. There was the Obstruction Committee (which Will accounted a redundancy, for what was any committee but an Obstruction), and the Scandalous Ministers Committee, and the Propagation Committee and the Indemnity Commission, and the Law Reform Committee, and the Plundered Ministers Committee, and the Compounding Committee that was at Goldsmiths Hall, and a dozen more, each with its own burrow in that great warren.

When they were all going to their work on a winter's day, the chimney smoke over the Palace was so thick that an eagle or a lark in the air above must have supposed some great disaster had afflicted London, a comet exploding or the like. The stench was so terrible that Mr John Evelyn in that rare work *Fumifugium* claimed that the prevalence of consumption and other pulmonic troubles was caused by Newcastle coal. Certain it is true that, though I was young, I was never free of coughs and spitting fits for so long as I worked in that place. Yet the College of Physicians esteemed the smoke rather a protection against infections, although one half of them who perish in London die of pulmonic distempers, and some parts of France, in the south-west of that realm, complained that the smoke from England was injuring their vines.

It was a year less a month when the doorkeeper Hodge came in to tell me I had a visitor at the King's Gate.

Who is it?

A woman.

A woman? Ah.

Yes, sir, a tall black woman.

Oh. Not one that looks like me?

Why, sir, so she does.

You must tell her I am greatly occupied.

But it was too late, for as he turned to take my message back to the gate, he met my mother coming in at the door.

I am not to be kept drumming my heels at a draughty gate. You must tell your fellow to be more civil.

Oh Mother. I came forward to embrace her because I thought Hodge would think it right, not out of love, but Hodge had already taken his leave with a smirk on his face, and she slipped out of my arms as though she were an eel, and began looking about her.

So this is your office, Jeremiah?

I share it with Mr Symons. He is my fellow Under-Clerk, though he is my senior.

I trust he is a sober influence upon you?

Oh exceedingly sober.

Then those must be your wine bottles that I see upon the shelf.

Ah, no, well, I believe Mr Symons is keeping them for his brother who is to take them down to Harwich.

My mother made that strange noise I knew so well, not quite a snort, nor yet a sniff, but somewhere between the two. And of a sudden I felt myself to be ten years old again, hesitating upon the threshold that I might detect whether her temper was out, and if I heard the snort-sniff I would creep off into the yard again.

And what do you here, Jeremiah?

We make out warrants and patents as we are instructed and deliver them to those they are made out to, and writs and instruments and summonses we make out also and deliver them to those they are made out against.

It seems light work.

But it is well paid, a hundred pounds a year. I told you, did I not, in my letter? (Which was the only letter I had written.)

So you did, she said. It is too much.

But it's a good place and since I'm at the hub of affairs I have reason to hope I may find a better one yet.

Your father rises at dawn and labours eighteen hours a day for less. (It was the first time I had ever heard her pray her husband in aid as an example of virtue unrewarded.)

I cannot help that, Mother.

She stood silent in her long dress of brown stuff, a hard look in her eye. Yet she was handsome.

You will come to no good, she said. You think you're so clever, but it will all tumble down around your ears.

You had best go now if that is how you think.

I am going. I would not outstay my welcome had there been any welcome.

Again the sniff-snort, and this time it pierced my heart and I wished that I were half her height again and could clasp her by the legs and hide my head in her skirts and she would pretend to search for bugs in my hair and call me Jemmy Junket, but those days were long gone.

I hope Mr Symons's brother will not forget to take his bottles, she said and went out without another word. Indeed, I remember those words very well because they were the last she ever spoke to me.

Now in recollection I am full of repentance and wish we had made up our differences, but at the time of our division, my resolution was as adamantine as hers. Neither of us would bend or break, and I plunged into the ocean of Whitehall in Will's wake without a backward glance.

Will found his first lodging in this great spider-web as Under-Clerk to the Scandalous Ministers Committee, but so diligent was he that within a month he was promoted Upper Clerk, and made me his underling, for which I was heartily grateful because there were fine pickings in this field and every cowpat brought up a mushroom. We would make a visit upon some suspect priest early in the morning while the dew was still upon his glebe and examine him thus: We have information that your wife is a Catholic. Not so, it is false, she is a proper woman who worships each Sunday at my church. You will swear an affidavit to that effect? Certainly, and so will she. That will be fourpence for her affidavit and fourpence for your affidavit and five pounds for the expenses of the examination. And then, and here Will would look at the ceiling as though to commune with a higher power, you would surely wish to give us something for our labour, that we may further the work of true religion in this country? Another five pounds. Or if he would not we would report to our masters in Whitehall that Mr G— in the parish of P— was widely supposed to be a delinquent priest and that his wife was said to be a Catholic, though for our part, we had no conclusive evidence for these rumours, but we thought it our duty to report them. This was usually sufficient for the man to lose his place to a minister of stout Presbyterian tendencies who had been recommended by the Plundered Ministers Committee. As for my former employment, I had now no leisure to trudge on scurvy wharves and solicit gruff sea-captains. Besides, who would labour at his own little pump when he might manage the great sluice-engines of State? Moreover, the King's coming in was soon to spoil the market for lewd books, there being so many published that a rare volume that had formerly cost ten shillings might be had for half-a-crown.

Will saw that it would be a great thing to be Clerk also to the Plundered Ministers Committee, since he would then have both sides of the balance in his hands: the minister that feared to be put out would pay to be recommended, and so would the minister that had cast covetous eyes on the parish.

Alas, the fellow that was Clerk to the Plundered Ministers Committee would not yield his place, nor would he appoint an Under-Clerk, for he preferred to keep all the fees for himself. And even the Scandalous Ministers Committee came to an end, when the desire for vengeance had run its course, and O.C. determined that reconciliation and tolerance should be his orders of the day.

O.C. is right as usual, we had squeezed that orange dry, said Will as he puffed at his pipe, for he imitated our master in such little things. He claimed that he had chanced upon our lord taking the air upon the bowling-green at the back of the Cockpit, and O.C. had congratulated Will upon the exquisite aroma of his tobacco.

Tomorrow to fresh woods and pastures new, in the words of Master Milton, said Will, and added: Whom I do not greatly care for, being a sour and extreme fellow, but he enjoys O.C.'s favour and therefore I have conned a bushel or two of his verses. He's not made for this trade, Jem, he won't bend and besides his eyes are as dim as a mole's. I have seen him scrabbling around for a sixpence on the pavement when it was winking up at him bright as the moon.

What fresh pastures have you in mind? I inquired.

Wait and the glory shall be revealed unto thee, Will said, it is such work in the service of the State as never was undertaken before, a most peculiar commission. Come with me up the river at the week's end and we shall make our first *reconnaissance* – a word which he pronounced in a frenchified fashion and explained that it was a military term for seeking out the lie of the ground.

But what is the ground we are to seek out, what is our mission? Hush, my dear underling, you shall know as much as is good for you when the time comes. Our mission is a delicate one and it should not be entrusted to babbling mouths.

I protested that I was a close man who could keep a secret as well as any, but he would tell me no more, until we met at dawn on the Horse-ferry on a Saturday where a waterman was waiting for us.

Why do we not take the Committee barge? I asked.

We don't wish to be conspicuous, Will said, that is why we are going today when honest folk will be lying indoors. It is most convenient that the State should smile upon these long week's-ends. In the traitor's time, we were lucky if we had so much as a half-holiday on Saturday.

The single pair of oars took us through the silent misty reaches of Chelsea and Putney and on past the tapestry factory at Mortlake and round the great bend at Richmond where the fields were white with hoar-frost though the sun had begun to shine and our waterman's face was dewed with sweat. As we left Petersham Meadows behind, I could imagine but one destination.

Is this true, are we going to –

Hush, Jem, or you'll blow the gab.

We landed at a dusty alehouse before the next bend on the river, and Will gave the waterman fourpence for his ale and cheese and told him to wait for our return, even though it should be after dark. I hoped we also might refresh ourselves after the journey but Will said we were on State business and we must look sharp about it. I could see the waterman grinning under his black hood and I fancied he knew more about the business than I did and that Will's hushing was for show. The waterman had dark brows and a raven's beak and I thought I might have seen him in one of the taverns frequented by Thurloe's spies, viz. the Horse and Cart in Old Conduit Street.

I shivered as I stepped ashore although the air was mild now and the sun was shining on the water. Will led me up the hill behind the alehouse which he told me was called Strawberry Hill for the strawberry field which girdled its lower slopes, although we saw no strawberries it being winter. As we came over the top of the hill, Will took my arm and with a grand gesture worthy of a tragedian exclaimed:

There, Jem, there's our mark.

It was as I had begun to suspect. Far off beyond the oaks of the Royal Park lay the red towers and lofty battlements of Hampton Court Palace.

Think of it, Jem, he wheezed, for the climb had left him out of breath, being a short-winded man because of the hogsheads he consumed, we are to be the first servants of the State to survey the Palace since the execution of you-know-who.

But why are we proceeding in this roundabout hugger-mugger fashion? We could have landed at Hampton Court steps and saved ourselves the walk.

These are delicate matters, Jem. O.C. is most particular that he should not be thought a snatcher. He wants everything to be accomplished in proper form. When he is proclaimed Grand Vizier of All England, then he may enter upon his own, but he must not seem to be previous. Yet *simultaneo* he is anxious to secure the property and dust it off, for it has been left vacant four years now.

We went through a little wood and came to a gate which was the boundary of the park. Beyond the gate there was a man setting snares in a bosky warren. He gave us good-morning.

By whose authority are you setting those snares, sir? Will asked in his solemn official voice.

Why, sir, on my own. I bought the lease of the hare warren off Mr Casewell who had it off the goldsmith Mr Edmund Backwell, a warm gentleman in the City, who had it off the Council and, so they say, made a profit of five hundred pounds and more on the selling.

Make a note of this fellow's name, Jem.

Tabbit, sir, rhymes with Rabbit. Are you from the Council? They were saying at the Palace that gentlemen from the Council were expected today.

Can no one keep any matter in this country private any more? Well, Tabbit, you will be hearing from us. Good-day.

Will was most put out, and he strode on so fast that I had a struggle to keep up with him as we dodged through the thorns and thistles of the unkempt fields. For in those brief few years nature had resumed her perpetual invasions and the meadows had become a wilderness. The grass was choked and the grazing was fit only for donkeys. Our path was many times blocked with fallen timber and the low ground was boggy so that we had to jump from tussock to tussock to keep our fine Spanish boots dry. I lost my footing none the less and splashed Will's new canary coat with the muddy water beneath the broken ice.

God damn you, Jem, how shall we cut a proper figure in these negotiations if we look like drowned rats?

By now we had reached the sunken ditch, or haw-haw as they call it now, which divides the park from the inner avenues and pleasaunces of the Palace, and as we were hitching ourselves up over the ditch, we were met by a richly dressed gentleman who was walking his black spaniel.

Good-morning, gentlemen, you look distressed, may I take you to my apartments and offer you a towel? You are from the Council of State, I presume? I am Edmund Backwell, lessee of these policies on the eastern side. Mr Phelps, who owns the manor and royalty of the Palace, is waiting for you in the State apartments. You will find them disagreeably mouldy, I fear.

In the face of this magnifico, Will began to muster his accustomed dignity. And after Mr Backwell had entertained us to a dish of coffee in his lodging next the old tennis court and his man had rubbed us down with a Turkey towel, we began to look more the part as Mr Backwell escorted us round the river-side of the Palace to the gatehouse.

But lord, there never was a more melancholy sight. All along the river the meaner sort from Kingston and Hampton Wick had fenced off portions of the ground for their pigs and cattle and chickens. There was scarce a blade of grass left on the long avenue, and the stench was intolerable. The bushes and shrubs which had been planted to make pretty walks for the late Queen and her ladies were all pulled about and half-eaten, and the parterres were trampled into mud. I chased off a mangy cur that was lifting its leg against the Italian statue of a goddess by the doorway that took us into the great court. A low busy personage in a coat of Genoa velvet came bouncing out like a puppy to meet us. This was Mr Phelps's man of business who had a bundle of papers for us to con.

Leases, sir, and contracts and assignments. When you have perused these, you will know the lie of the land from the attics to the drains and subterranean watercourses of the premises.

We are simply here to inspect and examine the State's property. We may come to these legal matters in good time, Will said, pushing these dusty papers away with a gesture which I thought somewhat lordly.

What *was* the State's property, sir. Matters have galloped on in the past twelve months, at a pace that would astonish you. Had you come here a year ago, I could have shown you whole ranges of the Palace buildings, its purlieus and its policies that were indeed the property of our most glorious State, but now, well, there is a verdurers' cottage or two in the corner of Bushey Park that has not yet been leased out, but as for the rest, this is a busy country, sir, a merchant's country, we do not loiter.

But the State apartments – Will bleated like a lost sheep.

Intact, sir, quite intact, too much so for there is a coat or two of dust on them.

Where is your master?

I am afraid Mr Phelps is not at liberty to see you today. He sends you his most profound apologies, he is engaged upon most urgent business with his cargoes from the Plantations. But he has asked me to show you everything and to let you have any particulars in regard to price that you may have need of.

Price?

Yes, sir, price. The man of business looked startled. You are here to repurchase certain items, are you not, on behalf of the State and of His Highness Oliver Cromwell?

You move too fast. We are here merely to survey the present conditions of the Palace and its purlieus.

Well sir, have it as you will. And the little man in Genoa velvet, much put out of his countenance, led us up the great staircase which was covered in dust and mould, ditto the windows, and there were bat droppings in the corners and old swallows' nests under the cornice.

Mr Phelps and his household do not come this way, having their own private entrance over towards the knot garden.

If the staircase was grimy, the great presence chamber was worse yet. The brocades were all torn, with dark patches where the King's Italian pictures had once hanged, and the dogs had got in and left a stink behind them and the wind was coming in through a cracked pane. The next room was no better, nor the one after it. But it was the emptiness and the sound of our echoing footsteps that made us reflect upon the damage that four short years of neglect could perform on so great a palace.

At the end of the range of great rooms, the little man in velvet unlocked a door for us and led us into an array of smaller chambers.

We are now in Mr Phelps's private apartments, that were the Queen's but are quite fitting for a private gentleman being of moderate size and well furnished.

And so they were. Every bedpost and chimneypiece was polished to a gleam, and the hangings of fine old brocade had not a hole or loose thread. The air smelled of beeswax and lavender and there was a fire blazing in every grate.

Mr Phelps is eager to assist the Commonwealth as far as may be in his power and has instructed me to strike the fairest price for any paintings or tapestries that belonged to the late Charles Stuart and ought by rights now to adorn His Highness's lodgings. Thus, this *Young Woman with Goliath Head*, fifteen pounds; this *Herodias with the Head of the Baptist*, from the hand of Titiano, one hundred and fifty; and this *Burning of Rome by Nero, a Dictator*, by Giulio of Rome, twenty-four. He jogged up and down the paintings and tapestries (which were very fine) like an auctioneer crying up a sale of goods.

Will, however, was set upon continuing in his severe vein.

I presume you have proof, sir, that your master came by these pictures honestly?

The little man went red as a turkey-cock. We have bills of sale for every item, sir, and if you would care to consult your own records at Whitehall, I dare say you would find copies thereof.

But Will was unmoved.

This close-stool now?

You mean the antique commode, sir. Note the fine red velvet, Genoa workmanship of course. It stood once in the King's apartments, so it did, and Mr Phelps had it from the Trustees for five pounds.

Did he? Well, we shall have it back for the same – and to my amazement Will went over to the commode and lifted the cover of it and pulled down his breeches and sat upon the close-stool.

There now, this close-stool shall have the privilege of entertaining the buttocks of three great men: Charles Stuart sometime King, Oliver Cromwell shortly to be Lord Protector, and in between Will Symons, Clerk to the Great Council. Fear not, sir, I have left no work for the groom of the stool – and he buttoned himself up with an expression of the utmost solemnity.

The little man stood, gaping-mouthed. He could neither speak nor move until Will led him gently by hand into the next room. It was the first time I ever heard the expression Lord Protector, for Will already knew the style that our master was to take, though it were not yet gazetted. Will knew everything. No sooner were we in the next room than Will started back through the door to the close-stool he had just quitted and took out one of the tickets that he had prepared for the purpose and pinned it to the velvet lid of the commode. Reserved for His Highness, it said.

But that is Mr Phelps's property.

Temporarily so, sir, temporarily so. I am sure we shall come to an accommodation. The ticket will serve as a memorandum for the valuers. You will not object if I attach another to this canvas of Giulio's. His Highness has a fine *connaissance* in matters of Italian art.

So we tramped on through the apartments affixing our tickets to likely articles until some of Mr Phelps's rooms looked as though a snowstorm had passed through them.

But that table is especially dear to Mrs Phelps. She plays at cards with her daughters upon it.

Do not fret, sir, the State will pay a fair price. There are other tables in this world.

Will was airy, almost monarchical in his demeanour. By the time we had finished, the little man was quite downcast, the bounce had gone out of him.

Yet as we came down Mr Phelps's private stairs and out into the knot garden, our business done, there was to be a reversal of fortunes.

Ah, there is Mrs Phelps now and some of her friends.

A stout lady with a high colour advanced upon us shouting even before we had come up with us: What do you mean by it, sir, you are robbers, rogues, you have no business here, take yourself off, begone, etc., etc.

We dodged round the yew hedge, tipping our hats to her *en passant*, for we saw no profit in holding conversation with her. And her friends appeared to be of a hostile disposition, waving sticks at us and uttering oaths of a foulness not to be expected of persons associated with a former royal residence.

Nor were we free of harm when we came out into the front court of the Palace, for there was gathered the other rabble, composed of those commoners who kept pigs and cattle and had squatted like hungry beasts upon the fields along the river where they had pasturage and water for free. They besieged us with their cries of sir, sir, please certify my lease, I fought for the Good Old Cause, I lost an arm at Worcester, sir, sir, this land was my father's, he had it of the Commission, sir, etc., etc. They clutched and pulled at us and belched their foul breath in our faces, and we could go neither forward nor back, and in my desperation to be gone I knocked over a weak little poxy man, with a bald head and he fell and cried that he'd broken his ankle. And the crowd said that I had trampled on him purposely. I said no no I meant him no ill, but I began to fear for my life, for I had heard how other of the State's servants bound upon unpopular business had been set upon and had not returned alive.

But at that moment the crowd was driven apart as though by a spear and through the evil-favoured rabble came a man with a black hood and a raven's beak and behind him two men whom I took to be constables.

I thought you might stand in need of help, sir, said our waterman in his strange formal mode of speech, so I took the liberty of coming up to the steps.

Quite right, take us out of here before we are destroyed.

Our dark escort brought us down the steps under the bridge and rowed us out into the middle of the river where we were out of reach of the rabble's grasping hands although not of the stones and cabbage-heads they threw at us. And their oaths pursued us down the river as they ran along the path taunting and abusing us.

But in the end they wearied of the pursuit and the afternoon was growing dark.

We sat in silence for a while with no noise but the waterman's oars and the mallards crying and the flap of their wings as they took off at our approach.

'Tis a grimy business, Jem.

Someone has to do it.

Do they? Does O.C. really need that place?

I suppose he was not born to it.

No, he was not. And if he needs pictures, can he not buy them elsewhere? There are plenty more Giulios and Titianos in Italy if he must plaster his walls with such gewgaws.

He is willing to pay for them.

He is not to pay for them. It is you and I, Jem, who are to pay for them. He is no more than a cloddish upstart and I do not see why we should risk our necks for such a –

This outburst was interrupted by a cough from the waterman. It was a harsh cough, as harsh as his raven's face, yet his voice was soft and courtly.

I doubt, sir, whether this conversation be well advised.

But we are alone on the river . . .

You place me in a difficult position, sir. I would rather not be compelled to –

Oh you mean, Mr Thurloe . . .

Just so, sir. He is most particular in these matters.

He will want an account of our voyage?

I fear he will, sir. A full account.

Well, Will was silent for a full minute by Richmond clock which I could just make out on the darkling hill above us.

He shall have it, by noon tomorrow.

I was talking of *my* report, sir.

Ah yes, well, no doubt we ought to compare our notes, that the two accounts may be fully reconciled. That would be desirable, wouldn't it?

Yes, it would, although I fear it may prove a costly business.

Costly? Costly to whom?

To you, sir, for a waterman's time is precious to him, it's his only stock in trade, as you might say, and if I'm to go about reconciling and recording and whatever, I shall lose hire, a considerable deal of hire.

You're not Welsh, are you?

No, sir. I thought something in the nature of a reconciliation fee might smooth out our difficulties.

A reconciliation fee?

Of five pounds, sir.

Will held out five sovereigns which glistened in the twilight before they disappeared under the raven's hood as though they had been grains of corn going into his crop.

We spoke no more. As we came below Putney Hill where the Ranters and Levellers and the rest of the trash had held their seditious debates (though what is sedition in times when there is an utter Revolution every six months), the waterman began to sing. It was a low song, of love, I fancy, though I could not catch the words.

Would you mind greatly not singing? Will asked.

No, sir, I shouldn't mind at all, if that is your wish.

My head aches.

Then I shall refrain from the refrain, sir, if I may put it in that fashion, though my singing *is* admired. My wife likes me to sing to her in bed.

I am not your wife.

No, sir. There's no disputing about tastes, is there?

He too fell silent although once he repeated to himself 'refrain from the refrain' and chuckled.

I fancied that Will and I were seized by the same melancholy fit. What were all our labours to bring settlement and sober government worth, if we were at the mercy of an ignorant and fearful peasantry on the one hand and an overweening general on the other? Could England ever be made safe for such as we? Decent people of the middling sort who wished no harm to anyone – I don't say godfearing people, for Will and I were not alone in having supped our fill of conformity and nonconformity, of oaths sworn or not sworn, of prayer-books and orders of service and quarrels about rubrics and vestments and Lord knows what else. We wanted only a church that would be peaceable, make no commotion and have no taint of popery nor yet of zealotry. Yet how were we ever to escape from the fanatics?

Will walked with me to my chamber at the Cockpit. We bade farewell as confederates in I know not what conspiracy. Perhaps we felt ourselves but puppets of an uneasy time and wished ourselves returned to the days of blossom and country matters. Yet we had quarrelled as we parted.

Five pounds was too much. He wouldn't have reported us, for he knew we would have denied it and it would have been the word of two honourable clerks against one scurvy waterman.

Mud sticks, Jem, and a scanty bribe is worse than none at all. But you need have no part in the matter, if you wish. It was my speech that was unguarded.

No, no, I'll stand my share. We're in this together.

O.C. removed to Hampton Court, although his mother and his wife thought the place was too big for them. Yet a palace will fill up like a water-butt in February, and it was not long before every lodging was taken and there was not an empty place at the long table on feast days, for O.C. was no fanatic for abstinence and men have been as merry at his table as at any cavalier's. Although he preferred honest English dishes, he liked a good Haut-Brion or a Mosel to accompany sweetmeats.

While the household at Hampton Court swelled; there was no lessening in the establishment at Whitehall. From dawn to dusk there was the knocking of builders and the slap of the mason's trowel, for there was always a new office to be converted or an old one demolished. My own little chamber was white with dust from plaster knocked off the walls of the great open tennis court that was taken down to make room for a garden for Mr Edward Mountagu being lately made President of the Council of State.

I had a longing to set eyes upon this gentleman, for he had won a rare reputation as a soldier. *Aet.* eighteen, he had raised a regiment and fought bravely at Marston Moor and Naseby, but then had retired to Huntingdon to manage his estates, whence he had but now returned to assist his old neighbour our lord and master.

A most affable fellow, Will reported. I would as lief be in his service as in any other Councillor's. He knew my name though we had met but once and he showed a quick understanding of the Exchequer's faults.

Would it be worth my while to –

No, no, he already has a creature, his cousin, a bright little fellow who is but a tailor's son from Fleet Street.

His cousin, you say?

Yes, Jem, we are in England where a tailor may be brother to a countess. The fellow has a little chamber behind where the tennis court stood, opposite the dedans. You will see him soon enough, for he has a powerful thirst.

It was in a tavern that I first set eyes on him, the Leg in New Palace Yard (not the one in King Street where the beer was but dogs-piss).

He sat with Will at a table in the back, a little man with eyes like children's marbles knocking together and a nose like a quill which he dipped into mine host's ink with a quick sucking motion as though he wished to empty the tavern before he was emptied out of it. He was all motion like a turbulent sea, yet neat.

This, Jem, is Mr Pepys.

He took my hand with warmth and pressed it to him in a fashion which I thought forward, though we were both but young clerks and why should he not be eager to make friends. He wore a high-crowned felt hat over his long curled hair and a new doublet of brown stuff.

You are welcome to the great fraternity of clerks, I said.

I am most fortunate to have the place, sir. My cousin Mr Montagu has been very good to me. My friends shall be your friends, Samuel, he says to me. I have already met Mr Downing twice.

Mr Downing is a popinjay, Will said. I perceived that Will had been in the Leg for some time, for he spoke in a heavy voice and his tankard came down hard upon the table.

It's said he may shortly be made Teller of the Receipt. I understand that's a post of great sway within the Exchequer.

A pop-in-jay, Sam, a parrot that sticks his arse out like, like a parrot. He is a vain man, sir, your Lord Downing.

Surely he is not a lord.

He is lordly, he sways like a popinjay. Why is there no more ale in this tankard? It's an empty tankard, a non-tankard, I hate it. Paulina, come and rescue me, I am dying of thirst.

Rescue me too, said the man with the bright marbles for eyes.

And within an instant he had become a toper like the rest of us.

He spoke no more of the Exchequer and Mr Downing's prospects, nor of his own, and devoted himself to pleasure. And he could carry the burden of a bawdy song as well as any of us. Was it 'Sweet, do not stay' that he sang that first night? He sang it many other times when we tumbled out into the smoky air to feel the frost. I give here the verse that is the most decent (if the hearer do not supply the verb that is missing):

> Sweet, do not stay, but come away,
> Stand a helpless maiden's friend
> That does you affection lend
> And ready is, poor heart, to—
> *Come away, come away —*

etc., etc. Well, that is the song he sang and we counted him an addition to our merry group. And it was not solely with his fellows that he was presumptuous. Paulina complained to Will that she could not pass his bench without his putting a hand upon her knee or fondling her behind. Upon Will saying that she was scarcely unused to such attentions, she was not working in a nunnery, she said yes but the other gentlemen were different, he was like that automaton Mr Evelyn spoke of, his hand went at her like a weaver's shuttle. Only his hand? Will inquired and Paulina struck him and said he was not to make sport of her.

Pepys was a brisk, impatient man and before long Mr Mountagu's service did not suffice for him and he was made clerk to George Downing that was now, as he had foretold, Teller of the Receipt in the Exchequer with another £50 a year supplemented by diverse fees and gratuities.

Soon after Michaelmas, I met him walking up Fish Street Hill with a pretty girl. She had a long neck and a sweet face like the portrait of the late Queen that used to hang in Mercers' Hall, but her teeth stood forward.

This is my bride, Elizabeth. We're to be married next month. She is French but a member of the true religion.

I wished them very well. As I was inquiring if I might kiss the bride as was our English custom, I saw how young she was and Pepys saw that I saw.

She is fifteen but has a mature mind and a ripe judgement.

The girl told him not to talk so about her but she did in truth seem well possessed of herself, although she was so pale and slight in body.

I heard that they were married by a magistrate at Westminster and they had plighted their troth at a service that was not lawful, though in which church I know not. But at any rate they were man and wife.

Will Symons also was married shortly thereafter to a fine woman, though quarrelsome. Thus I was the only bachelor left, at least until our trio became a quartetto. Little Peter Llewelyn looked barely older than Mrs Pepys. His head was fair and fluffy like a chick but three days old, and he squeaked when he was in his cups, and he had a body as scraggy as a chicken's too. Yet he was the best sport of all, as amorous as a rabbit and could drink a yard of ale without pausing for breath. And when we went clubbing at Woods at the Pell-Mell which was our accustomed house, he would drink us all under the table.

We clerks were clubbers all and would meet at Woods on Wednesday to sing a catch and drown our business in ale, though I would not wish posterity to fancy that we talked nothing but bawdy, for we debated many high matters of science, philosophy and the arts of prophecy, ophthalmics, geography and music, etc. In music we were most excellent, for Peter Llewelyn played the viol and Pepys was an *adeptus* upon the flageolet and Will Symons had a strong melodious voice so that our corner of the tavern was dubbed Woods Nightingales and we sang serious songs, too, not fooleries, for example, Mr Gibbons's 'Silver Swan' and the airs of Mr Lawes. When we were in good voice, the ladies would gather round our bench and we proved it oft that music was the veritable food of love.

When we met afterward, after the King came back, we talked of our old clubbing in Cromwell's day and how we had sung this or that and drunk too much and how Paulina would or would not that night. And we swore that such days would not come again, our salad days days were over, and such lamentations as men make in middle age.

Yet in truth I would not wish those days returned again, for though we took our pleasure of them they were precarious also. No man could think himself safe in his place, for each turn in affairs might accelerate into a Revolution, and he who was a proper man yesterday might on the morrow be denounced and turned out as a traitor or a heretic or papist or whatever was not to the taste of the times. Each knock on the door might determine one's fate, and Hodge, that pimply tosspot of a porter, might be the harbinger of doom.

Someone to see you, sir.

Not –

Not your mother, sir. This one's a tall gentleman and he's hard behind me for he would not be stayed either.

Nor was he, for the words were hardly out of Hodge's mouth when I heard that marvellous bass-viol voice, resonant like my mother's, but melodious as hers was not.

Greetings in the Lord, Jeremiah, you have not forgotten His Last Witness, I trust.

How could I?

But I had forgot how huge the Prophet was. His majesty seemd to fill my little office, his mane of red hair was as great as ever, though there was grey in it now.

And I do not forget my old friends who have stood by us in our most pressing hours.

I'm honoured by your presence, I said. It's a wondrous thing that you should seek me out.

It was in truth a very untimely and awkward thing. O.C. was tolerant of many religions, but he had to draw a line and Muggletonians fell beyond the limit in that outer darkness peopled by other malcontents such as Ranters and Fifth Monarchy Men. For all that the Prophet preached quietude and submission to authority, his teaching was esteemed too eccentric to be tolerated. And it would certainly not be tolerable that a clerk in the very citadel of power should be one of his flock.

It is a warm day, the Prophet said, his eye wandering, like my mother's, to the bottles Will kept upon the shelf.

Oh, I am most uncivil. May I press you to a glass?

We must not neglect the Lord's creatures, Jeremiah, those that he blessed at Cana in Galilee and has empowered his Witnesses to redouble the blessing of.

He sank the first glass with a hearty tilt and was scarce slower with the second (though I should add that I never saw him so much as half-drunk).

There is much work afoot, Jeremiah. I am to publish my responses to Cromwell himself. There is great call for them, and some of our following will have them bound up for better keeping. But the expenses of printing such things mount ever higher and —

I should be honoured to be of some modest assistance in the matter, I said, fishing in my pocket and thanking Providence that I found no less than £6 there.

You are of a generous humour, Jeremiah. This is not the first time I have had cause to pour down blessings upon you. You are rewarded, sir, in God's heart and in that of his Witness.

One thing I'd ask of you.

Anything, Jeremiah, anything that the Lord permits.

Since you're to publish your responses to the Lord Protector, it would seem strange, wouldn't it, if it were to be known that the printing —

— was paid for by one of his learned clerks? My dear sir, you may take my discretion as read. I would not breathe a word of it to any soul living or dead.

I had always known that the Prophet was of a quick understanding and, though I was glad to be rid of him, I could not deny that I felt the old power of his presence. He pressed me to attend his discourses which were held on Tuesdays in the Mitre in Turnagain Alley, but I could see he knew I would not come, for the State had agents everywhere.

But soon those agents had themselves to make shift, for the Revolutions followed so swift upon each other that only the most wide-awake could know for sure in what cause he was spying and to whom he was to make his report. The sudden death of O.C. set the whirligig spinning, the brief reign of Tumbledown Dick, his son, failed to halt it, and after he abdicated we were all spinning like tops to stay in the same place.

Then to me one thing above all strange and wonderful happened, or so it seemed at the time. The consequences of that thing were to cast a long shadow upon my life, but then it seemed like a miracle to rescue me from the drudgery of my clerkly existence.

My General was coming south from Scotland. 'Monck is coming' was all the word in Whitehall, on the Exchange. Across the water, the boatmen were holloaing it. In the dockyards, the merchants and the mariners were telling one another, each claiming to have the latest intelligence. He's at Newcastle, no, he's at Mansfield, no no, he's returned to Scotland. He has declared for the King, no, for the Republic, no, for himself. King George will not decline as King Oliver did. You're mistaken, he is a soldier, only a soldier.

Nobody knew what he wanted, nobody knew what he intended. Slowly south he came. We watched like schoolboys in a tedious lesson watching a fly crawling across a window pane. So slowly. He would pause, and take counsel, or send a letter, then wait for the answer or pretend so to do even though he knew it already. Never in all history was there a waiting game played with more delicate patience. So slowly – I believe never a man had an intellect more detached from his passions. How cold his brain was. When all the fiery republicans and the proud cavaliers had spouted their whirlwinds, he had barely opened his mouth.

Tomorrow he'll be at Westminster, he was at Barnet last night, Llewelyn told me in the tennis-court garden. We shall catch him in the Strand, he must march that way if he is to quarter his troops in the Park. And so we waited in the Cock alehouse at Temple Bar and consumed a deal of sack. When we heard the commotion, we tumbled out into the street and shouted Huzza Monck for ever (which I shouted with much sincerity, for I hoped that he might get me a better place). Although one or two did cry for a new parliament, it was the noise of the hooves and the marching feet that filled our ears, for the people, fearful or confused, were silent.

There he was, my landlubber Admiral, a squat low man jogging along on his old rusty charger, black in the face, a grim look upon him as he always had, as though he were going to his execution. Never has a conquering hero seemed to take less pleasure in his triumph. He kept tugging at the reins in order that his horse might not trample upon the men in front, for the horse seemed as ill at ease with the ceremony as its master.

And then: behind him came an old travelling coach with mud up to the tops of its wheels and the filth of the Scotch weather still upon its

roof, a lumbering old thing that swung about on its springs as though
it were about to topple into the ditch. And leaning out of the window
with her white arm waving was Nan, my Nan, my long-lost gaoler's
seamstress.

Nan, Nan, I cried reckless of who might hear.

He's crying to the General's whore.

No, no, the General's wife. He married her, you know.

I know that well enough, but a whore she was and a whore –

I turned to find the abuser and strangle him, but I could not be
sure which of the fellows it was, and by the time I turned back, the
coach had gone on.

But did I not know that Nan had married the General, that it had
been he whom she had waited on in the Tower? Surely all the world
knew that George Monck had married the daughter of one of the
women-barbers of Drury Lane. So they did, and so did I, but I had
had to keep the intelligence to myself, for the General was known to
be a jealous man and I owed my place to him and so I fancied it politic
to suppress my connection. Indeed, I wished I had not shouted out in
the crowd at Temple Bar and I swear I would have held my tongue
had it not been for the sack.

But those who are reading this story, the audience of my own
biography, should I not have told them earlier of my noble connection?
Well, I have often read a story in which the author keeps the secret to
himself until it shall make a grander effect upon his readers and I do
not see why I should not perform the same service upon you.

He's a black monk and I can't see through him, I heard one of the
Council say. No one knew which way he would jump: for a Parliament,
for the King, for himself. And none of us were any the wiser after he
had spoken before the Parliament. They had prepared a Chair of State
for him at the Bar, exceeding ornate with silver tassels and red velvet,
but he would not sit in it, saying he was but their servant. He took their
thanks for his services with humility, which he did most naturally, for
he was such a low plump inconspicuous man that you would pass him
in the street and not take any notice of him.

Then he spoke, most nonchalantly, leaning on the back of the chair
as though he were casually conversing with old companions. He told
them to look after the army and let the soldiers keep their lands in

Ireland, and he delivered himself of some proposals for the moderate governing of Scotland, for he said nothing was more dreadful to the Scots than to be overrun with fanatic notions.

But he did not say straight out what he meant, and what everyone in England meant, that this Rump Parliament had been too long sitting and it must be dissolved and new members elected who truly spoke for the people. And as for the Parliament, none of them complained that the General would not renew his oath against the Stuarts. Thus – as is our English way – no person spoke of what was in his mind, yet all claimed to be most content with the conversation.

Afterwards the members and their ladies repaired to the Prince's lodgings in Whitehall where the General had taken his residence and there were royally entertained to venison and carp and a hundred other costly dishes.

That, I believe, is Mrs Monck, though she looks like a serving-woman. She is homely certainly.

Well, she is serving with her own hands, and I call that uncommonly gracious.

I dare say she is used to the trade.

I stood in a rage behind these ill-natured females and waited my turn to be served from the long side-table.

She was wearing a low dress. Her cheeks had a high colour and her eyes the brightness of sapphires. Under the light of the great candles she shone like the moon at her zenith. For me, she was worth all the high-born ladies that were there. It was more than seven years since we had met. Even to see her was the end of one great hunger, although it was the beginning of another.

Nan was talking in her high throatsweet voice that I remembered so well from our first days amid the bales of cloth at the sign of the Three Spanish Gypsies. She was helping one of the ladies to punch with a silver ladle.

Now, she said turning to me, it is the gentleman's turn, I'm sure that – But of what she was sure I never knew, for she was struck dumb and could say not a word more but filled my tankard like a senseless automaton. Nor could I say a word in reply but bowed my head in thanks for the wine and passed on. Then I thought to go back but did not wish to cause her an *embarras*, as the ladies were pressed in, along her table. I went into the next room and cursed my dumbness, though I did not know what she would have wished me to say.

I was standing there moping by the mantel, feeling most sorry for my plight, when a commotion arose and that same low stocky man whom I had seen bumping along on his horse down the Strand came into the room with his attendants.

You, he said, pointing at me, I know you.

Yes, sir, you do.

You're the fellow sold me the maps I beat the Dutch with.

Yes, sir, I am. You are very good to remember.

I don't forget a face, and you looked like one of those Stuarts, that's why I remember. Don't shrink, man, it's not a crime. He laughed (it was more like a grunt than a laugh) to see how discommoded were his courtiers to hear mention of that name which was on everyone's lips in private, but never passed them in public. What are you doing now, hey?

Through the kindness of Your Highness, I'm Under-Clerk to the Council.

Are you now? Excellent, carry on the good work. We shall meet again, I trust. And he moved by.

This fortunate encounter restored my spirits greatly but I was still in a fever of passion and uncertainty at the sight of Nan and wondered whether I dare steal back into the great chamber just to see her again.

Just at that moment a small dull man who seemed familiar to me accosted me with an air of exasperation. Without troubling to greet me or inquire my name, he said:

I'm Clarges. I've a message for you from my sister.

Your sister?

Her Highness, the General's wife. She wishes to see you in an hour's time when the General has gone to the City and the other ladies have left.

Here?

Yes, in her apartment which lies beyond this one. I must add that you are to be extremely careful. That is my advice, not hers. She is a stranger to discretion, I fear, but I would not advise you to presume too much.

I have no such intention.

I am glad to hear it. These are dicing times. One false throw could lose the whole game.

It shall not come from me.

Good. He looked at me with his cold dry eye. I did not expect him to become my friend.

The interval was intolerable. The chamber seemed too hot to breathe in. I went out into King Street and paced up and down though there was a drizzle falling upon my head. W. Symons and S. Pepys passed by and mocked me for looking like a drowned magpie in my court finery (I wore my black surcoat with my new white justaucorps which was trimmed with silver lace, and my black Rhinegrave breeches edged with white ribbon, and a black beaver), but they were so impatient for wine that they did not stay to question me further.

But at length the hour struck upon the great clock and I went back into the Prince's lodging by the side-door that we clerks used as a short cut and came up into the apartments by a private stair.

There was only a young Scottish maid in the antechamber who bobbed and said I was to go on. I stood stock still in the middle of the room beyond, for a strange dizzy fit had come upon me and I began to shiver because my clothes were soaked. The room was dark and cold and I had almost started to wish I had not come. Was the trial too great for me? Had I the stomach for the fight?

But then the door opened and Nan looked round the edge of the door with a mocking smile on her face. Ah, she said, there you are. It's cold out there, come by the fire. She took me by the hand and led me into the next chamber, which was warm and hung with fine tapestries and had a fire crackling in the grate. She stood a yard away from me and regarded me as though I were a statue.

Why, you are wet to the skin. You look like ... like a drowned magpie.

So I'm told.

You must take off your fine feathers. Here off with this coat, and she pulled me out of my coat and vest as a mother undresses a child that has splashed his clothes in a puddle. I stood there in my linen underdrawers and after she had put my clothes on a chair by the fire she put her arms round me.

Now this is the Jem I remember. Come, sir, we have time to make up.

And I had barely kissed her in return before she had led me over the great bed with its blue hangings and laid herself upon it and thrown up her skirts so that her middle parts were quite exposed and that dark forest lay open to me as it had so often before. All my irresolution melted like snow in the morning sun and we resumed where we had left off in Cromwell's heyday. Jem, Jem, she cried with that nightingale gurgle which marked out her speech from all other women. You'll kill me, Jem, she said. But in the end it was I who expired first so that she had to rouse me from my sleep and tell me to make haste and be off down the back-stair, for it was not certain that the General would spend the night in the City, although lodgings were prepared for him at the Three Tuns by Guildhall.

Jem, how shall we manage?

I thought we managed well enough.

No, you silly boy, it must not be another seven years before we meet again.

I have a chamber in the Cockpit.

And you think the General's lady could be seen skipping through Whitehall to your lodging? The General is a good man, but he has a quick temper and many spies.

The General thinks well of me. He knew me just now, for I sold him charts before he went to sea.

Did you so? And he was not drowned either.

Nan, don't mock me. I can come again by the back way as I did just now.

No, you may not. Maids will not hold their tongue for ever. And what would a clerk to the Council be doing crawling up my lady's stairs every other night?

How did you know I was Clerk to the Council?

You see, we have spies everywhere.

Could I not be charged with some special business to you?

The General would spy out soon enough what that special business was. His eye is sharper than he pretends.

May I not at the least stay this night?

No, you may not, for there is another thing you must know.

She led me out the low door by her bed and down a dark passage, I buttoning myself the while. After a few paces she opened the door into a small side-chamber.

There, is he not beautiful?

I looked round the door and saw a child with dark tousled curls lying in a cot that was already too small for him and the moonlight upon his face.

Is he not an angel, my Christopher?

A cherub, madam, I said with all the *politesse* I could muster, for I had no great liking for children.

That is why you may not stay the night, for at first light the little darling crawls into bed with me. He is my rosy-fingered dawn.

Ah yes, I see.

Take his little hand. He will not bite you.

As I stretched out to fondle his chubby fist, a terrible thought struck me. The child might be as much as eight years old, in which case he might – but as though to answer my thought, Nan bent over the cot and cooed to her son like a pigeon in a hay loft:

Is he not like his papa? Oh he is my little general, yes you are, my Kitty Kit.

And in truth, I could discern even in sleep the lineaments of our nation's saviour.

How old is he?

He is but six years old, though many take him for eight or nine, he is so forward.

So he was born . . . ?

In a place we shall not speak of.

Ah, I said.

It was a full year after the General and I were married, whatever the ill-natured may say. You may see our names in the book at St George's, Southwark if you doubt my word.

I would not doubt it for all the world.

Yet I knew there were many who did doubt it and some who said that even if a true priest had married them he had no business to do so, for Mr Radford her first husband was not dead but had been dispatched to Tangier (or some said Devonshire) to be out of the way. But I was happy to believe every word she said and to observe the General's brow and nose and lips reproduced in the sleeping child's, all of which acquitted me of his paternity. Thus my first view of Kit inspired no apprehension in me. He seemed a mere attendant on our delights, a cupid who portended me no harm. If I had been able to peer into the future – but there, if we could foretell all that was to befall us, we would never stir out of doors. As we quitted the little chamber, the child turned over in his sleep and emitted a sturdy belch. That should have been an omen.

The rain had ceased as I came out into the court and the stars were shining in the sky again and I was as happy as any man can be, for there is no greater happiness than to lose your treasure and find it again long after you have given up all hope of it. And even though my affairs were to roll downhill afterwards, I still do not forget that glorious instant when I stood at the top of the hill.

It may seem curious but I did not worry about the difference in our situations or the danger that we might both stand in. I had such confidence in Nan, I could not imagine how she could fail me or undo herself. All the years in between now seemed like a sleepless night of fever and fret. Now true life began again. The destiny of the country lay in the General's hand, and my destiny lay in the hand of the General's lady.

Then to take my leave of the clerks of the Council; and thence Doling and Llewelyn would have me go with them to Mount's chamber, where we sat and talked and drank and then I went away.

Diary of Samuel Pepys, 22 March, 1660

IV

The Barge

And so I began to lead a doubled life. When my lady was out of town, I would carouse with my fellows that were turned out of office, viz. Will Symons and Peter Llewelyn and Mr Cooke (not the Mr Cooke that later built the new tennis court for the King) and Mr Chetwynd (his wife was sister to Will Symons). They would curse the name of Monck and look back to O.C.'s time when business was orderly and the fees were fat. And I and the two Leighs, Matthew and Thomas, that had survived the axe, would endeavour that we did not look too smug for that we had kept our posts. Thomas Leigh's wife was sister to James Chetwynd, so our old club was also a family, but it was a family that was sundered in two halves between the Ins and the Outs.

But when the General was away or detained on business, my other life would begin. I would walk past Nan's chamber and look up at her window. Two lit tapers standing together were a sign that I should duck down the alley and come in by the back-stair. Then we would re-create that first reunion as though we had not met for seven more years, and our brief giddy embraces would resume.

Yet this secret love had its inconveniences. Two times out of three that I walked past there was but a single taper in the window and I passed a solitary night, for I had sworn to remain faithful in gratitude for our reunion. Even when the two tapers were lit together, as often as not she would greet me at the head of the back-stairs and pray me to crouch there quietly until Christopher was asleep. And that was not the end of the brat, for after she beckoned me into her chamber she would insist that I hear all his exploits of the day, how he had fallen and cut his knee, what a merry sally he made at the butler's expense, etc. Moreover, I was so tall and the back-stair was so low that I must bend double not to knock my head. Even so my dark hair (of which I confess I was somewhat vain) was covered with white dust.

Sometimes you come to me like a drowned magpie, but tonight you are come like a camel from the Arabian sands.

Nan, don't mock.

You're in an ill-humour. Shall I put you in a better one if I tell you a secret?

I care nothing for your silly secrets.

Well then, I shan't tell you.

This teasing displeased me and I was too proud to inquire further about her secret which I thought would amount to little. Her thoughts were of jewels and gowns and brocades and hangings, for now she could buy for herself all the finery that had passed through her shop at the Three Spanish Gypsies, and much more besides came to her *gratis*, from supplicants for the General's favour. And she enjoyed her greatness. She called it her revenge for the ladies who had slighted her when she was but a female mercer.

Yet although she was severe with me, I could see that underneath she was on fire with joy. It was pardonable vanity that I should attribute her extremity of pleasure to my efforts, and I was the more flattered that when I was buttoned up she took my hand and said, Jem, I will come down the back-stair with you, for lovers should part at the door, should they not?

This seemed to me a foolish whim but I was content to humour it, for she had humoured me royally, and I led her down the winding stair, both of us crouched, she being tall for a woman.

Oh it's so cold, I'm all a-shiver.

I could see by the light of the taper she carried that her nose was quivering with mischief and her cheeks were flushed as a dogrose in July.

At the foot of the stair there was a store-room which I had not entered, for it was locked. And now I saw her take a key from the chain she had at her waist and unlock the door.

Look, Jem.

I peered into the dark. At first my eyes could see nothing beyond the taper, but as she moved it to and fro, my sight became accustomed, and I could see great piles of household linen, sheets and smaller cases for the pillows and other napery reaching almost to the ceiling. There must have been enough linen to furnish all the royal palaces.

I didn't know this was your linen closet, I said in tones of utmost indifference.

See, Jem, I bought it all wholesale, all of it . . . I must have saved the State five hundred pounds and more.

Has not the State linen enough already?

Oh you are a silly boy, she said and took me in her arms and began to unbutton the very buttons that I had just done up and started to fret me into life again there amid the linen. Yet this repetition of our first bout amid the bales of cloth in the Gypsies failed to stir my fancy, and with a sigh and a chuckle she put me away again, as one puts away a candle that will not light.

I was as tired as a dog after the chase, and it being yet early I dropped in upon Marsh's rooms in Whitehall, for I was famished and yearned for a beef pasty and some ale. There was no company to be had there, and I ate my victuals quickly and went off home to bed. But as I was putting on my nightshirt, there was a loud knocking at the door, and I opened it to see Thos Doling and Llewelyn who were both fully foxed and behind them in his high beaver which made him look like a mole was S. Pepys.

Sam is away tomorrow and we have brought him here so that you may have the honour to bid him farewell. Llewelyn spoke as slowly as a tortoise and he shook his head while he spoke, which *in vino* he did like some *paralytique*.

Well then farewell, Sam, I said curtly.

No, no, you must drink his health for he is going away. We must all drink his health.

It's very late.

It's never too late to bid farewell to a true friend who is taking ship.

Taking ship? For where?

Why, for Holland, of course. Where have you been, Jem?

That I was not at liberty to tell and had no mind to. My head ached and I was weary of their presence, especially of Mr Pepys who stood between them grinning like a monkey.

Very well, if you will, come in. I have some canary in my closet, if it was not all drunk upon your last visit.

No, but you don't understand, Jeremiah. Mr Pepys is bound for the Hague.

Very well, for the Hague, what of it?

At which little Llewelyn came up close to me and spoke almost into my face so that I could not breathe for the foulness of his breath, and uttered these words which made the hairs on my neck stand up like a porcupine's quills:

To fetch the King.

And I was the last man in London to know it, I whose lover was wife to London's ruler. Never was there such a humiliating ignorance. But I instantly resolved to seem unmoved.

Of course I know that, I said, but what are his precise orders? What are the commissions from Parliament and – and from the General?

I'd have thought you of all men would be privy to those matters, Mr Pepys said. For my own part I may disclose nothing beyond the fact that I am leaving tomorrow, with my lord and kinsman.

For one dreadful moment, I thought that Sam Pepys knew my secret, but then he continued in his sleek fashion:

For I recall, do I not, that you once sold charts to the General when he was our Admiral and that you owe your place to his favour?

I nodded and was glad that the room had only one candle lit, and that at the far corner (for their visit had surprised me), and thus they could not see how hot were my cheeks.

Observe, Jem, Mr Pepys's sword, isn't it fine? And his sea-boots, aren't they sturdy?

I had them of Mr Wotton in Fleet Street, and at a fair price. And the sword from Mr Brigden, a merry fellow. I took them both round the corner to the Pope's Head where we met Gilbert Holland the cutler and Mr Shelston who I believe is a grocer, and they paid all. I haven't laid out a penny on wine all day.

He sat down on my bed like a sack of coals and I perceived the magnitude of his achievement, for he had drunk a great deal. Yet foxed though he was, he kept his wits and discoursed mightily of the great business he was upon.

Enough of that, said little Peter Llewelyn, we must drink. He had found the cask in my pantry and was filling the bottle, which pained me since it was new Rhenish wine of the best quality which I had reserved for better purposes.

Now then my comrades let us drink to our lawful sovereign. God bless King Charles the Second.

I hear that they were making a bonfire at the Exchange, said Mr Pepys, and there was a man with a brush wiping out the inscription (only he said inshcrapshion) *Exit Tyrannus* and they were all crying God bless King Charles.

The second, Sam. There must be no holding back. The second. We cannot disallow his father. Charles the Second.

Well yes, the second it must be.

But Pepys hesitated, and so did I, for I had grown up in O.C.'s time and served him and I had no ancient love for the Stuarts. No, I was not a giddy republican of Mr Milton's stamp, but, if we were to be weathercocks, we should not swing round before we were sure the weather had changed.

Come, Jem, God bless King Charles the Second.

Little Llewelyn breathed his foul breath upon me again and my resistance expired, so with a great show of heartiness I roared:

God bless King Charles the Second, during which ejaculation I stole a sidelong glance at Mr Pepys and saw that he liked the oath no better than I did and for the same reason: he was not *contra* the King, but he would prefer that Charles *be* king before confessing undying allegiance to him.

It was past one o'clock before I was rid of them. They fell down the stairs on top of one another so hard that I thought Llewelyn had been suffocated which would have been no bad thing, for he shouted God bless King Charles the Second all the way across the Tiltyard and I could not imagine why the guards did not arrest him.

After they had gone, I looked out of my window at the stars in the black sky and wondered what would become of me. I had survived that first purge of the clerks because I was the General's man, but the new King would surely turn out all those who had served Cromwell

– whom we must now surely call the Great Satan or Antichrist – and who would now protect the Protector's men?

In the morning, I went straight to Nan and came up the front stair, asking to be admitted to Her Highness's presence without delay.

Are you mad? she said. (Her hair was down, her toilet only half-made, for it was still early.) You know you are not to come without the signal.

Madam, I said in high theatric style, Mr Pepys is gone to Holland to fetch the King.

Mr Pepys, who is Mr Pepys? Oh I know, that little man who now waits upon Mr Mountagu. I don't care for him, he is too busy.

It is nothing to me whether you care for him or not, he is gone to fetch the King.

Jem, do calm yourself. In any case, you should say Mr Mountagu is gone to Holland, it is he the Rump has appointed General-at-Sea and commissioned to parley with you-know-who. My brother, Dr Clarges, is also gone.

You knew all this when I came to you last night?

She laughed and began negligently to dress her hair, as though we were talking of some idle matter and not the future of our nation. I'm the General's lady, am I not? she said. Don't you think he would consult me upon affairs of state? And whether he like it or not, he never lacks the benefit of my advice, for after dinner I put on what I call my Treason Gown and say whatever has been burning in my mind. It has been evident to me ever since we came from Scotland that there'd be no end to this business unless the King came back, and I've told the General so many times, but he is a deep-revolving man and he takes his time.

Why didn't you tell me this last night?

Because you wouldn't listen. I offered you a secret and you refused it because I made sport of you. If you had asked prettily, I would have told you everything. And now you must go. No Clerk to the Council could have more than ten minutes' business with me.

Madam, I *am* here upon business, to beseech your favour, for I fear that if the King come back they will make a new purge of all those that served Cromwell, and the surviving clerks will be the first to feel the axe.

Jem, Jem, don't fret. The General will look after you, he will – and there she paused in mid-sentence, struck by a fresh stratagem.

Jemmy, my love, she said, suppose you left the Council and joined our service?

How, in what capacity?

Well, I would like you to be very close to me so that we might . . . converse when we wished. How would it be if you were to be my gentleman-usher?

Madam, to serve a woman in that fashion would be unmanly.

Don't madam me, Jem, remember the Three Gypsies, and consider, the proximity would afford you the opportunity to serve me in any manly style you can summon to your fancy. At the same time, you would be close to the General, you could be charged with important missions, missions to foreign courts perhaps, a species of ambassador. If you had been in that post last week, it might be you and not my brother that was going to fetch the King, for Thomas often has the seasickness. Though he be an apothecary, he has no medicine that will protect him. And there might be other offices that would spring from this beginning. For my Thomas is already appointed Commissioner-General of the Musters and Clerk of the Hanaper, although to be candid he has hitherto but served as Monck's messenger and he is only a blacksmith's son.

And your brother.

But you are my *friend*, and what blossoms may not drop from friendship's garland?

Garlands may wither.

You're surly this morning, Jem. I declare I never saw such a morose man.

My future is at the stake. I must be serious.

Well then, I have made you a serious offer. Most young men would thank heaven fasting for such a post.

I am not most young men.

But though I was reserved and hesitant of manner, I began to see the advantages of her proposal. General Monck was the first man in the kingdom, and if the King came back, he would owe it all to Monck. To be at Monck's right hand, to sit at his table, to make a threesome with his lady in their closet, that would be the high road to preferment. Mr Pepys would doff his beaver to me.

Seeing that I was beginning to yield, Nan pressed home her suit.

You shall be our Lord Chamberlain. Any man would be proud to have the place. You'll be sitting in the sunshine. The Council of State is a fine thing and in those former days it was the engine of the nation. But who knows how the King may dispose of the Council? He may explode it utterly, fearing it to be a nest of traitors. Then you would be cast out in the cold. But with us . . .

And she pressed my hand and bussed me on the side of my neck, and I was won over.

Thus I exchanged the service of the State for the service of General G. Monck and his lady. I exchanged public employment for the private and £100 a year for £200 ditto and a mulberry uniform. It was a fated step.

At first it seemed like the high summer of my days. My lady busied herself *in propria persona* for my translation. She found fresh linen from that store where we had fumbled, and she measured me with the old tape that she had had at the Three Gypsies and, when the tailor's man did not come to make the alterations, she herself sewed in a strip of cloth to make the waist easier.

Jem, you are waxing as fat as a turkey. You want exercise, and I shall provide you with an abundance of it.

Then she gave me a fine walking-stick chased with silver and surmounted by a Negro's head in black wood and told me that was to be my staff of office. I said the stick was too short, but she said that this was to be the new fashion, for she was setting the mode now.

I was apprehensive how the General would receive my employment. But it was neatly done the next morning while he was eating his breakfast in the little parlour.

My chuck, this is –

I know who it is. Said we would meet again, didn't I? By God, you do look like a Stuart. Perhaps we need not trouble to send to Holland.

He gnawed his chop, pressed my hand in his (which was greasy) and welcomed me aboard.

Revolving times, he said. We must slow down. Had enough of the whirligig.

I was proud to be a little ship in Monck's swelling armada, and when I told Llewelyn and Symons of my place, they paid for two glasses of canary at the Sugar Loaf by Temple Bar. I did not tell them the precise nature of my employment, for I was not sure of it myself. If there was no one else by, the General would tell me to take a message, or he would dictate a letter walking up and down the chamber with his short steps and his grunts in between each sentence. It was more often Nan who gave me instructions.

It was 23 May when Nan came to me flushed and out of breath as though she had just risen from my side in bed (although I had not visited that abode of delight for three days past).

We are off to Canterbury instantly. Put on your mulberry suit, for we must be splendid.

To Canterbury?

And then to Dover. The King has set sail. We heard it from Mr Downing, who took an earlier ship but went on board to see the King first and was knighted and looks like the cat that's swallowed the cream, and told me I must call him Sir George now. He is in the *Naseby*, the King is, only now it is to be the *Charles*, for all the ships are to have new names which wipe out the old times. Make haste, for it will be hard riding if we are to be there in time to greet His Majesty.

Within the hour Nan had taken her place in the old Scotch coach with her mewling brat, for her fine new chariot was still building down at Deptford. And I was on my new horse which was more mettlesome than I liked and off we rode up King Street to Charing Cross, for the coach was too heavy to go by the Horse-ferry and we must cross by London Bridge.

As we rode down the Kent Road on that glorious day, Nan called from the coach: We are like the pilgrims going to Canterbury, are we not?

But I was thinking of my earlier travels along that road, how first I had come to London full of hope and ambition and how then I had retreated cast down when I had lost Nan and how now all was restored both to the nation and to me. It was my intention to communicate the story of my pilgrimage to my dear Nan, but just then the General came by grunting and bumping along on his old nag.

Come on, come on. We've another dozen miles to Rochester yet.

I shall remember that journey along the old Roman road as my happiest yet, for the birds were singing and nesting in the greenwood and we were feathering our nests as well as they.

We slept the night at Canterbury, at the Mitre where I had thrown cherry stones down upon the people when I was in my uncle's service, and I laughed to think how I had risen since those prentice days. The next morning we took horse for Dover early. There was already a great crowd upon the road going to see the King and I had to go on ahead shouting out loud: Make way for His Highness the General. The people cheered, but for one disagreeable fellow who cried out some nonsense about me looking like a sugar plum on a stick.

Then we came down over the downs to Dover and got to the harbour under the white cliffs. We could already see the *Charles* lying out to sea and a barge coming away from it, for we were only just in time. The Mayor of Dover made haste to greet us and invited us under a blue canopy (in case it should rain, but the weather was fair). I hit my head on the roof of the canopy, at which the General said: You've made the canopy too low, my lord Mayor, for the King is taller than my boy. They say he's above two yards.

It was not until then that I remembered that General Monck had not seen the King for ten years, and the Mayor who was making ready to welcome him had never seen him in his life.

Longer posts were fetched and nailed up against the old ones, which answered well enough, although the canopy swung to and fro as though it was at sea.

But we did not mind it, for now we could see the barge coming closer to shore. As soon as they spied the King and his brother, the people began to cheer and huzza. I have never heard such shouting and joy. It would have moved the heart of the sourest Diogenes.

I cheered, too, when the King stepped out of his barge. He was tall and black as they had said. I was much pleased when General Monck murmured to me low, so that the other courtiers might not hear:

Could be your elder brother, Jem, couldn't he?

For that comparison I forgave the General for calling me his boy.

My heart was full of joy that, after all the travail, our nation was to enjoy peace at last. My joy was all the fuller that I did not see Mr Pepys among the great men surrounding the King, for I feared that he might have employed the voyage to some effect and insinuated himself into the King's counsels.

Therefore was my joy somewhat marred when I perceived another boat come in at the same time as the barge, with some footmen carrying little dogs, a personage I did not know – and Mr Pepys. Nor was I better pleased when he hopped out of the footmen's boat and scuttled across the beach like a little brown crab to step into the barge which I saw by the standard was his lord's.

For my own part, I was pressed to the back of the crowd so that I glimpsed only the black top of the King's head, and I could not see him receive from the Mayor that very rich Bible which he said was the book that he loved above all things in the world (I did not believe it but knew the words were the counterpart to the Protestant Henry of Navarre saying it was well worth a Mass to have Paris). Nor did I hear him thank my General for all the service he had done him (nor saw him knighted at Canterbury that same night).

But my spirits rose again when I saw a lady speak to Mr Pepys in their barge and hand him over a small boy about twelve years old. The boy did not wish to be entrusted to Mr Pepys and escaped his grasp, and climbed down the ladder on to the shore. Pepys gave chase and fell into the sand and the seamen laughed. The boy came back and wiped the sand off Mr Pepys's coat and led him back into the barge as though he were the tutor and Sam the naughty pupil.

As I was laughing, Nan came away from the crowd that was around the King and said, quick, Jem, we must be off. You must keep charge of Kit, for there is no room for him in the coach. And Dr Gumble is wanted at Canterbury (a sycophant that was with the General in Scotland). Behind her came Dr Gumble with the squalling brat who did not like being with me any more than I liked being with him.

I want to go with Mam, I want to see the King.

You can't, Kit, there's no room.

Yes there's room, etc., etc.

By this time the great crowd had dispersed. The King and the

General and their ladies were gone to Canterbury and had taken all the horses, for we had not thought to bring enough horses for the King's men.

So Kit and I must trudge back into the town and find lodging, which there was none because so many people had come to see the King. By an ill stroke of Providence, as I was turning away from the last inn with Kit (I'm hungry, I'm cold, etc.), we ran into my old uncle, now much decayed and withered.

Greetings, Jeremiah, the old scoundrel said, is that thy bastard then?

No, Uncle, not so, it's the son of His Highness the General, in whose service I have the great honour to be.

Highness, Highness, my uncle harrumphed, there is no lower man in the kingdom, for he has betrayed the good old cause and brought back Antichrist that he may reign in blood over God's anointed people. Thou shalt curse the day thou ever took his shilling, etc., etc.

I'm hungry, Kit began again. And I saw an evil calculating look come over my uncle's rheumy old eyes. He bethought himself that if he showed us some favour he might be appointed bookseller to the Parliament or some other such office.

Thou knowest, Nephew, how I cannot afford to keep high state in these tumbledown days, but I have a few poor victuals and my lodgings are always open to my fellows in Christ.

And so it was that I spent the first night of the glorious new era in that draughty hovel with this dismal hypocrite of an uncle whom I had thought to have escaped forever. Meanwhile, Mr Pepys rode in state on my lord's barge and, while his lord's boy might have led him a dance, he had at least approached the age of reason, while my grizzling infant was far off it.

I parted from my uncle with an ill grace since I was angry that I had missed the King. Who knows what place I might have got had I been by the General's side at his landing while Samuel Pepys was holding hard on to his lord's coat-tails? Nor were my gloomy prophecies baseless. Before the month was out, Mr Mountagu was become Earl of Sandwich, Viscount Hinchingbrooke and Baron of St Neots, and Mr Pepys was made Clerk of the Acts and had a suit of velvet from Pimm's the tailor and another of silk, the first that ever he wore in his life. He was so besieged by suitors that he might have eaten like a king without ever stirring from his office. One night that summer when he came with me and Llewelyn to the Bull Head, he told us that he had that same day received a vessel of Northdown ale from Mr Pierce the purser, a fine Turkey carpet and a jar of olives from Captain Cuttance and a pair of turtle doves for his wife, all in a day's space, that Mr Pepys might smile upon them and do their business.

My Nan was busy too. For the General was made Duke of Albemarle and Lord General of the Army, Master of the Horse, Knight of the Garter, etc., etc. and his whining brat Christopher was my lord of Torrington in Devon, and his Duchess lost no time in squeezing the juice out of the orange, a trade at which I knew she was no novice. In her greatness she sold places as merrily as ever she sold wash-balls and silks and linens at the Three Gypsies. A coachman in the Leg told me that she asked him £200 for the place he had held since the former times, telling him that now the King was restored they must start with a Clean Slate. I do not know how many doorkeepers and chamberlains and housekeepers and grooms of the wardrobe she did ask money from, but I know they all paid, for they were fearful of her tongue which was sharp and of her husband's power which was omnipotent.

I began to weary of this usurious coming and going, and asked her plain:

Nan, what favour have you stored up for me? Am I not your first suitor and ought I not to be first in the line?

You naughty boy, you've had more favours from me than any man in the kingdom. Now get me that paper about the Watermen. They've not had their warrants yet, and I've not yet had their fees.

But, Nan, you told me that my place in your service was the first step on the Ladder of Preferment.

So it is, Jem, but when you have the honour to be in such delightful company, why should you be in such haste to stir from that first rung? Now earn my love afresh and take Kit for a promenade.

So I was nursemaid again, for Christopher's first nurse Honour Mills, a low wench that sold apples and oysters, was left at Deptford, and his tutors in Scotland, who were also the General's chaplains, Dr

Gumble and Dr Price, now had other fish to fry. (Price, a royalist, was made a fellow of Eton College and Gumble, an amiable man but slow, was also sent to Eton and then to Winchester as prebend.) Price taught Kit theology and to write a fair hand, and a Mr Gunton taught him mathematics for £2 10s a month, and the dancing master had £10 for his services. I doubt that Gumble taught anything, he was too busy with intrigues. But now Kit had no permanent attendant except your humble servant (which was a part of the bargain that Nan had not forewarned me of, fearing my refusal) and I must go with him everywhere and keep him out of mischief. The boy had one great delight at that time which was to see the Traitors' heads, and so we would make a round march: first, Cooke's head on the top of the turret in Palace Yard and Harrison's on the other side of Westminster Hall, and then Hacker's and Axtell's and half a dozen more. Kit would jump up and down with glee and shout, more, more. When I told him how they had been hanged, drawn and quartered, he said why hadn't I shown him that too and couldn't the King have them hanged and quartered again so that he could see it? Later we found the limbs of some of the traitors set upon Aldersgate, near Crowe's the upholsterers, and Kit was happy again. But Lord, he was a bloodthirsty child, and I resolved never to have any children of my own if they were to be like him.

But when I told Nan of her son's antics, she only chucked him under the chin and said, he'll be a soldier like his father, won't he? Then she showed me a book that was richly bound being *The history of the thrice illustrious Princess Henrietta Maria de Bourbon, Queen of England.*

What of it? I said.

Look there, Jem, at the dedication: *To the Paragon of Virtue and Beauty, her Grace the Duchess of Albemarle.* And see how the epistle ends: *that the rising Sun of your Grace's Virtues and Honours may still soar higher but never know a declension.* There, Jem, isn't that fine?

I do not see that this rising sun shines greatly upon me.

Oh Jeremiah, you're too grudging. Can't you appreciate a pretty compliment?

It depends to whom that compliment is paid, I said pompously.

In the afternoon to the Privy Seal, where good stir of work now toward the end of the month. From thence with Mr Mount, Llewelyn and others to the Bull Head till late, and so home.

Diary of Samuel Pepys, 27 August 1660

To my office at Privy Seal in the afternoon, and from thence at night to the Bull Head with Mount, Llewelyn and others.

29 August 1660

In the afternoon Llewelyn comes to my house and takes me out to the Mitre in Wood Street where Mr Samford, W. Symons and his wife and Mrs Scobell, Mr Mount and Chetwynd. Where we were very merry – Llewelyn being drunk and I being to defend the ladies from his kissing them, I kissed them myself very often with a great deal of mirth. Parted very late, they by coach to Westminster and I on foot.

4 September 1660

From thence by water to Parliament Stairs and there at an alehouse to Doling (who is suddenly to go into Ireland to venture his fortune), Symons (who is at a great loss for 200*l.* present money, which I was loth to let him have; though I could now do it and do love him and think him honest and sufficient, yet loathness to part with money did dissuade me from it), Llewelyn (who was very drowzy from a dose that he hath got the last night), Mr Mount and several others.

6 December 1660

London was lit up again now the King was returned. The theatres were restored too, and I saw the *Moor of Venice*, the *Merry Wives of Windsor*, the *Silent Woman*, etc. Every man took wine with his neighbour, and there was much making of music and bawdry in the alehouses. The old crew that was in the Exchequer were not yet scattered. The Ins and the Outs still were on speaking terms, although little Peter Llewelyn was so drowsy that he could scarcely speak and great Mr Pepys was so full of his business that we found it more profit to beseech him to play upon his flageolet or the new guitar that he had brought with him out of Holland.

But when Sam was in wine I loved him better, for then he was a rogue unashamed. At the Mitre in Wood Street one night with the old crew, Will Symons and his wife, Mrs Scobell and Chetwynd, little Llewelyn announced that he would kiss all the ladies to determine whose lips had the most perfect shape and Pepys made him sit down (which was not difficult, for he could scarcely stand up) and said that it was his office as Clerk of the Acts to defend the fair sex against lewd acts of all kinds and that for the advancement of science he must carry out the experiment himself, at which he began to kiss the ladies so often that their cheeks became flushed and I was moved with desire to kiss them myself but they said that Mr Pepys's experiment sufficed. All the time I wondered that Mrs Pepys did not come with him to the alehouse as Will Symons's wife did, but Pepys said she had much to do at their new house and besides she believed him to be upon his lord's business.

On such capering nights I forgot my trouble and rejoiced with the rest of the *monde* that the easy times were come back. And when I returned to His Grace's lodgings and the soldiers saluted me I tripped on the step, and the captain of the guard said, it's a slippery night, sir), then it seemed my lot was truly set in a fair ground. Yet in the colder light of morn, there were less favourable signs and portents.

Nan was so taken up with her affairs that she had little time to spare for her attendant cavalier. Look at these pearls, Jem, aren't they fine? They come as a gift from the loyal citizens of Portsmouth, and this necklace of garnets, it's from Mr Warren the timber merchant who has grown great on the Swedish trade and is to supply the Navy. And she would hold up the jewels to her neck and stand near to the candle so that I might see the effect. Yet I could not but see that her neck had grown taut as two bowstrings and that the jewels would have looked better on Mrs Pepys, for she had a fine swan's neck though her teeth were so prominent.

Yet flattery has a cormorant's appetite. The recipient always wants more and better compliments. And she began to complain that the Mayor and Corporation of such-and-such a town had treated her in a very scurvy fashion and she knew that the jewels in the pendant were paste gems not worth sixpence.

Some people have no sense of what is fitting, Jem. The Verderers have asked for their licences to be renewed but won't pay more than £100 for the privilege which is no more than they paid in the time of the late martyred King, and hasn't there been a steepling rise in prices since then? It's too vexing and I've half a mind to abandon these troublesome affairs, were it not for the duty I owe to the General to see to these matters.

One night, I came into her chamber unannounced at my usual time when the General was away. And I saw her in the window-seat with the little round table before her and a fine walnut box chased with gold lying open. I could see the jewels shining in the box and her hands were dabbling in the jewels as a child will paddle his hands in the water.

She said, come here, Jem, and began to unbutton my coat. When my shoulders were naked she took some chains and necklaces out of the box and hung me with them. Then she instructed me to do the same to her, so that we were both naked but for the jewels. There, Jeremiah, she said, we are garlanded like the King and Queen of the May. She stood up against me so that the jewels rubbed against my bare flesh and vice versa. Lord but the cold stones made me shiver. Yet that cold shiver became another shiver that was hot. We tumbled upon the bed. When we were finished, she took the jewels off me and put them back in the box, as the leader of a troupe of actors will put back the properties after the play is done.

Now, Jem, she said, we are just as we began.

And as we shall finish, madam.

Oh, Jem, don't become tragical with me, I cannot tolerate tragedy.

I savoured these nocturnal rewards of my office, for the daytime had become a burden. Kit, although he was scarcely seven, had become conscious of his greatness.

You must call me my lord.

No, Kit, I will not, for you are my charge. I will call you my lord when you are grown.

No, now, you must call me my lord *now*.

I had to take His Lordship to his lessons in fencing and dancing and equitation, and wherever we went I fancied I could hear idle tongues saying: There goes Monck's bastard. It is a paradox, that the greater and richer Their Graces became, the more the tongues wagged. It was positively stated that Radford was not only living but had been seen at Whitehall and that the Duchess had paid him off or that he had been settled on a goodly estate in Devon under an alias.

It's none of your business, Jem, she said. Radford died soon after you and I first parted, and that's all you need to know. I have done that poor honest man enough wrong to let him rest quiet in his grave. If you wish to join that ill-natured company which refuses to believe my word that we were married, the General and I, you may go to St George's Church, Southwark and look at the register. And then you may go on to Africa or Tartary, for I don't wish to live with a doubting Thomas.

Nan, there was a man from Devon who called last week, wasn't there, when you sent me and Kit away to survey the building of the tennis court?

Jem, I have many visitors on business, and I will not be questioned as though I were brought before a magistrate.

Thus I knew that she had received such a visitor, and that the footman who had told me the man came from Devon upon private business had spoken the truth. What his business could be, I could not guess. I went secretly to St George's and asked the clerk to show me the entry, which was just as she had said, though it was not worth much without its being certified that Radford was dead.

Then came a dismal day. It took me so much by surprise that I had scarcely breath to respond when Nan called me to her chamber and said as follows:

Jem, you're an importunate boy and I know how earnestly you desire some extra duty that would befit your station more properly. Well, I have made inquiries during my peregrinations (a word she would never have employed in the old days) among the great ladies of the town. And I've noticed that the Duchess of York takes it as a matter of course that her gentleman-usher should wait upon her at table, in a superior capacity I need scarce say. This is a high historical function which ought not to be omitted.

But –

You may find it strange at first, but I beseech you to recall that an earl or a duke may be proud to assist his sovereign in putting on his breeches or to remove his *chaise percée*. Indeed, he will regard this personal service as a gilding of his office, for that it brings him the closer to his master. In your case, Jem, it may be said that you're close enough already, but the world doesn't know that, and I don't choose that the world learn it.

But –

I think that to perform this office would be to do honour to yourself, for the world would then recognise how intimate a member you are of the first family in the land, I mean, the first not of the royal sort. Moreover, it would throw the hounds off the scent, if ever they get wind of our amour, for they would not believe that a duchess could love one who waits at her table.

There was some contradiction in these latter remarks, for if my serving at table was to elevate my position, how then could it make me not more likely to be my mistress's lover? But I was too agitated to detect the contradiction.

Madam, I will not do it.

Sir, you will.

I am not a serving man.

Oh Jem, you'll grow fond of the office. Many young gentlemen acquire breeding and manners by serving in the house of a genteel neighbour. It is the best way to polish.

I am polished enough as it is.

Jem, I must remind you of where we stand. I have only to whisper to the General that you've become, shall we say, a trifle insolent of late, that you've presumed upon my favour, that you're an irreconcilable Puritan, that I don't care for you to be so near our son Christopher who is soft wax and may easily be impressed upon, that –

Enough, Nan. I'll try the experiment for a month or two in the winter, but I beg you to release me by the spring.

You are a good boy, Jem, I knew you would be. Here, take this. This shall be your chain of office.

And she gave me a gold chain that she had received from the Colliers Company of Newcastle that hoped to sell their coals to the royal household and the generals. It was a pretty chain, but to me it was a slave's halter.

But soon I was too busy to mind my humiliation. For the serving of great dinners requires great preparations. I was a novice, Nan a stickler. We must have forks, she would say, and a clean white cloth, to hide the stains under a jug or trencher is in vain, for when the vessel is moved during dinner the stain will be shown.

The General cared nothing for these things. He never called for food or drink, ate but once a day and drank only at dinner but could drink deep enough if there were other soldiers present, though I never saw him drunken.

The General's lodging was large, but it was not convenient. There was no separate dining-chamber such as modern houses have, but the dinner must be taken in the great saloon which was a mile away from the kitchens below. Thus Nan or His Grace would call for dinner at noon, when it was already half past eleven o'clock, and we must make haste to bring the table out from the side, set the chairs around, lay the cloth, and arrange the cutlery and flatware upon it, and then fetch the wine from the cask and put it in the new Flemish bottles that the King had given them, send orders to the cook to make hot the pasties and puddings and chines, take the oysters and anchovies out of the barrel, bring the bread and cheese from the larder and then carry them all up the winding stair past the privy which was on a sort of *mezzanino* and stank and might be occupied by the gentry who wished to void their bladders before dinner, so that there would be a crushing on the stairs between the laden serving men with their pots and dishes and the impatient gentlemen (the ladies' privy was on the other side of the chamber and was sweetened with herbs and flowers). Besides, the kitchen was so far away that the hot dishes were cold as stone by the time they reached the table and in hot weather the salads smelled of the privy, but His Grace did not care and Nan who was so particular about the silver and the napery was not particular about her person and did not always smell like a duchess (although my acquaintance among duchesses was slight as yet and, for all I knew, they might be as negligent as Nan).

Our first great dinner was in honour of the Duke of York, the King's brother, that was later king himself and a silly one (for he had no more notion how to keep a crown than his father had). But he was a gracious guest and although Tom, the new footman, dropped a venison pasty down the stairs, nothing untoward happened at table. When they were done which was not before seven o'clock (which Nan thought very creditable), the Duke of York rose from his chair, handed me his napkin and said: A fine dinner, a very fine dinner – which pleased me mightily.

Now I suppose we must entertain Sandwich, the General said the next day, when we were conducting an inquest upon the dinner.

Why, my lord, said Nan (her cheeks began to redden with anger), we owe him nothing, and he's no friend of ours.

That is why we must ask him to dinner, the General grunted, or he will think us his enemy.

If he's so hostile, one dinner won't cure his mistrust.

No, but it will calm him. He is an agitated man, the sort who has climbed high but fears he must go on climbing or he will fall. I don't wish him to think that I am shaking the ladder.

Very well, my dear, you are the strategist. Jem will set a grand pacifying dinner for him, will you not, Jem?

With pleasure, madam.

But there was no pleasure at all in the prospect. My lord Sandwich was nothing to me, I scarcely knew him, but I feared lest he should bring with him the new Clerk to the Acts that had risen with his master so fast, viz. Mr Pepys.

Yet all was well. My lord Sandwich came to dinner with his ladies and they were as merry as midsummer day, but I took note that, though they both drank deep, neither His Grace nor His Lordship said anything of how they had brought the King in, for they were both secret men who did not care to reveal their tricks lest they should have need of them again. Moreover, if they were to trace their previous path too plainly, they would discover their snipe's course to the public eye and lose credit. For there were men who swore that Monck was for the republic until the day when he sent for the King. *In vino, taciturnitas* was the motto of both. But it was a convivial meeting and its great quality was – *the absence of Mr Pepys*.

Nan was grateful to me for my work, and she showed me her love in the old way, and gave me a ring with an Indian stone to seal our alliance, she said.

You will come with me everywhere, Jem, I can't do without you.

How do you mean, my lady?

No my-ladies, Jem. When I go out to dine with these tedious greatlings, I have need of an ally, and why should not my gentleman-usher accompany me? Besides, you look so handsome in your gold chain.

You wish me to come as your servant?

No, Jem, as my friend and counsellor, just as my lord Sandwich is Master of the Great Wardrobe to the King and yet also his valued counsellor and friend.

The cases are not parallel, I said, and yet I agreed, for we were lying in that sweet state *post coitus*, which is all languor and delight and I could not refuse her anything (although in truth her power was superior, for I had no other connection and must continue to rely willy-nilly upon her favour).

So when she went out to dine, I must put on my chain and set off with her and His Grace, although he was more often absent upon business of the King. And for the most part, I did not mind greatly, for in foreign houses I was not burdened with preparing the dinner and I could talk with the ladies and participate in high discourse. Thus I was not much discomposed when Nan bid me make haste for we were to the Tower to take dinner with Sir John Robinson, a great merchant (in cloth): a colonel for the old King, he had played some part in bringing in the new King and had received the Tower as his reward. He was a boastful fellow who was always talking of his deeds in the war and how without him the King would never have come in. But it pleased me to go to the Tower as a visitor and ponder on all the tragic prisoners who had perished there, on the block or out of misery at their long immurement. And it pleased my fancy also to recall how I had looked over at those frowning walls and wondered what lay behind them and where my Nan had gone. For her too it was a visit to a scene of romance, where the General had wooed her while she sewed his shirts, though I could not imagine him in the guise of a wooer. He must have been like bluff King Hal in Shakespeare's play: Harrumph, Mrs Radford, well then, will you harrumph . . .

But I observed that His Grace made an excuse not to come with us, by which I deduced that he was not eager to visit his old prison.

As our carriage came close to the Tower, there was such a press of coaches and wagons that we were stuck stock still. Nan who was ever brisk and impatient said, let us get out and walk. So we dismounted and stretched our legs. As we were going down by All Hallows Church, I espied a familiar mop of white hair. It was my cousin Fluffy Ralph. He greeted me warmly as though we were friends long lost. I am a farmer again, he said. We have two sons and a daughter, our eldest Richard is to be apprentice to Mr Fisher when he is older, I hope that he may like the business better than I did, you must drop upon Mr Fisher's shop on Tower Hill, it is much enlarged, for with the revival of seagoing trade the demand for charts is very great. How goes it with you? Well, I said, very well, and to Nan: May I present a cousin? Her Grace the Duchess of Albemarle. I've the honour to be escorting her to dinner at the Tower, with the Lieutenant, Sir John Robinson.

Fluff made a low bow but not so low that I could not see how far his face had fallen to see me in such company. We promised to meet again, though I had no such intention, and I sailed on into the Tower with flags flying.

But within half an hour my self-esteem was a shattered wreck, for as we moved into the Lieutenant's dining-chamber and I took my place behind Nan's chair, some latecoming guests shuffled in: Sir William Batten, Surveyor of the Navy, Colonel Slingsby, Comptroller to the Navy, and horror of horrors, *Mr Samuel Pepys.*

All the morning at the office. At noon Sir W. Batten, Colonel Slingsby and I by coach to the tower, to Sir John Robinson's to dinner.

Where great good cheer. High company; among others the Duchess of Albemarle, who is ever a plain, homely dowdy.

After dinner, then to drink all the afternoon. Towards night the Duchess and ladies went away. Then we set to it again till it was very late. And at last in came Sir Wm Wale, almost fuddled; and because I was set between him and another, only to keep them from talking and spoiling the Company (as we did to others, he fell out with the Lieutenant of the Tower; but with much ado we made him understand his error). And then all quiet. And so he carried Sir W. Batten and I home again in his coach. And so I, almost overcome with drink, went to bed.

I was much contented to ride in such state into the tower and to be received among such high company – while Mr Mount, My Lady Duchess's gentleman-usher, stood waiting at table, whom I ever thought a man so much above me in all respects.

Also, to hear the discourse of so many high cavaliers of things past – it was of great content and joy to me.

Diary of Samuel Pepys, 8 March 1661

V

The Tower

A day in the bottommost pit of Hell would have been better. Four or five times I wished I had never been born. A dozen times I wished old Mrs Pepys had miscarried most foully or her son been eaten by rats in infancy. And it had begun so fairly. Nan presented me as a gentleman to Sir John and I entered upon my duties as though I were doing a kindness to a friend, the Lieutenant's household being short of hands. But then entered Mr Pepys in his new silk suit with gold buttons, doffing his new low-crowned beaver to my lady as though he were a veritable Castiglione and then turning to me with his Good-morrow, Jem, I hadn't thought to see you here, and he took my hand in a most condescending fashion. But as we were yet in the antechamber, the worst had not been revealed to him, and it was not until we had proceeded into the grand *salone* (in truth, a mean dark chamber, for the place was but a gaol) that the scales were to fall from his eyes. Or rather, they were to pop from his head, Mr Pepys's eyes being as prominent as his wife's teeth.

It happened thus. I took up my station behind my lady's chair, having helped her to the venison and the wine (of which in her greatness she was becoming passing fond). Mr Pepys was at the end of the table and was talking with Sir William Batten, his superior at the Navy Office. His glass was empty and he looked around the table for the bottle, and his eyes lighted upon me. His little woman's mouth (that had a swollen underlip) fell open so that he looked as though he had but lately swallowed an asparagus. Then he looked away in some *embarras* – yet I thought I saw him smile. Then he looked back again, for fear that he had made a mistake and I had merely been passing her chair on the way to my own, for there was as yet a chair vacant, Sir William Hale being retarded. But he saw that I did not stir, could not stir, for Nan had said that I must not move a muscle until she commanded me, that it was the sign of a well-bred household that the gentleman-usher did not fidget. Only when she commanded me with the crook of her little finger was I to bestir myself, help the company to more meat or wine, etc. That would be a truly genteel proceeding, she said, which would reflect well upon us in the mirror of society. I doubt whether you will be able to crook that finger soon, I had said, with the weight of all the jewels that dangle from it. Now, Jem, she had said, don't be sour.

So there I stood still as a statue, silent as the tomb, while Mr Pepys smirked and ogled and caught my eye and then ducked away again. I felt the most pressing urge to crush his greasy little body until it was no bigger than a nut. Then he turned to his neighbour Colonel Slingsby and began to talk in a most confiding manner, and I knew what he was saying as though I could hear the very words, viz. would you believe it sir, that fellow over there behind Her Grace's chair, that waits at table, yes him, not long since, last year in fact, he was a clerk to the Great Council, and much respected, and now he is but a common serving man, how the whirligig of time doth bring in his revenges.

Could I break a plate over his head or soak his popinjay's outfit with wine? No I could not, for Nan would fly into a fury and screech at me for a fortnight.

What think you of it, sir? I said, what think you of it?

Jem, wake up, Sir John is addressing you.

Oh, yes, sir?

I was asking what you thought of my proposal.

Your proposal . . .

To pull down all the shops that jut out in Canning Street and make a fine carriageway the entire distance from St Paul's to the Tower. A *dual* carriageway, wide enough for two carriages to pass. Don't you think that a rare solution to the problem of the wheeled throng that's so costly to our merchants in terms of delay and other expense?

Rare indeed, I murmured (for even in a state of distress I can play the sycophant as well as the next man). Might I venture to suggest that it be named Robinson Street in honour of its progenitor?

Sir, you do me too much honour. I would not wish that posterity should think me puffed up, yet it is well that the author of such a scheme should be commemorated. What think you, Your Grace?

Oh, Sir John, Nan said with a waggish laugh (for she was pretty near foxed already), it would be like trotting over your grave.

Hold hard, Your Grace, I'm not dead yet, said Sir John. More wine, boy, more wine.

This threw me into a rage. Until that minute, I had thought I was beginning to recapture my position, for it seemed Sir John was speaking to me as a guest rather than a servant, but now I saw that he was merely giving me the time of day, as one will to a porter or a groom.

In my rage, reckless of Nan's reproaches, I splashed the red wine over the sleeves of Sir John's coat which was of a pale yellow colour, much too gallant for such a pustulate old potbelly. He jumped to his feet and swore several oaths, then apologised to Nan who had heard worse in her time but bowed prettily in acknowledgement of his delicacy and then reproached me, but not as fiercely as I had feared, for she was wearied of Sir John's discourse of carriages and licences and easements and bills and committees.

But all Mr Pepys could see was my slopping and my consequent humiliation, and he chuckled into his plate so violently that I thought he would suffer an apoplexy. Then of course he drew Colonel Slingsby's attention to my mishap and the Colonel was stricken too.

To calm myself, I began to circulate with a fresh bottle of wine. In due course, I came to Mr Pepys.

Have you heard Colonel Slingsby's jest, Jem? If the Lieutenant's discourse will not *dry up*, at least his coat shall be soaked.

Very witty, sir. I emitted a little cough to indicate the degree of mirth appropriate to so feeble a jest.

He is an old sinner, is Sir John, he stands in need of regular baptising.

Very witty again, sir.

By now Pepys and Slingsby were paroxysmal at their own wit. I passed on, resolved on swift and brutal revenge.

But first I must make my true position plain to S. Pepys. He must be brought to understand that I was in truth a species of secretary to Her Grace, enjoying the confidence not only of herself but of her husband and entrusted with many important missions in their service. That I should be standing behind Her Grace's chair was a matter of convenience so that I be at hand to carry out any high business that might be in train. It was out of courtesy that I took my part in the serving of dinner, for a gentleman is never too proud to make himself useful.

Some such speech I had prepared for Mr P. on my next circuit. I suffered a mortification when he barely noticed my passage, waving his fat little hand in the direction of his glass that I should fill it promptly, for as usual there was not a drop left in it. Nor could I interpose myself between him and his neighbour, for their heads were knocking together as each boasted of his part in bringing the King back in, at which every man round the table then joined in, for it seems Restoration has a hundred fathers.

Soon I saw Nan's head beginning to nod which was a sign infallible of approaching stupor, and so I reminded her that we must make haste back to Whitehall.

So soon, Jem, so soon. I would rather stay with these jovial gallants. They are, they are – and she fumbled at some length for the *verbum justum* – they are such *cavaliers*. At which all the tousled old tosspots smirked and preened their feathers.

Madam, we must away.

Jem, you're a spoil-sport.

Madam, come. And at last she came. I had to drag her down the stairs and haul her into the carriage as though she were a sack of coals. And when we were in the carriage she fell to kissing me copiously, so that I was glad it was already dark (for we had been at the Lieutenant's five hours and more) and we could not be seen. To be kissed in a carriage by a duchess may seem like a fine thing, but when she has five pints of Rhenish inside her, it is more like being kissed by an alehouse.

She slavered me the entire way from the Tower to St Paul's, but all the while I was thinking how I might restore my credit with Mr Pepys and *simul* be revenged upon him. I resolved therefore to call upon him and make my peace with him while spying out the land.

My lady was to attend a *fête musicale* at Hampton Court on the water as a guest of the King, so I scampered off to the City, to the Navy

Board's house in Seething Lane, where I knew Mr Pepys had his lodgings.

Barely had I reached one end of the street when I saw Mr Pepys come out of the house with Mrs Pepys and some other persons unknown to me. I walked towards them, but while I was as yet twenty paces behind them they went into the little church on the corner (which I discovered to be St Olave's, that had a modern gateway with skulls grinning upon its top). I then remembered that it was Sunday (Nan and the rest at Hampton Court were to hear a sermon, which was not much to her taste). Nothing would therefore be easier than to join Mr and Mrs Pepys in church and walk home with them afterwards, perhaps be invited to dine, part firm friends, etc. I went through the door of the church and saw the tail of their party disappear through a little inner door, but when I attempted to follow them, a fellow barred the way, saying, you may not be admitted, the gallery is reserved for the Navy Board and their ladies.

So with a bad grace I went outside and sat opposite the gate with the skulls upon it. Inside I could hear the parson drone on concerning the persons of the Trinity and I fell asleep (for Nan and I had been late to sleep the night before, the General being away) and when I awoke the church was emptied, and my only company was the silly grinning skulls. Though I made haste back to the Navy Office, I arrived only to see Mrs Pepys shutting the door behind her. For a minute I delayed to reflect whether I should knock upon the door or whether that would make me seem too like a supplicant when I caught sight of my quarry, Mr Pepys, walking past the end of the street towards the Tower.

When he reached the corner he turned to the right along Thames Street towards Whitehall, where no doubt he had business. I resolved to track him in parallel, along Tower Street, then cut down Pudding Lane so that I could run into him by accident and not seem importunate. I walked at a brisk pace but even so when I came down the lane into Thames Street, no Mr Pepys. Had he taken a carriage? Or a boat? I went down to the wharf. Still no Mr Pepys. Returning in some perplexity to Seething Lane, supposing that he might have returned home, I suddenly saw S. Pepys at the end of the street walking at a great rate in the opposite direction, viz. towards the Tower. Again I gave chase, running past the skulls once more, that seemed to say 'you'll not catch him now'. But the more I hared after him, the faster his little legs seemed to carry him. By the time he came down to Wapping Steps, I was 300 yards behind him.

I thought he would go in at Warren's timber yard, for I had heard him have words at the Tower with Sir William Batten *in re* Warren's Norway deals: Colonel Slingsby had jested that a Batten could be made out of a wood but all that could be got out of a warren was a rabbit, which Mr Pepys did not think witty and no more do I. But that is by the by.

Mr Pepys did not drop upon Warren but went on down to the steps and took a pair of oars and bade the man row downriver. My blood was now heated by the chase and, I know not why, I looked for a sculler to carry me in Pepys's wake but it being the Lord's Day had to wait above a quarter of an hour. Yet Pepys's boat was still in sight, at the bend in the river, and we followed him down to Deptford Wharf at a sharp pace, for the tide was on the ebb.

At Deptford he paid off the man and went up the row of cottages where the Navy carpenters dwell. He knocked at the door of the last house and was admitted by a woman, whether young or old I could not see. I waited at the harbour end of the street. It was a fair day and the swallows were dipping in the water and I lost count of the time, but a sturdy fellow soon came out of the house with a disagreeable aspect on his face and took himself off to the tavern by the quay, the Dog and Fiddle. I considered whether to join him, but resolved to stay at my post. After an hour, near enough, out came Pepys with a smirk on his face, and a woman came half-out of the door behind him gathering her loose gown about her, a fine buxom laughing woman. She kissed him on the lips and patted him behind as though she were sending off a horse to pasture, and Mr Pepys came skipping down the road. He did not see me, for I skulked in the boatyard behind the tar barrels.

Well, this was useful intelligence to be stored up against a rainy day. Yet the day was only half done, and I followed my quarry back to the City, upstream, *seriatim*.

I thought he would have his boat land at the Tower Wharf, but they went on against the current under the bridge, which my man would not do, saying the tide was too low and he feared lest we might be dashed against the pier as had happened to three fish merchants the last Sunday but one. So we disembarked at the Custom House, and I walked on up Thames Street in search of a hackney to take me home, pondering to what advantage I might turn my strange adventure.

But as I came past Barnards Castle, to my amazement coming up from Puddle Wharf there was Mr Pepys again, well out of his ground, for the Navy Office was a good mile behind us. He stuck to the side of the warehouse like a fly to a window pane and looked as though he did not wish to be observed.

To my further amazement, he took the back cut that leads but to one place, viz. the notorious Fleet Alley. By now I was but twenty steps behind and had to moderate my pace. Even in the afternoon, the alley is dark enough to cover the deeds of darkness that are hourly committed there; and never at a greater rate than on the Lord's Day when the throng is idle and has money to jingle in its pocket. By chance, I was detained at the entrance to the alley by a woman I had had some dealings with and who declared, mendaciously, that I owed her 5 s. Well, I thought, why should Mr Pepys have all the pleasure? And so I offered her 10 s to include a return of our match, which she accepted. She took me by the arm and led me up the steps and along the gallery of the ill-famed house which boasts no rooms but wooden stalls fit for cattle with but a dirty curtain before each. As we passed along the gallery, she laughed and pointed at a torn curtain, through which we could see a man jiggling at the bare buttocks of some wretched woman. His breeches of a pale blue silk were at half-mast and his shirt-tail was streaming like a pennant in his agitation. He had not even troubled to take off his hat, which was a low-crowned beaver. I could not fail to distinguish the beaver and the breeches, for I had been pursuing them all day.

The woman took me on to her own miserable straw where we did our business, at the conclusion of which she complained that I was not as amorous as I had been.

I trudged home to Whitehall in low spirits. *Pro tempore* all desire for vengeance had fled. I vowed henceforth to lead a plain and continent life, though first to restore my spirits I called in at the Leg for a noggin. But no, it was not possible, there was Mr Pepys (he must have taken a hackney from Ludgate while I had walked). He was seated by the fire with Doll Powell and her sister and they called me over, crying: Come and join the Clerk of the Acts, for he will entertain us all.

And so he will it seems, I said to myself in great bitterness, Clerk of the Acts indeed, and there he was but four hours earlier nodding earnestly while the parson expounded the Three Persons of the Trinity.

On prattled Mr Pepys, of how the sun had shone so bright on the river that the boatman's face had burned like a lobster's; of how he had gone to see a carpenter about some Norway masts that would not stand in a gale, saying nothing of how his own standing mast had been dipped in pitch by the carpenter's wife, for which I was sure he had paid the carpenter 5s, no more, for he was a byword for parsimony. Of how on his return he had passed by the booksellers of St Paul's and purchased a book of curious tales – he said nothing of the other tails that were for sale in Fleet Alley.

Though we had ripened in the sunshine all day, the evening had turned chilly and disagreeable, and Clerke's man (Thomas Clerke that kept the Leg) had stoked up a rare fire in the back hearth where we sat. While Mr Pepys ran the course of his day, Doll and her sister hoisted their skirts to feel the warmth of the blaze. Pepys sat between them and felt a fat white thigh on each side with his fat little brown hand. It was as though two slugs were crawling up their legs. But the women were so intoxicated that they scarcely seemed to notice his attentions. I perceived that this was not the moment to enlighten Mr Pepys about the true nature of my position in her Highness's household.

Yet in truth, I had begun to chafe sorely under the burden of my duties. I was not brought into this world to count table-cloths or to scold serving men. But the heaviest of the crosses I had to bear was young Kit, now my lord of Torrington, a title upon which he was most insistent, as he was upon my waiting on him on every occasion.

Come, Jem, he would say, the dancing master is sick of the plague, you must play at tennis with me.

And so I would tumble out of bed and pull on my breeches and trot after Kit to the new-made tennis court next my old den in the Cockpit, where Monsieur Delatuile who was reputed the best player in Paris would be waiting with a dozen fresh newly sewn balls and racquets which he had strung himself.

I had little fancy for the game which seemed poor sport. I had rather watch a girl do up her garter than watch that ball rattle and roll along the penthouse and then drop dead in the nick from which no racquet could dig it out. Sometimes Kit's cuts would slide along the gallery and die like a mouse in the corner. Sometimes they would whistle past my head in a cannonade and come to rest in the nets of the dedans as sailors do drop into their hammocks.

Forty-love and chase better than half a yard, Kit sang, aren't you ever going to win a point, Jem?

Perhaps Your Lordship would do better to play with Monsieur Delatuile.

It's more sport with you, he doesn't fall about and go red in the face. Game and set, let's try another set, the court is free.

Excuse moi, milord, said the little Frenchman who had the skin and the mouth of an Egyptian alligator, but I zink *sa Majesté* has the court.

No, no, Delatuile, came a voice from behind the first gallery, I am sure the ladies would prefer to watch a young master than an old tiro.

Oh but your *Majesté* is a *joueur formidable.*

Tush, Delatuile, play on, play on, boys.

To my horror, the King settled down upon the bench in the dedans and signalled to the ladies that they were to join him. I could not see through the netting whether La Castlemaine or La Gwyn were of the party, but the delicate aromas of perfume wafted through the netting and weakened my already failing senses.

Come on, Jem, you're to serve.

That, I heard the King say behind me, is young Lord Torrington, Monck's lad. Isn't it strange that the General should have so young a son? He is scarce ten years old I think.

They say, sire – but I could not hear what they said, for the woman spoke in a whisper and then they all broke out laughing.

And the other fellow, said the King. He must be of Monck's household.

I felt it incumbent upon me to turn round and bow and inform my sovereign that I was indeed Her Highness's gentleman-usher. But Kit had not observed my manoeuvre and sent down a volley of balls, of which several battered at my posteriors, causing much mirth amongst the royal party.

He has a look of you, sire, said one of the ladies, I could not see which, for it was murky in the dedans.

A look of me, you say, that fellow? The King rose from the bench and took the netting aside (which was loose on the penthouse side), so that he might inspect me.

I don't see it, he said.

He is nothing like so fine in the face, said a female voice.

We are not alike, the King said. He is too black.

The company in the dedans fell silent.

There was no sound in the court but the rattle of the ball on the penthouse and the noise of Monsieur Delatuile calling out the score in his shrill popinjay's screech.

Five games to love, *bien joué*, milord.

Etc., etc.

Behind me the King was now laughing with the ladies, but I could not tell whether it was at my play or on some fancy matter, *scilicet* the parentage of my lord Torrington upon which subject the wits of the town discoursed frequently, some still insisting he was not Albemarle's, others that he was Albemarle's but not gotten legitimately.

Nettled by my ill-success in the first set, I began to play with more address and took the lead, which mightily annoyed little Kit, so that he began to bang the balls past my head into the dedans, causing the nets to belly forth like so many sails with the wind in them, and so to scrape against the faces of the ladies, which they did not care for, crying out with maidenly shrieks.

You thrash the ball too much, boy, I want no thrashing in my court, said the King. It is a game of finesse. Ladies, let us quit this battle-ground.

With dread, I heard the rustle of their silks and the door opening at the back of the gallery. I made a low bow, but there was none to bow to, for the royal party had gone. One more chance missed to advance my fortune. If I had cut a better figure on the court, if I had spoken winningly to my charge and demonstrated to him the delicate arts of the game (with which in truth I was scarce acquainted myself), how I might have shown myself a serviceable man. The King would have borne me in mind, spoken kindly to me on our next meeting, advanced my credit with my lord General who would have considered me for a great place.

Kit, you shouldn't have banged those balls into the dedans.

You mustn't speak to me like that. I shall tell my father.

This was no idle threat, for the General doted upon the boy. Indeed Christopher could charm away his ill humour, he being a lively frolicsome lad, and the General needing some distraction from affairs of state which weighed all the heavier upon him because his humour was naturally heavy and his health was growing worse. He suffered from distemper, from afflictions of the kidneys and from old wounds got on land and sea which troubled him when it was cold or wet or blowing a gale. At such times he would sit by the fire and grunt his way through his state papers, until either Nan or Kit came to tease him. For Nan loved him still in her peculiar way, and was not frightened of him, except that she feared he would discover our amour. Yet I wonder that he did not know, for his eye was quick. Perhaps he did guess in his heart but chose not to inquire for the hurt the knowledge would do him if he brought it to the surface. He was a deep man and in his deepness lay the secret of his genius. If he were so taciturn in public matters, why then should he not be more silent still in private matters and carry into the chamber of the heart his habitual practice of saying nothing that would do harm unless he intended harm?

It came to me that his was an example that might be imitated. This taciturnity was an art that could be studied and brought to perfection. I resolved therefore to play the Stoic myself and not to complain *sans cesse* of my situation, for it was not manly. I would bear all and be impassive, so that people should say: Did you mark that gentleman with my lady Albemarle? He is the power behind the throne, the *éminence noire*. I was much pleased with the effect I made as I stood at table, silent and erect, in a new black suit I had had made, for my revenues were now much improved, Nan having sold a dozen licences to clamorous monopolists (to sell playing-cards, silk-worms, ink, etc.) and deposited a share of the proceeds upon her faithful gentleman-usher.

I had followed this *modus vivendi* for two months, or perhaps three, when Nan said to me (we were in her chamber at Whitehall *tête-à-tête*):

Jem, we must have this out. Why are you so down in the mouth? It isn't like you. You used to be such a merry fellow. Aren't you well?

Madam, I am well, very well.

Then you love me no longer, you wish to be away from me, you are plotting your escape from us, you will run away to sea or to the Americas.

Nothing could be further from my thoughts, I love you as well as ever I did, I promise you.

I don't believe you, your promise does not come from the heart. You have a sidelong, slippery aspect.

No, nothing of the sort. If I sound different, it is because . . . well, because a man grows more serious as he grows older. One can't be a winsome pageboy all one's life.

You were never that, Jem, you were always older than your years.

Nan, I shall be thirty next birthday. I don't wish to be counting forks for ever.

Haven't I said a dozen times that we're looking out for a high place that will suit your talents? As you know, the General is much occupied at the moment, but as soon as he returns from his business with the Fleet I will speak to him and we shall see what we can do. In the meantime, there's no need to look so solemn. A woman must be amused, Jem. I'd swear you were studying to play Malvolio.

But as the months limped past in a tedious procession of dinners and levees and ceremonies, I had another part in mind, viz. that boy in the fairytale who was imprisoned by an ogress who promised that on the morrow he would be free if only she could suck a thimbleful of his blood, but on the morrow she said the same thing again and so on until he was a pale and bloodless wraith.

I knew that I must put some other irons in the fire and not rely upon my mistress alone. No sooner did I begin to reflect upon the matter than I saw that, if I was to explore every avenue to advancement, it would be folly to neglect the Navy Office, for it seemed that we were to be at war with the Dutch until the crack of doom, and that therefore there was an infinitude of business to be done in the commissioning of ships, their building and provisioning, the repair of harbours, the purchase of timber and sails and ropes and shot and powder, the getting of officers and men, not to mention the apportionment of prize money and a dozen other matters from which an abundance of juice might be squeezed. And there was no help for it. If I was to make a sally upon the Navy Office, my first port of call must be Samuel Pepys esquire.

Up by 5 a-clock and to my office – where hard at work till towards noon, and home and eat a bit; and so going out, met with Mr Mount, my old acquaintance, and took him in and drunk a glass of wine or two with him and so parted, having not time to talk together; and I with Sir W. Batten to the Stylyard and there eat a Lobster together; and Wyne the King's fishmonger coming in, we were very merry half an hour; and so by water to Whitehall, and by and by, being all met, we went in to the Duke and there did our business.

Diary of Samuel Pepys, 13 April 1663

I had been free upon the Sunday, but I recalled my former Pepys-chase on the Lord's Day and decided that he would be more of a mind to hear my business at his office. Thus it was on Monday a half-hour after noon that I presented myself at the Navy Office and finding my quarry absent walked on a few yards to his house where I chanced to meet with him going out in his low-crowned beaver and velvet cloak, a busy bustling fellow in a new wig that was too big for his head (though that were swollen enough):

Ha, Jem. It's a long time since we met.

Sam, it is indeed, you look well.

What brings you to my doorstep?

The hope of seeing you, what else?

Ha (again, disgruntled somewhat, as a man will say Ha when he is in haste and finds a barred gate in his way). Well then, come in and take a glass of wine. I have some Haut-Brion. You will never have tasted the like. I took a glass with Sir John Cutler in Lombard Street on Friday. It is a rare Bordeaux wine, and not cheap. Sir John fancies it tastes of blackcurrants.

So I followed him inside thanking him for his kindness at every step, asking after Mrs Pepys's health (which was indifferent for she has the toothache and other troubles beside which he would not tell me of), admiring his books and his hangings. Then I must admire his wig.

It's so long since we met that I haven't seen you in a wig before. That's a fine periwig, I haven't seen a finer.

Ah yes, I haven't worn it more than a month (and here he touched

it with both hands as though to prevent some wind from blowing it off).
I had it of Chapman, my wife thinks it becomes me and so do the maids.
It's a strange thing, but the day before Chapman cut off my hair, I heard
the Duke say that he was going to wear a periwig and they say the King
also will.

Great minds think alike, I said.

Yes, yes, well I must to Sir William's and then to the Tangier
Committee, heigh-ho these are busy times. What think you of the
Haut-Brion, excellent isn't it? I wish we had leisure to sip it, for it's
an old wine that exhales its fragrances slowly. (Where had he acquired
this manner of discourse? When we had first been acquainted, all he
minded about a bottle was that it should be full.)

But before I knew it, I was out in the street again and Mr Pepys was
bidding me farewell in that brisk fashion with which a man may dismiss
a tailor that has come to take his measure.

Thereafter I returned to my trusted and true companions, viz. Will
Symons and little Peter Llewelyn, men that had not been corrupted
by excess of fortune and in an age of dull dogs yet possessed the art
of enjoying life. Will had lost his place when the King came in. He now
earned his living as best he could, running errands on behalf of country
merchants and gentlemen that lived far removed from the hubbub and
had no friends in high places: thus a merchant of soap from Yorkshire
that wished to advertise the merits of his wares to the court ladies might
despatch Will as his agent to persuade their keepers of the wardrobe.
For such public relations as Will supplied to these bumpkins, he would
charge 5 or 10 per cent of any moneys that might be earned. It was
a dismal trade, but Will made as light of it as he could. He was also
much troubled by his wife who had discovered a cancer in her breast
and although the surgeon had cut off the lump (which was in truth no
larger than a grape) she continued on the wane and had lost nigh on
two stones of her weight.

Peter Llewelyn had also been turned out at the Restoration, but had
found a place as clerk to Mr Edward Dering (he was later to work for
his younger brother, Red Ned) and had gone with him into Ireland to
execute the Act of Settlement but was now returned to London on his
master's behalf to keep an eye on his timber business, in which capacity

he had dealings with Mr Pepys. I intend that literally, for he wished Mr Pepys to intercede with the King to buy his Norway deals.

And what a comedy Mr Pepys made out of it, Peter told me in the Leg one evening. He would say to me, Mr Llewelyn (he always calls me Mr Llewelyn now, I know not why, we're old comrades from O.C.'s time), there's no service I would not render you, but this is a hard thing you ask of me. I have a duty to His Majesty and to the Navy Office which I take most solemnly, to procure only the finest deals, I must buy where the wood is soundest, the cut is straightest and the price is best.

Then you must buy from my master, say I, the reputation of Dering's deals is unequalled in Kent.

That may be, says old Sam, that may be (and he settles his wig on his head like a hen settling on her nest), but there are many fine merchants of deals and it is an onerous task to choose among them.

Mr Dering has full cognisance of the heavy burden that your office lays upon you, say I (I was proud of that 'cognisance', for I know he has a fancy to long words), he would be happy to take that into account. I believe he has in mind a sum of fifty pounds as what we might call a cognisance fee.

My aim is *primus* and *solus* to serve the King, says Sam, that is my only end. I do not take bribes as do Sir William Batten and some other illustrious gents I could mention – but I can see the spark in his eye. Not five minutes earlier there had been tears in that same eye when I had told him that Will Symons's wife was dead. He had admired her greatly when we went to Will's house. And I told him that pretty story: how I had gone with my friend Mr Blurton to the Fleece Tavern by Guildhall and by my calling him Doctor Blurton, the mistress of the house a very pretty woman did think he was in truth a physician and disclose to him privately some infirmity belonging to women and he proffered her physic and she desired him to bring it to her some day and examine her which he did and had sight of her thing below and handled it – all of which much diverted Mr Pepys. But that is by the by, said Peter Llewelyn (for he is a roundabout fabulist and must be led back to the starting point). To return to the cognisance fee: I think he is well hooked, but to land the fish, we must go and dine there tomorrow which will be no hardship, for if the dinner is bad our eyes may yet feast upon Mrs Pepys.

So home to dinner; and thither came to me Mr Mount and Llewelyn, I think almost foxed, and there dined with me: and very merry as I could be, my mind being troubled to see things so ordered at the Board – though with no disparagement to me at all.

At dinner comes a messenger from the Counter, with an Execution against me for the 30 pounds ten shillings given by the last verdict to Field. The man's name is Thomas, of the Poultry Counter. I sent Griffin with him to the Dolphin, where Sir W. Batten was at dinner; and he being satisfied that I should pay the money, I did cause the money to be paid him and Griffin to tell it out to him in the office.

They being gone, Llewelyn having again told me by myself that Dering is content to give me 50 pounds if I can sell his Deals to the King, not that I did ever offer to take it or bid Llewelyn bargain for me with him, but did tacitly seem to be willing to do him what service I could in it, and expect his thanks what he thought good.

Diary of Samuel Pepys, 15 December 1663

On the way to Seething Lane, we had made a pause at the Globe in Eastcheap to wet our whistles. The mistress of the house had a fresh cask of canary which she spoke warmly of and after a glass or two (or three in Peter's case) we found ourselves in agreement with her and we gambolled down the street past All Hallows Church like lambs that have found their legs.

The knock we gave at Mr Pepys's door would have awakened the dead and indeed Mr Pepys looked as pale as a ghost when he opened the door to us.

I do not usually stand by the door, he said, but the maids are helping with the dinner and the boy is sick. Yet I suspected that he had been waiting by the door for some other visitor, for he seemed surprised to see us.

This is a handsome chamber, Peter said, I don't know when I have seen a finer, Mrs Pepys. And indeed it was handsome with a fire blazing in the grate and two portraits of Mr and Mrs Pepys, though somewhat gloomy, and two globes, for Mr Pepys was giving his wife lessons in geography and the planets. And beyond was Mr Pepys's study which contained a fine collection of books in an old press that he was resolved to replace, for it was too small. The firelight shone upon the backs of the books and brought me to the conclusion that books do furnish a room as well as any picture.

It was in truth a snug apartment and I could not but envy Mr Pepys his domestic contentments, and I wished that I too had a wife and an apartment of my own where I could stretch my legs and play the master instead of lodging like a cuckoo in another's nest and in a connection that dare not avow itself. What had Sam done to deserve Mrs Pepys who was so sweet in her ways and had eyes a man might drown in (though her teeth were imperfect, *vide supra*)? She too was pale but that was on account of her maladies which Peter tells me come from a swelling or *Fistula* in her privates (how does he come to know such a thing?) which Mr Hellier the surgeon hath lately cut her for. *Theorem:* that Mrs Pepys's incapacity drives Mr Pepys to the stews to piece up his lost contentments, which excuses him somewhat for such trespasses. But I do not believe this, for he is a lecherous fellow and would do it willy-nilly.

It was a good dinner, though not grand: a joint of salted beef and a fruit tart and Rhenish wine, but the company was dull. Peter Llewelyn told two or three of his stories which I had heard before, and which were too indelicate for Mrs Pepys's ears. Then he told a story of my lord Sandwich and the slut he keeps down at Chelsea, at which Mr Pepys told him to shut up his discourse, for it was a private matter and none of Llewelyn's business. To which Mr Llewelyn said that the matter was no longer private because the whole town was talking of it. At which Mr Pepys said that Llewelyn ought to find some better occupation than listening to idle tattle and that he had become embittered since he had been turned out. To which Llewelyn replied that he had rather be a free man than a whoremonger's lackey. And Mrs Pepys looked pale, and I fretted for I foresaw that the dinner would go by before I had asked Mr Pepys if he could advise me of any free place in the Navy Office.

But our quarrels were interrupted, for there came a rough knocking at the door and the maid flew down to answer it.

O sir, it is the man from the prison.

Mr Pepys went white. He could not speak. His wife ran to his side and put her arms round his neck. Mr Pepys recovered his speech enough to say, let him come up, but the man was already in the room, a little yellow fellow with a moustache.

Thomas, sir, from the Poultry Counter. Which of you gentlemen is Samuel Pepys, esquire?

I am he, said Sam, standing up, setting his wig straight and taking off the napkin from his neck.

I have a writ of execution against you on behalf of Edward Field, esquire for the thirty pounds ten shillings given him by verdict of the court on Friday last, which you must pay or go straight to jail, sir.

I'm aware of the matter, says Sam, essaying to speak as though there were a dozen such suits against him every day, it is a trivial thing. Will you go with my man Griffin down to Sir William Batten at the Dolphin so that he may settle it?

My orders are to settle with you, sir.

You know who Sir William Batten is, do you not? He is Surveyor of the Navy. The matter concerns the Navy's honour. I can't proceed in it without his consent.

Yes, sir, very well, sir. And the miserable little fellow trotted off with the doorkeeper to the great Sir William who was at dinner in Tower Street and within ten minutes returned saying:

He says: Pay.

Which Mr Pepys duly did with a flourish, as though it were an act of charity and not to keep himself out of prison. And after the man had gone he was at his ease again and told us the whole story, which was in truth long and tedious, *videlicet*: Field had accused the Board of failing to arrest one Turpin who had, he said, stolen timber, Field himself was arrested for slander but got free because he showed proof that the Board had no power to arrest a man within the City, Field then brought a suit against Pepys, and Batten brought a suit against Field, etc., etc. Lord, how tedious these lawyers' affairs are, and how they seduce the wits of ordinary men who get entangled in them. Mr Pepys droned on and I looked into his wife's eyes and listened to her gentle voice (there was as yet a touch of French in it, I fancied, for her parents were Huguenots) as she pressed me to another piece of tart. Then, ah what delight, I felt a silken leg alongside my own, and it began to stroke mine as a cat rubs its fur against a table – and then I saw Llewelyn laughing like a donkey and knew whose leg it was. Meanwhile, Mr Pepys:

It was a matter for the City magistrates in the first instance, I'll admit that, our counsel was poor, yet the gravamen of the original charge . . .

And I began again to despair of ever mentioning my matter to him, for he was in full spate by his own fireside and a regiment of Ironsides would not have halted him.

But little Peter Llewelyn, inebriated though he was, knew the trick.

If you are looking for an honest timber merchant, might I remind you . . .

Ah yes, said Sam, there is a small matter between us, isn't there? I had quite forgot, I've had so much to think on. Let us retire, then we shan't weary the company with the particulars of our business.

They went into the study and shut the door behind them. We were alone together, Mrs Pepys and I, for the first time.

Although it was winter, she wore a black silk taffeta gown, low at the waist, as was now the fashion, and open below to show the petticoat, which was of a lemon yellow. She wore her hair loose, for she was at home, and it tumbled about her bare shoulders. Her skin was fair, almost white, she could have been a child (she was only twenty-three years old) but that her breasts were as round as apples. There was a look about her eye which carried some such sly message as keep off but come again – or so I fancied. I have spoken before of her teeth, unkindly, but now by the light of her own face they seemed almost to bite into her lower lip as though she were tasting some succulent fruit.

It's so long since we last met, I said.

I don't go out much, except to my mother and Mr Pepys's friends.

Why not?

I was very young when we were first married, and Mr Pepys thought I'd be shy in company, so we have lived very quietly – or I have.

Don't you like to go out?

Oh yes, I am fond of the play and weddings and many other things, but – I don't like to say this for it has a presumptuous sound – Mr Pepys is a jealous man and he doesn't like to see a man talk to me unless he be very old.

And you – are you jealous?

She laughed and said, Yes I am, but you should not ask me such things.

We are old friends, Mr Pepys and I. There is no harm in the question.

He would not care to hear that I had talked with you so freely.

Well then, you need not tell him. But I think you should go out more often. A beautiful flower should breathe the pure air and feel the sun upon her petals.

I go to my parents, but the air is not very pure there, for they have a place in Long-Acre which is among all the bad houses and I don't like my husband to see them in such condition, so he sets me down upon the corner of Covent Garden.

What is your father by profession?

In the late King's reign he was a carver to the Queen, an excellent workman in wood, but he had a quarrel with one of her friars, upon some religious matter, and he punched the friar upon the nose and was dismissed, he is a Protestant but because he is French he has trouble in finding work. Mr Pepys is very good to him. He employs him to make fine rules upon the paper in his office and to repair the tables, but I weep to see him engaged upon such tasks, which are so inferior to his talents. You must know that he is an inventor – and her round eyes seemed to swell and brim as she thought of her father and his ill-fortune.

An inventor?

He has invented a machine for removing the smoke from chimneys, and for keeping the water in ponds clean so that horses may drink from them, and he has perfected a device for making ornamental bricks in any design you fancy – with leaves, or crowns, or letters upon them. And he has patent licences upon all of them, so that no one may copy his machines with impunity.

He must be a grand projector.

You mean a cheat?

No, no, not at all. I meant a man who sees further than others, one who has the visionary eye.

Sometimes I think he sees too far. I wish he would look nearer home and see to his own affairs, but he says he has no time. He is presently working on a project which is so private and so extraordinary that I am to tell no one of it, not even my husband, but then I don't think he cares to hear, for he thinks little of my father.

You may tell me, I'm as secret as the grave.

No, no, I must not, I promised him I wouldn't.

And I promise you I won't speak a word of it to any one. There is my promise – and I took her little hand and pressed it warmly and held it for above a minute that she might see there was more feeling in the pressure than was necessary for the promise alone.

Well then, if you are sure – perhaps it is really of no great consequence, so long as he does not hear of it, it is a – and here she bent low to my ear, so that I could feel her sweet breath upon my cheek, but we were both trembling so much that she could only mutter and I could not hear.

A what?

A *perpetuum mobile*. Do you not know what that is?

Certainly I know, I misheard you, that is all. It is a machine that operates in perpetuity, *ad saecula saeculorum*, without any horse to pull it, or water to drive it, or any other thing.

Oh it is such a pretty device with little iron balls that run along channels and into buckets that pass through other channels that are filled with water. He intends that Prince Rupert should come to see it when it is complete, for the Prince is a great projector and has but lately made a machine that draws pictures without a man's hand guiding it, and also a metal that is indistinguishable from gold but made all of baser metals, I know not which ones. Also he has made chemical glass drops which shatter to dust if you break off the little end, which is a great mystery and Mr Honeywood showed us. If Prince Rupert approves the machine, why then my father's fortune is made.

And does it work, this *perpetuum mobile*?

It must be built upon a larger scale, my father says, for then there will be less friction and the energy of the machine will never be exhausted.

I should not want there to be no more friction, I said and rubbed her hand with my own as one rubs a sore spot, gently.

Oh Mr Mount.

Jem, I said, call me Jem.

Just then there was a noise of a door opening. Llewelyn and Pepys must have finished their conference, and they laughed as they came along the passage.

Do you care for cards? she said quickly in a low voice.

Yes, yes, I said, although I had scarcely played at cards above three times in my life.

My husband doesn't. Though Mrs Jemimah Mountagu taught him cribbage, yet he can't keep the rules in his head, but he is often late at the office and I like to take a hand with Mr Pierce the surgeon and his wife, she is another Elizabeth and very beautiful.

She could not be more beautiful than the Elizabeth I know already, I whispered as her husband came back into the dining-room with Llewelyn, both of them being as smug as dormice. I spoke so low that I did not know whether she had heard me, but her eyes told me that she heard well enough.

Up and to the office, where all the morning sitting. And at noon to the Change, and there I found and brought home Mr Pierce the surgeon to dinner – where I find also Mr Llewelyn and Mount – and merry at dinner – but their discourse so free about claps and other foul discourse that I was weary of them. But after dinner Llewelyn took me up with him to my chamber, and there he told me how Dering did intend to be as good as his word, to give me fifty pounds for the service I did him, though not so great as he expected and I intended. But I told him that I would not sell my liberty to any man. If he would give me anything by another's hand, I would endeavour to deserve it, but I will never give him himself thanks for it, nor acknowledge the receiving of any – which he told me was reasonable. I did also tell him that neither this nor anything should make me to do anything that should not be for the King's service besides. So we parted, and I left them three at home with my wife going to cards, and I to my office and there stayed late.

Diary of Samuel Pepys, 29 December 1663

Every day thereafter I waited for an invitation from Mrs Pepys, for I fancied that she was of an ardent disposition, though she seemed so modest, and would not abide a long parting once the conversation between us was begun, for though she had not declared herself in speech, yet her eyes spoke. But a fortnight passed, and it was Christmas and I had returned from church with Nan but ten minutes earlier, and she was taking off her beaver fur when Griffin the Navy Office man came with a letter.

That's a woman's hand, Nan said, and tried to seize the letter from me, but I was too quick for her.

Oh it's merely an invitation to dinner and to play cards, from Mrs Pepys, the clerk's wife.

She is handsome, I dare say.

Scarcely. She is a pale thing, little more than a girl. We are old friends, Pepys and I. As I told you, we were clerks together in Cromwell's time.

Why doesn't Mr Pepys invite you?

He is a busy man.

Shall you go?

Yes.

I may have need of you that day.

Well, if you have need of me, I shan't go. The day is Tuesday.

Oh go then, go. You need the company of fledglings. You have roosted with old birds too long, no, don't deny it. I can discern the weariness in your look, I don't deceive myself.

Nan, you know that my passion for you burns brighter with each year.

Such stale speeches. I am sure they are more to Mrs Pepys's taste than mine. Be off with you, I await a delegation of Russian merchants who come smartly upon their cue, for this old beaver has become a nest of moths. Go take your ease with your little clerks and their little wives.

I left her with a sensation of relief. Of late she had become bitter towards me, seeing fault where I had sought only to please. She seemed to love her jewel-box more than me. I took refuge in the buttery downstairs, and more than once sat on a cask in the cool dark and drank a bottle of the old canary wine that the General loved. But even there, she would hound me – Jem, you drink too much, a gentleman-usher should set an example – so that I came to dread the rustle of her skirts on the stone stair.

Thus I lived through the three days before my dinner with Mrs Pepys in burning impatience. I foresaw the two of us with our heads together over the cards, her little white teeth biting her underlip as she pondered whether to play a knave or a king while my hand might brush against her thigh as I picked up a card that had fallen. The day before the *dies amoris*, I dropped upon the Golden Fleece for a glass of sack to keep out the cold and there chanced on Llewelyn who was finishing a glass of ditto.

Ha, Jem, I cannot stay, I must off to Deptford to view a fresh cargo of Norway firs, but we shall meet tomorrow.

Shall we?

Yes, with Mrs Pepys at cards. We are to teach her ombre which is a new game lately arrived from Spain and is for three persons.

When I presented myself at Seething Lane, there Llewelyn was on the doorstep before me. We went in together to Mrs Pepys who was in a white taffeta gown, with roses embroidered upon it, very pretty and costly. Not five minutes later, I was further sunk in despair for in came Mr Pepys with Mr Pierce, the Duke's surgeon, whom he had found on the Exchange.

This Pierce may be an eminent doctor, Mr Pepys swears by him, but he neglects one element in his profession, the one that Hippocrates himself imposed, viz. to stand mum about the affairs of his patients.

His manner of talk was thus (though I cannot remember the half of it):

All the world thinks that the King has set Lady Castlemaine by, but it is not so for he lay with her Wednesday last, having lain with the Queen but two days earlier and that was for the first time in a month, which gave her great pleasure, but Mr Frazer tells me that she, Lady Castlemaine I mean, complains of a great soreness in her parts, which I trust is but the result of the frequent traffic in that highway and nothing of more serious import, else the entire court will be poxed although the half of them are already afflicted. Mr Collins tells me that the Prince has the most fearsome sores rising up his body and likely to break out upon his head and . . .

And la belle Stuart, is she yet well? For I have a huge fancy to her, said little Llewelyn, rolling his eyes like a lovesick chicken (how did he come to be so soused so early in the day?).

I advise you to button up your fancy in your breeches if you don't wish to end in the Tower, for that maid of honour – now there's irony for you – is now Mistress in Chief and lies in her chamber in wait for him every night. Her chamber being below the Queen's, any noble who wishes to know where the King is must ask the sentries 'Is the King above or below?' meaning with the Queen or Mrs Stuart, but sometimes he dallies with La Stuart upstairs in the Queen's dressing-room, so that the Queen must stop and knock before she goes in, lest she surprise her husband bare-breeched with his mistress. I knew La Stuart's father, that was physician to the old Queen, a smooth man but not well versed in women's complaints and used to ask me for receipts for the flux.

Mr Pierce, there are ladies present. I beg you to take a glass of wine and turn to more fitting topics.

The royal surgeon refilled his glass and paused with a pleasant smile upon his face, as one will pause for the noise of a carriage passing in the street outside.

But little Peter Llewelyn came to our rescue: We came to play cards, did we not, and I perceive Mrs Pepys has a pretty walnut ombre table with three sides that is *à la mode* (I was astonished that he could perceive so much in his state of intoxication). Who will play?

I fear I have no time for such diversions, said his host, but we have a matter to discuss, don't we, Mr Llewellyn?

A matter? Llewelyn once more seemed incapable, quite dazed by all he had drunk since coming to Mr Pepys's, not to speak of all he had drunk before.

A matter of business.

Business?

Don't parrot me, sir. You know what I mean – and here Sam made a gesture as of counting money, then passing it to another.

Oh, you mean the fifty pounds, why didn't you say so?

Hush, hush, we needn't spell out such matters in company.

We're all friends here, are we not? Mr Pierce is a friend, Jem here is a friend, an old friend, he lodged in my lodgings, did you know that, I mean his old lodgings, well they were my old lodgings too, my old, old lodgings, so he is an old, old friend.

Now then, Peter, let us retire.

Let us retire to bed, that is what old friends are for, to . . .

No, not to bed, come next door and we can despatch our business without troubling the rest of the company.

We will despatch and you will play cards; one two three, knave, queen, king, no knave, queen, knave . . . for I see two knaves but no . . .

Come on, come on – and Pepys pushed him into the next room.

After they had gone, Mr Pierce fell silent, for he was one of those men who chatters like a jay when he is drinking and becomes taciturn when he is drunk. Now he dealt out the cards as solemnly as if he were dealing out prayer-books in church.

Three-two-three. There is your hand. I trust the deck had been well shuffled, for I forgot to do it myself. And we haven't fixed the colour, therefore it must be clubs.

I am content with clubs, I said, for all suits were the same to me, so long as I could look into Elizabeth's eyes.

Jeremiah, I may call you so, may I not, for I'm too drunk to stand on ceremony, Jeremiah, you mustn't peep at Mrs Pepys's hand, peep at Pepys, ha, that's good, but it's strange you don't pronounce it Peppis, the syllable would lend it dignity.

I was not peeping at her hand, but only at Mrs Pepys herself who must draw all eyes. This peeping is but natural, and I shall not apologise for it.

No more you should, a cat may look at a king and a . . . but here his speech dribbled into silence, for he was sorting his hand.

I'm the eldest hand and I ask, I said, for I sat on the surgeon's left.

Is it in colour? Mrs Pepys inquired.

Yes, I said.

Is it a solo? she inquired.

I'd rather it were a duo, I said.

You must not say so, the surgeon said. You must say either Yes or Pass.

Mrs Pepys knows what I mean, I said, for she was blushing.

I know what you mean too, the surgeon said, but we are playing at cards, not the other thing. I shall dub that a pass, and I am passing too and Mrs Pepys is to play solo in clubs.

Being eldest hand, I led my ace of hearts, with the king to follow, but my ace was trumped by Mrs Pepys's seven of clubs. She turned to diamonds and her little white hand played off the cards so fast that I put on the king of hearts when I intended the king of diamonds and put out my hand to take the trick.

Diamonds, sir, I played a diamond. Mrs Pepys spoke in a severe manner I had not heard from her before.

I pulled out my errant king, but she thrust it back into my hand.

You have revoked, Jem, you must pay all.

I made another attempt with my queen of clubs.

No, no, Jem, the game is over. A revoke finishes it.

Women are the devil at cards, are they not? Their fingers are so nimble. Seamstresses are the worst, never play cards with a seamstress. You must pay my loss too, I believe, the surgeon said, leaning back in his chair with a silly drunken smile on his face.

That is all we women are good for, I dare say, Mr Pierce, sewing and cards. Is that your mind?

Madam, I could add other purposes to the list, but modesty forbids.

I was speaking of intellectuals. I expect you think women have no place there.

On the contrary, madam, women are an adornment to the arts; I love to hear a woman sing.

Oh I love to sing, she said, but my husband says I sing out of tune. Music is the thing that he loves most in the world and he can play any instrument, you know, the lute, the viol, the spinet, the flageolet, and all by ear, for he does not know the scale of music. In the garden sometimes in summer he lets me sing while he plays, and the girl sings too and she has a pretty voice, although she is not taught.

While she spoke of music, her cheeks took on the flush of the Damask rose and my heart was filled with rage and envy at Mr Pepys. How dare he reproach his wife's singing? Her speaking voice was so sweet and low I was sure her singing voice must be just as fine. What would I have given to be of those summer night parties? With those dulcet voices chiming with Mr Pepys's lute and rising above the smoke of the City? And I drew in my mind the comparison with my own dark chamber in Whitehall, waiting to serve either at table or at bed a capricious mistress who was old enough to be Mrs Pepys's mother. How little I had made of my life, how the years had flown away.

When I was at sea, Mr Pierce was saying, I sang with several of the Court, sea songs for the greater part and some of Dowland's airs. You know this one?

And Mr Pierce began to sing, very low and with a sweet, baritone voice:

> *Sleep is a reconciling,*
> *A rest that peace begets.*
> *Doth not the sun rise smiling*
> *When fair at even he sets.*

It's a sort of lullaby, the surgeon said, and better fitted to a tenor, my voice is too far down the gamut.

It is very fine, I said, and in truth the tears were almost starting to my eyes I was so full of pity for my dismal lot.

But at that moment Mr Pepys came in with little Peter and he had a contented look upon his face as though to say the business is done while you are idling by the fire.

You have been at cards, I perceive, he said in a triumphal fashion as though he had discovered their presence by some necromancy.

We were playing at ombre, my dear, his wife said.

I thought I heard singing.

There was a little singing. Mr Pierce sang an air.

Cards and singing. What a pleasant afternoon for some. Well, I must away to the office. The Navy waits for no man. But please stay and entertain my wife. She is so fond of cards. I wish I had the time to learn.

You remember Mrs Mountagu tried to teach you gleek, my dear, and you could not get the rules of it.

Yes, yes, it is a fiddling sort of game. Well, I must take my leave of you, Master Pierce.

He scarcely spoke a word to me but nodded and left the room.

We can't play ombre now there are four of us.

O I'm too tired for cards, little Peter said.

So am I, the surgeon said. We'll talk and Jem shall play with Mrs Pepys.

Which pleased me greatly and proved that the wine had not addled his senses.

Let us play piquet, my beloved said, it is the best of all games for two.

And while she dealt the deck, she kept the tip of her little pink tongue between her white teeth as children do when they are studying.

There now, you are the major hand because I have dealt.

As I put out my hand to take up my cards, she was still putting them in a neat heap, and so my hand rested upon hers and I kept it there. But she took her hand from under mine with a hasty motion.

You must not, she said.

Must not what?

You know.

Friends may touch hands, may they not?

Only touch, she said.

They say that touch is the sweetest of the senses.

Do they? Why?

I could not answer at once because the maxim had only just come into my head. My first thought was to pretend some grand theory, but then it occurred to me that honesty might be the better policy, that she might be won by a show of humility and candour.

I don't know.

Do you often say things you don't know the reason for? she inquired with a smile.

Very often, but that is because I don't know a great deal.

My husband never says that he doesn't know the reason for what he has said.

That is doubtless because he knows so much.

Yes, she said musingly, he does know a great deal though not so much as he fancies. He thinks I am very ignorant.

There he is grievously in error.

No, he is in the right. I have not been well schooled, my parents were too poor, and when my father lost his place it was no time to think of such things. I would love to know Spanish and mathematics. I know a little French from my father, but that is all.

Couldn't your husband teach you?

He is so busy, and then he thinks I am so slow that he cannot bear to repeat the lesson when I make a mistake.

If only there were something I might have the honour to teach you, I should be very patient.

O there is, I am sure there is – and in her excitement she took my hand and squeezed it, but gently so.

I will teach you history, I said.

Oh would you? I should love to know the history of France and of those religionary wars which have cost my family so dear.

This was a stiff examination, for I knew little more of the history of France than of the history of China, although I could have given a fair account of myself on the Wars of the Roses.

I will see what I can do, I said.

She looked at me with her green eyes and I saw gratitude in them and felt humble that I had inspired such feelings in so noble a nature.

At that moment of moments, a loud snore came to our ears and we saw that Peter Llewelyn had fallen asleep in the surgeon's lap. Mr Pierce was not quite sleeping, his eyes being but half-closed and his lips emitting a low musical hum, though I could not catch the tune.

Oh, said Mrs Pepys with a start, I must go to my parents. I am reminded because my father hums thus when he is tired. But what shall I –

I will pack them off, I said.

You are a gentle man, she said.

But it is dark, Elizabeth, I may call you so, may I not? May I escort you to Covent Garden?

I mustn't trespass upon your kindness, Jem.

So I shook the two old soakers awake and they came to their senses with so many belches, groans and farts that I was glad Mrs Pepys had gone to her room for her hat.

Jem, you are a good fellow, Mr Pierce yawned, what time is it? I must wait upon His Grace, his piles are as big as apricots and he wants to have them cut, but I tell him to let nature heal them.

Peter Llewelyn said nothing, being too far gone, but scratched the chicken fluff on his scalp as though it were the lice that had intoxicated him and he would be sober again if he were rid of them.

I shuffled them off somehow and stepped out with Mrs Pepys in her neat beaver in search of a hackney. The coachman said the fare would be 5s.

You're an extortioner, I said. One of your fellows took me to Whitehall for half a crown.

It is Christmas, sir, you must pay the holiday charge.

It was Christmas four days ago.

The holiday charge runs between Christmas and Epiphany, he said.

Oh can we not get in? Elizabeth said. It's a wet night.

And because I did not wish to seem parsimonious I compounded with the fellow for 4s and we got into the hackney which smelled of leather and pickled onions.

But how blessed was that darkness with the rain coming down hard upon the roof and the rough motion of the hackney upon the cobbles, for the conveyance had old straps for springs. It was an antique hackney that had no glass windows but to me it was as glorious as Phaethon's chariot, for I felt her thigh next to my thigh and her heart beating close to mine.

We might be tossing about at sea in a storm, I said.

I would love to go to sea, she said. I wanted to go with my husband when he was bringing the King in but there was no room. I dream of sailing with my father back to his home in Anjou and seeing him restored to his estates there.

Estates? I said, diverted from amorous thoughts by this unexpected intelligence.

Yes, oh they had such a fine estate there, and my father was the heir, but he went to fight in the German wars and was converted to the Religion and so lost his inheritance. A cruel world, isn't it, to lose your birthright for your faith?

Very fine, I said, thinking: very foolish.

We were in Paris when I was little, my brother Balthazar and my mother and I, and they tried to make us into Catholics, but she said we must stay loyal to Papa – that's what we call my father. Was that not right?

Entirely right, I said.

Otherwise Balty might have had the property at my father's expense. But now we are proud to be Protestants even if we are doomed to a life of poverty.

I was so moved by her brave speech that I pressed her hand in a fatherly fashion and eschewed the grosser overtures for which the darkness and the bumping of the hackney were so convenient. Afterwards I cursed myself for this delicacy, but one cannot always overcome one's nobler impulses.

In all too short a time (the journey was never five shillings' worth) we came to a dismal, dripping, filthy street where the houses served as the cheaper sort of lodging, not old but so badly built they were already tumbling.

She led me up the stairs and as I saw her dainty feet in white stockings tread the dusty boards, I was put in mind of the low houses where I had followed other women up the stairs for shameful purposes.

Her father heard her step upon the stairs and came out to meet us. He was a tall man of choleric aspect with a mane of white hair like a mangy lion. And he had the roar of it too, for we were scarcely in the mean chamber before he was telling his entire *curriculum vitae:* viz., how he had been a gentleman-carver to the old Queen, how the said Queen had praised his work which might yet be seen in the Great

Saloon at Hampton Court, to wit a garland of fruit and partridges that the nobility now mistook for Mr Gibbons's work, though Gibbons had not yet the finesse of the French carvers such as he had learnt from, and how now he purposed to fight in the Turkish wars for, though he might seem old, an old soldier knew tricks and could outlast the young blades, but before he went he was seeking to arrange a conference with Prince Rupert who might assist him to a patent for his Machine which he was loath to manufacture without, for there were pirates everywhere.

And to all this I listened with a nod and a smile, and out of the corner of my eye I perceived Elizabeth nodding and smiling that I was so attentive. And soon there were two nodders of the company, for Mrs St Michel came in to join us and began nodding and smiling too. She was very like her daughter, but brown and withered, an old russet beside a fresh Kentish apple.

Some people think I'm French also because I am so brown, she said as though she could read my thoughts, but my father, Sir Francis Kingsmill, was from Devonshire and my mother was of the line of Clifford of Chudleigh who, as you may know, are foremost among the families of Devon, so I am as much of that country as was Sir Francis Drake. Will you take coffee?

She placed a coffee pot and China-ware cups amid the clutter that was on the table, and although the pot was dirty I could see that it was of silver which much surprised me, for it was not then the custom to take coffee at home, coffee beans costing 1s a pound and upwards, even the worst. Nor had I yet drunk coffee from a fine cup. Thus I perceived that although their situation was decayed their manners continued elegant.

We had better rooms, she said, in Charing Cross. But they were too dear.

Mr Pepys will not visit us here, said her husband, it would discredit him to be seen in our neighbourhood.

O Alexander, you must not reproach him. He is very busy and the Navy Office is some way distant. He is good to us notwithstanding. Last week Elizabeth brought us five shillings from him, though we had not asked it. And she brought up neat's tongue and brain as well.

We are grateful, very grateful, the father said, so grateful that we return him the compliment of not visiting his house, for he breathes more freely in our absence.

O Papa, he thinks often of you both.

Only when you speak to him of us, my dear. He has many other matters to concern him at the Office and at the Court. He has a hundred ships to think of, you cannot expect that he should think of your mother and me.

His daughter appeased his agitation with the soft touch of her hand and the liquid appeal of her eye, and his mind was soon diverted from the thought of his over-busy benefactor to his own projects and how he might bring them to the attention of great persons, which was not to be by his son-in-law, for S. Pepys had said that he would have nothing to do with that old man's whimsies and the sooner his father-in-law went off to fight the Turks and was cut in half by a scimitar, the better he would be pleased.

Yet, my Elizabeth's father was a man who had that art which Mr Pepys lacked, viz. how to charm. He told us tales of his youth in Anjou and how he had fought in the German wars and of the plague and dysenteries that had killed more men than sword or musket: he had been about to cut down a cuirassier in a fir-wood in Bohemia when the man fell and died on the spot from disease, so that his (Mr St Michel's) sword whistled through thin air. And as he told the story he swung his arm through the air as though it were his sword and knocked over a small carved cherub that stood upon the mantel which he made himself for the old Queen in the days when you could procure good pearwood that would not split.

And you, sir, what do you do?

I told them of my service with Their Highnesses, somewhat embroidering the nature of my employments.

How I admire your open English manners, Mr St Michel said. In France, we are so jealous that if a handsome young man like you, sir, were to play escort to my wife, even though he said it was but to her parents, I should feel compelled to challenge him.

Challenge him?

To a duel, sir, for the insult to my wife's honour. You came in a carriage, did you not? In France that would be unthinkable. A man and a woman in a carriage together, *ah mon Dieu*! And Mr St Michel made the gesture of running through me with his imaginary sword and almost knocked again the cherub that had been put back on the mantel.

But in England, he continued, you men trust one another, you are bound by the chains of friendship that are stronger than iron – and here he made a show of fruitlessly attempting to burst such chains, so I thought he might further endanger the furniture, and I wondered that he could master such delicate arts as carving when his gestures were so violent.

O Papa, Englishmen don't think such thoughts.

It is good that they do not, else I should be tempted to act like a Frenchman, ha ha – and he gave a desiccated laugh which I could not tell the meaning of, whether it was idle pleasantry or a threat, albeit a veiled one. I hoped that I had not gone red in the face but looked like a honest Englishman that was phlegmatic and had not an impure thought in his head.

When we took a hackney home – for I insisted that I must come back with her, for she was in equal danger coming back as going – I found myself hampered and doubly so: *primo*, if I made an assault upon her and she told her father of it, he would surely come and run me through as he had promised, for plainly he was a man of small inhibitions, and *secundo*, he had put the evil thought into her mind that if I did but take her hand or stroke her knee and say what pleasure I had taken in our visit, and how much I had loved her parents – which was nothing but the truth – this might be not out of pure friendship but a prelude to a vicious assault. So I did not attempt any such but burned inwardly and sat with my hands folded upon my lap while she talked of the price of coffee and how she wished her parents were more careful with money. Thus Mr St Michel's discourse had what might have been its desired effect, for he was not such a fool as he seemed.

At noon to the Change and there long; and from thence by appointment took Llewelyn, Mount and W. Symonds and Mr Pierce the surgeon home to dinner with me and were merry. But Lord, to hear how W. Symons doth commend his wife and look sad, and then talk bawdly and merrily, though she was dead but the other day would make a dog laugh. This dinner I did give in further part of kindness to Llewelyn for his kindness about Dering's fifty pounds which he procured me the other day of him.

We spent all the afternoon together and then they to cards with my wife (who this day put on her Indian blue gown which is very pretty), where I left them for an hour and to my office and then to them again . . .

We had great pleasure this afternoon, among other things to talk of our old passages together in Cromwell's time.

Diary of Samuel Pepys, 8 January 1664

You are bidden to the Great Bribe Dinner, aren't you? Little Peter could scarce keep from laughing as he inquired this strange question of me.

To what?

Old Sam is giving us all dinner to thank me for the fifty pounds I gave him from Dering, for future services to His Majesty's Navy, viz. masts, spars, timbers, keels, tillers, etc., etc. all supplied from the yards of E. Dering gent. You must know how to tip the quids in this game, Jem. Cast thy bread upon the waters and it shall return to thee an hundredfold. Will Symons is to be of the company, so it will be a reunion of old clerks.

And Sam calls it a Bribe Dinner, I hadn't thought –

No, no, dunderhead, *I* call it a bribe dinner, he calls it a vouchsafing of the great love he bears me and the gratitude he owes my master for the present which is merely a token of friendship, and if it were anything other, no torturer on earth could force him to accept it, etc., for in all things he seeketh only to serve His Gracious Majesty King Charles, *in saecula saeculorum*, amen. Pierce the surgeon will be there also, so it will be a frolic.

I hadn't thought to see Mrs Pepys again so soon. Amid the press at her husband's table, it would surely be possible to gain a few minutes' private conversation, for while I knew it would not do to alarm her, at the same time I must keep up a steady trot, or she would fear that my love was a feeble, inconstant thing.

But I needed bait for my trap and bought a pretty ribbon of green silk done in a knot which would sort with her green eyes. And as I gave the money to the girl in the shop, I remembered how Nan had sold such things in the Gypsies, and a melancholy fit overcame me at the thought of how she was changed and our love ditto.

I feared lest Will Symons should depress our spirits by his mournful mien. I should have known him better. Though his wife was but lately dead, he talked of her so tenderly that we almost fancied she was with us at the table.

I admired your wife, Will, said Mr Pepys. She was very handsome.

So she was, Sam, so she was. And she was extremely vexed by your admiration.

O I hope not, I do hope not.

She was. If I had sixpence for every time she told me I would have to fetch the constable if you went on making eyes at her thus . . .

I swear it is untrue. I admired her only as one will admire a picture.

When Mr Pepys waxed too solemn, Will knew how to tickle him out of the dark part of the stream and into the sparkling shallows.

Come, come, you goggled at her like a cod.

It's true, my dear, you did look at her so.

What, am I betrayed by my wife? Well, I am not ashamed. She was a fine woman.

O I loved her, Will said, and tears began to drop down his moonface and I filled his glass and he dried his tears, and began to describe how he had courted her in a hayloft and they had then gone to take tea with her uncle Scobell, for it was his farm and she hoped he might leave her some money, and her uncle said: I perceive you have been making hay, for they had not brushed the straws off her back. And then he told another tale of their courting which I will not set down here because, first, it is too obscene and, second, it requires a geometrical figure that cannot be represented on a page but he made plain with a series of gestures. And then he began to weep again, but the sight of all the fishes that Mrs Pepys had prepared cheered him, for she said: It is Friday and I know you're a great eater of fish, though there's a venison pasty for those that have no taste for fish, but here is Dutch herring, salted cod and haddock, and a lobster from Plymouth.

And then Will began to talk of our days together under the Usurper.

He served me better than ever our rightful Sovereign has, Will said. And we talked of our voyage upriver to make an inventory at Hampton Court, and of the commode that had received a Grand Triumvirate of Arses, viz. King Charles, King Oliver and W. Symons.

Where is it now, I wonder? Will mused. Perhaps my Lady Castlemaine sits upon it, after coming from the King.

Will, ladies do not like to hear such discourse.

Are you certain so, Sam? In my experience, ladies are not so refined, for they must deal with the grosser facts of our mortal existence, viz. empty the pots, wash the napkins, and the like.

It's true, said Elizabeth.

Well perhaps, Pepys said, but he looked ill at ease and though he laughed at Will's jests and stories, he harrumphed now and then, as though to say: This conversation is unfitting and I laugh but out of courtesy, because I am the host. And he was pleased when Will again turned solemn.

Yes it is so, Will said. Llewelyn told you rightly. Four days before she died she rose up in her bed as though the Heavens were drawing her to them. In four days I shall die, Will, she said, you must make preparation, for so many die at this season, you had better tell the parson it will be Thursday, no I am wrong, Wednesday, for it is Saturday today (for she was not in such a delirium that she had forgot what day it was).

But how did she know?

That is what I asked her. Because I have seen Uncle Scobell, she said, in a dream. He was wearing his old yellow coat and smelled of snuff, so I knew it was he. Hurry up, Niece, he said, you have only four days left.

I shouldn't wish to join Uncle Scobell, I said attempting to rally her, him being a mean-spirited old fellow.

I asked him, she said, where are you, Uncle, upstairs or downstairs?

There is no distinction, Niece, he said to her, we are all forgiven. Even the King of Spain is here. I took breakfast with him yesterday, he is much improved.

Said she really so? Mr Pepys inquired, greatly surprised.

She did, said Will, and you could not tell from his moonface whether he had added somewhat of decoration or whether his wife had in truth told him so, but herself had embroidered her dream even in her extremity, for she was a merry spirit.

And then Will began to talk of his great feat in O.C.'s time: that he had survived that whirligig year before the King came in when there were eight governments, viz.: Tumbledown Dick's, then the Council of Officers and the Committee of Safety that came in twice, and the Council of State and others that I have now forgot. And yet he fell at the last fence, when the King came in, and he was turned out along with Peter Llewelyn.

And we laughed at the recollection of his shifts and did not know that this was to be the last time we four were to drink together, for soon Providence was to scatter us to the four winds and our old friendship was vanished as though it had never been.

Well thank God I am still in the saddle, said Mr Pepys, which reminds me that I must jog off to the office to write a letter to Mr Coventry about the Deputy Treasurers, but my wife will entertain you to cards, and Jem, you can pour the wine, for you are practised in that art. I commend the canary. You will find a fair quarter cask below.

That was the Unforgivable, to contemn me as a mere cellarer, and a drunken one, and as he closed the door behind him, my blood boiled.

He was not five minutes gone before I turned to Elizabeth and asked her to show me the cellar.

You don't need me to show you, she said. It's down the stairs and on the left side.

I would not wish to lose my footing and break a bottle. You may hold the candle for me.

Very well then, she said, and she led me down the steps to the cellar which was narrow but well stocked with tierces of claret, and several vessels of tent and Malaga.

There, you'll know which is the canary. My husband is proud of his collection and says none of his friends now alive ever had so much.

Nor did any of his friends ever have such a wife.

You mustn't talk so.

I've brought you something.

And I gave her the favour.

It's green, it won't suit with my Indian blue dress, she said.

I'm sorry for that.

But I have a white dress that has green ribbons on it.

I love that dress.

You can't have seen it, for I haven't worn it in your company, she said.

I am flattered to think you should remember what you have worn when I am with you.

It's no flattery, I have a knack of remembering such things, I would remember it if you were the ugliest man alive.

Ah, so I am not the ugliest man alive?

You are a vain man, Jem, I perceive you are fishing for compliments.

I would fish all day if I could hope to hook one from you.

Well, you would have to fish all night too, because you shall not have one.

To the end of my life, I shall remember her standing on the lowest step with the candle held aloft. Her whole person was so pale in its light that you could not tell her dress was blue. But she had a smile on her face like a child that is out when she should be abed, and I knew it must be now or never.

We were of a level when we kissed because she was on the step. She did not resist and let me feel the warm press of her lips and broke away but to say:

Careful, the candle.

And I took the candle from her and placed it on a high step above her head so that it cast a flickering light upon her and would not spill. When I kissed her again, she shivered, I know not whether because of the cold in the cellar, and then tried to pull away, but I held her, loosely not fast and she let me draw her to me again. I was emboldened (and I was still angry for her husband using me as a potboy) and I put my hand up her skirts and felt her soft warm thigh but only a little above the knee before she pulled my hand away and said: No, no, you must not.

But I love you, you must know that I do.

No, you do not, you cannot, and anyway you must not.

I must, you deserve –

To be loved by you? – and I regret she laughed as she said it – You are yet vainer than I thought.

No, not to be neglected, was the best I could utter.

You think my husband neglects me?

I can see that he does.

You can see very little in that case. You don't know how he rescued me when I was penniless and gave me a good house and servants and gives money to my parents.

Money cannot warm a heart (how can I have gushed such cant, but we were both shivering in the dark and I held her still and felt her heart beating through the silk of her dress).

I have much to thank him for, and I do love him.

He is older than you.

Well, so are you.

But I am not so encumbered. My mind is not clogged with business.

Better that it were, and then you would have no time to pay court where you should not.

I can't help loving whom I love, my heart is not to be commanded (which is true, although hard to believe, for I might have done better for myself else).

O Jem, you're a rogue, she said, but said it sweetly.

A devoted rogue, I said and embraced her again – but she broke away.

No, no, I'm ill, you must not.

I didn't mean to offend, I was transported. Let me come to you again when you are better.

Yes, no, we must not. Quick, bring up the wine, they will be wondering that we are away so long.

O Elizabeth I am so fond of you.

Come on, hurry up, we must not delay.

I took the cask and followed her up the stairs.

Ah reinforcements, the surgeon roared, our powder was running low.

He seized the bottle from me and held it up to the light.

But this is claret if I am not mistaken. Didn't our host ask you to bring up the canary? Our fair hostess has fuddled your wits down there.

It was dark.

Of course it was dark. Doubtless that's why you took her as your guide.

You mustn't say such things, Mr Pierce.

I meant nothing by it, dear lady. If young Ganymede here would kindly fetch us up the canary instead?

Fretting with humiliation, I went down to the cellar again. It was cold and desolate without that lovely creature, and I resolved that I would pursue her to the end, whatever it might cost me.

This resolve came stronger upon me as I sat with them while Mr Pierce told us the tattle of the Court. But I was silent and glowering, and when Mr Pepys came back (which was not long, for he had not much business) he asked whether I was quite well and advised me not to drink so much canary in the afternoon when it lies heavier upon the stomach.

When I reached my room, I wrote a letter:

> *Elizabeth my dearest chuck, I hope you may be wearing your white gown with the green ribbons and that you may accordingly wear also my favour, for something of me must stay with you at every waking hour. Elizabeth, I am serious, this is no light fancy, I am hooked and will not be cast off. I am patient too and will wait until you see how true my love is. But I don't wish to importune you when you are not well, and I will call upon you in nine days' time to inquire how you do and to demonstrate quod erat demonstrandum that my love is no nine days' wonder.*

> *J.*

After dinner, by coach I carried my wife and Jane to Westminster; left her at Mr Hunt's and I to Westminster Hall and there visited Mrs Lane and by appointment went out and met at the Trumpet, Mrs Hare's; but the room being damp, went to the Bell tavern and there I had her company, but could not do as I used to do (yet nothing but what was honest) for that she told me she had those . . .

Thence, leading her to the Hall, I took coach and called my wife and her maid: and so to the New Exchange, where we bought several things of our pretty Mrs Dorothy Stacy, a pretty woman and hath the modestest look that ever I saw in my life and manner of speech . . .

So home to supper and to bed – my wife not being very well since she came home, being troubled with a fainting fit, which she never yet had before since she was my wife.

Diary of Samuel Pepys, 9 January 1664

That night I lay in torment. I must have cried out in my dreams, for Nan came to me and hushed me and asked me what was the matter.

You took too much wine with the little clerks, she said, that will teach you a lesson.

Oh leave me, Nan, do, I am sick.

Then I will minister to you, and she slipped under the sheets and began her business, but I was too weary and besides she ceased to please me.

Ha I see the little clerk's wife has had the best of you, which isn't much, for a sot will never make a lover, she said, and rose up out of bed, flinging her night-gown about her in a fury.

Tomorrow, she said, you will take Kit to the tennis court, for he is growing fat and he must be exercised.

And she left me to my dreams which in truth were but one dream, that Elizabeth said Yes and that life became a golden holiday. We would lie together in a boat by Richmond Meadows, we would take our pleasure in an inn where no one knew us and we would walk together in some remote gardens and there sheltered by the tall hedges that were shaped like peacocks – but these fancies were interrupted by the cold wet dawn stealing in through the grimy casement, for I had forgot the curtain.

I had forgot also Nan's last instruction and all my thoughts were upon the burning headache that bored in upon my skull. But in came Kit, bearing his tennis racquet that Monsieur Delatuile had newly strung for him.

Come on, Jem, up and away, for you are to be my Aunt Sally in the dedans.

I crawled along in his wake, buttoning my loose white breeches and shirt, cursing the day I had been saddled with this Incubus.

But my luck was in, for as we came along the gallery, a tall fair youth shouted through the net, Kit, I will play with you.

Crofts, I will give you fifteen points a game.

And lose every set six-love. No, I'll give you fifteen points and a hand.

No, we'll play level.

If you persist in calling me Crofts, I will call you by a worse name which you have heard before.

Do you mean the same name which you are always called?

Very well then, my lord, a truce.

Very well, Your Grace. You may go, Jem, I shall play with the Duke of Monmouth.

And with a wave of his hand, the little lordling dismissed me, preferring to play with the King's bastard that was lately known as Crofts, after his governor Lord Crofts, but had now been larded with honours, for the King was fond of him and he was a handsome gay lad, two or three years older than Kit and already a head taller.

I returned to my room, wet through from the rain, but as I was changing my shirt, a letter came to me.

Dear Jem

You should not write to me so. Yet because I am partly at fault, I must reply to you. As you know, I have not been well and my actions have not been such as I would they should be if I were well [she is all tangled up because her heart is fluttering]. Yet because I bear you a high regard, I do not wish that we should part as enemies [part? Who spoke of parting?]. Let us meet as friends and not the other thing, because it would grieve me not to see you again [she goes to and fro like a shuttlecock]. Therefore I will receive you at the time you spoke of. I shall not say aught of this to my husband, although our meeting shall be in all honesty, because he has a mistrusting jealousy and I would not do anything that would have him think ill of me and would shudder to be the cause of a breach of your ancient friendship, through an innocent cause. You must come in the morning for he will be at the office.

Your true friend
Elizabeth Pepys

I was much moved by this letter, and became even more tender in my thoughts towards her, for I could see how strongly she was drawn to me and yet how she fought within herself to save her honour and to protect her husband from injury. What a noble and delicate nature she showed. I could not but compare her with Nan who thought only of jewels and money, and had no more use for me than a farmer has for an old ram that will serve for tupping but cannot be sold.

What are you doing here? I told you to look after Kit.

He would rather play with the Duke of Monmouth.

I don't wish him to play with Crofts. He is a wilful boy who will lead Christopher into mischief.

I fancy your Christopher will prove a match for him.

If so, it is because you have had charge of him. He was never like this in Dr Gumble's day. He was such a sweet willing boy then, and oh lord what's this?

In came Kit, prompt upon his cue, with one eye all black and swollen like a beetroot and the other dropping tears.

He hit me, in the eye, with a ball.

Jeremiah, you will go and speak to Crofts instantly, and fetch a poultice from the apothecary. Oh that my brother were here, he was a magician with wounds of the eye.

I went with an ill grace. To be a tutor was bad enough, to be a nursemaid was worse – and to such a mewling ill-humoured boy. I was glad that Elizabeth could not see me, for I had given her to understand that I was engaged upon high state business for Their Highnesses, not fetching poultices for boys who could not dodge tennis balls.

I was passing Westminster Hall halfway to the apothecary's when I was surprised to see Mr Pepys come out of the Hall, looking somewhat flustered, though not with drink. He seemed to be in a great haste and took the first coach, then went back into the Hall to bring out – oh – my beloved and Jane the maid. Elizabeth looked pale as she stood on the wet pavement. Mr Pepys led her into the carriage and they were gone. And I was seized with jealousy of him that he had her company by night – and used her so ill – while I must plead for an hour of her nine days hence.

I by water to Westminster Hall and there did see Mrs Lane, and de la, elle and I to the cabaret at the cloche in the street du roy, and there, after some caresses, je l'ay foutée sous de la chaise deux times, and the last to my great pleasure; mais j'ai grand peur que je l'ay fait faire aussi elle même. Mais after I had done, elle commençait parler as before and I did perceive that je navais fait rien de danger à elle. Et avec ça, I came away, and though I did make grand promises à la contraire, nonobstant je ne la verrai pas long time. So by coach home and to my office, where Browne of the Minories brought me an instrument made of a spiral line, very pretty for all questions in Arithmetique almost. But it must be some use that must make me perfect it.

So home to supper and to bed – with my mind un peu troublé par ce que j'ai fait today. But I hope it will be the dernière de toute ma vie.

Diary of Samuel Pepys, 16 January 1664

That week drifted by as slowly as twigs upon a sluggish stream. I cannot tell how I passed the days or differentiate one day from another. My life seemed a dreary desert in which there was but one fertile patch, one Oasis as it is called in the Libyan desert, where palm trees and pine trees blow and there is an abundant spring of water. Elizabeth was my Oasis and all my thoughts were travelling towards her, for it was one consequence of my love for her that my affections for Nan had entirely fled, or rather they had decamped and gone to that fertile place where my hopes were now gathered.

And what of Pepys? Did I not scruple to cuckoldise my old acquaintance, for friend I could no longer call him? I will put the answer in the Italian tongue: *cazzo dritto non vuolt consiglio*, which being interpreted means: a standing prick will take no counsel.

A thousand times that week, I cursed my cowardice that I had withdrawn from the attack and had not pushed it straightaway to a conclusion. Even now it was not too late to breach the defence. I could call upon her, all wet from the rain, and throw myself upon her mercy, saying that I could stay away from her no longer and that I must instantly have proof of her love, or I would die. Yet if she were not yet recovered from her illness, then my breath would be wasted, and if I came at any time other than at the appointed hour I might run into Mr Pepys.

But as it turned out it was not I who was to run into Mr Pepys. It was but two days before our appointment, and Nan had gone down to Westminster Hall in the afternoon to inspect some linen. She liked to keep her hand in at that game, it being the prime source of her fortune at the King's coming in. There was no royal palace or State dining-room that she had not furnished at handsome profits and so she would visit all the linen drapers to compare their goods and prices that she might not lose touch with the market.

Who do you think I saw down at Westminster Hall? she said throwing off her bonnet.

How should I know?

Your little Mr Pepys.

He is none of mine, and I don't see why you should think it strange to see him there. It's a place of great resort. I dare say I have seen him there myself.

No, but wait. I was coming up to the linen stall that is kept by the Lane sisters in the Hall – they have good stuffs but dear because it is Westminster – and there was only the younger one, Doll, so I says to her, where is your sister today? Oh she says, Betty is away, but as she was rolling up a bolt of pretty cloth – a blue stuff the colour of cornflowers – I saw her sister through an opening in the curtain at the back. She was talking very low to a little man whom I instantly knew for Mr Pepys.

He may talk to a linen draper, I suppose. And you might have been mistaken, if you only saw him through a chink in a curtain.

No, no it was he. But why should Doll say Betty was away if she was only behind the stall and could have been called up to advise me, for she is the senior partner and Doll is an ignorant slut. So I kept watch, and after a minute I saw Mr Pepys walk off with what the French call *nonchalance* and ten paces behind as though she had nothing to do with him walked Betty Lane. If ever a couple were bound for an assignation, it was they.

Well, I dare say you're expert in assignations at a linen draper's.

So are you, Jem. Don't be a spoil-sport. Does the tale not entice you a little?

I would not admit it because I was so vexed with her, but her news did add fuel to the fire that was raging in my breast. If Pepys was taking his pleasure with female linen drapers in Westminster Hall, why should I not pursue my love that was so noble and sincere? He had forfeited the rights of a husband in consequence of his lewd conduct.

And so Monday dawned, that fateful Monday when I was to put my love to the touch. I wore my blue coat with the brass buttons that had anchors engraved upon them, and a vest of mulberry colour that she had once admired.

Where are you going? Nan said, as I passed her on the great stairs.

Out, I said, on business.

What business have you that is none of mine?

Private business, a family matter. I shall be away some time.

For some reason, I know not what, my tone alarmed her.

Are you not well?

I am well enough, madam, I said coldly. Good-day.

And she could say no more, for a footman came up the stair at that moment, and I went out into the damp street.

Up, being troubled to find my wife so ready to have me go out of doors; God forgive me for my jealousy, that I cannot forbear, though God knows that I have no reason not to do so or to expect being so true to me as I would have her.

I abroad to Whitehall, where the Court all in mourning for the Duchess of Savoy ... Thence home by coach to the Change, after having been at the Coffee-house, where I hear Turner is found guilty of felony and burglary; and strange stories of his confidence at the Bar, but yet great indiscretion in his arguing. All desirous of his being hanged.

So home and found that my clerk Will had been with my wife there; but Lord, why should I think any evil of that, and yet I cannot forbear it. But upon enquiry, though I found no reason of doubtfulness, yet I could not bring my nature to any quiet or content in my wife all day and night.

Diary of Samuel Pepys, 18 January 1664

She was wearing a dress of dark grey silk, the colour of a slate roof that has been rained upon, not the white dress trimmed with green, nor yet my favour. A bad beginning.

You are punctual, she said, but negligently as you might speak to a tradesman who comes upon his hour and has not kept you waiting.

I would have come at dawn if you had called for me then.

Jem, I beg you, it's too early in the day for such speeches.

It's never too early for me to pay tribute to your beauty, Eliza.

Jem, don't talk so, and please don't call me Eliza. We had a cat of that name and I didn't like to be confounded with it.

I'm sure it was a pretty cat.

No it was not, it was a mangy old thing – and she smiled at the thought of it, and I saw that I must tread more like a cat if I was to come nearer my goal.

Elizabeth then, I am sorry I was so forward. I was a little agitated, to see you again after so long . . .

Eight days –

Nine –

Nine days is not so long a time. If we are to bear misfortune as we should, we must learn to possess our desires in patience. My father –

I did not wish to hear about her father. Nor had I come here to be sermonised. But I knew I must be meek.

Please forgive me, I do acknowledge my fault.

You must not presume upon – upon what happened at our last meeting. I fear we had all taken too much wine.

It was a very merry dinner certainly, I said.

We wished to cheer poor Will. He must miss his wife exceedingly, she was such a beauty and of such a generous nature too.

She was. I admired her much.

As much as you admire me perhaps. I fear you are a ladies' man, Jem. You cannot see a woman without paying court to her.

You do me wrong. I admired Mrs Symons only as a friend and I was sorry for Will.

Upon my life, I do not know what I should do if my husband were taken from me. I would throw myself into the river, I think.

Don't fret, he looks healthy enough.

You don't know him privately, Jem. He presents a glowing front to the world, for one who will prosper in business must look the part. But he suffers, lord how he suffers. He had fevers very frequently, and the colic and such gripings, and he was cut for the stone seven years ago and every year he gives a dinner to celebrate his recovery, I wonder that you were not invited – but he fears lest the trouble may come back, I know he does. And then his eyes –

But I did not wish to hear about Pepys's eyes.

Madam, he looks well enough.

You think so?

I am sure of it. But he works too hard for his own good.

That's very true, she said.

And for your good also, I fancy. You are much alone here.

No, I have abundant company. There are the girls, and my mother and father come here often, and Mrs Pierce.

I meant company of your own age and sort.

Oh well, there's Will, he's here very often.

Will Symons?

No, Will Hewer, my husband's clerk at the Navy Office. He is such a bright spark. He makes me laugh.

This was bad news. A man who can make a woman laugh and is the same age, or younger (for if this Will were Pepys's clerk, he must be at the bottom of the ladder – indeed, it was wormwood and gall to learn that Pepys had a clerk already), such a man is halfway to winning her.

Have you room for another caller?

How do you mean?

Would it be agreeable if I came for a hand of picquet or a little conversation now and then?

Oh you may come if you please.

But does it please *you*?

If you are sensible, you may come.

Elizabeth, I am exceedingly sensible to your – you bade me not speak of your beauty – but to your presence. When I am with you, I am half-fainting with sensibility.

You know quite well I did not mean sensible in that sense. I meant discreet.

I can only say what I feel.

People say that when they had very much better say nothing.

Please don't preach at me. I can't help it, I don't mean to offend you, I would do anything in the world not to harm you, or distress you.

Well then, she said more softly, let us be calm.

And she took my hand. This voluntary action was the first encouragement I had received and I seized upon it as a loaf of manna in the desert and pressed her hand with mine and then, gently and with reverence, placed my lips upon that same hand, as though I were kissing a Bible and not the flesh of a woman.

She let the kiss rest there and stayed motionless for a minute in a kind of reverie. I heard her murmur something but so low that it seemed she was talking to herself.

I too stayed motionless, and silent too, apprehending that the absence of speech and motion might deepen our communion.

I counted to thirty (*sotto voce* of course) and then planted a kiss no less reverently upon her left cheek just below the little mole (which may be seen upon the sculpture of her that is now in St Olave's Church).

Oh, she said, very quietly, as though she were speaking to herself, now here's a thing.

Then I counted to twenty and put my lips to hers.

And thus we stayed in the silent room. It was cold, so that I felt her warmth more powerfully, and her breathing and my heart beating were all the sound there was but for the ticking of Mr Pepys's clock that he told me was given him by a Norway merchant.

Then we fell to kissing furiously and I tipped her velvet and felt myself to be at the gates of Heaven. But the gates had to be opened and, while a slow pace had been the best way to reach them, now I instantly summoned my forces for a direct assault before the moment was lost.

All of a sudden she broke away and hit my head with a huge swing of her fist so that my ear was bruised and then hit my wayward hand with the other fist which must have had rings upon it for I saw later that I was bleeding. Then almost in the same motion she was upon her feet shaking her skirts down to remove all trace of my invasion.

Go now, go, for ever, I shall never see you again. You know nothing of a woman. How could you have thought . . .

Please, I cannot go like this. At least permit me to offer my repentance.

Men like you never repent. You are like foxes, you will come back again and again until you have caught your poor silly chicken. I shall tell my husband, that is the only way to get rid of you. But perhaps — she paused and wiped the tears from her flushed cheeks, but she was weeping still — perhaps you would wish me to tell him, because you take pleasure from inflicting pain on humble honest men. He's worth ten of you, I am a vile creature to have let my thoughts stray from him for an instant.

This was too much. My own humiliation had turned to anger and the anger was compounded by my being compared to St Samuel.

I think he would be less amazed than you think, if you told him.

What? she said. You think he believes I am unchaste? She cast her eyes around for a projectile and saw a bowl of flowers that were kept indoors in earth out of the frost, but I was too quick for her and seized the bowl and clasped it to my bosom.

No, I said, I meant no aspersion on your character, none at all.

On my husband's then?

Well, I fancy he is not quite as innocent as you suppose in that respect. There is a certain place —

I don't wish to hear such horrible things, she shrieked, you're a monster, a liar, a lecher and I hate you for ever. Leave my sight now, *now*, NOW.

These instructions seemed tolerably clear. I put the flowers down on the table and said I was sorry that our friendship should end like this but was making haste towards the door as I said it, so as not to give her time to pick up the bowl. But when I closed the door behind me, I heard only the sound of her sobbing.

Halfway down the stairs, I met a young man with a mop of red hair coming up (the maid must have let him in just then, for she was at the foot of the stairs staring up open-mouthed). The young man addressed me familiarly in the way that London gallants will talk to a total stranger as though he were an old acquaintance.

Caught in the briars, are we? A touch of trouble upstairs? Choleric temperament, that's what it is, for all that she's so pale, it's the French in her. But I know how to sweeten her, don't you fret. Will Hewer, your servant, sir, clerk to Mr Pepys and friend of the family. My word, sir, you look as though you had been in the wars.

That was the last interview I had with Mrs Pepys. Although Llewelyn and I had dinner in that house once more, at her husband's invitation, Mrs Pepys and I did not speak one word to each other, and after dinner she went out straight to see my Lady Sandwich, for she had no thought but to promote her husband's career by which means she would have the advantages of better society.

Thence to the Cockpit, and there walked an hour with my Lord Duke of Albemarle alone in his garden, where he expressed in great words his opinion of me: that I was the right hand of the Navy here, nobody but I taking any care of anything therein – so that he should not know what could be done without me – at which I was (from him) not a little proud.

Diary of Samuel Pepys, 24 April 1665

VI

The Laboratory

You are always in the dumps nowadays, Jem. I remember when you were such a merry fellow and I was enamoured of you.

More fool you then, madam. At my base I am of a melancholy temperament.

You should not call a duchess a fool – but she was in gamesome mood and cuffed me lightly on the cheek in mock punishment, yet I would have none of it.

Madam, be serious, you treat me as a plaything and will not see that my occupation's gone like the Moor's.

Have I not given you occupation enough?

Yes, as a serving man.

No, as a major-domo, a counsellor and friend, a secretary – and something else.

Oh *that* something else, I said in a weary voice.

No, she said, I meant not that. And her tenor roused me a little, for I saw the old light in her eye and I knew that some game was up.

I have another profession for you, you're to be my architect.

Nan, don't mock me. You know I'm quite ignorant of Vitruvius.

I speak not of Vitruvius, whatever that may be, I speak of New Hall. The Duke of Buckingham has left it in a destroyed state and I can't undertake the refurbishment without a man of taste at my side.

New Hall? But it's as big as Hampton Court. I could not, I cannot –

You will, Jem, you will. We shall go there, tomorrow, you and Kit and I and the General – the four of us.

I had not yet seen this great palace near Chelmsford which my lord had of Bucks very cheap some months before, for the other duke was short of cash, and my Duke had been given £20,000 by the Parliament. They had first offered him Hampton Court which would have tickled me, for I could then have taken my revenge on Mr Phelps and the other saucy merchants who had usurped that royal seat, but the old General said he did not like to sleep in Cromwell's bed for fear he might catch the same disease (he meant overweening ambition), and so New Hall it was.

Though I knew Nan intended my new profession as a jest, yet I looked forward to our visit with a high expectation. Nor was I disappointed as we rode down the fair avenue planted with stately lime trees in four rows for near a mile in length and saw the long low palace built with brick, as wide as a small town but nowhere above two storeys high, with its spires and battlements and old windows of Henry VIII's time. And to hear the heels of our horses ring on the flagstones as we came into the Great Court and to see the Duke who had gone ahead helping his Duchess out of her carriage: I began to feel that my position had its compensations.

Well, Jem, what d'ye think? Not bad for a farmer's son? (In truth, old Sir Thomas Monck came from an ancient line in Devonshire, but I have noticed that great men who come from small beginnings like to make them smaller.)

Wonder of wonders! Honest George Monck, he who never spoke a word out of turn and made a profession out of keeping his feelings under lock and key, was as cheerful and garrulous as a schoolboy on holiday. He would show us round every door and picture and inscription:

Hey there's Henry's arms, d'ye see, Henricus Rex Octavus, he had it off old Sir Thomas Boleyn when he had his Anne, you tell me which was the better bargain. And there's Queen Bess: Viva Elizabetha, and an inscription in Italian which I cannot make out, and Queen Mary too, they all lived here. She was here when they told her she was no longer to call herself Princess – her face must have been a study then, hey? And here's a sea-piece, they tell me it's very fine, Sir Francis Drake's action against the Spaniards, *anno domini* 1580. A good Devonshire man.

We must find a painter to do a companion piece of another Devon man beating the Dutch.

Now, now, Nan, that's not for me to think of. If some mayor and corporation take it into their noddles to do such a thing, though I'm a poor subject for a limner, God knows, then I can't check 'em, but I won't do it myself.

Yet I saw the proposal had caught his fancy and I could see his cunning old brain working how he might have such a picture painted. Without seeming to have asked for it. Or paying for it.

Come into the chapel now, there's a painting by that Welshman, cost five hundred pounds.

What Welshman, my dear? (Though she knew well enough and so, I fancy, did he.)

Oh Inigo Jones, that's the fellow, though come to think of it, Jones didn't paint it himself, brought in old Gerbier.

Since he was acquainted with Sir Balthasar Gerbier, a considerably lesser man, he need not have hesitated over Inigo J., but his cunning was so habitual that he could not forbear to play the role of honest blockhead, which had taken him so far.

There now, d'ye see that window? It's a fine thing, is it not?

Indeed it was a glorious glass, the fairest I had ever seen: Flemish work, I fancied, more than a hundred years old. In the outward lights knelt a young prince and princess beneath two saints, St George for England with his red cloak and St Catherine in a blue gown with her wheel. In between, Our Lord on the Cross with the two thieves beside and above a band of angels playing musical instruments.

Robs you of breath, don't it?

The old man was touched by the beauty of it.

That's Catherine of Aragon below her patron saint, and there, that's Prince Arthur who would have been king if he hadn't died. Her parents, the King and Queen of Spain, had it made for the wedding, but Arthur caught the sweating sickness, and so when his brother Henry took her over he didn't want to be reminded. So he gave it to the monks at Waltham and they buried the glass pieces and then brought it here for safe keeping. Never engrave your schemes on glass, Jem, they'll come back to mock you.

The old General stood in contemplation. He who had himself seen one king executed and brought in another, was near to weeping.

Curious, is it not, I speculated idly, feeling that I must say something and not stand there like a lump of stone, that all the doctors could not say for sure whether such a marriage be legitimate or not?

What, what, what do you mean by that? His voice was loud and terrible and it came to me – too late – that he thought I intended some reference to the murky circumstances of his own marriage. And he stumped off in great dudgeon, for I had piqued him on the point where he was most tender.

As he went down the passage, we could still hear him wheezing like a grampus, for the asthma had come upon him in his latter years and sometimes he had to check his speech to gather his breath. He was of a distempered complexion also. Nan said he had an infection of the kidneys which he had contracted during the Dutch wars and could not shake off. An old Navy doctor, a friend of Mr Pierce's, had given him some pills that were reputed infallible for the asthma, which they may have been, but they were harmful to his other complaints and made him go blue in the face like a raw lobster, though his habitual complexion was jaundiced. Moreover, on an early visit to New Hall, when the place was new to him, he had fallen into a ditch and broken his ankle, which had not yet mended, for old men's bones break easily and mend only with difficulty. Thenceforward he walked with a limp which gave him a rolling gait like that of a sailor, which was ironic for a land Admiral.

Yet I had thought him immortal until that moment when I saw him walk off down the dusty passage and clutch at the door-post for support, for his ankle grew worse with standing still. All at once, I perceived that he would not live for ever and that, when he died, why, then, we should be in a new world. Nan would be looking for a new husband. I knew the gentry at Court laughed at her behind her back, and she knew so too. She was a bold woman, but she was not insensible to slights and sneers, and I fancied she would seek a true friend, and where else should she look but at her loyal servant?

Moreover, it was not unheard of that, in order to maintain the dignity of the loyal relict of such a noble duke, his successor (I mean me) should be ennobled also, though it might be to a lesser degree – as, for instance, Earl of Chelmsford.

A penny for your thoughts, Jem?

Oh they're not worth so much, madam.

No, but you're in a rare study. You have become more thoughtful.

Is that so bad a thing?

No but I wish you were more attentive to me, and not for ever a day-dreamer. The General is grown old and besides he is so often absent. I must have company to refresh me, Jem, I must be kept young.

So I bussed her upon the lips and chucked her under the chin, but it was uphill work and I foresaw that I must serve a hard sentence before I was to enjoy my reward.

We roamed the great rooms and cabinets and cloisters of New Hall with amazement that so large a palace should have lain neglected for so long, viz. ever since the Duke of Buckingham was exiled and deprived of his estates. There was dust upon every stair and banister and the grass grew long between the flags and the fish must have choked in the fishponds for the rubbish that was thrown in them.

We attempted to count the rooms, for it was said that there was one for each day of the year, that is, 365, but Nan said she had heard the same said of other palaces and did not believe it. So we counted, but we made several false starts because we doubled back upon our tracks without knowing it and counted the same room twice.

Have we not already seen that painted cupboard? she would cry, and back we would go to the doorway under Queen Bess's arms, and begin again.

It was upon our third or fourth attempt that we came to a little low door in a high dark chamber furnished with a bed which was of fine Italian workmanship. The low door opened but stiffly upon its hinges, and we were in a long room with windows as in a cloister. On either side of the room were long tables all covered with dust and upon the tables an array such as I have never seen: of phials and goblets and retorts and crucibles of brass and an alembic or still, of copper, and pans and basins and troughs of clay and iron, all cobwebbed as in a magician's cave. Behind these there were astronomical instruments – globes, monstrous brass telescopes, balances and prisms and perspectives. At the end of the room was a blackened furnace where great tongs and hammers lay negligently about as though a giant had lately dropped them there. Above our heads in the musty air, pulleys and rope cradles and an apparatus of wood that I knew not the purpose of depended from the beams, so that a man could hang himself in half a dozen ways, if he so fancied.

Bucks's laboratory, Nan said, this is where he chased after the philosopher's stone. They say he spent twenty thousand pounds a year on his chemistry. What silly toys will men beggar themselves to have.

How much do you know of chemistry?

As much as you, she said.

I hear his man has discovered a process for making glass equal to the best Venetian. He is to set up a manufactory at Lambeth. The Venetian Ambassador has already complained to the King.

Pooh, if you believe all that, she said.

But I moved about the laboratory in a trance, for I had long wished to dig into the mysteries of Nature but lacked a spade. Now here was a chemist's utopia, a place where I might retire from the futile bustle of the Court and devote myself to the pursuit of true science.

So you fancy yourself a chemist, do you? You will doubtless soon consort with Mr Boyle.

Don't mock, Nan. Why shouldn't I better myself?

Because you have no grounding in that science, my dear boy. You will weary of the pastime in a fortnight. Let's leave this place, I don't like the smell.

I was determined to prove her wrong and had the maids sweep out the laboratory and clean the windows. There was a case of learned books under the table, and I began to delve into *Principia chymica* and other works that might teach me how to make such trials and experiments as would assist me to a deeper understanding of chemistry. I had no overvaulting ambition to become a Grand Master in that science, but it was an agreeable prospect that I might club with the *Illuminati* of the Royal Society and talk together of experiments, for chemistry was then a profession for gentlemen.

Each day I devoted an hour or two in the afternoon to study of chemistry, when the household was quiet, and I soon chafed to put my art to the practice. It was about this time that Nan began to be struck by intermitting fevers, which I dare say was on account of the marshy country that lay round about. The doctor came out from Chelmsford and commended a decoction of willow bark which he had not with him but would bring tomorrow.

I had read the method in Mr Culpeper's *English Physician* and begged Nan that I might be allowed to prepare the medicine myself, for there were many willows growing by the ponds.

Poison me if you will, she said, I'm good for little else now – and lay back upon her pillows as though about to expire.

I stripped the bark from the low trees leaning over the water and then boiled it in canary wine in the duke's copper still. It made a foul smell and I resolved to dilute it that it might be more potable.

Ugh, said Nan, and instantly vomited and went into minor convulsion. You'll gain nothing by murdering me, she said, when she had recovered herself, I've left you nothing in my will.

You ought to have used the Peruvian bark, the doctor said the next day, though it is so dear. The white Essex willow will not do, and it needs drying first besides.

But her fever is abated, I said.

It would have gone in any case, he said. These fevers are short-lived at this season.

None the less, I chalked my first venture a success, and resolved to advance to more composite experiments that would bring into play more instruments in the Duke's armoury.

The other Duke (I mean Albemarle, not Bucks) had lately complained about the costs of governing the State:

In the old days, all it cost was breath. You told a fellow to go and he goeth, but now everything must needs be written down and a copy kept, that if there be any dispute proof of the true order shall be to hand. I never knew such expense, the cabinet's full of reams of old paper, new offices built to lodge 'em, even the ink costs a king's ransom.

The ink ... there perhaps I could help. I dreamed of patents and commissions, of saving the State a fortune, of men turning as I passed and whispering: You must know him, that's the fellow who invented the new ink. Accordingly I turned to Grimwade's *True Chemist*, which was in Bucks's case, and acquainted myself with the prevailing method.

To manufacture vitriol which makes the best ink

First you must gather from the foreshore of the Thames (or some other great river where they are to be found) the copperas stones or gold stones. Contrary to the suppositions of the foolish, these stones contain not one particle of copper or gold but are made entirely of iron, and the finest of them will serve as flints for muskets.

Place the stones on ground raised like the beds in gardens, one above the other, and let the rain come down upon them and dissolve them so that the liquid drains down into a trench or pipe that conveys it to the house wherein you are to set great pans, at least twelve yards long, of beaten clay where they are to be mixed with iron, then when the liquid is sour, let it flow into lead tanks where it is to be boiled for some days until it be thick, then let it run off into vats where it cools and affixes itself to branches of birch which are to be laid there a-purpose. Thus the liquid will come down to a candy that will hang upon the branches like a bunch of grapes. Then the branches may be taken up and the crystals shaken off them. This is the green vitriol, which is the iron sulphur, and makes the best ink as attested by the Company of Stationers.

I lay in my bed as the great clock in the court chimed two and rehearsed these instructions in my mind as though they had been some witches' incantation. I could not wait for the morrow to prepare my experiment. But first I must procure the goldstones.

The next morning while the dew was still on the grass, I rode out to Maldon and along the shore to Tollesbury, inquiring of all I met where goldstones were to be had. At length I found an old woman who had been paid a penny a bushel by Mr Stephenson that had first found out how to turn copperas into brimstone for the making of gunpowder (which was a use I had not thought of, but which might prove profitable, for wars we have always with us). Mr Stephenson having removed into Kent where the stones were more plentiful, the trade had dried up.

I told the old hag that I would pay her threepence a bushel if she and her husband could carry some stones to New Hall, which she said she would, and within the week. I left her and cast a last look upon that melancholy shore, across the sea to my native land of Kent, reflecting upon the providence of Nature that the very stones on the seashore may be transformed into powder and flint for us to murder one another with, or, conversely, into ink that the word of the Lord may be broadcast among the nations.

While I waited for the goldstones, I metamorphosed my laboratory (for it was now mine in all but name) into a copperas house, that is, I had the gardener raise the ground outside into three beds, so that each bed was lower than the next, and along the lowest he put a gutter that ran into a pipe through a hole I had made in the wall into my laboratory.

What's this, hey, what's all this disturbance? The General harumphed as he saw the new beds and the gutter.

Jem is inventing a new process for the manufacture of ink, Nan said, for she was becoming proud of my endeavours. It is to cost half what the government now pays.

Well, well, humph, the General said, but he was pleased at the scheme as I described it to him, for though he gloried in his palace, he liked that it should be put to use and was himself full of schemes for the cow-byres and the sheepfolds, and had plotted to plant grapes, for he had heard there had been a vineyard there once.

Inside the laboratory, I had put the Duke's boiler in the furnace with a pipe coming in from the garden and another pipe going out to the trough where the birch twigs were to be laid. All was ready and with scarce any fresh expense, for Bucks's laboratory was furnished royally.

On Saturday, the old woman and her husband came puffing up the lime avenue with a cart laden with stones that winked at the sun and I saw why foolish folk had thought they were made of gold. The ancient nag that pulled the cart could scarce reach my beds without falling down, but the old people laid the stones out on the ground and raked them level and promised me more if ever I should need them.

The next requisite which nature obstinately denied me for the next fortnight was rain, for the dew was not enough to rust them.

Your stones stink damnably, Jem, the General said. Have you put some rotten eggs in among 'em?

But the next Sunday the rain came and began to dissolve the stones. It rained every day that week as it does in March, so hard that you could not see your hand in front of your face, and the liquid began to run off the stones and then to flow through into the boiler. Then I kindled the furnace, which filled the laboratory with black smoke, for the chimney wanted sweeping. But after it was swept, the fire began to heat the boiler and I heard my cauldron bubble and felt like a true chemist.

While I was sitting by the furnace and wondering how many days I should let the potion boil, for Mr Grimwade gave me no exact counsel on that point, I heard a great commotion from the garden.

What is this, sir? What in the name of Beelzebub? etc.

I ran out through the side-door and there was the General in an apoplexy pointing to my copperas beds.

A trail of noxious bubbling green slime was running over the edge of the gutter (for it would not go higher, back into the beds) and along the grass into his new French roses that he had had sent from Provence in Champagne (which is now the red rose of England).

Damn you, sir, damn you.

I swiftly perceived what had happened. The pressure within the boiler had sent the precious liquid back down the pipe into the garden where it was running to waste for I had not shut off the pipe. I hastened to pour water on the fire, to douse it, which made another great smoke, so that I came out again smoked from head to toe, like a blackamoor, which made the General and his lady laugh.

Copperas, is that what you call it? roared the General. I'll give you copperas – and then, for he was never quick on to a jest though he was fond of them – You are a copper-arse in truth.

Copper-arse, went the General again – for when he had caught hold of a joke he was not one to let it go.

Copper-arse, said Nan, by now helpless in her mirth and scarce able to get the word out.

Thus they stood there, this noble pair, incapacitated by the crude jest, each buttressing the other, while I began to shovel the odious liquid back into my beds.

It was the last time that my General laughed.

Yet I was undaunted, and when the stones had quite dissolved and the gutter was full, I made a fresh trial of the experiment. At the end of the pipe I fixed a valve or shutter that would open but one way, viz. towards the boiler. Thus the copperas-water could go into the boiler but not go back out again until I opened the tap that let the liquid out into the trough. Soon I had a full trough (it was not above two yards long, my experiment being in miniature and not in gross, for I was an Inventor not a Manufactor).

Then I must spend two days attending upon Kit now grown

boisterous and overweening. The country air suited him and every day he would clamour to be taken hawking or coursing the pair of greyhounds that his mother had given him or to see the bear-baiting in Chelmsford or the cocks, etc. I would come home tired as a dog after the chase and would take refuge in my laboratory where only I had the key.

The sun was still shining through the windows, for the laboratory faced to the west, when I looked idly into the trough, expecting to see the same dull green liquid like that of a river that has been fouled. But the trough was dried up and there, clinging to the birch branches as though they had been some rare fruit of the birch, there were the green crystals. I took up a branch and held the crystals to the light so that the light shone through them and made them look like emeralds, but finer by far because they were so bright and huge. In my joy I held a branch in each hand and shook them so that they made a faint tinkling.

Copper-arse, I said to myself, I'll give them copper-arse.

I perceived then that the true joys of our existence are those that we manufacture for ourselves and not the trumpery shows of greatness which men prize so highly. I resolved that I would pursue these material arts with the sober diligence that becomes an *Illuminato* and not chase after the deceiving pleasures of the Court. If only I had adhered to that resolution, I might be now a respected Fellow of the Royal Society with a chronometer or some invention for computation that would bear my name. But we are as we are, or as Nature has fashioned us, and though we may see the true path, brambles and thistles often keep us from following it.

So it was with me, for the success of my first experiments was not followed up. The copperas crystals gathered dust in the trough. My distillations turned brackish through neglect, and Nan had forbidden me to try my medicines upon her household. Besides, we grew dull, for the neighbours were mostly country boors and sycophants. I began to count the days before we should return to London which was to be after Easter (it fell early that year, at the end of March). His Grace was already gone and April was half done, but still we tarried at New Hall.

Nan, when are we to go to London?

Soon, soon, she said.

Then there was another change of plan, for she was to go to
Whitehall to be with her husband, but I was to stay at New Hall
with Kit.

But, madam, I have heard you say you can't live without your
darling son.

Well, you say he does better in the country.

So he does, but I don't.

He must have a guardian, Jem, for there are envious persons that
want to do the Duke ill. And how better than through his son?

Grumbling, I obeyed, though I did not believe she had told me all
she knew. Yet, as a consolation, she said I might come to London once
a month to bring them fresh fruit, salads and other eatables and render
them a report of the estate, for I would keep an eye on the housekeeper
and the wardrobe-keeper and read over the bailiff's accounts.

Thus it was towards the end of April that I set off in the Duchess's
old Scotch coach (the new one already being at Whitehall) which was
loaded to the roof with spinach, cabbages and plucked chickens, so that
I felt like a travelling shopkeeper.

I was four hours tossing about among the cabbages and onions and
must have smelled as bad as a bumboat woman by the time we rumbled
down King Street and under the gate that was named for Mr Holbein,
painter to Henry VIII.

My first thought was to go to the tap by the upper privy (near my
old chamber) where I could wash myself privately without being seen,
and thence to the butler's cupboard where I kept balls of Castile soap,
for I was most careful that our footmen and servingmen should be clean.
But to reach that pantry, I must pass through the Duke's garden and
there to my horror I saw His Grace walking up and down with a low
bustling fellow much the same height as he, who was none other than
my old acquaintance Mr Pepys.

This was a great disaster. To be seen in my foul dishevelled
condition by the Duke was bad enough, but for that humiliation to
be witnessed and reported by Mr S. Pepys was to double it.

Then I espied a hedge of box along one side of the garden. It was
low, not above four feet high, yet it might serve to hide me. And so
I bent myself as low as a spaniel and at the same time went lightly

upon my feet, for it was a gravel walk and there must be no noise. Thus I padded along until I came up with them (I could see their feet through the roots of the box trees) and caught but intermittently some phrases of the Duke's – his voice was low and difficult to catch at the best of times.

... first-rate work ... excellent care you take of the masts ... that fellow Batten, do you trust him ... none like you, sir ...

Then I heard Pepys babbling his thanks: deeply grateful ... Your Highness's gracious patronage ... etc., etc.

Nothing but the truth, went the Duke, Navy couldn't get along without you ...

To hear these odious compliments rained upon so unworthy an object and to hear that object fawning and bridling at this ill-deserved praise and myself to be unable to say a word or even shift my legs to ease the ache that came from stooping – was such indignity ever visited upon an innocent man who was but delivering the fruits of the soil? I crawled to the end of the hedge and made my way to the cupboard, but some officious person had locked it, so I must deliver my goods to the cook, smelling as bad as he did, then make my way to the Duke's apartment resolved to bare my teeth at Mr Pepys. But he had gone and the Duke with him.

I wished I were dead. At least, I could be drunk and therefore went straight to the Leg. There I met Peter Llewellyn who already was three-quarters cut.

I had not seen him or any of the old crew for an age and I fell upon his neck and we made up for lost time. To my astonishment however he insisted that he would pay.

How's this? I said. You never were a treater in the old days. *Per contra*, you would feign sleep when old Stone came with the tally.

Ah but then I was poor. Now I am a man of business. These are great days for Mr Dering and I live well enough upon the crumbs that fall from his table. You would not guess how much I am worth now.

There was ale spilled upon the table and with his long finger (which was white and delicate, like a woman's) he traced out: £750.

That *is* a tidy fortune.

And there's more where that came from, namely my master's leavings. Climb aboard, Jem, and we shall capture the golden fleece

– at which he began furiously to scratch his own golden fleece (which was scanter yet than when I had last seen him) as he always did when he was in liquor.

It's true I have a few pennies saved.

Invest them, Jem, invest them. Money will do nothing if it lie idle. Remember the parable of the talents.

It was so strange to hear little Peter quote Holy Scripture at me, and in a tavern too, that I laughed out loud, but I was thinking the while. For my eggs still lay in their nest, *videlicet,* that ship's chest which I had brought with me from Dover and though I had considered of putting some of it into Mr Backwell's hand at 6 per cent interest (which was then the law's maximum), I feared that Backwell though honest was but mortal and his heirs might be thieves. Will Symons had counselled me to venture my money with Morris and Clayton instead, but since they speculated in land which pays but 3 per cent the rate of interest would be inferior though the money were safer. And so I had done nothing with it (these memorials being private, I may say that the sum was now advanced to £620). Yet I felt a dull fellow, for these were great days for speculation, and every blockhead was boasting that his investment was surefooted and could not lose, though it might be with a company to promote some crazy project such as Mrs Pepys's father might have invented. And if Llewelyn had made an accumulation, having started from naught and being a careless tippler, what might a more sober calculator not come to?

The difficulty of the timber trade, Jem, said my old friend leaning forward gravely as though he were a pedagogue, is its fluctuations. Fluctuations, he repeated solemnly in case I had not heard him, they're the curse of the business, but also the main chance of it.

How so? I said.

Listen and it shall be revealed unto thee, Jeremiah. When a good parcel of timber comes in, let us say of Norway deals, worth three thousand pounds of anyone's money, it may come in at a moment when my master has just laid out all his ready cash. He could borrow from Backwell or one of the others, but that would wipe his profit. So the captain goes to Winter or Sir William Warren, but he finds them in the same plight. All the great men are cleaned out for the time being, so he must go to the small fry.

Like you?

Even so. But what the good captain doesn't know is that we small fry agree among ourselves to tell him that we are broken too, for we're a species of club, and so the price must come down further. Then, and not until then, we buy, when the price is as low as a caterpillar's paws.

And then?

We wait, Jem, until the market is cleared and the Navy comes along, as it might be in the person of my old friend S. Pepys, and says we must have a parcel of straight oak with sufficient knees and other compass-timber, for the Dutch are coming. But Sir William and Mr Winter cannot supply the whole deficiency – at which moment your humble servant steps forward and coughs: You remember that timber you so kindly let me store at your yard? I could perhaps . . . And your master is so keen to keep the business that he will pay you twice as much as you paid and everyone is content, for everyone has a profit and the King has his timber. Thus one serves one's master and one's country and oneself too, Jem, there's the greatness of it. One cannot fail, for one is dealing with the Royal Navy.

Exhausted by this discourse, he called for more drink and then his head fell upon his arms, before the pot-boy had come with the ale. While he snored lightly and even in his half-sleep scratched his sparse hairs, I began to think that there might be something in this way of doing business. So I resolved to wait until he was sober and to go shares with him in his next venture.

This I did, and left £200 with him when I next came up to town, which I repented of all the way back to New Hall, for though I knew he was honest he was not careful. However, he sent by the post a week later news that we had between us bought £400 worth of Eastland Fir which would surely be worth £700 by the autumn, for there was a great call for plank coming and Mr Dering's yard and others were but half-full. And he sent with it a note setting out the number of timbers and their situation in the yard, so that there should be no confusion. And I began to read the *Intelligencer* which Nan had sent from London that gave me news of the timber that had been landed and the price that had been paid for it, so that I could estimate whether my investment was waxing or waning. Thus I began to know the pangs of the Investor, how he starts with anguish at news of a fall in his stock yet cherishes the hope that it will be but a temporary setback, and throbs with joy at the news of a rise yet fears it may not last, though doubting whether to seize that chance to sell in case the stock might go higher still. So he is in a constant state of suspended anguish, never utterly downcast, yet never enjoying a secure contentment.

For the first month, I was in despair, for a veritable fleet of ships from the Eastland trade came into London and the price for deals fell like a plummet. So I cursed Llewelyn and wrote to him inquiring what we should do. And he answered that we should bide our time, the Investor must have the patience of Job, for Jeremiah did nothing but lament whereas the Lord blessed Job's latter end. I purposed to respond that I would not wait 140 years to have my latter end blessed, but then I read in the *Intelligencer* that all of a sudden there was, as Llewelyn had foretold, a great call for timber, matters having gone badly with the Dutch, who had captured the Hamburg convoy that was laden with naval supplies.

I wrote quickly to Peter: Was this now the time to sell, or should we wait till the price should rise again, and if so how long?

When the tide is rising, Jem, the wise sailor crowds all the sail he can. You must send me another £100 and we shall double our money by Michaelmas, for the Navy is short of timber and the merchants can get no more credit. Thus cash is king.

But I was resolved to make no further investment by faith alone and on my next journey to London I met Llewelyn by appointment at the Old Swan in Fish Street Hill.

First, you must show me the timber before I take a step further into the business.

Show you the timber? Peter looked at me as though I had uttered some blasphemy. A seasoned man of business works upon trust. If he insisted on seeing every scrap of canvas or every stick of timber, trade would never go forward.

Well then, take me for a beginner. I will see the timber.

If you will, you will, though much good it may do you, for the quality of a parcel cannot be judged by a novice.

Still grumbling, he led me along East Smithfield, a scurvy highway, down to Wapping along a narrow lane by a high wall through a forest of wharves and yards and across a narrow plank that bridged the cut to the yard (which he said was the back way in) where the timber was kept at Sir William Warren's. In the back shed up against a high wall, he showed me good oak timbers heaped as high as a house with the crooked pieces kept upright by ropes like so many gibbets.

There, you see.

Peter pointed to a label affixed to the timber, upon which was the legend: property of P. Llewelyn Esq. and partners.

Partners? I said. What is this?

You're the only one, Jem, but the plural has a ring about it, does it not?

And indeed my heart did swell to see this great forest of shining timber. I would that my weaselly uncle or Fluffy Ralph could see me thus in front of my joint stock.

We're wasting good drinking time, Peter said. And he seemed strangely anxious to quit the place.

Could you present me to Sir William Warren that we may cement our partnership?

Another time, Jem, Peter said, taking me by the arm. I've a terrible thirst.

And his thirst was not for liquor only, for in no time he had got the £100 out of me and taken me along the Lane to Dering's office where he gave me a receipt he had written out in advance, so that I should not have a chance to repent my investment.

Now that I had ventured half of my capital upon timber, I was anxious to return to London.

But Nan was adamantine.

I've told you before, Jem, she said. Kit must abide at New Hall and you must abide with him.

But why?

Don't you love the sweet air of the country? I beseech you to wash yourself from head to toe when you get home, for the London vapours are notorious. And will you tell Mary those cabbages she sent me were rotten, they must be picked sooner?

So I held my tongue and went back to New Hall. The sun shone and the days passed. It was our pleasure (among other sports) to take the two greyhounds, Willow and Dancer, into the cornfields beyond the river to

see if we might not start a hare from his form in the long grasses. First
we had to go through a low wood of old oaks.

Hush, Kit said, who's that?

His hearing was sharper than mine. As we stood still and listened,
it seemed that there were too many voices to be a poachers' gang (which
is seldom more than two or three men).

We crept very quiet through the brushwood with the oaks shading
us until we could see them on cleared ground where the Duke had had
the trees felled to make the new roof in the Hall. There were eight or
nine and they were camped there round a fire with two or three rough
tents of ferns and branches. There was a woman and two children, and
they were all ragged and burnt by the sun.

These are vile Gypsies, Kit said, we must throw them off.

Before I could counsel caution, for they looked wild and might be
armed, my foolhardy pupil strode through the bracken and out into the
clearing.

What are you doing here? he cried in his cracked treble, for his voice
was not yet fully broken.

To my surprise, they did not make a violent front but cringed at his
approach.

Sir, we were in a barn at Brentwood, sir, but the barn was taken.

Why are you babbling of barns? said my precocious charge.

Bless you, sir, we are all honest tradesmen, sir, but in Spitalfields,
sir, where we live, our homes are all shut up.

Why shut up?

A silence fell upon them and they looked at each other.

Why, sir, at length resumed the tall man who had spoken first, do
you not know – but he broke off.

Know what? Come on. Out with it. When he talked in this peremp-
tory fashion, Kit was his father in miniature.

But they would not speak.

Then at last I saw, and shouted to Kit (for he had come close to the
tall man in his anger), come back, come away, come back.

What do you mean, Jem?

They have the plague, I cried. And cursed myself.

Now I knew why Nan had kept Kit down here at New Hall. She
must have had private intelligence of the spread of the distemper,

perhaps from the Lord Mayor. Yet she would not tell me, for fear that I would have demanded to stay by her side (though in truth I don't know whether I would have). But I was angry that she had thought so little of me. I vented my anger upon the trespassers:

I'll have a trained band sent to evict you, and they'll be armed and impatient men. You'd be wise to take your leave now.

But where shall we go, sir? the woman said. My child has a fever and cannot walk, but it is not the plague I swear to you, for he has not the swellings.

I held a handkerchief to my mouth as I retreated and bade Kit do the same. The child I did not care to look upon. It was a pale skinny thing in a bundle of rags, and if the rest of them were not infected already the child would do the trick soon enough. That none of them had the swellings was by the by, for there had been cases reported from Holland (whence came this plague) of men dropping down dead and the swellings coming out only when they fell. It was the uncertainty of the signs that spread such fear through the City, for a man might know he had the distemper, yet have no visible signs of it, and thus be able to revenge himself upon his enemies by consorting with them and breathing his foul vapour upon them and infecting them – of which wickedness there were many tales told, though few fairly attested.

When we had returned to the Hall, I despatched the bailiff and the carters and two of their men to chase off the trespassers, though I did not tell them why or the bailiff would not have gone, he being hypochondriac. But the Londoners had already vanished into the forest, like a throng of diseased ghosts.

For some days afterwards, I looked out of my windows at night and when the mist came up from the river, I fancied that I could see their thin shapes stealing up the lawns to take their revenge upon us. Yet when I opened the casement, there was no sound but the hooting of the owl in the wood.

Nevertheless though that gang had gone, there might be other wretches roaming the country and I prepared to defend the Hall against them. The gate on to the Chelmsford road was shut up and a guard posted night and day, and the back gates were locked. The servants had orders to admit no one, however plausible his errand, and I retired to my laboratory to mix Venice Treacle for which I had an ancient receipt.

To make assurance double sure, I sent Tom the carter, an honest fellow who would not peach, into Chelmsford for plague water, telling him that he must tell no one, but the apothecary sent him back, saying that the plague water was a false remedy for fools and the only sure medicine was avoidance of those who had the plague. Kit would not take the treacle until I put more honey in it and said the potion was so nasty he would rather have the plague, but I told him he must take it or his father would have him whipped, which he laughed at, for that tough old soldier had a heart soft as butter in regard to his only son (that is, the only son surviving, a younger had died as an infant; there was rumour also of an elder son who had died young, yet that would have been before they were married, and so he could have been no duke or viscount either).

But while I busied myself with these precautions, my heart was sore and for several reasons: *primo*, I did not like this nursemaid's part which was an ignoble one; *secundo*, though our love was not as hot as it had formerly been, yet still I pined for Nan, for she infused a vital warmth into my solitary life; and *tertio*, I was sixty miles away from my Investment, whereas hitherto all my wealth had been within arm's reach, to wit, under my bed, so that I could be sure it was safe until the instant before my throat was cut.

Nan had still told me nothing of the plague and sent word that I should bring a cart with the victuals, for it was now the season for plums and apples and onions and potatoes and many another herb. What an Irony it was that Nature should prove so abundant and the weather so fair when Death was stalking every street. You may wonder that I was so ready to enter these infernal regions, I mean London, when the danger was so great (for my memorials have not hitherto shown great record of stoutheartedness). Yet I did not wish to lose credit at this crisis in affairs, for I knew that if I did not come everyone would remember that I had not. Besides, as I have said, I must take care of my Investment.

We came up the long road to Whitechapel, past the Miles End post. Lord how quiet it was. The hooves of our two horses sounded as clear as though we were walking at midnight, though it was two o'clock in the afternoon. The houses were all shuttered, and there was no one at their doors or upon the pavement. Those who had business to do walked down the middle of the thoroughfare that they might be as far away from the infection as they could. Here and there grass was growing upon this great highway for lack of traffic, as though it had been a country lane.

When we came to Aldgate Barrs, Tom and I soaked our handkerchiefs in the jar of vinegar that we had brought and tied them round our mouths and noses so that we looked like highwaymen. We had covered our provisions tightly, that the infection might not reach them. And then we tramped through the empty streets of the City that was formerly thronged and noisy. We looked out for houses that had the cross upon them, but they were few. The emptiness was more fearful to us than the thought that we might be infected. Nan told me after that the Lord Mayor estimated that 200,000 persons had fled.

She greeted me at the door of her apartment – oh how she greeted me:

Oh, Jem, I should have told you earlier, I know, but I didn't wish you to come rushing to my side when the infection was at its worst, for it's better now, everyone says so. Dr Heath says the crisis was a fortnight ago, the last week in September, that henceforth those that haven't yet got it should prove hardened to the infection. The bill was decreased a thousand last week, but the General says we must not relax our precautions, for the distemper may recover its wind and come again as it did in Holland, but how pleased I am to see you, I can't say how pleased.

She took me in her arms as she had not done for so many months, even when we had been together at New Hall, and though Tom was unloading the carts down in the courtyard, she kissed me upon the lips, for she felt as though she had been in a besieged city, she told me, and she must needs break out. It was not much longer before we were in her chamber and in her bed. There was in it a feverishness, which is the true word, for the fever left its mark even upon those who never got it and those who came through thanked the Lord for it and resolved to enjoy His gifts while they were yet alive to do so.

While we lay together under the white-bear rug that had been given her by the Muscovy merchants, she told me of all that had happened while I had been nursemaiding at New Hall: of the Lord Mayor receiving visitors in his glass case at Guildhall that he might be spared the infection, of the dead carts going through the streets so full that some toppled over into the plague pits carrying the horses with them, of how the Anglican ministers had mostly fled and the Dissenters filled their pulpits, of the amulets and phylactories and other trumpery that the simple wore to protect themselves from the plague, and of the charlatans that preyed upon them, promising Infallible Pills and the like, and how the Court had removed to Hampton Court and then to Salisbury, but how the General had stayed to look after the City and to beat the Dutch, and how he had been ably served at the Navy Office by –

But here I shut her mouth with kisses, for I did not wish to hear that name, and besides the bells of St Margaret's started tolling for another poor wretch that had gone to meet his maker, and then the bells of another church further off, and she began to tell me of all those she knew that had been carried off: the woman that made her ribbons, and the best baker and all his family, and two of the girls that had been with her at the Gypsies, and the gatekeeper at the Cockpit and all his family that had lain dead in their lodgings for a week before the physician had gone in to them, but few persons of quality, for they had all fled and the Court had set them a bad example. For though she knew they called her a dirty slut, she was better than they were.

And she was.

Thus I rejoiced that out of all this misery had come one good thing, I mean our finding again that which we had lost, our love for one another. And we stayed together for an hour or more, at which she had to shoo me out, for the General was coming back.

So I retired quietly to my chamber and looked out of the window on to the court. Beyond King Street, I heard yet another bell toll and gave thanks to God that I had been spared – which was I think the first time that ever I prayed of my own free will and not in church. But then a cold air came up from the court and I began to look in my walnut cupboard for a heavy coat, having brought only my summer vest with me. Everything in the cupboard was covered with dust, and the moth had corrupted a wool waistcoat that I had left behind. Then I went to the pantry to seek out some wine, but there was only an old cask of sack that had been opened too long and gone sour. Since my own chamber gave me such a pauper's welcome, it was better to go out to a public tavern where I might find Peter Llewelyn and learn of the progress of my investment.

The Leg in New Palace Yard was my first port which was our favourite, but old Stone had not seen Peter for a fortnight. Then I tried the other Leg, Clarke's on King Street, and afterwards Harper's, but old Mrs Harper had not seen him for a year, then the Heaven and Hell, which the members of Parliament and their hangers-on much frequented, but they were both shut up, for the members had all gone to the country.

I did not know where Llewelyn lodged, for since he had been turned out, he had no official residence, and I had known him sleep where he drank, I mean let his head fall on to his arms and snore soundly till breakfast when Paulina or one of the others would wake him with ale, which he called a hair of the dog that bit him.

But I could not find him anywhere, and by the time I had ended my inquiries, I had drained so many tankards to celebrate my return (for all the taverns were suffering from the plague because they were reckoned a prime source of the infection and only the foolhardy continued to frequent them) that I fell asleep on my bed, dog tired, and woke in a sweat to hear the bells tolling again though it was past midnight.

The next morning, a dark and rainy one, I resolved to set out and inspect my timber, where I might also hear news of Peter. I found a hackney with ease, for the coachman told me that they were all starving for lack of custom because no one would take them, fearing an infection bequeathed by former passengers. And we rumbled down to Wapping where the rain was coming down hard. I walked along the narrow lane by the Wall and across a bridge to the back shed where our wood was stored up against the high wall. But I could see no ticket on it. Fearing that the label might have fallen off in the storm, I inquired of a fellow that was passing whether this was Mr Llewelyn's timber, but he said no, it was his master's, and he had never heard of any Llewelyn. I told him I had a receipt for it, but the fellow said I might have a dozen for all he cared, the timber was his master's.

This sent me mad with grief. Every sort of terror coursed through my veins: Llewelyn had sold the timber and absconded with the proceeds, he had lost it all in a wager, he had never bought it in the first place but had pinned on the label to dazzle me when the timber had always been Dering's or Warren's, he was in gaol for some felony and the timber had been forfeit, or . . . but my head ran on and on as the rain ran through my hair and down my cheeks where it mingled with my tears.

Then I recovered my senses and bethought myself that someone must know where Llewelyn was if he was still Dering's clerk, so I went to Dering's office along Wapping Lane and inquired where I might find Mr P. Llewelyn, his clerk. They had not seen him for some days, but that was not unusual for he roamed the town on Dering's business, but they sent letters on to his chamber in St Martin's Lane, hard by the Goat.

Another hackney took me back along Fleet Street and the Strand where I was sad again to see so few people out and them walking in the middle of the street, so that my coachman had to dodge them.

We turned the corner up into St Martin's Lane and an abominable dread seized my heart, which was soon to be fulfilled. For there on the door of the lodging house next to the Goat was a red cross painted a foot high as the Lord Mayor said it must be, and the next house to it painted with the same. I leapt out of the carriage and battered upon the door with both my hands.

No answer. Again I battered. No answer again. And I felt myself roughly seized from behind.

You must not, sir, for the house is shut up.

But my friend is there.

They are all dead, sir.

And the two watchmen led me away, but gently, for this was not the first such scene they had assisted at.

They told me at the Goat that he had died two days before and had left me his ring which the landlord had instructions to give me at his funeral, but if I would rather avoid the stench and the danger, he would give it me now. It is a fine ring of agate and gold. I wear it still in the guise of a mourning ring, although it is not in that mode.

And so took horse for Nonesuch, with two men with me, and the ways very bad, and the weather worse for wind and rain. But we got in good time thither, and I did get my Tallies got ready, and thence with as many as would go to Ewell; and there dined very well, and I saw my Bess, a very well-favoured country lass there. And after being very merry and having spent a piece, I took horse and by another way met with a very good road; but it rained hard and blew but got home very well. Here I find Mr Dering come to trouble me about business – which I soon despatched; and parted he telling me that Llewelyn hath been dead this fortnight of the plague in St Martin's Lane – which much surprised me.

Diary of Samuel Pepys, 20 November 1665

Never was there a more dismal awakening. I could hear the rain beating down on the flags outside my chamber which was cold and dusty. My head ached. My friend lay dead. My timber was gone. All around me were houses shut up with the dead and dying. For all I knew, I myself had the infection already. Perhaps that headache – and my pulse seemed to flutter like a bird's when it is caught in the hand. I lay in bed thinking on the merry days we had in Cromwell's time – Peter and I and Will Symons and his wife, yes, and Samuel Pepys although he was a latecomer to our club and now they were all dead or disgraced, all save he who yet basked in the sunshine.

As I lay there between the damp sheets, I began to compose a lament for my friend. It ran easily enough for the first few lines, thus:

Elegy for Peter Llewelyn, Esq. lately perished of the Plague

> Farewell! Companion of my happy time,
> Who never slept before the midnight chime,
> Thou that ne'er felt the turbulence of sorrow,
> Bequeatheth us the dolour of the morrow.

But then the task disgusted my palate, for true sorrow leaves no room for poetry. A man who can pen an epitaph is already half-recovered from his grief, and besides I began to think of my timber and to wonder whether it might not have been shifted to another yard because Sir William had not room for it, but Peter had not thought it worth the while to tell me. So I dressed, and went off down to Wapping yet again, though with small hope.

After I had paid off the coachman, I trudged off down the same narrow lane by the wall and crossed the cut by the same plank – the *Plank*! When I had gone over the cut yesterday, I had crossed by a little bridge. I ran over to the other side to the back shed and there I saw the white label winking at me where I had seen it last, in the middle of the high masts with the compass timbers hung to the left. No jewelled parchment in the world could have been more precious. On my former journey, I had missed the little turning to the plank and taken the broader path that led over the bridge and to another yard where they knew nothing of Llewelyn's timber. I clasped a stout Eastland mast to my bosom and wept again, but this time tears of joy, though my friend lay stiff and cold in the pit if the quick lime had not yet consumed him. All was well, my Investment was safe.

But to make assurance double sure, I went afterwards to Mr Dering's office, and to acquaint him with Peter's death. He was standing ready to go out, a bustling red man (that was known as Red Ned to distinguish him from his half-brother the baronet who was also christened Edward).

What, what, Llewelyn dead, oh that is miserable news. He was a good lad, I loved him, and a trustworthy lad. And he sat down heavily as though his legs had broken, and began to weep – which astonished me for I had pictured him a hard man of business, but Llewelyn had the power to melt hearts, I mean in particular the hearts of sober men that would shrink from living as he did but loved him for his excess.

Oh dear, oh dear, this Dering went on clucking like an old woman, till I almost wished to tell him to recover himself that I might inquire about the timber.

A joint venture, ah so you are the partner? That was a good Investment in truth, and you have come at the right time, for I have just had an Imprest from Mr Pepys though I had to give him another present for it, which disgusts me because he makes such a pretence of shrinking from the bribe. Oh poor Peter – and he sat down again – he was in Ireland with my brother who loved him too.

Then he looked with another look and his face was as sharp as a fox's.

I could give you the money now, he said, but if you value my counsel, you will let the investment run.

Run?

Well, how much do you stand in for, three hundred pounds I fancy (all of a sudden he appeared to have a precise insight into my affairs). That timber will soon be worth a thousand pounds, and I will give you five hundred pounds for it here and now – and he slapped his empty hand down upon the table, as though he were putting the money down – but Peter's death intricates the matter.

How so?

His will must be proved. We must respect the wishes of his heirs, he has a brother living, a father too perhaps. The law is a tortoise in these matters. It would be no light business to disentangle your half-share. And besides, you'd do better to let the Investment run, much better. With the Dutch on our shores, that timber will double again before next year is out. You leave your £500 with me, sir, and I guarantee you'll not regret it.

At what rate of interest?

Interest, sir, I don't trifle with interest. I deal in timber. When we sell your present parcel, we'll buy another with it, and so you shall rise with me, sir. Here, here's my note.

And with remarkable dexterity – and I could not but marvel how quickly these merchants wrote their receipts – he gave me a bill stating that he was indebted to me *solus* in the sum of £500 which he was to invest in prime timber on my behalf, in consideration of which I was to give him a note stating that I had received from him the sum of £500 in consideration of which he was to have my half-share of the timber now standing in Sir William Warren's yard, labelled the property of Peter Llewelyn, Esq., now deceased.

My head was spinning like a child's top and I stumbled out of Red Ned's office with my papers, knowing nothing but that I had received no money. Yet I was too proud to complain, for I could see that Mr Dering would have thought me a fool for signing the papers.

My humour was not improved by Nan's command that I should take back with me to New Hall all her dirty linen, for she did not trust the laundresses about her, believing that one of them had been carried off by the plague but they had hidden the intelligence from her. So I bumped about down the empty road amid great bundles of foul washing which was as likely infected as the laundresses.

But no evil lasts for ever. In the end, the plague purged itself and those who escaped it needed no other physic, the running sores which were kept open by order of the physician having sufficiently cleansed them, and by degrees people came back to town and began to air their houses and sweeten them by burning incense, benjamin, rozin and even gunpowder to blast out the infection. I mean the poorer sort of people came back but the rich made no such haste. Many of them did not come up till the spring came on. The precious Kit and his poor nursemaid your servant were among the latter, by Nan's order – although the plague was nearer New Hall than ever it had been, for it had broken out at Colchester, some said because of the wanderers such as we had met in the woods. But when Nan came down to see us, all thought of the plague had flitted from her mind.

Oh he is not to go! he shall not go!

Madam?

He is not to go, I say! I am his wife, and he is an old man. And he's no sailor. Why won't they send that coward Mountagu? They are all cowards, those gentleman-captains with their feathers and ribands. Why will the King not send out the old plain sea-captains that he served with formerly, men that fight so their ships swim with blood, though they can't play the gallant and make legs as captains nowadays can? Mr Pepys agrees with me, Jem, although he is Mountagu's man.

Madam, I care little what Mr Pepys thinks.

Then you will be made to care, Jem, for he is a cunning little hedgehog. There he is snug in the Navy Office where all the bribes and presents come in to him like the tide, and there is his master Ambassador in Madrid enjoying all the ladies of Spain, while my poor husband who has the asthma and a severe complaint in the veins will be clinging to a mast in a storm as the Dutch pound at him day and night.

He will beat the Dutch as he beat 'em before, I said.

Oh I don't doubt it but he will be carried back dead in a mizen shroud. And the nation will mourn and they'll all tell me I must not sorrow but rejoice in his immortal greatness, but I don't want him dead, Jem, I want him at my side, here, snuffling, grunting, drinking, even laughing at me which he does when I counsel him though he knows there is sense in what I tell him.

And a great heaviness fell upon me because in her distress she had betrayed that she loved the old General, body and soul, and that consequently I was no more than a toy to her (one may be fond of a toy but it is a light fondness).

That day, she wept as she unpacked the treasures she had brought back from London and I helped her disperse them about New Hall.

These chairs I had of the Genoa merchants (sob). Is not the leatherwork fine? A little nearer the wall, I think, Jem (sob). There is a walnut table to come which will go well there that the Lord Mayor of Norwich is making for me, for he had one that I admired, oh Jem he will die. I wish ladies could go with their husbands on flagships as they may on merchantmen. Now I must dry my eyes, for Kit is to come and show us his uniform. He is to be a captain of a regiment, you know, although he is but thirteen. I wouldn't have it so, but his father says he must though he promises he shan't serve as a soldier nor see action till he is sixteen, but I mean to stretch out that time.

And in came the Brat plump as a pigeon in his bright new uniform with his greasy black curls falling down over his cuirass.

Is he not the image of his father?

I did not say what was in my mind, that he was but a hideous parody, as an urchin may ape the dignity of a nobleman but only to mock it.

Oh Mamma, it is too tight, under the arms.

Loosen the strings, Jem.

They will go no looser, madam.

You have fed him too many puddings, there is a tendency to corpulence in his blood and it must be resisted.

Madam, I cannot keep him out of the kitchen.

Mamma, the suit is ill-made, it is not my fault.

Thus they went on, the distraught mother and her spoilt son, while the old Duke set off for his ship.

Up, and walked to Whitehall, where we all met to present a letter to the Duke of York, complaining solemnly of the want of money. And that being done, I to and again up and down Westminster, thinking to have spent a little time with Sarah at the Swan, or Mrs Martin, but was disappointed in both, so walked the greatest part of the way home – where comes Mr Symons, my old acquaintance, to dine with me; and I made myself as good company as I could to him, but he was mighty impertinent methought too, yet; and thereby I see the difference between myself now and what it was heretofore, when I reckoned him a very brave fellow.

Diary of Samuel Pepys, 13 May 1666

Well, all the world knows what happened in the Four Days Fight, how the General and Prince Rupert set sail together to find the Dutch, and then it was rumoured that the French had sailed out of Gibraltar and were coming up the Channel, how it was accordingly resolved to divide the Fleet and send the Prince after the French with twenty ships, how then the Dutch put to sea and the King sent orders to call back the Prince but the order went in the night to my Lord Arlington's who was asleep and his servant would not wake him, so that the Prince did not receive the order until the next day when the tide was out, and how the General was thereby left with fifty-five ships when de Ruyter had ninety and forced him back up the River, and he lost so many ships that there were two Dutchmen for every one of his and at last the Prince joined him and they beat off the Dutch, how the *Royal Prince* was stuck in the Galloper Sand and was burnt by the Dutch and the *Royal Charles* grounded too but got off, and how Master Sheffield spied the General charging a very little pistol and putting it in his pocket, for he would never be taken prisoner and would blow up the magazine if the Dutch boarded her, and how the General blamed the Captain saying that he never fought with worse officers in his life, not above twenty of them behaving themselves like men (for he hated a coward as ill as a toad), and the Captain blamed the General for dividing the fleet and when it turned out that the report of the French leaving port was false the Court blamed the General also, for the losses of ships and men were very great. But the common people still loved the General, because he had stood and fought. Even Mr Pepys rejoiced, though he tried to hide it, for he had no love for the General and his own lord was safe and sound in Spain.

Out at New Hall we had heard the guns not fifteen miles away off the Gunfleet and I had to calm and cheer my lady, for each broadside that echoed across the river and along the long avenue might be her husband's last. It was in the afternoon after Whitsunday that an old seaman was carried up the drive, his face covered with dirt and pitch and powder and his leg wrapped up in dirty cloths, it being broken. He had been set on shore from Harwich that morning with twenty more wounded men from the *Royal Charles*, with orders to tell Her Ladyship that the General was well, the battle was over and it was a great victory.

It was no such thing, though the General always swore there had never been a greater fight against the odds and, if they had not fought, the Dutch would have been singing their hymns in Westminster Abbey.

But my own heart was light, for surely my Investment would now come safely into harbour, as the call for timber was at the flood.

No man ever lost money by taking counsel from Edward Dering. Your timber is worth twelve hundred pounds today if it is worth a penny, said the bristly red man and he lay back in his chair and laughed as I thanked him. You'll have the cash by Michaelmas.

No sooner? That is two months hence.

Trust me, Jem. Wait for high water. When you see the merchandise, you will understand why it would be a crime to let it go too early.

He took me across the little plank – that blessed plank which had proclaimed the safety of my fortune – to a different part of the yard. And there standing high and proud against the water was a veritable forest of masts, in comparison to the which my earlier store was but a little copse. And there was a ticket with my name on it and the sun shining on the river. I was a man of property. And Mr Dering, the great merchant, shook my hand and congratulated me.

Then I swaggered with him to the Old Swan to christen our partnership in wine. As we came in, I saw a familiar face, as red and round as a dutch cheese, though I did not know him at first, for he used not to be so red, but it was Will Symons.

I have seen that fellow here before, Dering said, he is always half-cut.

He served with me under Oliver, I said, we are old comrades, but he lost his place.

I don't wonder at it, said Dering (for though he was red in the face too, and had a red pimple on the end of his nose the size of a billiard ball, he was a prim and sober man).

Jem, Jem, my old friend. Will came up and embraced me as though we were lovers though I could not have loved a woman who stank as he did. Yet I loved him, we being the last of the old brigade.

We are the last of the old brigade, I said. Llewelyn gone, your wife gone and –

And Pepys gone too, he interjected, to Hell, for all I care. You must know he spoke to me like a servant and when I rehearsed a tale or two of the old days he pretended that he remembered nothing of it and told me not to vex him with such impertinent stuff.

Pepys? said Mr Dering. Now there's a sharp fellow, he feels the pulse of the times. You know Mr Pepys?

He was lately a colleague of ours in the Great Council, a *junior*, said Will with his old dignity that would have graced a lord mayor.

Well, he's overtaken you now. I tell you, gentlemen, there have been times when he's outdone me, or come close to it. There was a parcel of Gutenberg timber, once, he was nearly too quick for me. Oh that Mr Pepys – and he chuckled at the recollection, whilst Will and I sat with faces of stone.

I fancy he is not quite so nimble as you think, said Will, speaking somewhat slowly as though to an imbecile, by which I saw that he was drunk.

No? How so?

That business of the East-Indiamen last summer did for his master, he had to go and hide his face in Spain.

Well, that's all water under the bridge.

Pepys was in with Cocke the hemp merchant and they had a thousand pounds' worth of the captain's share of the goods – mace, nutmegs, cinnamon and cloves, silks and indigo and I don't know what else. And they had no right to it, he abused a physician of trust.

A physician?

A physician. He must be impeached. And I shall be the one.

You?

Your servant, sir, the very same. Will made an attempt to rise but knocked his knees against the table and spilled the wine upon Mr Dering's russet silk coat (though he was an ill-looking man, Dering was also vain and took much thought that the colour of his clothes should sort with his beard, which made him look like a fox that had fed upon half a dozen chickens).

Mr Dering shook off the wine and laughed. You won't harm a hair of his head.

We have papers, Will said.

Oh if papers are your weapons, you are done, he is a *virtuoso* with papers.

Parliament will not be so indulgent, Will persisted. Parliament will look at the state of our ships that could not catch the Dutch, and they will look at men like Pepys with their thousand pounds' worth of nutmeg and calico, and they will say these men are thieves, these men have betrayed us, these men –

Mr Dering cut short Will's peroration: I thought that Mr Pepys had sold his share to Captain Cocke, that he was out of the business.

Ah, so you know the facts, sir, said Will, you shall be a witness. We'll have a cloud of witnesses as thick as seagulls on a rubbish heap.

I fear I'll be unable to oblige you, said Dering gathering up his gloves, I've an appointment. I wish you good-day. And he was gone as quick as a fox to its earth.

There you see, Jem, they all take fright because they know that a great scandal is brewing, for there is never a great defeat without a great scandal and we shall be in at the death. There will be a committee and we shall be on it, it will be like the old days. Do you think your purse might accommodate a little more wine?

I filled his glass and we drank to our success and disgrace to S. Pepys, but I must confess (though I did not say so) that I had little faith in our conspiracy. Will seemed too much decayed to carry it off and Pepys was too strongly entrenched for us to dislodge him.

Yet it was upon that hot August day that I not only became a man of property *pro tempore* but also embarked upon the prosecution of Samuel Pepys. My fellow prosecutor dragged me along in the business. Every week, whether we were at New Hall or the Cockpit, came fresh news from Will about the progress of the affair: 'I have an affidavit from Captain Cuttance that sold the goods', or 'A serving woman will swear that she heard SP and Cocke discourse of prize goods in her back room', or 'I have two members that will vote for a committee and promise to bring a dozen more with them'.

Then I caught the infection and began to pursue my own inquiries, for I knew many men that had dealings with PS, for we now reversed the initials that we might throw the hounds off the scent (George Cocke was CG).

What are you doing? What are all these letters you send and receive? Nan became jealous and wanted to know my business, but I chose to keep it a mystery.

I cannot tell you now, but it is business that will do great credit to the General when it is revealed.

This was true, for I had cogitated upon the matter thus: my fate was bound up with the General's and he had shown favour to me; if he fell, we were all undone; so if we could demonstrate to Parliament that he had been betrayed by dishonest underlings in the Navy Office and that stout fighting men had been starved of ships and powder and sent to watery graves while the clerks were heaping up their gold, then Parliament and the Court would continue to worship the General (the common people never ceased from worshipping him) and Pepys would be sunk or grounded as fast as one of the General's ships.

So on it went: 'Clerk in CG's office will swear that PS importuned his master for a share in the goods but bound him to secrecy for he knew it was illegal' . . . 'receipt for calico made out in PS's name then scratched out and CG's put in its stead' . . . 'silversmith's apprentice says CG had half a dozen silver plates made for PS in April but will not swear to it unless paid. *Quaere*: connected with prize goods, or is there another parcel of hemp in the wind?'

By the end of August, I had a mass of papers that almost filled my old sea-chest (apart from the gold that was yet in it), and my blood was up. Nor were my feelings those of revenge alone, for I saw the old General stumbling about the flowerbeds at New Hall grunting to himself and I could not abide that he should be brought so low by little men.

I beat 'em, I could hear him say as he passed by my laboratory where I now conducted my researches into the mysteries of human not chemical affairs. I beat 'em off and I'll beat 'em again if I can get the officers. The King believes in me, I brought him in, he needs me.

It was a low muttering noise that he made, like a scuffling of rats behind the wainscoting. He seemed to be speaking to his own soul. Nan would try to cheer him by saying those same things that he said to himself, but when she said them he stood mute and looked at the ground and only grunted.

But it was not for the old man's sake alone that I conspired, nor yet because I was so envious of Pepys, though that was the principal reason, but the truth is, I loved the chase and opened each note from Will or bent my ear to his messenger with a keen expectancy.

Tonight – his note said – come to the foot of Seething Lane at ten o'clock and we shall have him, for I have infallible intelligence. Bring pen and ink. Daniel. (For the purpose of our conspiracy, he called himself Daniel, while I was to be Toby.)

Will's intelligence was hitherto anything but infallible and I did not like that we should meet so close to Pepys's, but I was in too deep to draw back.

It was a hot night – we might have been in Spain with my lord Sandwich – and the people were still taking the air by the river and along the parapet of the moat. But it was not difficult to spy out Will, for he alone was muffled to his eyes like a bumble-bee.

Hist, Toby, our prey is almost in the snare.

Can't you speak plain English? What are you talking about?

PS is to meet with CG and another (and here he spoke very low so that I had to burrow my ear into his cloak to hear him), I mean the Commissioner of the Navy.

Sir William Penn? But he sees him every day at the Office.

This is to be a private confabulation for one secret purpose, viz. to cover up what they did in the matter of the prize-money. And we shall take a record of it. I've my new fountain pen which carries its own ink, and it is well charged. See, like a dagger: shall we not stab PS to the heart with it?

His silver pen shone in the moonlight very like a dagger. I had never seen such a device and wanted to inquire into its mechanism but there was no time for any such diversion.

Now come, Sir Toby. And he led me up a small alley and into a narrow winding stair that the nightsoil men must have used when they emptied the house of office, for it stank though it was open to the sky. Up, up we went until we were upon the leads and I recovered my bearings for I could see the Tower and the bridge beyond it and the bend of the river.

Now, Toby, he whispered. They will be but ten yards from us here and we shall hear every word.

We crouched like fieldmice behind the chimneystack and settled to wait. Will whiled the tedium with a flask of sack which he passed to me but infrequently.

Are you sure they will come?

Penn's man swore to me that this would be the place. They could be certain of their privacy here. Penn's man mislikes his master and his master's friend and he is on the *qui vive* for another place which I have told him I will help him to.

It was not above half an hour before we heard the noise of someone climbing another stair a little beyond the stack. Then I heard Pepys's voice calling down encouragement:

I'm sorry for the climb, but it's not far now.

But a minute later to our astonishment we heard women's voices, and there came to our nostrils some delicate scent, not lavender but bergamot or the like.

Oh that was a pretty thought, it will be airy up here.

It was the voice of my dear Elizabeth, and my heart throbbed to think of her so close and yet so far.

We often come up here, Sir William, to sing and play. Husband, have you fetched your viol?

No, I don't like to bring it up that stair. I have the flageolet.

The flageolet makes thin music. Mary, go fetch the master's viol.

No, no, Mary, don't trouble yourself, but sing to us. Will you sing my song?

What song is that? Is it one from the play? Penn's voice was drowsy like a bee's buzzing.

Sing, Mary, sing my song. Pepys's voice was drowsy too. Sing, Mercer.

And a woman's voice began to sing, carelessly, not troubling to be true to every note, yet with a sweetness and fluency that I never heard equalled.

> Beauty retire, thou dost my pity move,
> Believe my pity and then trust my love,
> At first I thought her by our prophet sent
> As a reward for valour's toils

– but here I lost the song, for the words were carried away from us by the wind, then came back to us at the verse's end, thus:

> I break the hearts of half the world
> And she breaks mine.

Well sung, Mercer. That's a fair song.

It's my own, Sir William.

Is it by God, Pepys? It's a fair song.

Mercer, fetch us some wine.

Never have I known such beauty and such torment. To listen to that nightingale on the rooftop on that sweet summer's night and to hear my beloved speak to the nightingale as a servant, and me not able to say a word.

Shall I sing now, Sir William, while Mercer is downstairs?

It will break the spell. My wife sings well, Sir William, but she has not Mercer's voice.

Let her sing, Mr Pepys.

No I shall not, for my husband thinks nothing of my singing.

Sing, my dearest, if you will.

So she sang the next verse but with an ill grace, and in truth her voice was not so strong, but I loved to hear her sing and to think of what might have been if the fates had been kinder.

Shall we go down to the garden? It's not so warm up here as it was.

And so they clattered back down the stair.

What do we do now? I whispered: We can't hear what they say in the garden if we stay here.

We wait, Will said. They'll come back up for the serious business.

Thus we waited an hour and then another, until we heard doors shut below us and a cry of good-night from one of the ladies. The city was silent below us and now we had finished Will's flask.

They will not come.

They will, I swear it. The clock has not yet struck midnight.

I began to get a cramp in my hams and I laid myself out along the leads to ease it. Then Will did the same and laid himself beside me, and soon we fell fast asleep side by side like dead men in a graveyard while the city slept below us. We must have slept two or three hours, in which I dreamed that Mrs Pepys and I were in a boat together and we floated down the river and out to sea where we passed the Dutch fleet grounded on a sandbank and all the sailors pressed along the gunwales to see us for we were quite naked . . .

And then I woke with a start and a strange smell came to my nostrils. I was at first too drowsy to determine what it was: Then I began to cough, and I knew. Smoke. Fire? *Fire.*

We stood up and I felt that east wind cool at my back ruffling my shirt. Ahead of us plumes of smoke were rolling over the rooftops, black and foul as the rivers of Hell. The smoke was thickest above the bridge but already it had crept up Fish Street Hill and Watling Street so that we could scarce see the tops of old St Paul's. And though the wind was carrying the stench from us, yet the scent of destruction was so strong that it came back to us. But Lord what a sight it was, so black and foul, yet the sky all around was bright and blue and the dew glistening on the chimneys and the hills of Surrey exceeding blue and the sun just coming up on the river and gilding the wharves so that they looked like the palaces of Venice and not the filthy docks they were in truth.

Then we began to *hear* the fire, for the air was still (it was barely half past five in the morning). That noise will never escape the memory of those who heard it, for there was never a worse noise in the world. It was a low harsh grinding cackle, as though a giant were cracking walnuts in the next chamber.

My God, we shall all perish, Will said.

Down below, the cries and shouts began, yet the people could not like us see how far and wide the fire had already spread.

We scampered down the back-stairs and along the alley. As we came to the street, a thought struck me like a lightning bolt.

My timber!

You've no cause to fret, Will said, you told me it was in store at Wapping, and the wind is from the east.

So it is, but we had best make sure.

I ran like a stag with Will lumbering 200 yards behind me. As we came past the Tower, we had to dodge between the people who were already coming to see the fire with pale eager faces.

At the Wapping yards, men were already astir, some barricading the gates with stones and iron bars against the fire, while others were loading their timber into boats to float it downriver, for the wind might change and a single spark could destroy all.

Where's Dering? I inquired of a man, but the noise of timber being hauled on the boats was so great that he could not hear and I had to cry louder. Where's Dering? But the man would say nothing save point upriver, towards the fire.

Why is he there?

The man cupped his hand to his mouth and shouted: He moved half the timber there last week, to Botolph's Wharf, we had so many fires here.

Botolph's?

But even as I repeated that terrible word after him, I was sure my fate was sealed, for Botolph's was just below the bridge where the fire was worst.

Come on, said Will, there's time yet, we'll take a boat and bring the wood off.

A boat? said the old wharfman. There's no boats left here, even the skiffs have been taken, you should have been here an hour ago.

There must be a boat.

Well, there's my old bucket, she's sprung a leak but if you hammer a plank across her bottom, she'll hold, but I've given the oars away.

We'll row with these staves, Will said.

I could not speak, for a strange paralysis had seized me, and I stood shivering in the cold morning air, as insubstantial as a ghost, so that Will had to shake me before I would help him carry the filthy old hulk down to the slipway. Evil-smelling water swirled about her bottom and dripped through the leak on to our heads. At the water's edge, we hammered a plank across the hole. I cared little if we made yet another hole in the hammering. In truth, I did not care if we drowned and said so to Will.

Come on, Jem, there's life in us yet.

But even he must have doubted as we struggled up the river, rowing with our sticks like castaways in the South Seas. As we came up past the Tower, there were already boats laden with families fleeing the fire with their children in their arms and their dearest possessions weighing down each vessel so that it could scarce float. There was an old woman carrying a parrot in a cage and weeping as though her heart had broken. And when we came close to Botolph's Wharf, the heat of the fire was very great and we could hear the hiss of the lead melting on the church roof, and the wharf itself and the mast-store behind was one continuous sheet of flame so bright that the eye could not bear to look at it.

We could go no closer and rested upon our makeshift oars to watch the wreck of all my hopes.

Is Dering in there, do you think? Will asked, but I was past caring and hung my head in the miserable boat and blubbered like a baby.

My head was so low that I did not see a black man wave at me from the boat alongside.

Gone, he cried, all gone, yours too, and it was only from his voice that I knew him. Dering the red fox was as filthy as a chimney-sweep.

Well, said Will, after he had allowed me a period of mourning for my timber. Your tears won't put out the fire. The Bear at the Southwark end of the bridge opens early for the hopmen. Do you fancy –

Thus we rowed away from the fire, the heat of it burning down ever more fiercely upon our backs. Now and then we rested upon our oars and looked back to see the foul plumes twist and belch all along the river, then we turned away and rowed on.

My feet were wet but I thought little of it for there had been water in the boat when we boarded her, but now I felt the water lap at my calves and looked down and saw that she was filling fast and within a minute more the water was up to the thwart.

She's sinking, Jem, we must get out.

We dived overboard like a pair of ducks bobbing. I thought to swim, but we were at the edge of Southwark spit, so that the water was barely a yard deep and my face and knees were cut by the stones in the foreshore.

It was an awkward business, but we found our feet and slipped and slithered across the mud – a loathsome substance which contained half the ordure of the parish and covered us from head to toe and mingled with the blood from the cuts. At the top of the bank we halted to catch our breath and let the water stream off our clothes.

Thus we stood, smeared with shit and blood, the scum of the river dripping off us, while across the river the flames fulminated as though Hell had broken loose from its moorings. By now the smoke was billowing over the whole city from the outer gate of the Tower to the apse of St Paul's (from the bridge-foot where we stood I could now see the towers of that ancient church).

We must be the only two men in London who are shivering, Will said and he put his arm upon my shoulder to console me in my loss. Yet I saw upon his shining face a delight in the conflagration which he could ill conceal, for he had nothing to lose by it, and men do love a great fire.

We drank all that day at the Bear, and we were not alone. Many a poor wretch came with blackened face across the bridge bearing only light baggage and a heavy tale of woe. Some had no money and old Abraham Browne the vintner who was a fair rogue let them drink for free and we drank along with them, so that by the day's end as the stench of the burning blew across the bridge we were almost insensible to it and lay across one another on the benches outside the tavern (for it was still warm) with the ashes falling gently like thistledown on us, and after we slept we woke to find ourselves as grey as ghosts.

For many months after that day, my spirits would not buoy, I cared little for the world.

It was a June morning that we sat in the garden at the Cockpit, the General shading his eyes against the sun while I read to him his narration of the Four Days Fight which was to be an apology for his conduct in dividing the fleet.

Good, very good, he mumbled as I read, for he liked to hear his own words, but he was drowsy now. Doubtless it was his sickness (the dropsy) that made him fall asleep after dinner or when the sun beat down upon his greasy old head.

That passage again now, read it again, he said – but at that minute came the sound of feet running upon the flags and here was a messenger falling over himself into the box hedge as he told the General that the King had sent for him, for the Dutch were come up as high as the Nore and there were eighty sail of them.

Monck was up as quick as a boy, his eyes very sharp like a crocodile's that did but seem to sleep to deceive his prey.

The General sent messengers on by horse to warn of his coming. And behind the messengers rode the most absurd army I ever saw, for every gallant and feathered fool that was at Court was resolved not to miss the spectacle. I saw them go off on their mincing steeds across Lambeth Marsh with their plumes nodding in the wind and their hats cocked back (as was then the fashion with the blades) so that they looked like a gaggle of silly cockerels crowing to the heavens. And they had women riding with them (but only as far as Greenwich where they dined) which made them crow the more and twirl their pistols like heroes. I thought I saw the Duke of Monmouth there as we now named him in public (though amongst ourselves we still called him Crofts) and many another bufflehead and windfucker.

I was glad that I was not among them but rode in the *Swift* with the General.

By nightfall we had come to Gravesend and the General in a rage, for there was not a man in the batteries and not an ounce of shot or a barrel of powder anywhere.

Where are they all? Where's Pett? Where's Mennes? I'll have them all shot. Where's the enemy, hey – you? Bring those frigates in a line, do you hear, between the two block-houses and run chains between them, now while the tide permits, and I must have ammunition. Where's Pepys?

Sent for, sir.

He should be here already.

They are gone down from the Hope towards the Medway. Will you go to Chatham?

No, he said, I'll rest. Jem, fetch me the guard's bed. I brought out the filthy old pallet (the straw was almost black) and put it in the lee of the bulwark as he directed that he might see downriver, and he lay down on it in front of us under the stars and closed his eyes.

We stood a little around him as though we were standing watch over a corpse – though his breath was stertorous – and then dispersed to find corners to lie in. But we had no sleep, for within the hour, a furious cannonade began over towards Sheerness, and Monck rose up as quickly as he had done before and took horse over the hill for Chatham, with the moon lighting his way and the stars as bright as daisies, the General cursing his officers.

Where's Pepys?

He came, sir, to Gravesend while you were asleep but he went away, to attend to the business, sir. He didn't think it right to bring the frigates in a line, he said.

Did he not so? Perhaps he would care to sail 'em himself. When I need advice from Admiral Pepys, I shall ask for it.

Yes, sir.

And I laughed in the darkness, for the General's words were midnight music to my ears.

The sun was coming up as we rode over the cliff and looked down upon the Medway. We could see our great ships lying idle upon the tideway and downriver shimmering between the islands were the Dutch.

By God, they're near, said the General.

We clattered down into the battery which was an old castle, much decayed, called Upnor. Again, there was not a gun mounted and only one filthy old fellow to guard the place rubbing the sleep out of his eyes and feeding his chickens in the courtyard.

Where's Pett?

Pett, sir?

Pett the Commissioner that has charge of the defence here.

Oh that gentleman, sir, a fine gentleman indeed. He's gone down to take his baggage to safety and he must use the fireships for there are no others, and the Dutch are coming, you know.

Is that so? – the General seemed marvellous mild – and could you tell me, Captain, what preparations that fine gentleman has made against the coming of the Dutch?

Oh I'm no captain, sir, but a common soldier, an ordinary sort of soldier though I had the honour to serve Your Grace in Scotland, you may recall at Dalkeith —

The *defences*, Captain.

Well, sir, there's the chain — and it's an excellent chain, as thick as your arm, sir, no ship could break it . . .

I take it there are no guns to defend it, no boats?

Oh bless you, sir, that chain don't need no guns, it's as thick as —

Spragge, send to Gravesend for the artillery. We must have batteries on the flanks, one here below the castle and another across the river, there. Where are the stores, Captain? We need tools for the platform and carriages to take the guns down.

The stores, sir, are in the store-house, which is in the outer court, but you cannot open the door.

Cannot?

Cannot, sir, without a requisition.

I am ordering you to break open those stores.

I can't do it, sir. I must have the requisition. Besides, my wife has the key and she is across the river.

Break open the door, Jem. And I took a great log that I doubt not the old fellow meant to use for firewood and broke open the doors of the store-house although they were already half broken down.

When we had the tools, we slithered down the cliff through the mud and brambles till we found a flat place where we might set the battery. Then the General told me to go on down to the river, for he had spied a guardship coming up on the tide and I was to tell the captain to come up to hear his orders.

My heart pounded to be in the thick of things, the General's man, the last line of defence of old England, whilst Mr Pepys was slinking back to London, having left us fighting men with no shot or powder. That should add fuel to the flames of our bonfire when the fighting was done and the recriminations began again.

My mind was whirling through such happy thoughts when, all of a sudden, my foot caught — at first I thought it was on a tree stump, but as I fell down the hill, I knew it was a rabbit-hole, for the foot stayed upright as though encased in a long boot and my body tumbled down.

I heard the crack, it seemed as loud as the crack of lightning splitting a tree, and I knew my leg was broken.

Never was there such agony, I was sprawled down the hill, my head hanging below my legs, my face in the brambles, unable to move.

Help me, help me, I cried, but at that moment the Dutch guns began to boom and my cries were drowned out.

Then I think I must have fainted away from the pain, for the next thing I recall is that feckless gallant, Mr Holles, gazing down upon me with a look of terror upon his silly long face and a red plume falling across one eye and saying in a batsqueak: He's dead, sir, I swear it, he's dead.

Not my Jem, we'll not rid ourselves of him so easily, he needs a surgeon, fetch Mr Pierce from Gravesend.

And the General patted my head as though I were his favourite horse. My Jem – I had not thought of him being so fond of me, for he was never one to open his heart. And I wept from the pain and from the compliment.

The gallants made a rough litter from some hazel branches they had cut from the hill and carried me back up to the castle, where I lay in the old man's cottage which smelled of chicken's shit, and his hens ran in and out and over my broken leg.

Thus I lay all that day and the next night, being the first casualty of the Battle of the Medway. I could hear the boom of the guns below me, for the Dutch came up on the tide and the General was in HMS *Monmouth* that was the only one of our ships proper ready to defend the chain. He had sunk five ships to block the channel but there was a way through, though the Dutch could not find it on the first run. And outside my window I heard the clatter of soldiery and the rumble of the guns on the cobbles. Mr Pierce came and gave me a draught and he set my leg as best he could though he feared I would always limp.

Thus I slept, but in my dreams I still heard the clash of arms and the noise of the great guns and the cries of dying men, and saw the flood-tide of the Medway dyed bright red (but I heard Will Symons declare once that no man dreamed in hues).

What day is it? I asked the old chicken-keeper.

Wednesday morning, my lord, and the Dutch are coming up again with the tide. They would have come through yesterday but it took them so long to clear the river that the tide had turned.

And today?

Every man in Rochester has taken his treasure out to the country. You can't move on the roads, for it'll be a second conquest and we must all learn to say mynheer.

But I was too weak to take fright and I was soon asleep again, while the guns fired from the castle tops and down on the river the Dutch came through and seized the *Royal Charles* that had been the *Naseby*, the ship that had brought the King in, and took her away to Amsterdam where she remains to this day to England's lasting shame.

Indeed, this was the most shameful day in our history and I am thankful that I was not awake to see it, but they say the General wept salt tears to see our flag humbled as he stood on the shore with eight great ships gone and the flagship a Dutch prize.

But the pain from my leg filled all my thoughts as I was taken back in the General's carriage to London. On the way, we met a flock of merchants and their ladies in their carriages returning to their homes with stout chests hidden under the seat and all professing *nonchalance* as though they had but been taking the air on the high road and not flying for their lives. For the Dutch had gone, it not being their purpose to make an invasion as we had thought but only to destroy our fleet that we might no longer injure their carrying trade.

Thus, by a strange mischance, the hour of the General's greatest shame was soon accounted his hour of triumph. For the common people thought he had saved them from invasion and there was a ballad sung to him on every street corner and Mr Dryden wrote a poem in his honour and Mr Marvell another, though that was mostly done to speed Pett on his way to the Tower whither he was presently taken for his negligence. But Pett was let go, when in former days he would have been hanged, for these were kinder times and men that had felt the axe against their own necks were loth to see others lose their heads.

So Monck's reputation was preserved by disaster, and mine too.

Jem, Jem, oh you are pale. Nan took my hand with great *empressement*, which was the most she could do, for the grooms were carrying me to my bed.

Leave us, she said, I shall nurse him, for he has served the General valiantly – though at that moment she knew not the inglorious particulars of my injury. When we were alone in my little chamber, she covered my face with kisses and my old love came back and I looked upon her pert lips and bright eyes as though she were thirty and I were nineteen again. If she was plumper and her cheeks redder than they had been then, her affection for me made up for all and was like a magnetic force of attraction so that even half-asleep I knew when she was in the room, though she was silent.

Towards one o'clock in the morning she came in and lay down beside me.

May I touch you?

You may.

Ah I'm glad you're not broken *there*.

If I was, Mr Pierce could mend it.

You think so?

He's learned in such matters.

He is a saucy fellow.

Am I not saucy too?

No, Jeremiah, you are a proper man.

Perhaps some sobersides will reproach me for setting down such fooleries which are best kept secret. Yet I would show only that a duchess may have a warm heart and that a poor wretch who has nothing else to commend him but his person may inspire love that will outlast age and infirmity.

The General was not safe yet, Pett was in the Tower but he could not be the sole scapegoat for so great a disaster, being but a little man. Why had the great ships been laid up, why had Upnor Castle not been provisioned, why were there no batteries on either river (the Thames or the Medway)? Why had the sailors not been paid, so that half the Dutch crews were English tars that had deserted for pay and jeered at the General on the shore saying 'Now we fight for dollars' and calling to their old comrades asking how Tom did and the like, which was a sorry sight?

Parliament was not to be appeased by the coming of the peace. There was to be a Committee of Miscarriages to look into the late disasters and a Committee of Accounts to discover where the money had gone and what had been paid out in bribes and presents so that the seamen were left penurious.

Great news – Will put his moonface round the door of my chamber where I was lying to let my leg heal. I'm appointed Clerk to the Committee, we're to sit in Brooke House and I'm to have an under-clerk and the power to call witnesses. It will be like old times.

Well, I said, affecting a certain *taedium vitae*, I care not for these posthumous inquests, the ships are sunk, the men are drowned.

No, Jem, but think of Pepys. He is left at the prow of the Navy Board. He is the one that must answer all the charges. This time we shall have him.

I have heard that tale before.

Ah but you have not seen my witnesses. Haul yourself down to the Leg tomorrow and I'll show you a thing.

I confess he had caught me and I hobbled to the Leg the next morning with a keen expectancy. Will was sitting in the corner with two villainous fellows who were strangers to me.

Gentlemen, this is Mr Mount, my lord General's lieutenant. He is but lately recovered of his wound that he got at the Medway. Jem, this is Mr Carcase, Mr James Carcase, a friend of Lord Brouncker and was formerly at the Ticket Office until he fell out with Pepys but was lately reinstated. He will testify that Pepys and his friends paid off a privateer which was theirs with money that was due to the King's tars, is that not so, Mr Carcase?

As true as I'm sitting here, sir. I was so affronted by the news that I wished to bring the matter to the notice of Sir William Coventry or some other person in the Office, but they were all in league so that the only honourable course was to depart until my actions should be justified before the Council – as they have been.

Indeed it was, your action did you credit, I said, but looking into his yellow eyes, like an old cat's, I was certain that he had not told one quarter the truth and that he had been dismissed for some crime or another and had got his place back by influence.

And here is Captain Tatnell that served in Cromwell's time.

The other fellow was a veritable old sea-dog with fine moustachios and a high colour that betrayed that he was no enemy to the glass.

Your servant, sir, Valentine Tatnell late of the *Adventure*. I tell you, sir, the Navy is not what it was in O.C.'s time. We knew our trade then, sir. There was trust and there was fellowship. One might send a man a barrel of oysters by way of fellowship — I sent that fellow Pepys a barrel once and precious little he did for me — but there was no corruption in it. A man of talent had a fair run, but now there are no commands to be had for one that won't bend the knee. So you see me, sir, reduced to service with the press, for if the seamen are not paid the true rate, they must be pressed.

You've not been to sea of late then, Captain?

Not since the *Adventure*, sir. There was an incident thereafter — but we won't speak of it.

Pray do, I'm a glutton for sea stories.

Not a story of the sea, a story of villainous landsmen, a story of calumny and false witness. I shan't speak of it, it is too painful.

Captain, don't spare our feelings. Injustice must cry to Heaven.

You're right, sir. It is an injustice and I shall air it. There was a widow of a brother officer, a dear lady, whom I attempted to aid in her distress. If fortune had smiled, our friendship might have ripened into some nearer relation, but she had evil counsel. Poison was poured into her ear.

Poison?

They told her I'd embezzled her late husband's pay, stolen it. A foul lie, sir, I had merely lent it out upon interest, that it might return to her fourfold just as the Bible tells us.

But then you had only to return her the money, had you not.

The captain looked at me with displeasure.

That was not possible, sir. The rogue had fled with my money when he heard the Dutch were coming. I was destitute, sir, and they imprisoned me, threw me into the Clink without listening to my story. They're a nest of vipers, sir, a nest of vipers, I could tell you a dozen tales — and I shall tell *them* a tale (here he nodded towards Westminster Palace) — that would make your eyes start out of your head. Thank you, sir, another glass of the canary would be most commodious.

Nothing you may say about S. Pepys, esquire would surprise me.

You're right, sir, there are no lengths to which that fellow would not go to line his pockets. I have seen him take two pound in five for a common seaman's ticket. The privateer that he and his fellows have bought is provisioned like the King's barge. If the Navy's ships had been commissioned so, the Dutch would never have dared pass the Nore, I'll warrant you that, you never saw such a ship. This canary is a first-rater, sir, a first-rater.

And he sunk his great pimpled nose deep into the glass as though to cool it, which let in Mr Carcase again.

These are unpleasant matters, sir, I wish my duty lay in other paths, I'm a gentleman, sir, an alumnus of Westminster School where I think I may say my Latin verses are remembered yet. The poverty of my family, poor, sir, yet of some antiquity, compelled me to seek employment in the Navy Office. I wish that I had never set foot in that

– nest of vipers – Captain Tatnell brought up his nose that it might breathe a little before diving again.

– abode of abomination. They're all corrupt, sir, every manjack of them. At first I preferred to avert my eyes and bury myself in my studio, for I am elected Fellow of the Royal Society. Indeed in my mistaken kindness I assisted Mr Pepys to follow me into that society of *cognoscenti*, which he has no right to, for he had no more notion of chemistry or astronomy than a pig.

I am something of a chemist myself, I said. I conduct experiments in the Duke of Bucks's old laboratory in Essex.

Ah then we are both men of science. It is a cruel fate that brings us into association with men like Pepys. How hard it is to touch pitch and not be defiled.

He sighed and looked into his empty glass. I perceived that he was as much of a tosspot as the other, though he was a skinny fellow. His coat was torn at the hem and his shirt was dirty. His yellow eyes flickered round as though he was looking out for spies.

Let us drink to chemistry, he said, and damnation to S. Pepys.

Perhaps we should make our prayers in silence, Will said, for we are in Westminster and the walls have ears here.

You are right, sir, we must be discreet, let us but mouth the words, as monks do when they read the office.

So we mouthed the words: To chemistry and damnation to Pepys, so that Paulina who was filling our glasses said, once I thought you were all mad, now I know so.

I have maintained the practice of versification, Carcase continued, I believe it helps me to cleave to my sanity. I write satires, in the Horatian mode. I have written a satire upon Mr Pepys.

We must have it now, Will cried.

It is a little rough yet, it wants polish.

Now, *instanter*.

Well, if you must, and he rose unsteady to his feet and declaimed in his reedy sour voice, but very quiet so that none but us should hear:

> It Helen was that launched a thousand ships
> But who sunk a hundred? That was Pepys.
> He stole the seamen's pay to line his nest
> Denied them powder so they failed the test.

He sat down. Captain Tatnell shouted: Well done, that was bravely rhymed, I'll drink to that. But Will and I were struck dumb by this doggerel.

When my verses are all complete, I mean to have them published under the title of *Carcase's Satires*.

Is that so? I said.

There are not a hundred ships in the Navy, Tatnell said suddenly, be he never so bad, he could not have sunk a hundred.

That is poetical licence, Captain, have you never heard of poetical licence?

And *ships–Pepys* don't rhyme.

That, sir, is assonance.

Is that so? Captain Tatnell grunted, but he went on muttering *Pepys–ships* into his glass.

Satires won't sink Pepys, Will said. We must have witnesses, clerks who will bring up a ticket that is made out for seven pounds ten shillings to Jack Tar but inscribed paid to Mr Pepys with Jack Tar to swear he had only four pounds.

Tickets? I have dozens of tickets and men that will swear. There is John Capps of the *Lion* and his brother Thomas, and three men from the *Flying Greyhound* that will swear they were paid in Pepys's own interest and his lord's while the King's sailors starved, and Endicott Jones from the Navy Office and his cousin who has a boxful of tickets that were broked, and Sir William Warren's man Edward that knows the truth of the matter of the masts and the imprests for them but he has a defect in his speech and will do better with an affidavit.

And so on, etc., etc. My head was aching with the wine and his voice was so low that I could not be sure of hearing it. Nevertheless his sour catalogue was music to my ears. There must have been thirty names on it, all prepared to swear that Pepys was a cheat whose frauds and ticket-brokings and bribe-takings had cost the King's Navy dear and left her defenceless against the Dutch to the near-ruin of the nation, were it not for the heroism of one little old General and, whisper it not, his gentleman-usher that had first given the alarm to the ships in the Medway (we could forget about the rabbit-hole).

I must have dozed, for when I came to my senses he was talking of other fantastical matters, of the Queen of Sheba and the Whore of Babylon and some mathematical calculations which he said would unlock the Great Riddle, by the which I saw that the man was as mad as a March hare and was no more use to our cause than a fart in a thunderstorm.

Finally he too subsided and fell into a low babble and then into a profound sleep on Will's lap, so that we sat with our two witnesses between us, each as dead to the world as the other.

Will, you're a fool, I said, we must have spent thirty shillings on these two tosspots.

Don't fret, *amico mio*, Will said. I shall have them rehearsed so that they are perfect when they come before the Committee. I am expert in these matters.

But I was doubtful, and as the day approached I could not sleep for fear that they might miss their cues and confound their evidence.

Yet to my astonishment Will was right. He kept both of them sober and then slipped them to the dogs and each ran a frisky course. Carcase had been the better, Will said, for he had all the facts at his fingers' ends whereas the captain stopped and started. Yet both sounded like honest men and you would not have thought that Carcase was mad, for at an interview he was capable of rational conversation for half an hour at a stretch and, as luck would have it, Will said the Committee broke off to dine halfway through his evidence, so he was not taxed too hard.

Thus when Pepys was to come before the Committee on the morning of 6 March, to defend the Navy Office and his own conduct, there was an abundant indictment against him. The only trouble for the members was where to begin. And to answer it all there was but one little clerk, for the great men of the Navy Office were all melted from the scene like snow in April (and Sir William Batten, one of the prime malefactors, was dead).

It was a cold wet day, and I paced the streets like an author that has written a play but dare not put his head in at the door of the theatre to see how the audience like it. To warm myself, I went into the Dog and had half a pint of sack. Hargrave the vintner said:

Your friend Pepys was in here but an hour ago, shaking like a leaf he was, pale as a ghost. Steadied himself with a pint then went off.

Ah, I said.

In the Hall, where I was to wait for Will to bring me news, I called at Mrs Howlett's stall.

My nephew Samuel was in here a quarter of an hour gone. Took a dram of brandy, for his nerve.

Your nephew?

Mr Pepys, that is Clerk to the Navy Office.

Ah, I said.

I took a glass of brandy with Mrs Howlett and then a turn about the Great Hall and thought how many chapters in our nation's history had passed under that high roof and how today a fresh chapter was being written, namely, the downfall of the upstart Pepys that would be reckoned with the histories of the great impostors of our past: like Perkin Warbeck and Lambert Simnel, one that passed himself off as a loyal servant of the King, yet was no such thing, but a covetous, grasping, scheming rogue.

As I passed down the Hall, I greeted Mrs Lane, a pretty woman with fine *mamelles*, that I had seen making an assignation with Pepys. I bowed low to her as though she were a great lady and not a clerk's whore. She was white and barely nodded in reply. I dare say she was fond of the fellow, for though he was plain and warty, he was assiduous in his attentions to women, which is the first *desideratum*.

After Pepys's disgrace, there would be empty places at the Navy Office, for he would assuredly carry others down with him. I could surely prevail upon the General to instal me as Clerk, with Will Symons as my deputy. Thus would the Augean Stables be cleansed, and Englishmen be proud to serve the King at sea once more and not need to be pressed by drunken fools like Captain Tatnell.

I must have passed nearer three hours than two in the Hall, drinking, discoursing with old friends and dreaming of the golden days that were to come. I cannot recall a more pleasant expectation in my whole life. To this day, I remember the cooing of the pigeons in the rafters, the hubbub of the shopkeepers in the aisle, the never-ceasing noise of footsteps upon the great stone floor, and the cold air that made them that passed breathe puffs of steam into the high vault.

But the time began to drag its heels, and I to wonder what kept them. At length there was a huge commotion at the top of the stairs, and men poured forth from the lobby.

Will was among the first half-dozen.

Catastrophe, he said.

And spilling down the steps behind him came a further multitude, of fops and clerks and Parliament men. And in their midst, all smiles, Mr Samuel Pepys.

He wore a yellow vest and he looked like a canary-bird amidst a flock of starlings, a canary-bird that had fed on apricots.

Up betimes, and with Sir D Gauden to Sir W Coventry's chamber, where the first word he said was, 'Good morrow Mr Pepys, that must be Speaker of the Parliament-House' – and did protest I had got honour for ever in Parliament. He said that his brother that sat by him, admires me; and another gentleman said that I could not get less than 9000*l* a year if I would put on a gown and plead at the Chancery-bar. But what pleases me most, he tells me that the Solicitor General did protest that he thought I spoke the best of any man in England. After several talks with him alone touching his own businesses, he carried me to Whitehall and then parted; and I to the Duke of York's lodging and find him going to the Park, it being a very fine morning; and I after him, and as soon as he saw me, he told me with great satisfaction that I had converted a great many yesterday, and did with great praise of me go on with the discourse with me. And by and by overtaking the King, the King and Duke of York came to me both and he said, 'Mr Pepys, I am very glad of your success yesterday;' and fell to talk of my well speaking.

Diary of Samuel Pepys, 6 March 1668

The old Duke was dying. All that year when I had been bent upon my own business, viz. the vain pursuit of S. Pepys, he had been sinking. His dropsy was a heavy burden to him, and he could not breathe for his asthma.

Nan said, it will not be long, then you and I must look after Kit.

Day after day we sat at his bedside or rather by his chair, for his dropsy gave him discomfort and he could not abide to lie down.

The Archbishop of Canterbury came to see him and left behind several sheets full of spiritual counsels to prepare him for death. The Grand Duke of Tuscany also came, being upon his Grand Tour. He was a person of exquisite manner and showed much respect not only to the General but to Nan, which pleased her mightily, since she said with an English duke you could always picture him saying to himself I'll be damned if I'll bow and scrape to a seamstress.

These visits cheered the General, for he did not care to lie in a backwater but wished to be back in the swim. Otherwise for days upon end, he would sit by himself and grunt and stare into the air, taking little nourishment and less pleasure of our company.

Then came to New Hall one Stothard that had served with him in Scotland and had won some reputation in the plague as a doctor, though he was but a quack. He told Nan that he had a sovereign remedy against the asthma which had proved of especial efficacity in cases of elderly gentlemen. It was a secret compound of many herbs which he would not reveal for fear of the receipt being pirated, but he would say that it was based upon the milk of gum ammoniac and syrup of squills and thus fitted to rarify and thin the viscid cohesions in the pulmonary vessels.

I perceived that this was all sham but Nan was at her wits' end and ready to try any remedy. She gave the General the pills and whether though some inspiration of faith or because nature had afforded him a respite, the next day he was somewhat recovered.

London, he grunted, we'll go to London.

London? said Nan, but my chuck, you –

London, the General said in a voice which was low yet had recovered something of its old command. We must marry the boy.

Marry Kit? But he is barely sixteen.

He has a seat in the Parliament House. He is old enough to marry. I cannot leave this earth unless he is married.

I had forgot to say that the Brat had been furnished with a seat in the House of Commons, for his family's native country of Devonshire. It was a horrid imposition upon that ancient and venerable House and I blushed to see the Brat sit alongside the great men of our country and tip his hat over his brow and laugh his strange corncrake's laugh, but the Parliament men had been used to worse humiliation in their time and there was not much to be gained by treating the General's son with disrespect.

So to London we went. Each turn of the carriage wheel was a fresh torture to the patient and we must needs travel along the busy road at the pace of a snail, so slowly that some thought we were a funeral procession and took off their hats. It was autumn and the leaves muffled the road so that the noise of the hooves was faint. It was a sad journey and a silent one.

The General continued much improved from Stothard's pills and though he was fatigate when we came to the Cockpit, yet he lost no time, for he feared that he had not much time to lose.

Where is Pierrepont? Has he the papers? We sent to Welbeck a week ago.

I do not like the terms, Nan said, twenty thousand is a poor dowry for a duke's granddaughter.

He has other daughters to provide for, my dear.

That may be so, but they may marry well and not need dowries.

Kit will not be poor, the General said.

No, but the thing looks bad, as though we should be grateful for twenty thousand.

It is done, Nan, the General grunted. When will Pierrepont come?

It was old Pierrepont's granddaughter that was to be Kit's bride, though in the antique fashion he had not met her yet. She was the Duke of Newcastle's granddaughter too on her father's side, but it was old Pierrepont, a friend of Cromwell's and the General's too, that had made the match.

She is a quiet girl, they say, and has not been out of Nottinghamshire.

Is she handsome? Kit asked.

You've seen the miniature, his mother said

She has a thin look.

That will do you no harm, for none of us is thin. She comes on Tuesday with Pierrepont and her mother.

Tuesday? And for once the Brat shed his cock-a-hoop mien and looked like a frightened boy.

It was a strange cold day, soon before Christmas, when Kit, and I too for that matter, first set eyes on Elizabeth Cavendish.

She was thin indeed with a long face and a mouth that was puckered as though for a kiss and eyes that slanted like a Chinese, and seemed half-asleep. She was frightened, too, and gave her hand to Kit as if he might bite it off.

We stood stiff as playing-cards in the narrow room where the General sat in his chair all day.

Well, William, so this is the girl.

Here she is, my pretty Betty.

She is very welcome in our, in our – this was Nan who for the first time since I knew her was at a loss for words. She could not speak and must sit down. She had been pale for some weeks and I had thought that the fatigue of nursing her husband was injuring her health. Nor was the impending loss of her son at so young an age an easy thing to bear.

You are not well, madam, were the first words I heard Elizabeth utter. She spoke in a reedy voice like the squeak of a carriage wheel that wants oiling.

No, I am only a little tired. Then I saw for the first time clearly, as one does not notice gradual changes in one's familiars, that she had grown grievous thin, thinner yet than her daughter-in-law that was to be.

It was then, and not before, that I saw how vain my dream had been, that the old General would die and she would take me to her husband and I would be raised up, to a barony it might be, or a knighthood at the least, and people would overlook the difference in our years, for nobility is a great leveller in that sense. Now I saw she would not outlive him by much, and all her old strength and liveliness were gone from her. She looked on me kindly yet and would stroke me now and then but was absent, as one may stroke a spaniel while thinking of some other matter. Her affection for me was not gone, I was sure of that, but it was hollowed out by her weakness, it no longer had the carnal bloom upon it. I could scarce recognise in her the hoyden who had tumbled me amid the bolts of cloth.

The next day she could not rise from her bed, nor the day after that, nor ever again. The canker that she had was slow-growing, the doctor said, and only at the last pulled her down.

For those days I was glad to do the office of her usher and move her in her bed when she ached and change her linen, for thin as she was the maids could not lift her.

It's ironical, Jemmy, that now you can come and go freely in my chamber when there's nothing left to come for. Look at my sticks of legs now.

You'll soon be plump as a turkey again.

I think not. Shall I outlast the General, do you think?

Don't ask me such questions.

I don't wish to outlast him, Jem. You don't mind me saying so?

No, no.

I don't wish to leave you either but our wishes on these matters are not generally respected. She lay quiet for a minute, then –

Jem, I can't find the keys, they were under my pillow but half an hour ago.

Here they are, in the same place still.

You will not let the girl have them, will you, Jem, none but Kit is to have the keys to my jewel cabinet, do you understand?

Yes, Nan, I understand.

Again and again, she came back to that great tortoiseshell cabinet that stood beside her bed and seemed more precious to her than her son's happiness.

They grew weaker together, she and the General, so that sometimes I thought his grunting was an answer to her groans, though it was but coincidence.

It was five days after Christmas that the handfasting was set for (the settlement had been signed a week before). So the two young persons stood before Monck, Kit dark and squat, Elizabeth slender and fair, and the old General gave her away though in law she was not his to give, but her father Lord Ogle was not there.

Nan could not rise for the ceremony, but they had to go into her chamber afterwards and receive her blessing.

After the wedding, the General's old officers came to stand watch by him as though he were already dead. They did not have long to wait. Three days later, at about nine in the morning, he gave out a quiet groan and died, with the utmost discretion as he had lived.

We were called in to see him sitting there with his officers beside him. He was already waxen as an effigy and the old frown had gone from his face.

He is like an antique Roman, is he not? said Dr Gumble who was on hand to speed his passage to Heaven.

He is like an Englishman, I said and wept, for though he had said scarcely more than two dozen words to me in our years together, yet I felt secure in his affections and comfortable in his silences, for such is true friendship in men of our race that we do not need to prate of it.

I passed next door to tell the melancholy news to Nan, but she said only in a low voice:

I know already. I felt the moment. I shall not be long now.

I sat outside her chamber on a little folding chair like a guard-dog. In the great passage beyond, the preparations were made for the General's lying-in-state at Somerset House, but I took little part in such obsequies being abandoned to my own private grief, and was much astonished to hear from Nan's waiting-woman, Mrs Lascelles, that the sorrowing people were not to be admitted to see the corpse.

Why not?

Because there is no black velvet to hang the walls of the state rooms.

But the King has promised to take care of the funeral.

There is no velvet and they are ashamed to let the people see the poverty of the King's promise.

So the old General's body lay mouldering, that had saved the King and the country and was now forgot by both. And I dozed on in my folding chair.

My good sir.

Yes – I was half-asleep – ah, my lady. It was Lady Ogle, Elizabeth's mother.

My daughter the Duchess, that is the new Duchess, wants the keys to the jewel cabinet. The Duke is to have his father's Garter and my daughter must have something to wear on her black satin gown. Mourning is a fine garb, but it needs tricking out.

The Duchess keeps the keys herself.

Oh I am sure she is past caring for such matters.

I will inquire.

Do not trouble, this is a woman's matter. I will inquire myself.

Wait a moment, if you would.

And I was as quick out of my chair as a flushed partridge that I might reach the door to Nan's chamber before Lady Ogle.

Nan was herself half-asleep, but I saw the keys firmly grasped in her fist.

Lady Ogle requests the keys to the jewel cabinet for her daughter, I said.

Nan did not speak but shook her head twice and clasped the keys more firmly.

I returned to Lady Ogle, and said that Her Grace was unable to let her have the keys and would in my opinion surrender them only to her son.

Fiddlesticks, said Lady Ogle, and went off downstairs.

Twenty minutes later, up comes Kit sweating and flushed.

Where are the keys, Jem?

Keys?

You know which keys.

Your mother has them.

He went in.

He came out carrying the keys.

A fortnight later, she died as quiet as her husband. I went in to her to kiss her one last time. The pale waxen figure was a stranger's. I remember only how grey her hair had grown as though death had silvered it overnight (it was only that she had ceased to dye it).

I stood beside her bed and prepared to weep for her, as her waiting-women (Mrs Lascelles and the other one that limped) were already weeping. Yet my ducts were dry as a river-bed in the desert. Indeed my whole being was dried up and withered so that I could scarce breathe and I coughed as though I was an Asthmatique which I never had been. Nor could I speak, even had I words to say

Then, I remember thinking to myself, how should this be? When my mother died, in the year before the Great Plague, I thought little of it, for we had met but once since I had joined the service of the State, yet I wept easily enough, and for my father too who had predeceased her, but less so, for he was only a dull farmer, no more worth grieving over than a tree that had got the scab. Yet for Nan, no tears.

Go now, sir, you are tired, the waiting-woman said. You must sleep.

Then in my little narrow bed that had been poor Peter Llewelyn's before me (he had sold it me for 5s though it fitted his miniature frame but not mine), there at last I began to shed tears, not so much for Nan as for myself, no, for both of us, but more for me. For she had triumphed over her low birth, over the whispers against her chastity and the lawfulness of her marriage (it was said that as she lay dying old Radford had been seen skulking round the back-stairs of the Cockpit), over the contumely of the Court. She had served her husband loyally and faithfully – well, after her fashion – and she had served me – ah how she had served me. Through my tears, I remembered our first meetings at the Gypsies and the Turk's-head knocker behind and the night when we had decked ourselves with her jewels though we were naked and many another night under the great fur coverlet that was a gift from the Muscovy merchants. She had melted my frozen heart and taught me the fluent habits of affection. At times, I was angry with her that she had degraded me to a servant and had betrayed her promises of advancement. Yet I was proud to serve her, and when I stood before her at some great banquet of State and bowed even as she curtsied to the King or the Duke of York, I was happy and thought that to be in her service was no more than the minstrels of old Provence had prized as their dearest wish on this earth.

She was not admired as a beauty – Pepys had spoken of her once as ugly – yet she had more true beauty than all the sickly ladies of the Court, for every atom of her being was instinct with life. Yet – this was ironical – now that life had ebbed from her, she was beautiful in that classical sense also, for her colour had fled and her cheeks were of alabaster, her brow ivory, and the last wrinkle had vanished from her face. Only her hair was grey.

My tears ran down my chest, and I shifted in the bed to dry them upon the bedsheet, when I found that these inward memorials had stirred my flesh. At first this rising seemed an impious recreant impulse. Then I thought, well, at least I shall sleep. Then I thought, Nan would say, go on, do this in remembrance of me (for she had a free tongue when the old General was not by). So I did it, and I slept. It was a final salutation.

The next morning, the tortoiseshell cabinet was taken down to the chamber that had been prepared for the new Duke and Duchess, and they spent most of that day trying the jewels, for Nan had a collection that was second only to the King's.

Meanwhile the old Duke's body lay unburied, unvisited, rotting, at Somerset House. Nan died almost a month after him but was buried two months before him. After she was buried, I crawled from one tavern to the next to souse my sorrow, and when I came back to the Cockpit, I preferred to lie downstairs on two old bolsters in the dusty linen store where Nan had kissed me once, for my own chamber was too near the young couple's, and I did not care to hear the noises of their pleasure that were so like and yet unlike the last groans of their predecessors dying.

The time came when even that dallying Court was ready to bury its last hero, though the leaves were already on the trees again by the time the procession set out from Somerset House. It was the greatest funeral known to history save that of kings and queens.

First marched the troops of the guards with the Coldstreams at their head, as having been the General's own regiment, all in excellent funeral order. Then a train of poor men in mourning gowns with their conductor. Then trumpets and heralds and banners, and the principal officers of the King's house, bearing white staves; barons, bishops and earls.

Then came the great banner, the horse caparisoned with black velvet; then an open chariot covered with black velvet and a canopy of the same, in which lay the effigy of the Duke in azure armour (the body itself went privately by water to the Abbey), a golden truncheon in his hand, having on his ducal robe and coronet, a collar of the order about his neck and a garter on his left leg; the chariot drawn by six horses caparisoned with velvet, with escutcheons, chafferoons and plumes. The Poele was supported by three barons and the Treasurer of His Majesty's Household and on each side of the chariot were carried five banner-rolls of arms of the Duke's paternal descent. Next after the chariot came Garter principal King of Arms with a gentleman-usher preceding His Grace the present Duke of Albemarle, the chief mourner.

The gentleman-usher was I.

After his mother's funeral, Kit had said to me:

Now, Jem, you've got no one to serve. So I had better take you, for no one else will.

Oh, I said.

Well?

Yes, I am obliged to Your Lordship.

Grace, Jem, Your Grace.

Just so, Your Grace.

It's our turn now.

So it is, I said.

VII

The Hospital

She is dead, you know.

Yes I know, how should I not know? She was the one love of my life, Will, and I was with her to the end.

I never knew that. I had thought her faithful.

And so she was, oh so faithful – and I began to weep.

I did not see you at the funeral, Will said.

What funeral? She isn't buried yet, the King won't appoint a date.

The King? Jem, I am talking of Mrs Pepys.

Mrs Pepys?

Yes, she died in November, of a fever. They had made a journey, to Holland and Paris, so that she might see her old haunts, and she took a fever in Flanders when they were coming back and died at home three weeks after. She wasn't yet thirty. I didn't know you were so warm toward her.

She – but I could not think what to say, for I repented of my earlier confession, that I had loved Nan, because I did not wish Kit to know of it and to tell a secret to Will Symons (if he should understand it) was to tell the town crier. And I was struck dumb to hear that Elizabeth was dead too. I felt as though I were a ghost wandering a graveyard and upon every tombstone was carved the name of one I had loved.

But Will had no patience with lacrimosities. He had lost his own wife so long before and his heart was now adamant.

She was a handsome woman, he said. Too good for Master Pepys. I hear he is broken-hearted, and remorseful too, I trust, for he used her shamefully.

He did, he did, I said. And to my mind came the image of his pure young wife resisting my clumsy approaches, then, *simul*, of his joggling buttocks in Fleet Alley, and I wept again, for all the imperfections of this world.

Come, come, Jem, no more blubbering. Think on the bright aspect of the matter. Pepys is weak and griefful now. He survived the Committee for Miscarriages, but the Committee for Accounts will be too much for him. Once they have the evidence, Jem, the evidence will do for him.

What evidence? I said, but listlessly.

Carcase, Jem, he's the key that will unlock the door.

He's a madman.

I have rehearsed him thoroughly. And being the Clerk to the Committee I can have him shut off when he is prolix and lead him back when he strays.

He's a madman and –

Hush, here he comes now. Be gentle to him, for he is easily downcast.

Not easily enough, I muttered, as the bedrabbled figure stumbled across the tavern floor, knocking against the other topers as he came. He looked like a scarecrow that had been left out in a ploughed field all night, but his yellow eyes were alight with triumph.

I have the ticket, boys, I have the ticket – and he waved a stained old sheet of paper.

Hush, Mr Carcase, sir, do you want the whole world to hear?

Look, there, to John Capps of the HMS *Lion* seven pounds ten shillings and there – that is the hand of Carteret's clerk – 'paid to Mr Pepys'. He'll deny it but there it is, ticket-broking plain as a pikestaff. He'll go to the Tower for it, sure as –

Now, now, Mr Carcase, stop waving it around like a prick in a bawdy house and give it to me and I'll deliver it to Lord Brereton.

You'll let me testify, won't you? I have so much to tell.

Now then, sir, you shall testify but you must take direction, you must not wander.

I looked at the stained and tattered piece of paper as Carcase handed it to Will who shut it away in the little satchel he carried his papers in. Could so mean a paper destroy a man? Could this shrivelled unsteady creature really break the Secretary to the Navy? Well, stranger things had happened.

But I could not be there to hear the outcome. My new master was whirling about the country to view his estates, which were vast and multitudinous, for the old Duke had squirrelled away every acorn that rolled into his path. New Hall was but the seat principal. There was the royal park at Theobalds, and Norton Disney, Lincs, and the ancient Monck demesne of Potheridge in Devonshire, and Midgeham Hall with its tide mills, and Moore Park near Windsor which the King had later, and Grindon Manor in Staffordshire that came with Elizabeth Cavendish, and half a dozen more that we scarce knew the names of.

They say Ormonde and Buckingham have more, but I'm the third subject in the kingdom, the Brat said, you're fortunate to be in my service, Jem. This afternoon we'll course the greyhounds. They want exercise. Monmouth has a dog that he wants to match against mine.

He talked only of dukes now that he was one, and although he had not reached his eighteenth birthday, he looked nearer my age than his.

Yet I cannot say that I hated him, for he guided me through a realm of pleasure that I had not known of, and wherever he went his lightest whim was jumped to, for every servant wishes to endear himself to a new master, knowing that if he be not turned off at the beginning he may well survive till the end.

We went first to Devonshire where his aunts lived. The weather was wet and windy and the ground had turned to a red mire. Kit (I shall call him the Brat no more in deference to his new dignity) took it into his head that the two villages which were his (Potheridge and I forget the other) should play at football.

You shall be the captain of one, Jem, and I of the other.

Sir, you forget I limp still from having broken my leg with your father in the Dutch war.

God, man, I didn't mean that we should *play* with these varlets. I'll have a platform built that we may judge the match.

His woodmen put up a dais of plank and canvas above the road between the two villages, and we and the young Duchess and the aunts and their people sat upon it, while the muddy bodies, fifty of them to each side, pushed and kicked each other. At the outset, they had worn white and blue favours to distinguish them but after half an hour all were obscured by the red mud.

Isn't this great sport? Kit bellowed, to make himself heard above the noise of the rain upon the canvas canopy.

I would rather be indoors, my lord, his wife said, she being a pale and peaking thing.

Look, there goes the ball, he shouted, paying her no heed at all.

And there was the muddy bladder, sneaking out of the ruck down the hill like a fox stealing out of a covert while the hounds are all faced the other way.

After her, boys, after her – and he leapt down from the platform and charged down the field, giving the ball a mighty kick which sent it soaring high into the leaden sky. And fearing to seem deficient in sportful spirit, I limped after him but was overtaken by the besmirched throng and trampled to the ground with my face down in the mud.

Such was the introduction to my new life which was to be one unbroken riot of sport: wrestling (in both the Northern and the Grecian mode), coursing after hares, hunting wildfowl in the flat boats of the Fenland, more football, hawking on the Essex plain, and above all else racing and gambling on Newmarket Heath which was for Kit a veritable *Paradiso*. And indeed it was pleasant to rise early at New Hall and trot along the lanes while the frost of morning dispersed the fumes of last night's wine. At Saffron Walden or Chesterford, we would change horses. Before dusk, we would come down the straight old Roman road into Newmarket where you never saw such fine carriages or such ladies tossing their heads as if they too were pure-bred like the horses, which they were not. In that confusion of nobility, with my height and carriage, I passed off well enough as a minor gentleman of the Court and took my share of the beauties that were displayed. Ah such a curve of breast, such swan-like necks, ivory and alabaster alighting from gilded coaches, the smiles beneath the nodding plumes, the high-stepping racing horses with bright sheen on their quarters, the click of cards at the tables, the windows thrown open to the starlight when the room grew hot, the noise of hooves trotting off to greet the dawn. None who did not know Newmarket in the first years of its splendour has known what true pleasure is.

But there were days after the racing and gaming when even

Newmarket staled and we must stare out of the windows to see nothing but the rain and the flat ground and the cabbages growing. Then was the prince among men the one who knew how to entertain the King with a lewd jest or a masque made impromptu or – a sermon.

We sat in the long hall, I think it was at Lord Cornwallis's, on such a dreary Sunday afternoon, when a minister, a tall man in gown and bands and spectacles, came in and begged leave that he might make the King a sermon. Picture the fellow rolling his eyes and sniffing and snuffling like the Puritan preachers that pour hellfire down upon their congregations.

My text, dearly beloved, he began, is divided into three parts. First, a lewd woman is a sinful temptation. Second, her eyes are the snares of Satan. Third, her flesh is the mousetrap of iniquity.

The King began to smile.

The conversation of a lewd woman is dangerous, for she flatters with her tongue and charms with her tail till her languishing looks and lecherous kisses have roused up the devil in the flesh. There then arises a hurly-burly in nature. He embraces the temptation in his arms, and casting her on a couch full of crackling infirmities she tussles, he bustles, the couch shrieks out to discover the baseness they are acting – But alas! it being in the tents of the wicked, nobody will hear till they have glutted their souls with forbidden fruit and sowed their polluted seed amongst the thorns of abomination.

The King was laughing now, and even the slower gentlemen had begun to smile. The fellow whoever he was had so well caught the ranting manner of the Puritan.

I shall now proceed to the second part of my text, viz. her eyes are the snares of Satan. That is, my friend, they are the deluding baits which first influence your frail natures by their pinking and winking, their rambling and rolling, their long and languishing motion. They are the very allurements with which Satan baits his mousetrap of iniquity; this is the *ignis fatuus* that leads you into dark pits, stinking bottomless pools, and filthy water-gaps of destruction.

They had ceased smiling now, so powerful was the preacher's denunciations. But with a swirl of his gown and a pointing of his bony finger at his royal hearers, he went on:

I come now to the third and last part, wherein I shall endeavour to handle the mousetrap of iniquity, which I fear, dearly beloved, you have all been handling before me . . .

– at which the entire company broke out laughing.

. . . This trap of Satan lies hid like a coney burrow in the warren of wickedness between the supporters of human frailty, covered over with the fuzzes of frailty which grow on the very cleft of abomination. A lewd woman, beloved, I say is this warren of wickedness; therefore let not her eyes entice you to be fingering the fuzzes which grow in the cleft of abomination, lest Satan thrust you headlong into the mousetrap of iniquity.

Thus shall I conclude with all my hearty wishes for the congregation here present. May Providence hedge you and ditch you with His mercy and send His dung-carts to fetch away the filthiness from among you, that you may enter undefiled into the congregation of the righteous. A – a – men.

At which conclusion the preacher took off his spectacles and his cap and revealed himself to be – the Duke of Buckingham, that chemist, republican and reprobate who cared naught for God or man and least of all for the King whom he played with and tickled as one does a child or a kitten. But when he set the table on a roar, the King was the first to applaud and none of us dared be the last.

I was older than the young lords. They called me Uncle. I could not keep up with their giddy pranks and was *ultimo* glad to go back to the Metropole where I might retire to the solitude of a quiet tavern and catch my breath. And it was in Harpers (where we had clubbed as clerks in O.C.'s time) that I met by chance Will Symons, and learnt of Mr Pepys's proceedings before the Brooke House Committee.

You would not believe it, Jem, the fellow had the impudence to write what he called a full and sufficient Answer to the Commissioners' charges, fifty folios of it, composed he said at enormous labour not only while other parts of His Majesty's service called for his daily attendance but also during the sorrowful interruption lately given him by the sickness and death of his wife, when I saw him down in the Leg with Mrs Bagwell but three days after the funeral. But what was worse, when he had read his answer over to Brouncker and the Duke of York, he brought a fair copy of it over to me and said, Will, be a good fellow and tell your masters to trouble me no further with their vexatious inquiries, for I have better things to do with my time. But I saw that he had no notion of my true feelings towards him, for these men that are puffed up with themselves never pause to think what others may be thinking of them.

We had the matter well prepared, but what I had not counted on was that the King himself would hear the case to support his little clerk throughout the proceedings, and oh how the little clerk repaid the favour.

Thus when it was said that £514,000 which was to have been laid out on the Navy had been diverted to the private pleasures of His Majesty, Pepys declared that not only had the money gone to the Navy but the King had spent £300,000 of his own money on it besides. And nobody durst contradict him, the King sitting there in the Council Chamber.

And so when Pepys said that in exchange for ten years' service, and these the most valuable of his life, he found not his estate bettered by £1,000 from his employment – which was a foul lie, for he boasted to me last year he was worth £11,000 – again, they dare not speak against him.

And then again, when Pepys was garrulous about his accounts so that Colonel Thomson was yawning and scratching his wooden leg and the other Commissioners were impatient, the King came in to say that he had it upon very good information that the expense of the Dutch in the late war had amounted to £11,000,000, whereas ours does not exceed £6,000,000. Which claim none of the Commissioners knew how to challenge.

I do not say that Pepys himself was not a ready answerer. When old Thomson was accusing the Navy Office that they had used foreign plank to build their ships, Pepys replied that like Thomson he too had served in the Navy, and was as much in love with English plank as he, and would give him thanks to direct us where we might be furnished at this day with 2,000 loads of English plank, which struck Thomson dumb – although I know that Pepys preferred Gottenburg plank because he got 5 per cent more from the merchants.

Yet still I placed my hope in the business of the tickets. There it was, in black and white – 'paid to Mr Pepys', and when Lord Brereton brought it out with a flourish, I thought we would win. Pepys spoke very high, said he defied mankind to prove that this or any other ticket was ever paid him. He would assert in defiance of the whole world that it was a lie, etc., etc. But he had no proof positive to offer.

At last he was doomed. All the exits were locked, I was convinced of it. Alas, all the exits save one.

For the King smiled and shook his head and said he thought it a vain thing to believe that one having so great trust should descend to so poor a thing as doing anything unfit in a matter of £7 10s. And that was *finis*. The Commissioners had no answer. The bystanders began to murmur against them. The King and the Duke took Pepys off to supper, and the Council never met again.

So the King rescued him, I said. Who would have thought it, to trouble himself so much, only for Pepys.

But look at it from the other side, Jem. Our little Sam rescued the King with his fervent protestations that all was done properly in the Navy Office and not a penny was wasted. Don't you see? The Committee was after greater game. To catch a little Pepys with a seaman's ticket is like snaring a rabbit. To prove that the King had spent the Navy's money on Lady Castlemaine's jewels, now *that* is a chase worthy of any high-spirited republican. Therefore the King sat there all day long day after day when he might have been at Newmarket or wenching, for though he seems an idle lover of pleasure, he can be as diligent as any man when he smells danger to himself.

But if the King protects him, then Pepys is safe for ever, *ad saecula saeculorum*.

Hmm, Will mused, looking deep into his tankard bottom, we must divide the fleet. We must sow suspicions, we must make the King think that . . .

But I could see he had no notion what the King was to think, for Pepys had floored us and rode high in his gilded coach with the black horses and cared not whom his wheels plashed. Some of us were on the pavement, some of us were in the gutter, some of us were in the grave. And he cared not a fig for any of us, nor for humankind entire with the exception of Samuel Pepys, esquire. For he was self-centred and his motto was *solus ego*. And I resolved to think no more of him and to leave Will to his plots and stratagems, while I removed to pastures new. But there still lingered in my mind what the King had said about the ticket, viz. that Pepys was dealing in contracts that might bring him £100 or £1,000, whether honestly or otherwise, so why should he trouble himself for £7 10s. Though it is true that great thieves must begin with small thefts, yet I pondered whether there might be some other explanation. Then I recalled that in his cups (when was he ever out of them?) Mr Carcase had boasted that he was not only a scholar and a gentleman but he was also an excellent penman, nay a *Calligrapher*, which he told us as though we were turnips was derived from the Greek *kalli* meaning beautiful and *graphia* meaning writing. Might not a calligrapher as well be a forger of evidence where true evidence were deficient?

Leave your brown study, Jem, my master interrupted me. Remember, tonight we are to become learned lawyers.

I'm sick, mayn't I cry off?

No, Jem, we're to be admitted members of the Honourable Society of Lincoln's Inn, it will be a great feast, the King will be there, and the Duke of York, and other gallants.

But I'm not to be admitted. I shall not be missed.

You will miss the revels. A glass or two of the Benchers' wine will mend your humour. I command you to come.

As Your Grace wishes.

No but do it gracefully, Jem, you must surrender gracefully.

His voice had a whining tone like that of a keen wind through a keyhole. He wished to be thought well of, yet he behaved so ill that none could honestly approve him, and so we his servants caught his grudging manner as though it were an infectious disease.

In truth, I had no more than a chill, but it was the last night of February and raw wet weather and I had supped my fill of banquets and balls. There was to be a grand ball at Whitehall two nights later and I hoped to be recovered in time to step it there with my new lady, whom I had met with at Newmarket, a widow only a year older than myself and well provided for.

But off to Lincoln's Inn we must go and drink deep into the night while the lawyers regaled us with their venisons and oysters which were excellent and their discourse which was dry and spiced only with stale lecheries, for it seems a rule established by divine ordinance that every lawyer believes two things of himself, first, that he is the cleverest man in England, and, second, that his lewd stories are the wittiest and most original when they are for the most part second-hand goods.

Thus I sat glum while some Justice of the Queen's Bench told me of the infallible manner by which one may tell whether a woman be virgin or not by the use of an orange, which I had heard a hundred times before, when Kit slapped me on the back.

Come, Jem, the King is gone. We must be off, the chase is up.

I think I'll go to bed, sir.

No, Jem, you will not. I would not pardon myself if I let you go to bed without seeing Dolly. It would be a sin, wouldn't it, my lord?

A very grave sin, Your Grace, the old judge replied, toppling off the bench and catching my arm to steady himself. She is, she is . . . Dolly, in short, is . . . she is in Whetstone Park.

There you see, Jem, come along.

So I stumbled off out of the hall in the wake of the soused crew. I can still hear their cries calling to one another to try the echo as we meandered through the old pillars of the crypt.

This Whetstone Park was then (is now for that matter) no Park but a foul alley behind Lincoln's Inn which is convenient for the baser sort of lawyer who cannot afford to keep a mistress and is too idle to traipse as far as Covent Garden for his pleasure. He may slip out for ten minutes between one brief and the next and his clerk not know he be gone.

Where's Dolly? Come out, Dolly! Dolly, there are three handsome dukes come to see you. No, there are three handsome pricks to . . . No, no, three handsome dukes *with* three handsome pricks . . . Dolly, where are you? You needn't be shy.

Well, there were three dukes, none of them yet twenty, but only one was handsome, and that was Jemmy Monmouth, with his noble brow and his bright eyes, he was like a spoiled angel and even when he was standing there, three-quarters cut, in the wet street with the rain streaming down his cheeks and bawling for this poor whore that was too frightened to come out, even then he had a noble aspect. Beside him my master looked like a sweaty bumble-bee.

Dolly, where are you, Dolly my darling, don't be frightened, for we are loving lords.

Then two men came out of a dark alley with long staves and began to belabour Albemarle (who was the smallest of the dukes) about the head. The other two and their hangers-on came to his aid. I saw the flash of someone's blade. And still they cried Dolly, Dolly, as though it were some sacred battle-cry though none of them, I dare say, had ever set eyes on the girl.

Then together with Dolly, Dolly, they mingled in the cry 'slit his nose, slit his nose' – for this was the cry of the moment among silly young gents, and every one such as claimed to be of the bolder sort would boast of having slit the nose of some inferior who had offended him, *videlicet* an impudent coachman, or a moneylender who was proving troublesome – although I cannot recall ever having seen anyone with a nose thus slit.

Roused by the clamour, men were now pouring out of the dark doors and alleys, waving sticks and holding up lanterns that they might see who the miscreants were.

Then from the far end by the turnstile came a little man with a bigger lantern crying peace, peace, I am the beadle.

Slit his nose, slit the beadle's nose came the roar back from our party.

I did not see what happened, for I was stricken with a sudden fit of giddiness (the wine had sorted badly with my chill) and I sat down upon a mounting block and thought I was about to vomit – which I then did.

And it was only after I had done so that I heard the terrible cry of the beadle. It was a great groan, like the cry of some far-off bird.

For a moment, there was silence. Then a voice (I thought it was Kit's) shouted: He's down. And then another voice said, not so loud, no, he's dead.

There was a clattering of heels as some of the rioters ran to the end of the alley, but the beadle had locked the turnstile. By his final act, he at least ensured that his murderers' names were recorded.

The three silly young lords and their fellows stood, quite crest-fallen in the gutter that ran down the middle of the alley, with the rain running down their clothes, the fine lace and silks all sodden now, while the beadle's assistant took their names, and his neighbours held up their lanterns that there might be no prospect of concealment or escape.

How young they looked, these murderous innocents, with scarcely a word to say between them, their beautiful tresses straggling down their backs like wild animals that had been trapped and skinned and were worn home as trophies of the chase.

The beadle lay a few yards from them, a fair man though he had not much hair and what he had was muddied in the gutter. His face had no hatred on it, only surprise. He looked like poor Llewelyn, who had also met an untimely end. One of the men took off his cloak and wrapped the beadle and carried him off to his house. I wondered that they did not fall upon the murderers and take swift revenge, but they stayed quiet as though they had been standing at a peaceful deathbed.

But why were they in that place? the young Duchess asked.

Madam, it is just by Lincoln's Inn, not two hundred yards away.

But they had their carriages at the gate, they had no need to walk anywhere.

I fancy they wished to stretch their legs and clear their heads of wine.

You think I'm a fool, Jem. I know what Whetstone Park is. It's a dreadful place, the resort of *putanas*.

Well then, madam, if you knew, why did you ask?

I wanted to test you, Jem, to see how you would lie for him. Will they hang, do you think?

She asked the question as calmly as though she were asking whether it would rain tomorrow. She had a capricious humour. You could not tell what she was thinking. And the expression of her face was no sure guide to her heart. She would wear a bright smile when she was accusing me (which she did often) and then look grave when she paid me a compliment which she did less often and when I least looked for one. She seemed to look sidelong at me with her Chinese eyes.

Oh no, madam, I said, surely not. They were heated with wine. It was a brawl, there was no purpose to it.

It was murder, Jem. And she said 'murder' with a strange relish.

I don't think so. And besides, the King's son . . .

We've executed kings before now, haven't we, Jem? And for less cause. Tell me, who struck the blow, was it Kit?

That I cannot say, madam. I was . . . otherwise occupied at the time.

Oh yes, Kit told me, you were vomiting like a dog. Let us hope you were observed, for that will prove you innocent.

Until that moment, it had not struck my mind that I too might be indicted for the crime, but now I saw that it might as well be me as another.

But her mind had passed to other matters.

They have put off the ball, you know. That is a tragedy. My new gown is ready at last, the one of sea-blue silk with the silvered lace here – and she caressed her bosom – I was to have looked like Venus arising from the foam, Madame des Grieux said. And now nobody is to see me, isn't that a tragedy, Jem?

There'll be other balls.

Yes, but not before the spring, and one does starve of pleasure in these dreary months. I had thought to go skating, but the ice is all melted. What are we to do, Jem?

Then again she said:

Will he hang, do you think?

But he did not hang, not he, nor any of his fellows. Nor did they go to gaol or even come before a court. For the King loved his son and he loved Kit, and there had been executions enough. And so he pardoned the lot of them. They were none of them to suffer punishment for all assaults, woundings, crimes, misdemeanours, trespasses and forfeitures whatsoever committed alone or with any other person from 28 February to 14 March, whether the assaulted or wounded person shall die or not.

March the fourteenth, do you see that, Jem? They could have gone on murdering for another fortnight and not be punished for it. The King is very kind, isn't he, Jem?

Very kind, madam.

It is a fine thing this pardon, I shall put it in a gilt frame and hang it where my friends may see it, that they not forget how close my Kit came to hanging with a silken cord. Or would he have been executed like a traitor? I know so little of the law. Now will you show me your pardon, Jem?

I have none, madam.

No pardon? But Mr Savage and Mr Fenwick have pardons, and Mr Griffen too, I think. The gentlemen are to be forgiven along with the dukes.

My name has not been mentioned thus far.

Well then, I do earnestly hope there was some witness to your vomit. It would be a tragedy to me if you alone were to hang.

I am grateful for your solicitude.

Are you, Jem? How grateful?

And she smiled at me in a dark way that was near a scowl.

There was a ballad written upon the affair, some say by Mr Marvell, though the verses were too lumpish for his pen. I tried to keep the ballad from my lady, but one of the waiting-women brought her a copy and she read it out to me trippingly.

Listen to this, Jem.

> "Tis strange (but sure they thought not on't before)
> Three bastard dukes should come to undo one whore.'

Three? Is Somerset a bastard then? Not that I believe the tale about Kit, for his mother swore with her last breath she would show me the register.

> 'Then fell the Beadle by a ducal hand
> For daring to pronounce the saucy stand.'

Saucy stand? These are weak verses, Jem, very weak. But let us persevere.

> 'This silly fellow's death puts off the Ball
> And disappoints the Queen, poor little chuck
> I warrant 'twould have danced it like a Duck.'

Duck, for mercy's sake, he was short of a rhyme there. Still, it's true, the Queen was disappointed.

> 'Near t'other Path there stands an aged tree
> As fit as if 'twere made in the nonce for Three;
> Where that no ceremony may be lost,
> Each Duke for State may have a several Post.'

—Oh, he wants them all hanged, but only the dukes, not Mr Griffen and Mr Savage, and not you, Jem, for you were otherwise engaged, were you not?

Madam, enough of this, I pleaded.

Do you think so? There are but two more lines:

> 'What storms may rise out of so black a Cause
> If such turd-flies shall break through Cobweb Laws?'

Turd-flies is not kind. I don't think Kit resembles a turd-fly, do you, Jem? Or perhaps he is only a little like.

Kit himself never talked of the matter and continued his carouses as though no beadle had never crossed his path. But she liked to tease me. Some months later at a water pique-nique she said: You see that man over there.

The one in the black hat?

The same.

What of him?

He swears he saw you vomit in Whetstone Park – and then she laughed and went off.

Another time, I was going down a dark passage at New Hall when I met a young gentleman in a snuff-coloured coat who said in a gruff voice:

Surely you remember me?

No, ah that is, you have the advantage of me. I can't recall the exact occasion on which –

I saw you vomit in Whetstone Park – and with a laugh, my lady threw off her velvet beaver and shook out her long fair curls.

She was much given to masquerade and once with other ladies of the Court acted in a masque which greatly vexed her parents who were sober country folk and her mother wrote to rebuke her, though she was glad it was a woman acted the man's part with her and not some young man.

But though she had her giddy flights, she was much given also to melancholy – and to suspicion.

Why are you all whispering against me?

What? Nobody was whispering, my dear.

I heard whispering. I heard someone say, she is too stupid to understand.

No one would say such a thing. Jem, tell her nobody was uttering a word before she came in.

It's true, I swear, madam. I was reading the *Mercury*, and His Grace was polishing his new pistols. Perhaps it was the noise of His Grace's brushes.

Hah, you think I shall believe that? Too stupid indeed.

Madam, it is the truth.

Then she laughed as if it were she had been playing some prank on us, but I do not know what.

Don't look so solemn, she said. I'll not betray you.

What is there to betray?

I must write to my mother, she said thoughtfully, breaking off the former conversation as though it had never been.

She called for my company if she had none better, when Kit had gone off to the new Dutch wars in search of glory, though he heard not a shot fired, or when he was drilling his militia, for he was Lord-Lieutenant of two counties now, of Essex and Devon. 'Playing at his soldiers' his wife called it, for she thought little of his martial prowess. Then he must go to the House of Lords, and to the King's, for he was lately made a Gentleman of the Bedchamber and enjoyed a pension of £1,000 a year, though God knows how little he needed it.

Thus willy-nilly I became escort to Duchess Elizabeth, but not in the same sense as I had been to her mother-in-law. Elizabeth was very young and she wanted a guide to the sights of the town. So it was that I showed her the shipyards at Deptford, and the Tower of London and the new churches in the City that was yet all dust and clangour with the rebuilding after the Great Fire and many another palace and temple.

Jem, will you take me to New Bedlam?

It isn't a fitting place for ladies. Your husband would not forgive me if I caused you distress.

But the Duchess of Grafton has been there, and the Duchess of Portsmouth. They say the lunatics are greatly diverting.

They're not put there for our diversion.

Oh Jem, don't be so pompous. Besides, we may give them money for their lodging and I've heard the hospital is very fine.

So we went to the New Bethlehem Hospital on Moorfields, to call it by its proper name. And indeed it was a fair palace with a French spire and gable in the centre and long wings with a French pavilion at either end, not unlike the hospital that Wren also built at Chelsea, but Bedlam is more beautiful. As we came in, men upon a scaffold with ropes were bringing two great stone figures up to the top of the gate-piers. The statues were naked and couchant. One was in chains and snarled like a dog, the other bore an expression of sightless vacancy. They swung in the air above our heads like horrid phantasms in a nightmare.

Mania and Melancholy, said Matthew the porter, our *cicerone* in his blue gown and bearing a fine silver staff. They are carved by Mr Cibber, after the statues by Michael Angelo at Florence.

But isn't it cruel to show the sufferings of the Mad to the world?

You'll see them soon enough inside, madam. The governor is much pleased with the statues. May I also draw your attention to these ingenious figures here? See the boxes they carry. If you drop in a penny, it goes straight down into the pedestal. You see, they're in blue, same as me, that's our livery. They were made at the expense of Mr Foot, one of our governors.

As our coins went chink, chink down through the figures of the begging gypsies, I could see an unhealthy excitement had taken hold of Elizabeth. Her cheeks were flushed and her hands trembled, as she put a shilling into each of the poor-boxes.

We passed through these Penny Gates, as Matthew called them, into a large hall. On either side were long galleries from which we could hear a dim hubbub as of a crowd gathering with evil intent.

That room there is where the physician and the apothecary examine the patients when they come in and before they go out, though they must stand before the court first to see whether they are cured. Oh they're tigers that court, I've seen many a patient look as sane as you or me, butter wouldn't melt in their mouths, but give 'em ten minutes before the court and they are raving and gibbering and it's back to the lock-up and no appeal, I can tell you.

Elizabeth was scarcely listening but was already off out of the hall down the gallery. I followed her through the press of people who were standing in idle chatter, some eating and drinking, others smoking their pipes or playing at cards on little folding tables. We might have been in Covent Garden or Westminster Hall.

Which are the lunatics? Elizabeth whispered to Matthew.

Oh they are mostly in the cells, though some of the quieter ones have the liberty of the gallery.

What sport it must be to distinguish which is which. Jem, that sad-looking gentleman over there, is he a melancholiaque, do you think?

That, madam, is Dr Allen, he keeps a private madhouse at Finsbury, but he takes care of patients in Bedlam too. His methods are said to be very modern. The masculine patients are on this floor. We have separated the females on to the floor below that there may be no lewdness.

We stared through the iron grilles that pierced the high gallery every five yards. The cells were high too and airy like bare chapels in a cathedral, but instead of an altar in each there was a piteous creature upon a heap of straw, moaning or communing with himself in a ceaseless low babble. Some among them seemed unconscious of our presence but others stood up against the bars and bared their teeth at the idlers or held their hands out for alms and other gifts that were thrust at them.

Ha, I heard a sharp voice louder than the rest, there goes the Mad-Quack, that's him, Allen the torturer. You want bleeding or vomiting or purging, go to Finsbury, he'll suit you with his rusty lance.

There was a crowd gathered around the cell from which the voice came. And it was a minute or two before I could make my way through them to see the speaker who was still ranting.

I'm a gentleman, sir, and a middling scholar and something of a poet. The Quack tried to beat the poetry out of me. He beats the madmen at Finsbury, you know, birching's his Physick. You wouldn't think it to look at him. Hey Quack, where's your birch?

We looked for the sad-looking gentleman, but he had vanished in the throng.

Suddenly I came face to face with the man behind the bars and knew him instantly.

Mr Carcase, sir.

More people know Tom Fool than Tom Fool knows. You've heard me read my verses perhaps. They're to be published shortly, the first poems ever to be written at Bedlam. I advise you to subscribe for a rarity. I shall entitle them *Lucida Intervalla*.

Don't you remember me? Jeremiah Mount? We used to meet at the Leg.

You have the advantage of me, sir. The Duchess of Portsmouth was here last week and Mistress Gwyn. I upbraided them both on the grounds of their loose behaviour. As a minister of the Established Church I could do no other. The Quack will have me unfrocked. He had me committed here while I was about the Lord's work, bringing damnable Dissenters back to the true Church. I told Mistress Gwyn that the King should cleave to her, being a Protestant. The Quack has me locked up here claiming that I am no priest, but my flock are not deceived. As you see, they come and I absolve them. The Duke of Grafton looked into my cloister and asked me how I did and I wrote him a poem. Mr Stackhouse presented me with a periwig, and I wrote him a poem. No matter how small the gift – an orange, a sixpence, a bottle of ink – they all have a poem. Thus they have absolution and immortality together. Is that not a fair bargain?

Do you not remember . . . the matter of Pepys?

Pepys. He spat out the word. There is the author of all my misfortunes, he and the Quack. Yet it was the design of Providence that I was removed from the Navy Office to Bedlam, for I became free to do the Lord's work and reduce Dissenters to the Church. Hear my words, O Israel.

And in his high sour voice, he recited:

> *I'm a minister of God's most Holy Word:*
> *Have taken up the gown, laid down the sword.*
> *Him I must praise, who open'd hath my lips,*
> *Sent me from Navy to the Ark by Pepys.*
> *For the Duke's favour more than years thirteen.*
> *But I excluded, he high, fortunate;*
> *This Secretary I could never mate.*
> *But Clerke of th'Acts, if I'm a parson, then*
> *I shall prevail: the voice outdoes the pen.*

Some among the crowd snickered when they heard the verses, at which Carcase shouted, those who mock the Lord's word shall be cast into outer darkness.

Of course he's not a parson, Matthews murmured in my ear. They brought him here for breaking up a Dissenters' meeting. Six strong 'uns to hold him down, then he broke the windows of the coach, we put him in a cell with no glass, but nowadays he's harmless enough, except he still thinks he's a reverend.

As Matthews finished, Carcase crooked his finger at me to signal me to come up closer. I pressed my nose against the bars so that we were only two inches apart (his breath was foul and fishy).

I knew you at once, he whispered to me, I have to feign madness, this is the only place I'm safe from my enemies. But I'll be released soon in time for the great conflagration.

Conflagration?

Now we see through a glass, darkly, but then face to face. Come here tomorrow at the same time, when the people are gone, and I shall unfold more of the matter you spoke of.

While I had been conversing with Carcase, I had lost sight of the young Duchess and for some minutes could not find her again in the throng. She was handing apricots through the bars to an old man who could say nothing by way of thanks except to set his teeth chattering. He wore only a dirty white robe which fell from his shoulders as he stretched forward to receive the apricots and uncovered his filthy privates. He laughed and my lady laughed too, as though they had hatched the trick between them. I began to wish to be free of the place, but the Duchess insisted we must stay and talk with each of the lunatics in turns.

The next day being Sunday, there were no visitors but by appointment. The gallery was as quiet as a church aisle and as chilly though it was yet September. To my surprise Mr Carcase was not alone.

At the bars of his cell stood a tall gentleman in a long black coat edged with lace. His eyebrows and beard were black as night. As he turned to look at me, I perceived that he squinted so that he appeared to examine me with a magistrate's eye.

Colonel John Scott, sir, of Scotts Hall in the County of Kent, at your service.

Don't I know you? I burst out, for there was something profoundly familiar about the man, yet I could not recall having seen anyone like him.

I wish I could claim the pleasure of your acquaintance. Perhaps we met in the Americas. Are you acquainted with Long Island?

Not at all.

Or New York perhaps. I have considerable property in both places.

I was never there in my life.

Indeed I've so much property there, continued the Colonel, paying me little heed, that I lately found it convenient to sell two or three expanses to the Governor of Barbados. I removed to the West Indies to lead one of our regiments against the French, you may have heard some mention of the action. That was before I returned to my native land to assist Lord Sandwich's Committee on the Plantations with informations on conditions in America. There are so few white men who are conversant with the Indian tongue. I count Sunk Squaw as a particular friend, a remarkable woman, she is queen of the Indians of Long Island. Have you ever had a Indian woman?

Ah no.

There is no experience like it. I don't say they are clean, but they are perfectly formed for the arts of love. They sing, you know.

Sing?

As they fuck. Sounds much like a lullaby. I speak of the Indians of Long Island. In the Carolinas they are silent. You're a friend of Mr Carcase?

We have had dealings in the past.

And shall have again. For we'll soon have you sprung from this trap, sir. But not before we are ready. All our bells must chime together.

Bells?

I cannot say more at the moment. All depends on the great bell that must be tolled. Here, sir, I've brought you some victuals.

The Colonel thrust a bag of oranges and some bread and cheese through the bars. Carcase took them and placed them carefully under a blanket. He looked pale this morning, but wide awake. He might have been an attentive clerk who hoped to win favour with his master. One could scarce imagine him ranting or raving as he had the day before. Only his yellow eyes flickered to and fro between us.

He knows S.P., Carcase said in a discreet whisper.

Do you, sir? Then you know a damnable villain who has defrauded the Navy. But I will tell you what is worse, sir . . .

Colonel Scott leant very close to me. He smelled of some exquisite fragrance, bergamot or jessamine.

Then very quietly: Popery, sir, that's what's worse. That's what will bring the whole of England tumbling down.

Pepys a p—?

Hush, sir. But you may depend upon it, he's the worst sort, sly, deceitful and, I scarcely need say, in the pay of a foreign power.

But –

You doubt me, sir. You are wrong to doubt me. I shall overwhelm you if you doubt me.

We were clerks together in O.C.'s time.

Then you know, sir – or ought to know (here he withdrew from me and looked at me sidelong with his squinting eye, as though I might be keeping information from him) that his late wife was a Papist, his musician – one Morelli – is a Jesuit to whom he makes confession, his house is a veritable devil's cauldron of altars and crucifixes and rosaries and incense –

Of course, I said. Jack Scott. Bare-arse Jack.

What? he said. What?

You must remember. We played together, down by the stream, and you pushed me in as your mother came out of the mill with the parson. Is she still alive, your mother?

And you are – ?

Jemmy Mount from Churn.

Ah yes, he said, discommoded, a faint recollection does come back to me. How far our paths have branched.

We were so poor.

It is true that my family's fortunes were temporarily eclipsed. Scotts Hall had not then –

Your cottage was even smaller than ours.

A cousin –

You remember Emm, I'm sure.

Emm, Emm? I was in love with all the girls. What rascals we were, said the Colonel managing a laugh.

You must remember her.

Certainly I do, he said. Beautiful girl, very fair.

She was brown as a berry but I did not say so, for my temper was hot.

Far-off days, the Colonel said, let us hear no more of them. My mother would be delighted to entertain you on her estate.

In Kent?

In Long Island, the Colonel said in a decided manner.

And where do you live yourself?

Scotts Hall is let, temporarily, while I've been travelling. I was compelled to come to London at short notice, on this great matter, and I found lodgings in haste, above the Dog and Dripping Pan in Drury Lane. They are modest enough, but there is no harm in that. When one is about business of state, *Incognito* must be one's watchword. I trust you will visit me there, but we must be sharp about it, for the great bell is to toll very soon. Mr Carcase, sir, I must take my leave of you. Good-day, good-day.

And the Colonel swung upon his heel, the silver lace of his coat-tails flashing like the wings of a pigeon disturbed from its roost. I wondered what caused this haste and then perceived a group of strollers come into the gallery. He must have heard their voices and taken fright, though I could not see why, for what did it matter who might be visiting a poor lunatic?

Two days later I called at the Dog and Dripping Pan which was a wretched tavern that I had never noticed before though I had walked along the street a hundred times.

I went in to inquire after the Colonel's lodgings when I saw the man himself taking his ease at the foot of the stairs in conversation with a young woman. While they talked, he was painting his eyebrows and beard with a little black brush.

Hail, friend, one must always be prepared, the Colonel said, seeing my eyes light upon the paintbrush. Greatness lies in detail, as the philosopher said. I beg your pardon, Mrs P., have you met my childhood friend Jem –? I am afraid I forget your surname. We met through a common acquaintance, the Reverend Dr Carcase. Jem, may I present you to my delectable landlady, Mrs Paulett. Well, have not matters sped forward since we met but a couple of days ago?

What matters?

You haven't heard? The terrible plot is uncovered. The worthy Mr Oates, a patriot if ever there was one, has gone to the King and told all.

All what?

I would have told you at our last meeting but the place was not private. How the Jesuits plotted to burn London and land an army from France, then kill the King and put his brother on the throne and if he would not do it kill him too. The Queen's physician was to slip a potion in the King's drink, or if he lacked the opportunity, Coniers the Jesuit stood ready to murder the King in the park, run him through with his knife a foot long which he has had consecrated for the purpose, some say by the Pope himself.

But surely this is all very great nonsense, I said, the King can't believe a word of it.

Jem, you're an old friend and therefore I offer you my most solemn counsel. If anyone but me hears you talk in that fashion, they will tear you apart like a pack of dogs. Mrs P., you heard not a word of what my friend said, did you? Mr Oates has a dozen Jesuits in Newgate already, more are to be arrested today. The Duchess of York's secretary is arrested too and his letters seized. There are riots everywhere. The fury of a righteous people is a terrible thing.

He tucked his paintbrush into a little walnut box and put up a mirror on the back of the box to admire his whiskers.

Mrs Paulett took advantage of this to ask whether she might have the five shillings that was outstanding by way of rent.

Jem, would you oblige me by letting Mrs P. have a sovereign? My purse is in my other coat upstairs?

As though in a trance, I handed Mrs Paulett the coin.

You're a good fellow. You and I must put our heads together and prepare our evidence.

What evidence?

Mrs Paulett, might I with the greatest respect beg you to leave us, for we have private business to conclude?

Why don't you go upstairs then? Mrs Paulett said. She seemed a tart shrew who was immune to the Colonel's charms.

Dear lady, *rem acu tetigisti*, as always. The Colonel smiled at her and led me upstairs.

Now then, he said to me, as we were scarce in the little low chamber that was strewn with empty bottles and the Colonel's fine clothes. This time we shall have him. No, no, I will not mention his name but you know of whom I speak. Mr Carcase has told me of the doughty work you did on the last occasion but alas in vain, for he was too quick for you. But this time, there will be such a hue and cry across the nation that he will be swept up in it as a piece of driftwood is shattered on a spring tide.

But what has he done?

Done, sir, what hasn't he done? Corruption, sir, and piracy and popery and treachery. He has stolen from the Navy and stuffed her ships with Catholics, and he has been treating with the French.

Treating *with the French*?

You don't believe me, sir? I have the evidence here, maps, the Navy's own secret maps with the dispositions of our ships upon them which Mr Pepys's associate Sir Anthony Deane gave Monsieur Pellissary, the late Treasurer of the French Navy. I have a man who will swear he saw it with his own eyes through a window.

I looked at the charts. They had been sewn with silk fringes and on them, in ink, some hand had written the positions of our men-o'-war, viz.: *Quaker* (60 tons), *Firecat* (2nd-rater), etc., etc. But I knew the maps at once.

Why these are my charts that I sold to sea-captains. Can the Navy be using them still? And these fringes . . .

The Colonel looked displeased.

Sir Anthony wanted forty thousand pounds for the plans, he said. If the French had 'em, they could sail in any day they chose and burn the English Fleet without losing a man. It was the basest piece of treachery I ever heard of.

Well, Colonel, I said, I must confess I find this hard to believe. Sir Anthony is the King's favourite shipwright and a true man, he would not—

Didn't he build two yachts for the French king?

Yes, it is true, Louis had seen how fine was the yacht our King travelled in—

If I was to tell you that I saw him with my own eyes trafficking with Monsieur Pellissary—

But you spoke of another witness, you didn't say it was you yourself—

Sir, these are very secret matters, I may not say all that I know, even to a trusted confidant such as yourself. He stroked his whiskers again. I wondered whether the paint would run in the rain. I had myself inked over faded figures in the old Dutch maps where one could not see whether the depth might be three fathoms or nine and the plate-maker had copied my guesses: any French fleet which sailed by such charts might not sail very far.

But those charts— I began . . .

Sir, we shall speak no more of it. We must stay mum until the great bell tolls.

This phrase stuck in my mind. It seemed apt to the times. For after the first uproar and the arrest of the Jesuits, there was a week in which the world was expectant but no event of note occurred, so that it was like the pause that came after some great clock has tolled the three-quarters but before it begins to tell the hour.

The King had gone to Newmarket. Although he seemed an idle man, yet he knew when to let things lie and could judge the *tempo* of affairs, just as his jockey Fletcher was famous for letting his horse run easy until the last furlong of the race and then would steal through to win by a short head.

Kit must go too and I with Kit. To be near the King was to show one's loyalty and to be safe from accusation. For that reason, I was not astonished to see Mr Pepys come down to join the Court at Newmarket, but it turned out the King had sent for him, fearing that he might have need of his counsel if Parliament should renew its broadside against his conduct of the Navy.

Pepys looked mournful and he was tetchy. What are *you* doing here? was his only greeting. I answered that I had as good a right to be there as he.

The King sent for me, Pepys said, to which there was no answer, and he passed on his way into the King's study, affecting to take no notice of the ladies playing ombre in the small saloon, although they offered a cornucopia of delights.

But we all had the fidgets and would roam restless from room to room, as though someone in the next room might explain what we were there for. Men would go out into the rain for no purpose except to hear if there were any news from London.

And then the news came. At first, we did not grasp its meaning.

Sir Edmund Berry Godfrey, magistrate, found dead in a ditch at the foot of Primrose Hill, with his own sword run through him, but no blood on the sword or the body, yet there were bruises on his breast and his neck.

Who had murdered him? There could be but one answer: the Jesuits. Terrified, the Catholics sought to show that Sir Edmund must have committed suicide.

But how could he get to a ditch in Primrose Hill without a spot of dirt on his polished shoes? And how could he have run a sword through himself after he was dead, for it had passed through his body as dry as a butcher's knife through a well-hung carcase which showed the injury to be posthumous. Those cruel bruises proved that the Jesuits had strangled him first and then run him through with his own sword to counterfeit suicide. O the villainy of it!

On my return to London, I found a note from the Colonel:

The great bell has tolled.

The upstairs room at the Dog and Dripping Pan was swept clean. Where once there had been high disorder, now not so much as a stocking of the Colonel's was to be seen. He sat on a stool in the middle of the room that was as bare as though the bailiff had but lately called.

When I spoke of this transformation, he seemed distracted.

I've been on my travels. I daren't leave traces of my whereabouts. There are enemies everywhere. If we don't strike first, they'll have us. Tonight, I must remove again to collect more evidence.

Evidence of . . .

He thought he was too clever for us. I will admit it was a master stroke, to place himself in the one spot in the kingdom where nobody can deny he was, at the King's side. But we'll have him yet.

If you mean Pepys, I saw him at Newmarket.

A master butcher does not do all his own slaughtering. *We know the butcher's boy.*

The Colonel stroked his whiskers which had gone grey since our last meeting. Indeed, he was altogether dishevelled and moth-eaten.

But why would Pepys want to kill Sir Edmund?

Why would— the Colonel squinted at me with astonishment as though at a man with three heads. Are you an imbecile, sir? Have I the honour to be addressing a three-year-old child? Pepys and Godfrey had been acquainted, well acquainted and in the course of their acquaintance Godfrey had learnt Pepys's secrets – his popery, his dealings with the French, his conspiracy with the Jesuits – and as an honest Englishman, and a magistrate, don't forget he was a magistrate, he was about to carry this information to Mr Oates who would make it public in the proper quarters, but being a good Christian, O fatal innocence, he thought it right to advise Pepys of his intentions. In so doing, he signed his own death warrant.

The Colonel slapped the table as though slapping such a warrant down upon it. Then he paused, struck by another thought.

Do you think we might go downstairs for a glass or two? I have been riding all night on State service and my throat is dry.

In the Dog and Dripping Pan, he told me of his adventures.

I had command of a regiment in Holland, you know. De Witt swore I was the finest commander there. If I had been present at Texel, the outcome would have been very different, though it would have been obnoxious to me to defeat my own countrymen, however badly they may have treated me. But it was not to be. My wife, that is, my Dutch wife, for my American wife was at my estate on Long Island, took it ill that so many women should run after me. I do not account myself a *Beau Garçon*, but there is a certain good humour about me. I never come into the coffee-house if there are a hundred other men in the room but the women will come and flock about me to hear me discourse. I think I shall marry Lady Vane in the end, for she will settle three thousand pounds a year on me and I may marry myself into Parliament. The people of England like a man who has seen something of the world. Did I tell you I killed a man in St Kitts? They took me to the gallows and I had the rope round my neck while I was persuading them that the man, a sugar-planter by whom I was employed, was a rogue and should have been on the gallows in my stead. So instead of hanging me they gave me command of a company against the French.

Together we disposed of glass after glass, and the Colonel's exploits grew more remarkable yet. Because I did not wish to seem a dismal simpleton I told him something of my own past, how I had made my fortune in Cromwell's service, how I had won the love of the Duchess of Albemarle and become the trusted counsellor of Honest George Monck and fought side by side with him at the Battle of the Medway – of which action my body still bore the marks, and of the place I now held among the young rakes and bloods of the town, how I saved the young dukes from the gallows after they had run the beadle through and so earned their gratitude. And I could see that I had made some impression upon him.

We're navigators, sir, on the sea of life. We shall help one another into safe harbour yet. The butcher's boy will save our bacon. Hush, not another word.

He put his finger to his whiskers as I tried to ask him who this mysterious butcher's boy might be.

But I was to know soon enough. For no more than a week later one Samuel Atkins, clerk to Pepys, was arrested and taken before the Committee for Examining the Plot, which was in truth a committee for destroying Pepys and, through Pepys, the Duke of York that was now his sole patron, for Sandwich (*olim* Mountagu) had perished in the last Dutch war.

It is a first-rater of a committee, the Colonel said, the Duke of Buckingham is a member and Lord Shaftesbury and many another great gentleman that have the welfare of this realm at heart (*anglice*: a crew of libertines, republicans, sodomites and other riff-raff).

I will ask you a favour, Jem, he said. I dare not attend upon this Committee myself, my person is reserved for great business and I must come fresh to it so that they will know my testimony comes from a sincere heart and has not been prompted or confected by artful plotters. Will you keep watch for me and let me know what passes?

I will, I said, not quite knowing why I said so.

Thus it was that I saw Samuel Atkins, a fresh-faced youth, brought in from Newgate and taken before the Committee.

Did you ever say that there was no kindness, or a want of friendship I think it was, between Mr Pepys your master and Sir Edmund Berry Godfrey? (This was Lord Shaftesbury, a little man with a canting whining voice like a dog that will be let out.)

No, my lord.

I think you did. We have your namesake Captain Atkins who will swear that you told him Sir E. Godfrey had very much injured your master, Mr Secretary Pepys, and would ruin him if he lived.

I said no such thing, my lord.

Well then, let us hear it from the horse's mouth. Bring in Captain Atkins.

And they brought in a big fellow with a face that was well weathered, by liquor as well as by storms at sea, I fancied. This Captain Atkins then testified as he was meant to, though his manner was somewhat rehearsed.

Did you not say those words, Mr Atkins?

No, my lord, not in my life, not one word like it.

You know, said the Captain to his namesake, the discourse was between us in your large room by the windows.

Captain Atkins, sir, the boy answered, God, your conscience and I know it is notoriously untrue. We have not met since last summer, when you came to borrow half-a-crown of me.

Come, Mr Samuel Atkins, said Lord Shaftesbury in his most wheedling manner, you are an ingenious hopeful young man. Captain Atkins has sworn this positively against you, he bears you no malice, besides, to tell you truth, I don't think him to have wit enough to invent such a lie.

No, my lord, I said no such thing.

What, we admit Captain Atkins to be a man that has loved wine and women, but would you have us think him a liar?

Well, sir, I would not have spoken a word of the matter, were things otherwise, but you will recall that it was two years ago that Captain Atkins was captured by Algerine Corsairs and let himself be towed into Algiers by them that he might save the gold he had on board, which he ought not to have had aboard a man-of-war, and he lost his command.

There was a silence, very heavy, and Lord Shaftesbury was greatly out of countenance.

Then they began to inquire of the religion of young Mr Atkins, and he swore that he was a stout Protestant and was due to receive the Sacrament on Sunday.

Foiled again, his accusers returned to the principal accusation.

Well, Samuel Atkins, said the Duke of Buckingham flatteringly, I never saw you before, but I'd swear you are an ingenious man. I see the working of your brain. Pray tell us what you know of this matter. You may be sure that you will come to no harm so long as you keep nothing back, and otherwise a great deal of harm must attend you.

My lord, said Atkins – and my heart leapt to hear him – telling a lie will do me a great deal of harm.

They could not shake him, however hard they talked of honour and truth and religion – of which their hearts knew nothing. And as Bucks pressed him on matters of conscience, I recalled that bawdy sermon he had preached to the King and wondered how so great a canting rogue should be esteemed the first gentleman of Europe.

They came at him again a week later. Same questions put, same answer given:

My lord, I avow to you Mr Pepys never in his life committed any secret to me of any kind, nor ever mentioned to me upon any occasion one word about Sir Edmund Berry Godfrey. And this you'd believe if you knew how totteringly I stand in his opinion, having been turned away from him, and am this minute in his very ill apprehension.

Why, said the Bishop of London (who was an ill-natured fanatic), are you given to drink and debauchery?

And though the Bishop thought it a great thing to throw discredit upon the character of Samuel Atkins, yet, curious to relate, in that direction lay Atkins's salvation. For he did have a secret, but it had nothing to do with popery or treachery or the poor murdered magistrate.

Bucks and Shaftesbury and the rest had him committed back to Newgate to await trial, that is, to give them time to assemble more false witnesses against him to bolster the ungallant captain. There was a swindler named Bedlow who told the House of Lords that the murder had been committed in Somerset House by a gang of desperadoes hired by Jesuits and that Atkins had been seen there later at nine o'clock on the Monday standing over the corpse by the light of a lantern – or so he was meant to swear, but all he would say was that he had been told the man he had seen was called Atkins and he did look very like the prisoner.

And still Atkins refused to bend, and still the great lords pressed him, promising, wheedling, threatening. But all the while, his master Mr Pepys was bustling to and fro to find evidence that might save his clerk and himself. This delay while the great lords were bribing their witnesses gave Atkins's friends a breathing-space.

And into that space stepped another Navy man, one Captain Vittles who had command of the yacht *Katherine* then lying off Greenwich. The Bishop swore him, and then he told his tale:

It was four o'clock on the Monday, I mean the Monday after that poor gentleman was murdered. I had come up to London to take my orders from Mr Pepys, but finding him to be away at Newmarket (a sigh from some great lord here), I fell into discourse with Mr Atkins who told me that he had pledged himself for the afternoon to two young gentlewomen. Might he bring them to see the yacht, he said. Yes, I said, by all means. So I went back to Greenwich, cleaned the ship that it might be fit for inspection and waited till half past four when Mr Atkins came with his friends. Well, we drank some wine, and the wine being good and just come from beyond seas, we drank some more. It was past seven o'clock when I put them into the ship's wherry with a dutch cheese and half a dozen bottles of wine. I fear they were very much fuddled. But the tide was flowing too strong for my seamen to make London Bridge, and so they set them down by the iron gates at Billingsgate at half past eleven.

Half past eleven?

Yes, sir.

They could not be mistaken as to the time?

No, sir, nor as to their condition, for they were much in drink and Mr Atkins was unable to stand, being asleep.

Thus two hours after Bedlow claimed to have seen Samuel Atkins by the light of a lantern standing over the corpse, the said Atkins was dead drunk in a wherry rowed by four seamen, and thereafter one of the young gentlewomen, Sarah Williams, would swear that she could prove that Mr Atkins had spent the rest of the night in his own bed, for she had been lying next to him.

It was this circumstance that he dared not confide to his particular master, though, Lord knows, his master had been in the same pickle more than once when he was younger.

None the less they sent him for trial, hoping that Captain Vittles would break, but Vittles was stout as English oak, and Scroggs the Lord Chief Justice was no flincher from the glass and acknowledged the Captain as his fellow. And the jury found him Not Guilty, and Atkins knelt down and called out, not once but three times, 'God bless the King and this honourable Bench.' He was weeping as he cried out.

I must confess that tears came to my eyes too, when I saw it, tears of joy that virtue could yet triumph in this naughty world and that the whining hypocrites had been beaten. And that joy diminished my hatred for Pepys, for the loyalty that young Atkins bore him could not but reflect upon his own character, as the sun's light will brighten the darkest corner. I had rejoiced in the acquittal of one Samuel, could I rejoice in the conviction of another?

Well, this is a damnable nuisance, the Colonel said. Curse that lying drunken Captain. Never trust a Navy man, Jem. There is nothing for it, we have no recourse but to try the route direct.

Yet the disaster that now fell upon Pepys was not of the Colonel's own making. It was a grand calamity that went by the name of a general election. The people were inflamed with terror of popery. There was no room in their noddles for any other thought. Everywhere but in the Crown's own boroughs the King's men went down, and the republican fanatics were in. The King tried to keep his friends, but Parliament would not have it, and he had to dismiss them and let in the mutineers. Within a fortnight, Pepys was out of his place. Within another month, he was brought before a committee of the House of Commons charged with Piracy, Popery and Treachery.

Now's your moment, Jem, the Colonel said.

How so?

I have the information here. All you need say is how, looking through the window, you saw Sir Anthony Deane in conversation with Monsieur Pellissary and how you then saw him give the said Monsieur a packet of plans. Deane and thereby Pepys will be sunk for ever and we shall make our fortunes.

But you said you had another witness who would swear to all that.

Did I? You must have misheard me. You would swear much better to it. You are an old comrade of Pepys's. It would come well from you.

But it isn't true.

But it is, Jem. Haven't I told you the story a dozen times?

I was not by, I have seen nothing of the sort.

Two witnesses are better than one Jem. Corroborate, corroborate. That is the art in legal matters.

I know nothing of the business. And I will say nothing.

Sleep on it, Jem, you would not wish to miss your part in Pepys's downfall. The business will appear in a different light after a good night's sleep.

But all that night I lay awake and all I saw was the fresh young face of the other Samuel, and it seemed to me a vision of goodness that was sent to speak to me, just as the Lord spoke to Samuel in the Bible and he said Here am I.

On the morrow, I went to the Dog and Dripping Pan and said to the Colonel straight out:

I cannot do it. Even to destroy Pepys, I will not perjure.

What is perjury? the Colonel said, a lawyer's term, a thing of no account. But don't fret, Jem, you can't catch a fish without spreading the ground-bait. I shall speak to Elephant Smith.

Elephant Smith?

The first man in the kingdom for broadsides, squibs and libels and lampoons. He has a marvellous delicate touch. No man can recover his reputation, once the Elephant has trodden on him.

But as it turned out, the matter came to the House before Elephant Smith had published his notorious libel upon Mr Pepys and Will Hewer his clerk (on whom Mrs Pepys had doted to my displeasure). And Mr Carcase? He had been so gladdened by his release that he had not drawn a sober breath since and, according to the Colonel, lay in a brothel across the river in a species of delirium, so that he could not be moved, still less come before the Bar to discourse of tickets and treachery.

Thus when Pepys was arraigned before the mob of republicans and Green Ribbon men, there was but one witness principal, viz. Colonel John Scott. He looked fine in his silver lace but for his squint. He might have been one of the King's ministers. When he met an acquaintance whom he had known in Paris, a seal-graver named Browne, he hallooed him with a 'Welcome friend' and begged him to do his King and country a service by testifying how, in the autumn of 1675, looking through a window, he had seen Sir Anthony Deane give Monsieur Pellissary, etc., etc.

I can't, for the life of me, sir, said the poor bewildered man, for I saw no such thing.

Well, it is all true as light shines, said the Colonel and swaggered on to tell the House of Commons the self-same story with himself as the witness of it. Then in addition he told of the interview he had then had with Monsieur Pellissary who had showed him the papers Sir Anthony had brought, each signed by Mr Pepys, for which he was asking £40,000 and if the King of France had 'em, he could burn the English fleet entire as it lay at anchor. Was there ever treachery like it?

The House gasped, the House gaped and gabbled. They had heard of Sir Anthony's piracy, how he had diverted the sloop *Hunter* to his own use and furnished it out of government stores together with Pepys's brother-in-law Mr St Michel and caused her to prey on English shipping. And now they heard of Pepys's popery, how he had filled the Navy with the Duke of York's Catholic nominees and how his butler James swore he kept a tame Jesuit named Morelli, with whom he would whine out masses in the Romish manner. But it was the Colonel's evidence that was the clencher.

Pepys rose and did his best. It was strange that no word of these charges had been spoken before him. As an Englishman and a member of the Commons he should have been acquainted with the charges beforehand. He had nothing to do with the business of the *Hunter*. Morelli was a harmless musician whose only fault was to catch the servant James in bed with his housekeeper, for which James was turned away. As for Colonel Scott, he had never met him, though he had had occasion to attempt his arrest at Gravesend under another name, and later to present the House with papers which showed him to be guilty of the same crimes with which he himself was charged.

But it was all in vain. They mocked him without mercy. Some friend of Colonel Scott's got up to say:

You are unfortunate, are you not, Mr Pepys?

Unfortunate to be here, I am indeed, sir.

No I meant unfortunate in your servants: one accused to be in the Plot; your best maid found in bed with your butler; another accused to be a Jesuit. Very unfortunate.

It is no crime to be unfortunate, sir.

But then a flock of members – Harbord, Sacheverell and their ilk – got up, rehearsed to say that it was indeed a crime and one that had come to light only through the patriotism of Colonel John Scott, who was the finest man in all England for a West India voyage and a man of honour and sagacity.

Moved, that Mr Pepys and Sir A. Deane be taken into the custody of the Sergeant-at-Arms. Carried.

Then, two days later, Moved that the said Mr Pepys and the said Sir Anthony Deane be committed to the Tower. Carried.

There were bonfires lit beneath the windows of the Green Ribbon Club, and republicans throughout the length of England drank to the confusion of Pepys, Plot, Popery, Piracy.

But as the gates of that dreadful place clanged shut behind Pepys and his faithful friend, there was no bonfire in my heart. I had not testified myself, yet I had not spoken against the Colonel's false testimony. I had wanted Pepys disgraced, but it should have been by fair means, not by foul machinations.

So it is, I dare say, that what we thought we most wanted in life reaches us by the back way if at all and we do not welcome its arrival, for it comes tainted by the times. I cannot say that the late proceedings had brought to me a fondness for Pepys himself. In defending himself, he was an irksome, arrogant little fellow who must always be in the right of everything. Yet he had kept the love of young Samuel Atkins, though he had treated him severely. Pepys had abused his office, that was true, but he was zealous in his attendance to duty and I could not swear that he was greatly more corrupt than the rest of us.

It was his zealousness that saved him now. From his chamber behind those frowning battlements he sent out agents all over the kingdom and to France and Holland to bring witnesses who might shake the Colonel's testimony. Many of these witnesses were papists who would not be credited in an English court, some were too old to travel and their written depositions would be of small account. But little by little cracks began to appear in the smooth walls of Pepys's prison.

I was leaving the Duke's house on a fine June morning when a beggar tugged at my arm.

A word in your ear, sir, a private word.

He was a filthy fellow, in soiled rags and a large black hat, doubtless filched from some gent he had robbed.

Why should I speak to you?

Pepys, the beggar whistled through his broken teeth, it is of Pepys I must speak.

I let the man lead me round the corner to a private spot behind the porter's lodge.

What is it then?

See here, Jem, said the Colonel unbending to his full height and shaking his hair free of the black hat. This fellow Pepys is beginning to vex me.

How so?

He has put spies on my track in half the countries of Europe. My every movement is followed and recorded. He even has a man in New York compiling my history.

You must expect that he will defend himself.

I have been discoursing with the Attorney-General who is a first-rater and an intimate of mine. He is of the opinion that we cannot hang Pepys on my evidence alone.

Hang?

I spoke metaphorically, the Colonel said. You remember, I told you – corroborate, corroborate.

And?

You're the key, Jem. You're the one man who can sink him. You speak as the trusted counsellor to the present Duke of Albemarle and to his father who saved the nation. You speak also as an ancient colleague of Pepys's, one who has witnessed his career of crime and misdemeanour at close hand. The Attorney-General told me that he had Lord Shaftesbury's authority to say that certain high places in the Navy Office must be filled as a result of these proceedings and that he would know where to look to fill them.

No.

You don't believe me. Perhaps you'd prefer to converse with Mr Attorney directly?

No.

You mean –

I shall not, cannot and will not do as you ask. Here's sixpence for your pains.

This last gesture was not solely to humiliate the Colonel, but was brought on by my seeing Kit stump across the court with his greyhound Patch which he was to course at Barnes that afternoon. Quick as lightning, the Colonel was crouched back into the shape of a hoop and thanking me for my sixpence as he hobbled off into the street.

That was the last I was ever to see of the Colonel, for though he came and went, he could no longer stay openly in London, for Pepys's witnesses began to arrive in clouds like flies hatching in May. Within a month, Pepys was out of the Tower, and removed to the Marshalsea. Within another month, he was out on bail and free to pursue the Colonel which he did without mercy until the whole case melted into thin air and when he and Deane came before the Lord Chief Justice, that cheerful old tosspot Scroggs, and Scroggs asked the Attorney-General what he had to say against the prisoners' motion for a discharge, the Attorney answered 'Nothing' – and they were free.

For all that, Pepys had lost his place and lived quietly in retirement, but his downfall gave me small pleasure. Indeed, I was weary of life. All my fond hopes had shrivelled into husks. Kit grew fat and greedy for office. Because he was a stout Protestant he became a great man in the kingdom, the people being so distracted and fearful that all they wished to know of a minister or a magnifico was that he was of the true religion, caring little whether he be imbecile, of which the prime example was Kit being made Chancellor of the University of Cambridge, when never in my life had I seen him read a book through. But Monmouth who had the place before him was put out of it because the King (though fond of him) thought he had grown too big for his boots.

Which he had, for when he came back to England he struck the baton sinister from his arms, putting it about that the King had secretly married his mother (a poor whore from Haverfordwest) and went down to Somerset where I believe he touched for the King's Evil, claiming to be the Prince of Wales.

So the King dismissed him from all his posts and made Kit Captain of the Life Guards in his stead, and so the two old friends fell out and nearly came to a duel, when Monmouth said the guards did not march as well as when he had had command of them.

Yet though Kit was cock of the dunghill, he was not a happy man, for it was then that the first dread whisper began to attach itself to his name, viz. DEBT. Even a year before, I would not have believed it. He had rich estates in half the counties of England, he had a place at Court and vessels upon the high seas. When he lost a thousand or two playing at basset at Madame Mazarin's, it was as though you or I were to drop twopence in the street. He entertained all the great potentates from overseas: the Prince of Orange, the Muscovite Ambassador who was dirty and the Ambassador from Morocco, a great gentleman though barelegged who gave the King two lions and thirty ostriches, and who much enjoyed the Bear Garden and the horse-racing at Newmarket where he raced his Barbary steeds and borrowed money from Kit which he did not pay back. But all the time the money was leaking away.

Then came the bitter reckoning. Albemarle House was to be sold and we returned to his old childhood lodging at the Cockpit. It was a mournful homecoming.

In his despair, he listened to the counsels of his secretary Arthur Farwell, a giddy gent, who had married his cousin Mary Monck (a miserable sallow creature whom my lady could not abide). Farwell had always half a dozen schemes bubbling in his mind's cauldron, most of them harebrained. His latest was to present to Kit one Captain William Phipps from the New England plantations who told him of a Spanish galleon laden with gold and silver for the King of Spain which had been wrecked off the shores of Hispaniola, a year before the King came back (I mean King Charles). Many a ship had been sent to search for the gold and silver, from France and England and Spain, but none had found it. But now Kit must be taken in by this crazy mariner from the Americas, persuade the King to lend him the frigate *Algier Rose*, eighteen guns and ninety-five seamen, and pay half the costs himself at a time when he needed every penny to maintain his estate. The expedition failed, to the amazement of none and the delight of Kit's enemies, and he was left worse off than before.

But Kit had contracted the gold fever and whenever a rumour of a wrecked galleon reached the Lords of Trade and Plantations, his ears pricked fastest, though we all told him it was but foolishness.

Worst of all was the plight of his wife. How thin and distracted she had grown, how wearisome her complaints against her husband and his cousin Mary Farwell.

Where is he?

Gone to Wapping, madam, there was a great fire, and he's gone with the Lord Mayor to direct the water engines.

A pretty story, did he think of that himself? No, he is too stupid. You invented it, Jem, you're his artificer.

No, madam, I did not. You will read of it tomorrow in the *Gazette*.

He will pay the *Gazette* to say he was a hero, and saved a dozen burning babies.

No madam, I swear he –

Why can nobody see how unwell I am? I have such an ague, Jem, but Dr Barwick says there is nothing wrong with me.

Dr Barwick is a learned doctor.

Dr Barwick is a quack. I'm not a fool Jem, I know he has been sent here to guard me because my husband thinks I am mad. Besides, he knows nothing of women.

Who does, madam? I mean, what man?

You do, Jem. I think you do. You look much like the King, has anyone ever said so? The King knows women though he is foolish with them, but he will die soon.

I hope not, madam.

But he will, you know, I am sure of it. Please place your hand there – and she undid the buttons at the front of her dress and took my hand and thrust it in upon her slender belly.

Madam, I –

Do not madam me, there now, can you feel my barrenness? Perhaps you can cure me, Jem, perhaps you are a wizard.

And she laughed her high laugh like a magpie's chuckle.

Would you like to call me Eliza? You called his mother Nan, didn't you?

I –

You did, I heard you call to her so when she was dying, and then I knew why you were so sad.

Madam – She still held my hand against her naked skin which was warm and trembled to my touch.

I will not let you go until you call me Eliza.

Very well – Eliza.

Now I shall not let you go because we are friends, and she laughed again and held my hand more tightly against her.

Please, I said, I don't think this is right.

Many things are not right, Jem. It's not right that I should be cooped up here with Dr Barwick and that horrid Farwell. It's not right that my husband should cut my income so that I have barely a thousand pounds a year to feed on and dress myself and my women. It's not right that my mother should reproach me with being undutiful. Nothing is right, so one more wrong will do no hurt, don't you agree?

Eliza – I managed to get out the word, though it came hard to me – I am . . .

A servant? Then you should be willing to serve me.

No, I was about to say that I'm so much older than you.

Well, you were so much younger than his mother. It is a pleasant fancy, is it not, to make an echo in the next generation.

It's only a fancy, madam.

Eliza.

Eliza, I can't do what you ask.

What I ask? You don't know what I ask. Did you think I meant – well, upon my honour, I was never so insulted. And she gave me a basilisk glare, tearing my hand out of the opening in her dress.

I am sorry for –

Sorry? I should think so. I have a mind to tell my husband of your indecent conduct. No, don't look so frighted, Jem. I'm mad, he won't believe me.

Madam, I would rather you –

Rather I did not tell my husband? Then I shall not. I shall be generous, for I have a generous nature. That is why people say I am mad.

Yet she was not generous even before she was mad. She was sly and suspicious and miserly also. At night she would roam the kitchens and store-rooms, fancying she heard some poor wretch stealing bread or cheese. As to her own person, she was extravagant, and seldom wore a gown more than once, claiming that it was so old and dirty that people would think her a scarecrow.

Dr Barwick who was a good enough man but ponderous was much concerned that she might do herself an injury if she was not watched. I was more concerned about the injury she might do me.

The Duke for his part wished to see her as little as possible and would use the Cockpit as one might use a lodging house to sleep and change his clothes. She became fretful in his company, would say what was most likely to displease him even when she intended to please, but she knew that the only way she could please him greatly was to bear him an heir, and that was beyond her. Dr Barwick filled her with pills and infusions which he esteemed infallible remedies for non-conception, but they did not work.

She had conceived a son soon after they were first married and bore him, but he barely survived his first breath and I think his coming into the world was more painful to both of them than if he had not been born.

They did not speak of it to one another, at least not when I was by, but you could hear the grief hover unspoken in the air like a ghost that will not leave off its haunting. There was a cat in the alley behind the tennis court that would cry at night very like a child in pain and the Duchess put her hands to her ears and told me to go down and chase it away.

It was a hellish place, for the Duchess continually bemoaned the loss of Albemarle House and their state of poverty and the new measures that must be taken to stave off the creditors. I escaped to the nearest tavern whenever I could and stayed as late as I dared, though I found few of the old companions to beguile me, for even Will Symons was gone off to Norfolk, and all the world seemed to have grown stale.

I was returning from the Leg late one night (midnight had already struck) and coming along the passage past the same linen store-room where Nan and I had embraced so long ago, and I heard a scuffling as of several rats. Looking in to chase them away, I saw the pale shining figure of the Duchess bending over the sheets in their wooden racks.

Ah there you are, Jem, she said turning to greet me as though she had sent for me.

I thought I heard a noise . . . Rats . . .

Rats indeed, Jem, look, there were two dozen best sheets when I last counted and now there are but eighteen. I will inspect La Farwell's chamber, for I told her she could not have my sheets.

She raised her hand to put back the sheets she had counted and her hand touched my cheek.

You're warm, Jem, yet it's a cold night.

I've been sitting by a fire.

In a tavern, Jem, I'm sure it was a tavern, you drink too much, don't you?

And her hand stayed upon my cheek and began to stroke it.

Oh it is a pretty warm cheek.

Then to my horror – you must believe it was to my horror – her other hand, her right, began to fiddle with the strings of my breeches, and, oh she was quick, she had undone me and was stroking me with her other hand. It did not take much to get me ready, for I was not too drunk. She was as quick to hoist her own skirts, so quick that I had no time to consider what I thought before she was pushing against me so hard I could scarcely keep my feet. The business was finished as soon as is the coupling of chaffinches. Indeed, she gave a distracted cheep such as a bird might make. She clung to me for a minute afterward, then thrust me away from her.

You must be gone or Farwell will see you. She follows me everywhere.

I found that hard to credit, for I had heard her snores many a night. But I could see that Eliza – as I must now think of her – wished to see the back of me. So I left her, wondering equally at her strange fancy and her haste.

As I passed the door to the great chamber, which was open, I had a fright, for there was Kit sitting in a chair by the fire with a glass of wine in his hand, half-asleep and three-quarters drunk and I wondered that she should have engaged in such proceedings with me, for the linen store was directly beneath.

The next night, after supper, Eliza and I were alone in the great room, for Kit was waiting on the King and Farwell had gone to visit friends.

Will you come with me to the linen store, Jem? I must complete the inventory.

I followed her downstairs, not displeased. When we came into the dark room, I made to embrace her, but she put her hand on my chest and kept me distant from her.

Not so, Jem, not so, she murmured.

Then she began to stroke my cheek as before, and then to fiddle with my strings again as before. In fact, all went on as before, except that my pleasure was the fiercer because I was not so drunk. Again the chaffinch cheep and the clinging afterwards. But this time she said:

We shall remember this night, we shall remember where we were.

I shall never forget it, I said.

No, you mistake me, we shall remember because it was the night the King was dying, not for the other thing.

Dying? I knew he was sick.

Yes, dying. I warned you, didn't I? You must always believe me, Jem, for I can tell the future.

And she laughed as though she were mocking herself or me or both of us.

The King died the next morning, between eleven and twelve.

They said at the last he had been reconciled to the Church of Rome. Every man's heart was full of foreboding, for if we had steered so uncertain a course through treacherous shallows with such a cunning captain, how would we fare with his brother who lacked the politic arts? And the worst of his brother – which showed his lack of judgement – was that he was partial to one I thought we had seen the back of, viz. S. Pepys who had been living quietly in disgrace, though at liberty. I heard he had been sent to Tangier on the King's business, where he might have been taken by pirates or died of a fever. But no, he returns in triumph, gets back his old place at the Admiralty, indeed a greater place, there being now no Board to oppose him.

King Charles's funeral was a pitiful shabby affair, not one tenth as magnificent as General Monck's, for it was not thought fitting to prepare a great English ceremony for one who had died a Roman

Catholic. Kit was much concerned with the management of these shrunken obsequies. Even Eliza roused herself to have made a new gown trimmed with jet and a sable collar that showed off her white skin and made me ache for – I cannot say her embrace, but for her body. In fact, when I saw her come down the stair, from her bedchamber in her mourning gown to go to the funeral, it was the first time I consciously desired her.

Do you like the gown? she said playing the coquette to me for the first time.

It's beautiful.

And the owner of it?

Oh beautiful too, but I'd rather tell her that in the linen store.

You may not say such things, Jem, it is not the right time.

Well, so it was not and I thought no more of it until I renewed my approaches a few days after the King's funeral. Kit had gone to New Hall, La Farwell had not yet returned from her friends, and we had the house to ourselves once more.

Madam, I fancy the linen needs counting again.

She looked at me not unkindly and shook her head.

No, Jem, it is not the time.

I assumed that she had those, but her manner deterred questioning. I could not help but compare her to Nan, to whom I could say anything, but that was no doubt accounted for by the difference in birth between a blacksmith's daughter and a duke's. So again I thought little of it.

A fortnight later, without a word spoken and Farwell in her chamber and Kit barely out of the house, she took me by the hand and led me down to the linen store and had me – I must say it that way around – so quickly that we were back upstairs in ten minutes. Then again the next night, in defiance of very present danger of discovery, then again the night after that.

Then nothing. I made a few hesitant approaches but received a firm rebuff, though not unkindly, as a mother will rebuff a child who has begged for something that he should not have but is too young to know why he may not have it.

By now the spring was coming, the trees were in bud in the courtyard and my spirits began to revive, for although I could not make head or tail of this strange amour, yet I was not one to spurn its pleasures, and hoped that, though I could not plumb her mind, I was conferring pleasure on her in her peculiar fashion.

But then one morning – it must have been at the beginning of May – I found her sitting on the bench at the oriel and weeping as though her heart would break.

Oh Jem, it isn't working.

Not working – how not?

It was a foolish fancy. Well, we must try once more.

Eliza, I don't understand.

It's not your part to understand, she said, but not unkindly, as though her mind had wandered to some other theme. Indeed, she often spoke in this manner which, I must confess, we who were in her household had come to prefer above her other mien, which was querulous and distrustful, finding conspiracy in the smallest thing: if there was no butter on the table, the butler must be selling it to the taverns in Palace Yard; if some great lady failed to take notice of her, there must be a conspiracy to exclude her from Court. What was ironical was that, at this season, the whole nation was in a ferment of rumour about plots and counter-plots – devised by the Papists, devised by the Protestants, for the Court against the Country, for the Country against the Court, plots in Newmarket, plots in the City, plots in Scotland, plots in Holland. Yet Eliza paid not the slightest heed to any of these public matters. Her thoughts were all turned in upon her own plight.

It was a dry spring, we had had no rain since March, and the oak trees had died and caterpillars devoured the fruit-trees. The Cockpit had become too dusty and the smoke from the chimneys provoked Elizabeth's asthma, so we had removed to her father's house in Clerkenwell.

Kit had the gold fever again. Governor Molesworth of Jamaica had passed to their lordships a report of a sunken treasure ship wrecked upon a reef off Hispaniola. A sailor, one John Smith, claimed to have seen several ingots of silver and one of gold, but the wind had freshened and they could make no further search. Their lordships yawned, except for Kit who made King James promise that this ship should be his, which the King did quite readily thinking he might as well promise Kit an estate of 10,000 acres on the moon. But Kit was greatly pleased and would spend hours in foolish discourse on the matter. Eliza seemed happier in her father's house. And it was there that she summoned me to the little room where they kept the linen that had come with us from the Cockpit. Everything was the same, as regular as in the prayer-book: the stroking at arm's length, then the fiddling with the strings and the quick thrusting and the brief clinging when the business was done.

And the same the next night, though I almost failed her, for I thought I heard Kit's tread on the floor above us, and I wondered why she always chose the nights when he was at home or nearby. I had heard that some women found greater pleasure in the danger of being discovered. Certainly she was distracted enough for her mind to run in such a fashion. Yet she never spoke of Kit to me, nor uttered any private opinion that might prove her desire to provoke him or defy him.

What I thought was Kit's tread must have been the creaking of the floorboard, for we were safely upstairs again and I was reading to her from the *Gazette* when in came Kit glowing like a comet.

Have you heard the news? Monmouth has taken ship from Holland.

So? He has come from Holland before.

But this time he is to declare himself King and join with the Scots and the Cheshire Whigs.

You are too hot, my lord, said Eliza, reaching for a sugar-plum which was her principal diet. It will all come to nothing. He will prance through the West Country, silly girls will throw flowers at him, he will touch a few scrofulous old women for the Evil and then he will go racing and we shall all forget him again.

No, no, this time he has brought trained bands with him, a thousand Orangemen, it is said, and some Scotch exiles, hardy, bitter men.

If you believe that, my lord . . . all he will have with him is his groom and that pretty whore what's-her-name and a few idle prattlers.

I will hear no more of this. The King has ordered me to Exeter to raise the militia. I am to leave tomorrow.

Well then, you had best go to bed, for you'll need sleep, but I fear the expedition will be a wild-goose chase. Come now.

And she took his arm firmly and led him off to bed, before I had time to inquire what I should do, whether go with him, or stay with her. For myself, I did not know which I would rather, for I had taken a fancy to our brief couplings, the denial of any prolonged embrace serving rather to heighten the pleasure of them. Yet if there was a rebellion to be snuffed out, there was glory to be won and the prospect of an independent place and an end to my life as a household servant. I was advanced in years to be a soldier, and my leg was sure to trouble me in the damp air of the West, but an old wound had never kept my former General from the Fight, and had not Mr St Michel at the same age as I had now attained purposed to go fight in the Turkish wars? (But had he gone?) Thus I lay in my bed on the upper storey pondering what role in this great play might best become me when I heard from below those sounds which I knew all too well, that old part-song between the bedstead and the bedfellows. On and on went the chorus. If I had been lying in a tavern, I would have beaten upon the floor and told them to be quiet, but in my position I was condemned to listen to the ducal groans until they came to their appointed end and issued, not in a chaffinch squeak, but in the full-throated gurgle of some greater bird.

Anger, humiliation but most of all puzzlement overcame me. Was this pale wretched creature the greatest whore of them all?

The next day, it was decided. I was to go with Kit as his *aide-de-camp*, for though my limp might debar me from active part in battle, my experience would serve him well in gathering intelligence and estimating the size and disposition of forces, matters likely to be of the highest import in the slippery campaign which might lie ahead.

I expected no tearful farewells from Eliza and got none. As I left Clerkenwell, she stroked my cheek none the less, and said, Jem, take care of yourself, as one strokes a horse that is being let out into the field.

Kit had already set off with his principal train. I trotted off on my own the next day. It being a dry and dusty morning, I stopped at the Leg before my long ride to the West. There I found none other than my old friend Will Symons, the Norfolk squire.

I meant to rally him on his bucolic costume, ignorance of the Metropole, etc., but we had barely greeted one another before he, seeing my travelling garb and the leather bag I carried containing certain valuables and papers, launched the first assault:

Off to beat Monmouth then?

Oh, I said, where did you hear that?

It's all over London. Your master is to hold the West Country and some other fellow is to beat off the Scots.

I doubt if it will come to that.

It will, if you don't make haste. They'll flock to him, if you let him have half a chance. You must strike instantly before he bewitches 'em. Have you seen the look in men's eyes as he rides through? A Monmouth! A Monmouth! A Protestant Duke!

Keep your voice down, Will. This is no time for foolery. The people know he can be no legitimate king.

Ah, but Jem, remember that pamphlet of Junius Brutus? He who has the worst title always makes the best king. William the Conqueror was a bastard. Besides, every Anabaptist and Quaker and disappointed Nonconformist is looking for a hero, and they will not much mind whether his parents were married or not.

You sound as if you might go over yourself.

Oh me, I take no part in public affairs, I grow my corn and feed my pigs. By the by, I intend to marry again, did you know that? A widow, very handsome, with a farm in the next parish, but I fear she may be a little cold.

Ah, I said. On that very subject, a friend of mine is in some perplexity. A lady of his acquaintance, I mean a proper lady, one whom he had no reason to think loose, the very opposite . . . she thrusts herself upon him one night without warning as though she were a drab in Fleet Alley. Well, he did not resist, for plums that drop into our laps are all too rare, and he fancied that perhaps he might have proved irresistible to her, even though he had given no sign of attraction on his part.

Such things do happen, though not alas often enough, Will sighed.

Just so. But wait. Our friend then learns that after leaving him she goes straight to her husband and lets him take his pleasure of her also and willingly so.

How does your friend know this?

Well, we won't go into that. But he knows. And, what is stranger still, when her husband is absent, she won't let my friend approach her but keeps her distance as though they were barely acquainted. What can be the explanation of this weird behaviour? Does she require the services of my friend to heighten her pleasure with her husband? Or is it vice versa? Or what?

Hum, said Will, frowning over his spectacles like a learned doctor, tell me, has your friend told you whether she lets him spend in her?

Well, I said, yes. I mean, he says yes she does.

Your friend is very confiding.

It's most capricious behaviour, is it not?

On the contrary, your friend's friend is merely following medical practice. I have heard of half a dozen cases similar.

How peculiar, I can scarcely believe it.

The explanation is simple, Jem. There are men whose seed will furnish a regiment of women with sons. One coupling and nine months later a child is born. But there are others who are poor breeders. This is no aspersion upon their vigour, they may be mighty men, but their seed is too weak to reach the ovaries of the woman. Thus they need reinforcements. Many doctors therefore advise an admixture of some other man's seed at a certain time of the month to increase the probability of conceiving. I have heard of many cases in which this remedy has cured barrenness when all hope of a child had been abandoned.

But –

The birth of the child answers any buts and who is to say whose seed had the larger part in the creation of it? Besides, one cannot be blamed for taking the advice of one's doctor, so long as there is no ungodly pleasure taken in the reinforcement.

Well, I said, my friend will be most surprised.

Was I always to be disappointed in matters of the heart? Was there ever to be some ulterior purpose, some hidden affection, which my lover would not discover to me? And what perversity that it should always be the husband who was the true apple of her eye. No printed romance ever contained such matter, it being too indecent to be spoken of that a woman should use a man for her own advantage without thought of his. To the old Duchess I was a plaything, to the young Duchess an auxiliary stallion, to Mrs Pepys – nothing. And I had no child of my own to comfort my old age that was fast approaching. Even had I a son, I could have taken little pleasure in him, nor he in me, for I had no land or title. Truly, as that cynic of Malmesbury has said, the lot of man is brutish, nasty, solitary, and, were I to be struck down in resisting the usurper, short too.

Burdened with such reflections, I rode out along the high road, to the West. Until my first post (for I was riding at my lord's expense, it costing half-a-crown a stage) I was sunk in inspissated gloom. It seemed as though I had fallen into a well so deep that I could not see the sky and with sides so slippery that I could not climb out of the foul bog at the bottom of it. But then I came to a decent inn at the turnpike and had two mutton chops and a pint of cider, and by the next morning, which was as fair as it had been for weeks before, my spirits rose again and the brisk motion of the post-horse restored my vitality. And the day after that, when I rode out of the heathland and on to the undulant plains of Sarum, with the larks singing above me and the fragrance of the burnet roses in every hedge, I felt young again and scorned my earlier inner discourses as empty chop-logic.

In Salisbury, I met my master at an inn by the market cross and we embraced, for we felt ourselves to be on the verge of a high adventure.

This time I shall do it, Jem, he said. They'll remember me after this as they remember my father. Old Monck and Young Monck – that's how it will be in the histories and they'll think of us in the same breath.

So they will, I said, and for an instant I too believed it.

We rode on to Exeter with destiny lending us wings and the hot sun in our faces.

By nightfall the next day we were in Devonshire and Kit was among his own people and with his own militia, and Feversham and Churchill under him, to resist the invader of whose forces we knew nothing: was he in one ship or many, with field-pieces or no, if so, large or small, and how many men?

The castle at Exeter was much broken down, and though the late King had left money for its repair, there was no time but to patch up the worst of the decay. And I thought of the piteous decay of Upnor Castle, when I had broken open the store to get the tools to repair the batteries against the Dutch. Was it always to be the fate of our unlucky nation to be unready? Were we by nature late wakers to the alarum?

Kit threw himself into the preparation, drilling the militia himself, overseeing the repairs to the castle, demanding reinforcement from the other towns of the county, and then sending officers out to see to it that the men were being brought in and properly armed. By dusk, he was as tired as a dog, for his intemperance had brought the jaundice upon him and though I was twenty years older than he, I could outlast him.

Read me the letters over, Jem, I have no patience left for reading.

And so it was that I read him the first letter his wife sent him from Clerkenwell, of which I have kept a copy, for it pierced my heart. I will not correct the grammar of it nor the spelling, for gentlewomen in those days were not taught as they are today.

It began:

My deare Lord— Ye confusion I am in you will eseylay emagin by Dayley ill nuses (she meant news). *I have not sleped all yet last night my feares have incresed soe fast and with such Great reson. Dearist cretuare, you will wonder at this letter foloeing ye outher soe fast, excuses ye trouble I give you and when you consider ye danger that is round you, you will pardon me eseyat for being soe Tender; did you know my thoughts your love to me would mocion you to Greeve for my presnet Torment. I am to ignorant to advises and my Deare has so large share of Jugment in ware matters to feare anyting can goe amis for want of conduckt, nether doe I think you will be a rash ackter. God spare your life, you will be as Great as Good, I being for ever your affectionate Dutyfull wife.*

E. Albemarle

Her untutored sentiments may give some modern ladies to smile, but they struck me deeply and I carried the letter in my vest and kept it under my pillow at night as though it had been written to me.

She's a good little bitch after all, was all Kit grunted. Pour me another glass, Jem, be a good fellow.

I remember sitting at the table by the wine jug and looking at my master sprawled in his chair, corpulent now, his long greasy hair falling over the wing of the chair, his yellow face reddened in the firelight, and wondering what she could see in such a creature and thinking that I was beginning to love her only now that I knew she had no love for me but was employing me as one might employ a syringe. For a moment, I thought of crashing the jug down upon his greasy head, but then there came the noise of running footsteps upon the stair and a little bald man half-fell into the room.

Sir, Your Grace, he is landed.

And who are you?

Gregory Alfred, sir, the Mayor of Lyme. I was there to see him on the Cobb, sir. It was a terrible sight, there must have been a thousand of them. They ran up their flag in the market place ...

armed to the teeth ... barely escaped with my life ... the guns, oh the guns.

When we saw there was no more to be got out of him, we thanked him for his pains and packed him off to bed with a glass of wine.

So there we sat in the Commandant's lodging in Exeter Castle, the two of us, none other by, the local officers long gone to bed. The logs sputtered on the hearth. I heard the cathedral clock strike I know not what hour. Outside, it began to rain, not a storm but steady rain that soaks through to a man's bones.

Yet for all that, I have never known such a silence. I fancied I could hear the pulse in my temple beating. It was a profound, chilling quiet, and when Kit spoke, there was no flush of wine in his voice, but only a quality of awe as of a man speaking in church when he knows not whether he may.

Well then, Jem, he said.

Well then.

Do we take him now? Or do we give him more rope?

Another dreadful silence, while I thought what was the right answer, and what he wished me to say, and whether these two answers were the same or not.

My commission is to Devonshire, he went on. I have no authority to cross into Dorset to take him. That is for the Dorsetshire Militia, but they are a dismal rabble.

So I've heard.

What would my father have done, Jem? You knew the old man. What would he have done?

He would have taken him, sir.

So he would, so he would.

For a moment, Kit looked encouraged, then again began to muse:

But you're thinking of battle on the high seas, when the only argument is a broadside. In this matter, there are delicate threads embroidered, it may be a time for being politic. Remember how slow and patient my father came down from Scotland without telling a soul that he meant to bring the King back in? This may be such another time. Perhaps my wife is right to tell me not to be a rash actor.

We should strike now before he gathers more men to him (I did not disclose that this sage counsel came by courtesy of Colonel W. Symons).

But we don't know how many men he already has. It would be fatal to let him win a cheap victory at the outset, then he might be irresistible.

Silence again. The rain was coming down harder now.

Kit got up, quite briskly, all his languor gone.

I shall ask the King for reinforcements. Will you write a letter to Lord Sunderland to that effect?

And?

And what?

What are we to do here with the militia?

The militia will go down towards Lyme to seal off his escape to the West. Then we shall meet with the other militias and when we are ready, pin him down until he has nowhere to run but back to the sea.

But not take him now?

Not yet. He must hang himself first before we hang him. Goodnight, Jem.

I did not sleep much that night, even with Eliza's letter beneath my pillow, for the middle way between two extremes which Kit had proposed might bring us the worst of both, viz. that we would have given him enough time to recruit more Dorset and Devon men while our forces would not yet be strong enough to destroy him.

The next morning we set off for Axminster, where we were to meet Sir Edward Phillips and Colonel Luttrell with their men.

The rain still came down and the high banks of the lanes were streaming with red mud. The lanes were so narrow that our boots grazed the hedges. Our horses were like mudlarks before we had gone a mile and the bright uniforms of the militia turned to drab. We lost the way in the lanes and came back upon ourselves, which wasted I don't know how much time.

We came over the brow of a hill and there was smoke and noise beyond the next hill. Then more noise of feet and hooves clattering towards us.

The breathless muddy wretches who burst over the brow of the hill looked like men fleeing from Bedlam rather than Luttrell's militia. *Monmouth has taken the town! We are all betrayed!*

They pressed around us shouting that all was lost and half their comrades had gone over to Monmouth and he would be at Taunton by nightfall.

The more Kit tried to restore them to order, the more they wept and wailed.

It seems he got first to Axminster, Kit said.

My leg was beginning to ache and my martial enthusiasm was waning. But as I got off my horse, Kit roared:

Back in the saddle, that man!

For a leader who had just lost half his army, he seemed less downcast than he might have been.

On boys, on to Wellington! We'll cut him off from the West.

I was sore from being so long in the saddle and my thighs itched like the fires of Hell, but Kit rode on like a Roman through the bedrabbled mass, telling them to take heart and reform their ranks, which they did after a fashion, though not with zest, for half of them were with Monmouth in spirit and dreaming of a hero's welcome in Taunton and a hot supper.

Then as we trudged over the hills towards Wellington, a despatch rider came to meet us with the news: 'He has proclaimed himself King, the whole town is for him.'

Thank God, Kit said, now we have him.

Or he us.

I told you, didn't I? He needed more rope. He has no hope of pardon now.

I forbore to point out that it was not yet certain around whose necks this 'more rope' would be knotted. Yet I could not but marvel at the facility with which Great Persons represent the accidents of fortune as the outcome of their designs. If any general had deliberately brought it about that his enemy should slip through his fingers on the main high road taking half his militia with him to Taunton in order that the said enemy should thereby be emboldened to declare himself King and thus render his life forfeit, then such a general would be carted off to the mad-house.

Kit was less pleased by the letter which came from London the day after the non-Battle of Axminster in which Lord Sunderland said: 'His Majesty commands me to tell you that the forces with the

Duke of Monmouth are not near so great as the Mayor of Lyme has represented them to you' – which, being interpreted, meant that a bolder commander might have annihilated Monmouth before he left the Cobb – but Kit skipped over that passage and saw only the place where His Majesty declared his 'Entire Confidence in Your conduct and zeal for his service', leaving it to Kit to decide when and where to march, though the next day Sunderland sent another letter telling him to forbear to attack 'Except upon great advantages', which was another example of the brilliance of Great Persons, viz. to issue contrary instructions, so that one or the other of them may be remembered as having been the right one for the times.

But then came the finest moment: a letter from James R. (alias Monmouth, alias Scott, alias Crofts) addressed:

'To our Trusty and Well-beloved Cousin and Counsellor, Christopher, Lord Duke of Albemarle'.

In this absurd and vain screed, he spoke of troops raised up for James, Duke of York 'in opposition to Us and Our Royal Authority'. King Monmouth signified 'Our Royal resentment', but said that it was no doubt through inadvertency and mistake. Albemarle would think differently when he had received 'this information of Our being proclaimed King to succeed our Royal Father lately deceased'. If his well-beloved cousin would cease all hostilities and repair to 'Our camp', he would have a kind and hearty reception.

Etc., etc. Never was there a more imbecile piece of boastfulness.

I quickly composed a short and dignified reply to the effect that Albemarle 'never was and never will be a rebel to my lawful king who is James the Second' and that 'James Scott, late Duke of Monmouth' would have done better to let this rebellion alone and not put the nation to so much trouble.

We sent the letter by the same trumpeter that had brought Monmouth's letter and we despatched copies of both to Lord Sunderland.

My reply answers him well, Kit said. It is a sharp and weighty reply, isn't it, Jem?

It is indeed (Kit had already forgotten I had written it for him).

We soon heard that the whole Court was laughing at Monmouth and praising Albemarle's reply – the whole Court bar one person, but that one not the least, namely the King.

It was there in the letters from Lord Sunderland if Kit had had eyes to read them. Though he praised the Duke of Albemarle for subduing the country and penning Monmouth in like a sheep for the shearing, yet each letter ended with a lament for the disloyalty and cowardice of the militia or a complaint that Albemarle was very slow to hang the rebels he had taken and that no man should live who had proclaimed Monmouth King and such like.

It was true that Kit was loath to see these simple miners and shoemakers hanged for being led astray by Monmouth and his plotters (often when half-fuddled with cider). But he thought his credit with the King was strong enough for him to be forgiven such clemencies.

Yet still Kit hankered for a great victory that would cement his fame. And it was his schoolboy friend and manhood rival who denied it him. If Monmouth had taken flight to the West, he would have met our Devonshire men who would have overwhelmed him, I do not doubt, for Monmouth's straggling band was now tired and desperate. We would have harried them in the high lanes from which there was no escape and trampled them into the red mud.

But it was not to be. Monmouth turned northwards, with some crazy design to stir up his friends in Cheshire and march down to London through the Midlands where the girls had thrown him so many garlands five years before.

It was a foolish fancy but then Monmouth's whole excursion was misbegotten from first to last. On the boggy moors of North Somerset, his evading army was caught as soundly as eels in a Sedgemoor trap. The whole county was a maze of ditches and mires and plungeons and rines.

Feversham had sixteen guns to Monmouth's three and Feversham had the credit of the victory, though he was still tying his cravat-string when Churchill was already cutting Monmouth's foot-soldiers to ribbons.

Sedgemoor. A famous victory, but even had Monmouth carried it off there, he would have lost the next engagement. His army was encircled and he was doomed. He himself escaped until they caught him forty miles to the east, asleep in a ditch in the New Forest under the bracken. His hands were trembling, he could not speak, his beard was grey.

Well, you could say that Kit's strategy had worked. He had given

Monmouth rope and the rope had tightened round the rebel's neck. But our celebrations were muted. For just as we heard that Monmouth was taken, we heard also that Feversham had been put over all His Majesty's forces and all Lords-Lieutenant were to obey him – when until that day Feversham had been under Kit's command.

For a whole day Kit stayed in his bed and would not speak. Indeed, his rage was so terrible that his whole body was suffused with it and he could not speak. He came out once and waved an empty brandy bottle that I might fetch him another. Then retired again.

The next day, he came out and ate a venison pasty and drank some ale, but he would say nothing, except: It is finished, which he said several times.

Then the following day, a transformation, or so I thought. He came out into the court to drill his troops, make arrangements for their return, the safe stowage of arms and ammunition and all the other after-battle business. He was calm and sober but still spoke little.

When we returned to London at the end of the month (a fortnight after Monmouth had been beheaded), Kit still kept this calm and sober mien. He even said he would take his part in electing Feversham to the Garter.

It happened after the ceremony. Kit presented himself to the King in the Royal Bedchamber and they had private discourse for a quarter of an hour. Kit never revealed to us what had transpired, though Lord Lucas said the King had rebuked him till tears stood in Kit's eyes.

That evening, he asked the King openly what employment he had, now that Feversham was Lieutenant-General.

Why, said the King, you are the first Colonel.

But, sir, I had a patent to command all the forces and I know not how to serve under these I have commanded (I had all this from Lucas who is an old tattler).

Then he said: If Your Majesty pleases, you may see my Commission.

The King: That ended with my brother's life.

Kit: If Your Majesty please, you may take my Commission and confer it on somebody you think better of.

King: I would not have you quit my employment, I will not take back your Commission, think better on it. Sleep upon it.

But he would not. Pride surged up in him like hot coals in a volcano. The next day, Kit resigned his Commission. At the same time, he resigned his lieutenancies of Devon and Essex, and he wrote to the University of Cambridge telling them that he was of no more use to them, because he was retiring from Court.

If only he had gone straight to Lyme and arrested Monmouth. If only he had led his militia over into Somersetshire and paid no heed to Lord Sunderland's prevarications. If only . . . But his chance of glory had gone. He would never be remembered as his father is yet remembered.

How many of us can stop time's moving finger and point to that exact instant at which our bright future shattered into a dismal past? In Kit's case, it was when the wet Devonshire logs were sputtering on the hearth after the Mayor of Lyme had been packed off to bed. He knew that he had come to a tide that must be taken at the flood, and deep in his heart he feared to take it. And so he missed the tide. As for me, I had missed it also, even as I had missed it at the Medway fight. I wager there is no man alive who was more nearly present at the two great defences of old England, which is to say absent.

VIII

The Island

'He has retired from Court and gone into the country' – the words sound well enough. They speak of rustic tranquillity, of the fragrances of the herb garden on a summer's evening, the barking of dogs after rabbits in the warren.

But with my master it was not so. All through that dry dusty summer at New Hall he mourned his fate, cursed the King, cursed the Devon militia, cursed his wife and her friends who were conspiring against him to make him change his will in her favour, and especially he cursed me, because I was the nearest at hand.

He slept but little, his nights were broken with bad dreams. He ate little too, nothing but crusts of bread washed down with great draughts of Lambeth ale. He suffered from headaches and often his speech lost coherence and I had to feign understanding of what he said, which inflamed his anger when I mistook him.

Listen you fool, I called for Flier to be saddled, I said nothing of the flies.

But Flier is gone to Newmarket, to run against Brown Betty.

I forgot, I had thought it was next week.

He dressed in rough country clothes who had only the year before been a magnifico in gold lace. He was much jaundiced from the bleedings which Dr Barwick prescribed, though I could not see that they did him any good.

But his prime sickness was Failure, a disease which doctors cannot cure though a loving wife might. But Elizabeth would not come to the country and stayed in Clerkenwell. She had, it seemed, no desire for her husband's company, nor for mine. I looked back at our couplings in the linen store with wonder, as though it had all been a dream, though in my mind I could still feel her bony body against mine and hear the chaffinch squeak.

There was only one gleam in the clouds that lowered over my master, and that, I feared, was a false gleam and one that might lead us from the Slough of Despond to utter perdition.

The ships are to leave tomorrow, Jem.

Are they so?

Captain Phipps has the command and he has with him Indian divers from the pearl fisheries who have great acquaintance with the art. They have brought *diving-bells*, Jem, that will trap the air and double the time they may stay below water. Did you ever hear of such a thing?

If only there be something to dive for.

The seaman, John Smith, saw six ingots of silver and one of gold in the hull of the ship. Saw them, Jem, with his own eyes and has sworn it in an affidavit.

And upon this affidavit, you are venturing?

Eight hundred pounds and I shall have a quarter of the treasure. None of the other Gentlemen-Venturers would put in more than a hundred pounds.

Because they have more sense.

You'll rue your timidity, Jem, you'll wish you had come in with me.

His yellow eyes, so dull of late, were now ablaze with Spanish gold. He had quite forgot the *Algier Rose*. Now he was sending two ships, the *James and Mary* and the *Henry*, and venturing twice as much money.

You're wrong, I tell you, you are always wrong. You were wrong about Monmouth at Lyme, and you're wrong about Captain Phipps.

Well, if I'm always wrong, then I should leave your service.

No, no, it doesn't signify. I never listen to you. Come, my throat is dry, fetch me some ale. If we're to live like bachelors, at least we need not be sober.

So we rattled about that great house like peas in a pan, two lost men on retreat from the world.

His wife wrote so mockingly of the folly, of his treasure-hunting – she called it Monck's moonshine – that even Kit lost heart and tried to sell some part of his share, to Lord Sunderland and, I think, to Lord

Dartmouth. But they were all too worldly-wise and, truth to tell, Kit now had a reputation for ill-success which clung to him as a mephitic vapour.

It was six o'clock on a June morning when the courier came knocking at our door and roused the porter who woke Kit who came running into my chamber in his nightshirt and jumped on my bed as wild as a schoolboy on holiday.

They found her, they're back, we're rich, they found her. The ship's so full of gold it ran aground.

Aground?

They floated her again, she's here anchored in the Downs. We're rich.

And we were, or rather he was. Captain Phipps and his divers had found the galleon just where the seaman said she was, caught in a moon-shaped reef, her planks all covered with sea-feather and coral, and the bones of her seamen whitening where they lay by their brass cannon and their great chests of plate and coin. Such treasure was never brought up before – or, I fancy since, though many men have wasted their fortunes in the attempt. For three months, they had dived and dived and dived again. They could stay as long as three-quarters of an hour under water in their ingenious diving tubs. Even on a bad day's work they brought up more than 3,000 dollars.

And who took the lion's share, more than the King (who had his 10 per cent) and all the worldly-wise gentlemen adventurers? Why, my poor silly master who had not done another thing right since the day he was born. Whatever Lord Rochester and his wits might say, there was a God in Heaven after all.

We made speed to Tilbury where Captain Phipps was to come ashore. There were to be no dirty country clothes for this ceremony. My master put on his embroidered satin shirt that Mr Riley painted him in and his great blue velvet coat with the gold tassels and his full-bottomed wig (though that was dirty, but his tall feathered hat hid it). As he strode along the quay, you would have thought here was a man had never known an unhappy day in his life. Only his little eyes flickered from side to side like an animal that fears some hidden danger.

But there was no danger, only crowds that were cheering, for every man likes to see another bring home treasure so long as it be undeserved, for then he fancies how he too, being undeserving also, might win such a prize in fortune's lottery.

And what was this? Who was this great lady, so pale yet so radiant, hastening along the quay from her carriage? Why it is Her Grace, hot from Clerkenwell, the first to congratulate her lord on his farsighted daring. Had she not always known that the gallant Captain Phipps would find their galleon for them? For fortune has not only a hundred fathers but a hundred wives and sweethearts also.

But Kit was in no mood to remind her of Monck's moonshine, for he was gay and nonchalant. He embraced Captain Phipps, a weatherbeaten little nut of a man, as though they were lovers; and skipped aboard the *James and Mary* to view the treasure like a lamb that has lately learned the use of its legs. He chattered to every fellow and shook him by the hand and laughed at nothings.

The hold was so full that when the captain took off the hatches the treasure seemed to burst up on to the deck: the chests of shining dollars creaking and chinking when the seamen took them up that we might see the chests of plate beneath that shimmered like some subterranean paradise.

We were silent, awestruck by the spectacle. None of us had ever seen, oh half the like. Beside it Nan's jewel box was a plaything for children. Captain Phipps began his recital: the first finding the ship, the waiting for a favourable breeze to bring them on her quarter, that not coming till the Lord's Day, and they thought it trying God's Providence to hunt for treasure then, and so on.

But we could scarcely listen, our eyes were so dazzled by the sight.

Kit embraced his wife and she kissed him back. They might have been lovebirds who had never quitted the same branch. She hugged me too and whispered, oh Jem, dear Jem. But it was the Spanish gold she loved, not me. I was no more worthy of a remembered tenderness than is a stallion who has failed to get a mare in foal.

The King came to see the treasure, a tenth of it being his, and the other fearful lords who had backed the venture (though Sir Richard Haddock, who had sold out his £100 share for £90 only a month before the ships came back, could not bear to come).

And the King said: Well, you must go to Jamaica now, for I see you have a nose for gold.

All on a sudden, everyone at court remembered that Kit had been appointed Governor of Jamaica during his year of disgrace, though he had made no preparation to go to the island, and indeed everyone thought the King had thrown him a worthless bauble, for who would wish to settle in an island full of snakes and fevers and pirates?

But now this previous appointment was taken for further proof of my lord's foresight, and fresh commissions and privileges were rained down upon him. Under a royal patent, Kit was granted 'all mines of lead and copper and other mines, all earths for the making of saltpetre and all minerals, stones and salts whatsoever, whether they be already opened or discovered or not opened or discovered in all our plantations or colonies in America or colonies of New England, Virginia and all parts northward of our colony of Carolina'.

Furthermore, he was to be Generalissimo of all forces in any of those colonies he might choose to visit. He was to keep Outsiders from engaging in the slave trade and he was to 'protect all our Roman Catholic Subjects in our island of Jamaica'. Oh and one last thing, he, His Grace the Duke of Albemarle, was to have the monopoly for all sawmills in America for a period of fourteen years, the colonies of New England only excepted, and the patent upon all diving-bells that had been or were yet to be invented for the same period.

Thus he was to be lord of the forests through all the New World, and of the mines that lay beneath them, and of the treasures that lay in the waters round about. Was there ever such a commission given to an Englishman? Even the King of Spain in his days of greatness had scarce conferred such powers on his *conquistadores*.

That night Kit was foul stinking drunk, and he broke a chair of his father-in-law's and at the same time broke half a dozen of his father-in-law's fine Venetian glasses that had been set out for the celebration. He called his wife a barren whore. Then he turned on me.

You shan't come, no, you bring bad luck. You're a surly idle fellow and I've had enough of you. If you come to Jamaica, I'll have you hanged.

I do not mean to come.

Oh yes you do, you're greedy for treasure like the rest of this scurvy, canting crew.

My lord, mercy, Jem has done nothing wrong.

The Duchess was sitting the other side of the table sobbing as the insults rained down upon her. I looked at her with gratitude for her protection. But Kit would have none of it.

He has done nothing right. He is an idle drunken rogue.

Oh Kit, don't if you love me.

I'll wager *he* loves *you*. I've seen his filthy eyes follow you round the room. I'll wager he's had you, what's more. I'll . . .

Kit, Kit. She cried in distress which was the more piteous because it sounded so innocent.

All at once, he was quiet and meek again.

I don't know what I was saying, I've drunk too much, I'm tired, let's go to bed. It has been the happiest day we have known, has it not? There will be happy days to come, many happy days.

Thus he stumped off to bed, on the greatest day of his life, and even that he must spoil. I resolved that I would not go to Jamaica, I must make a worthy life for myself and not trot along for ever behind the coat-tails of this mad couple, for they were both of them sick in mind as in body and when they were together they gave each other no comfort but only scratched their sores.

On the morrow, though, he was bright as a sparrow and bustled about the house tossing out orders.

Charts, Jem, didn't you say you were once a chart-seller? Go buy me some charts of the West Indies, that we may plot our voyage.

Out in the streets, everyone was talking of the Duke of Albemarle, how he had ventured his fortune upon the report of some Biscayan diver – already the tale was somewhat embroidered – or how his father with his dying words had told him the whereabouts of the wreck which he had seen go down with his own eyes when he was on the West Indies squadron (which he never was).

I took my way down Cheapside, for I resolved to visit my old master, Mr Fisher, at his shop on Tower Hill. At the back of my mind, I had a project that I might offer to become his partner and resume my old trade profiting by my association with the great treasure-seeker and being appointed map-maker to the West Indies trade. Dwelling on this pleasant fancy, I had arrived at Tower Hill before I knew it and was about to turn in at the old familiar sign when I saw that it had been freshly painted with ... no ... RICHARD M— ... my own name – MOUNT – swinging from the pole.

Who could this be? What cousin or kinsman had inveigled himself into old Fisher's favour? I flung open the door in a fever. Out of the gloom, a tall young man, very tall and black, came to greet me. When he came into the light from the windows, the apparition robbed me of my breath. I could not speak.

The young man, *aetatis suae* twenty five or thirty, I should say, was me. Everything about him was the image and *simulacrum* of myself, the long figure, the black hair and swarthy skin like a Spaniard's, the eagle's nose a little bent at the knob, the resemblance to the late King, even the voice which seemed to come through the nose but was, I flatter myself, not unmelodious, even the way his head cocked a little to one side as though he were considering a fine painting – all, everything, was me.

There could be but one explanation, though my furious-beating heart could scarce admit it.

You are, you are – I stammered, the proprietor of this shop?

Yes, sir, or rather joint-proprietor (how like the voice was, or as like as I could tell, for who knows what his own voice is like, since it sounds not the same to the speaker as to the harkener and we have no way of recording a voice but on parchment), for Mr Fisher was good enough to take me into partnership two years ago, after I married his daughter Sarah. Our families were old friends and –

Your father was bound apprentice to Mr Fisher once, was he not? His name was Ralph?

Why yes, sir, that is he. But how did you know?

Careful, be careful, I said to myself.

I am a cousin of your father, and thus of yours also. Jeremiah Mount, sir, at your service.

I am pleased to meet you, sir. Alas, my father is dead these ten years past. Not a day goes by without my thinking on him and wondering what he would have done in such and such a case, for he was not only the best of fathers but the wisest of men.

Thinking on him even thus far induced a severe fit of melancholy in the young man and he took out a cambric handkerchief and put it to his nose.

Did you know the shop, sir, in my father's day?

Ah, a little, that is –

It is much changed. Since we acquired the patent to publish Captain Collins's marine charts, we have come to engage greatly in that business, although we publish much else besides. We have taken the shop next door to accommodate our stock. Perhaps I might show you some of our choice items?

This was a cruel trick, perhaps the most cruel that fate had yet played me. How often I had wondered if I might one day have a son, never suspecting that all the while I had already sired one. That brief meeting with poor Mary Court had borne more lasting fruit than all my couplings with duchesses. It was my great revenge upon Fluffy Ralph, or so I had thought. Yet in the long run it was he who had had the revenge upon me. For he had brought the boy up to be an unctuous sycophant, the worst type of shopman, so that while his figure was the very image of mine, his character, his soul indeed, was the very image of Ralph's.

This son-who-was-no-son droned on interminably describing the different qualities of paper they employed and how buckram was now quite out of favour and whether the future lay in binding up charts or in selling single sheets. I might have been jogging along besides Ralph thirty years before while he described the principal manufactures of Kent and the tonnages that were sent out from each of the county's ports.

And now, sir, I have the honour to show you our very newest work. It is based upon Captain Collins's latest sounding of Harwich Harbour. The Captain assures me that the pilots of the vicinity had never seen such precise work. But I have not yet told the summit of our fortune, which is that we received gracious permission to dedicate the plate to the Member of Parliament for Harwich who, as I am sure you are fully cognisant, is none other than our lately restored Secretary of the Admiralty, the worthy *Mr Samuel Pepys*.

No, I cried involuntarily.

Yes indeed, sir, for there is the inscription and there are his arms. And what is more, I had the honour myself to present the chart on behalf of the firm to Mr Secretary in person who professed himself profoundly gratified by the honour and remarked on the quality of workmanship, as well he might, for it is very fair work indeed, though I do say it myself.

I stared at the thing and the obsequious words that were inscribed upon it:

> *To the Honble Samuel Pepys, Esquire,*
> *Secretary of the Admiralty of England*
> *President of the Royal Society*
> *Master of the Trinity House*

There was the outward and visible sign of Pepys's greatness, the standard that fluttered upon his indestructible battlements. Pepys was immortal.

Then it was that I saw as clear as though the whole scene were lit by a lightning flash that I could not remain in London a day longer. It was impossible to tarry in a city where S.P. lorded it so and where my son, my only son who must not be acknowledged, spoke of this bandy-legged little clerk as though he were a god.

I must quit these shores and seek my fortune beyond the seas. Thus I was shackled to my master as surely as those felons who are chained together and despatched to people our colonies. And though I might die of a fever or be murdered by the Caribs or enslaved by cut-throat Biscayans, yet any such fate were better than to sit out my last years in London in humiliation and obscurity. Westward I must decline with the sun, to borrow the words of Mr Dryden.

I would return in triumph like a Roman general and those who had not been with me on the voyage (*videlicet*, one S. Pepys) would think themselves accursed they had not been with us. I had besides a design for the long term that I had scarcely confided even to myself. Kit had sent me upon business to Alderman Gauden that had been chief victualler to the Navy, who lived in a great house at Clapham on the north side of the common. The house was of red brick and white stucco with figures of gods upon its pediment. The garden had an avenue of peach trees in espalier that led to a round carp-pond. At the corners of a wall the alderman had built two pavilions in the same taste. It was a pretty retreat and though it was in the suburbs the alderman swore to me that on a fast horse he could be in the City within the hour. Yet I doubted whether he had made this journey since the press of coaches and carts had become so great, he being ancient and much decayed. The house was already broken down though it was modern, for he was now a pauper, the government being unable to unwilling to pay his bills for the Dutch wars, so it was doubtful whether he would die first or be bankrupt.

Either way the house must be sold and I resolved that if I could further augment my fortune I should be the purchaser when it came to the market. I had given instructions to an agent that lived upon the common to send me the latest news of the matter. Thus I would have that greatest of blessings as I set out upon my voyage, viz. something to look forward to.

Yet while I watched my son parcel up the charts I had bought, I could not repress a tear at the recollection of what might have been. For did not this Fisher who had made my son his partner and married him to his daughter himself also have a sister? If I had married *her* and had kept to the trade, might it not have been me who – but then I recalled the sister, a pale puking thing, Emma, Emilia, some such name, and knew that I could not have borne such a life. You were begotten for adventure, I said to myself, as I took the maps from his long hands that were as soaped and scented as a lady's.

Pray send your mother a hearty greeting from me. I knew her also (I should not have said so but I could not forbear).

Thus I strode out of the shop with the charts under my arm.

So you're coming then, His Grace grunted.

Only if you take me.

Well, the rest of the crew will be ruffians, so one more will make no odds.

I am obliged to Your Lordship for the commendation.

Quick, Jem, pour me a glass. I must drain it before the doctors come.

But he had drunk only halfway when no less than four quacks were brought in, led in by old Dr Barwick who looked in a fair way to sign his own death bill before the year was out.

Dr Hobbs, Dr Brown, and this is Dr Sloane whom you have already met. In my opinion, he is one of the finest young Scotsmen to come out of Ireland since they were planted there.

Well, Sloane, will you come?

The learned Dr Sydenham told me I had better drown myself in Rosamund's pond than go to Jamaica.

Pay no heed to Sydenham, Dr Sloane, he is not even a member of the College and you will recall that at the coming of the Great Plague –

You stayed in town, Dr Barwick, and he did not. But I will come to Jamaica, Your Grace, though not to flout Dr Sydenham whom I much respect, but because I want to learn the truth about tropical diseases, of which so much nonsense is spoken, and I hope I may have the honour to cure you and your household of any such which you have the misfortune to contract on the voyage.

This Sloane was a lean, sharp young man with a long nose and a crinkle about the mouth. He knew his own mind, that any fool could see at first glance, but I doubted whether I would care for him.

You shall share a cabin with Jem here, Jem is my trusted counsellor (a description which I had never had applied to me before).

The sharp young man bowed to me.

Hans Sloane, sir, I am honoured to make your acquaintance. And he gave me an up-and-down look as though I were already his patient.

Now then, Your Grace, Dr Barwick said, we are all agreed on the best medicine for the tropics.

I think I can guess at it.

No more than a modicum of wine, plenty of water, making sure only that it be fresh, and no late nights. I rely on you, Dr Sloane, to ensure His Grace's obedience.

Here Kit grunted an oath which made the doctors jump out of their skins and which I will not set down. Dr Barwick turned swiftly to talking of fees. Dr Sloane, it came out, had already secured that he should be paid £600 per annum with a previous payment of £300 for his preparation for this service. My respect for him grew greater by the minute.

It might be thought from all this high bustle that we were to weigh anchor on the morrow. That was not Kit's way. First, his humour was lethargic and, second, he was a lover of preparation. He could spend a morning in determining what types of oatmeals and pease we should take and whether they would keep better in large barrels or small. And my lady could match him, for she must have a dozen gowns, and shawls and veils and stockings made for Jamaica that would be as light as gossamer and yet protect her from the fierceness of the sun. Meanwhile Dr Sloane was collecting his medicines and his instruments and having chests and cabinets made for his specimens of the flora and fauna of the islands.

Am I a doctor or a botanist or a zoologist? He pondered. Can one be one without being all three, for Nature scatters her secrets without regard for our subtle divisions?

Quite so, I said, thinking only that there was now scarce room on my side of the cabin to keep a shirt or any change of underlinen.

It was September before Captain Lawrence Wright advised us that we might at last step aboard His Majesty's frigate *Assistance* which was lying at Spithead with two large merchant ships for company and the Duke's yacht, which was to lodge His Grace's household, to wit, one mad duchess, one Ulster doctor, myself and a dozen others, and a queer young man whom Kit presented to me as his cousin Thomas Monck, who was to captain the yacht, but how he was related I could not fathom. If illegitimate, he seemed too old to be of Kit's spawning, too young to be the Lord-General's. And if he was either's bastard, I could not see why the Duchess tolerated him, for he was taciturn and ill-favoured. But then I recalled that morose fellow that had skulked about the Cockpit in the General's day and was sometimes called in to dinner when there was room and presented to the company as 'my worthy cousin Colonel Thomas Monck', though colonel of what regiment was never disclosed, nor his kinship to my master, so that I fancied each generation of Moncks must have its byblow.

My theory found its confirmation the first night after we had weighed anchor.

What think you of my cousin the Captain? His Grace inquired.

I have not yet had enough time to gauge his merit. He is a near connection?

Kit grinned. He was halfway through his second bottle.

The nearest, my boy.

Oh, I said, affecting amazement.

I was barely sixteen at the time. She was three years older and must be sent down to Devonshire so as not to blight my wedding. My father told me you must always settle your bastards to a profession. He put his in the Army, so I chose the Navy for young Tom. He's done well – as he must do, for he can expect nothing more from me.

Then I saw how the arrogance of greatness had filled his soul and emptied it of those sympathies that we are born with. For my own part, if I had had the means to assist my own son (and he the necessity to receive assistance), I should have been generous.

Does Her Grace know?

Oh she could know if she wished to. But she prefers to be mad and know nothing.

We made but a stuttering beginning, for no sooner had we set sail than bad weather compelled us to take shelter behind the Isle of Wight. Once more we weighed anchor and this time were driven by the equinoctial storms to take refuge in St Helen's Road outside Plymouth harbour, where we swung about for a fortnight, being most foully seasick (Dr Sloane advised us to drink small beer as an emetic). While we were at Plymouth, a party of Devon gentlemen came out to wish us godspeed, for Kit had never ceased to command the love of his fellow Devonians. What must they have thought as our party staggered to the rail, as green in the face as a row of ghosts and scarce able to thank them for their kindness.

Thus we took leave of our native shores, with pale countenances and uneasy bellies, but for Dr Sloane who seemed very well and much occupied with observing a sea-bird which he called a Greater Sea-Swallow or *Hirundo Marina major* but a seaman from Pembroke told me was only a common shearwater that nests on the cliffs in these parts.

When we had passed the Lizard, the Duke ordered his Admiral's flag hoisted on the main top mast, and several huzzas and guns discharged marked the drinking of His Grace's health, for he was Vice-Admiral of those seas. Kit stood there in his admiral's uniform on the deck, rolling a little with the pitch of the vessel and a greenish-yellow in the face, but with a complacent countenance, for were not the waves his to command as far as the eye might see? His wife stood at his side, deathly pale also, and shivering in the breeze. Huzza! we all went in her honour, though in truth they were a melancholy pair.

As we sailed south, the weather began to smile upon us. A grampus followed us all one day, about forty foot long, and spouting great plumes of water from two channels in his head, and porpoises came to play about us, swimming past the ship and then coming back at us again, whereat the sailors would throw out harping irons and bring them in quite easily.

Oh the poor creature, the Duchess cried as they brought one up on the deck and began to skin the fat off it, and then, oh but it stinks, as the fishy smell began to spread through the ship.

But she would watch for hours the dolphins play in our wake and when a lark was blown into our rigging and perched there too weary to sing, she wanted one of the seamen to climb up and catch it, that she might keep it in a cage and listen to its music in her cabin, but when the ship's boy had climbed up to within arm's length of it, the bird flew off to one of the other ships and perched there.

The Duke spent much of his time on the *Assistance*, busying himself with the dividing of the stores and matters of navigation of which he knew little. Even the Captain was ignorant how to set a true course for Madeira, and had to take counsel from the old Pembroke seaman who had voyaged that way many times before. But we were only sixteen days from Plymouth when we came to anchor in the Madeira road. It seemed as though we had already passed the tropic-line, for the sun shone down upon the palm trees above us and the natives came out in their boats which were heaped with oranges and lemons and other southern fruits. There we took on wine and fresh water and provisions and weighed anchor and set sail, but with little wind. For three days we idled along the shore of the island, and there we first took dolphins with what they call *fisgigs*, viz. sharp arrow-headed or bearded irons fitted with poles of about ten feet long and a rope tied to them. The seamen then put out lines and hooks baited with rags which dabbled in and out of the water as we sailed, so as to imitate the flying fish which the dolphins pursue with great greediness. Thus lured, the dolphins were easy prey for the seamen waiting with their fisgigs on the yardarm or the poop.

It is cruel sport, the Duchess said, but still she hung out over the side to watch. For our part, we lolled upon the deck of the yacht on cushions that we had brought from our cabins and talked idly of many matters that had nothing to do with our voyage, while Dr Sloane made observation and noted down all that he saw: the tropic-bird with the two feathers in its tail, the Portuguese men-o'-war that have such a terrible sting, the flying fish and the dolphins leaping after them. At night he brought us out on deck to see the sea-water alight along the bow of the ship where the water is more broken, like sparks of fire leaping up as if a flint-and-steel were struck together, and then vanishing. He had a bucket of water drawn and as the water struck the bucket-rope, the sparkles lit up along it, so that it was a slender rope of fire.

Oh it is so pretty, the Duchess said, leaning down over the side. But now it is gone, so soon. Is that not sad?

I think it must be phosphorus, the doctor said. Mr Boyle showed me a suspension of it. He called it the Aerial Noctiluca.

It shines only for us, I think, the Duchess said. If we had not sailed this way, those sparkles would never have been lit.

It may well be so, madam. The action of the rope –

Our passage leaves a trail of light. Is that not a poetic thought, Jem? She took my arm.

Very, madam.

I incline to believe, persisted the doctor, that the phenomenon may proceed from particles of fish floating in the water, too small for us to see. I have observed the same sparkle on parts of dead fish lying on the shore.

Ugh, said the Duchess.

As she spoke, I felt her thigh against mine and the press of her hand grew firmer. The gentle motion of the yacht seemed to fasten us together.

Good-night, Doctor, take care (for he was observing the sparkles halfway down the rope as it swung round in the water).

Good-night, Your Grace.

As we went down into the cabin, she rubbed herself against me with a slow lascivious motion.

His Grace has sent word he will sleep on the *Assistance* tonight. He says he must be up betimes to take the sun, so, Jem, we may take the moon.

Now we were in her cabin and she was taking off her light cotton gown, of an ivory colour so pale it was as though she was slipping off a second skin. I could see her ribs by the light coming in through the porthole. Round her neck a gold necklace shone in that soft light.

Is that phosphorus, do you think? she said stroking the necklace. Perhaps I am a creature of the deep.

We must ask the doctor to examine you.

No you examine me first, Jem, you first.

It was as though the boat was rocking us, we being motionless but carried on by the boat. And as my mind flew off from the cabin to that distant realm to which the amorous sense transports us (though still I felt her hips rub against mine) so it reverted to my first recollection of love, my lying with Emm in the field at home and watching the distant ships at anchor swaying together in the breeze, or so we fancied though it was we who were swaying. Now I was come full circle and we were moving in time with the boat in a universal motion. Yet as that flame of passion sparkled, blew hard, so hard and then dwindled again, so a dismal intimation came upon me that this might be my last of love, just as Emm had been my first, for such sad thoughts come upon a man after the flame is quenched.

Do you feel sad afterwards, Jem?

Yes, sometimes.

Now? Do you feel sad now?

A little.

So do I. Do all women feel so?

I don't know.

I must have a child, Jem. If it should be yours in part, you must say nothing.

I know that.

And I'll say nothing, but I shan't forget your part, so don't forget me. You promise not to forget me? And she pressed her fingers into my shoulders, so hard that the fingernails might have drawn blood.

I promise.

They say I'm mad, Jem. You don't think I'm mad, do you?

No, not the least.

Sometimes I do fear I am out of my mind. It's true I'm a little distracted, but I am not gone mad.

Your health is fragile, that's all.

I'm better now. The sea air makes me better. Oh I wish this voyage could go on for ever. Do you think the doctor is still turned round that rope?

By now he must be sailing behind us in the bucket.

All the next day we lay upon the deck and watched the dolphins. The sun grew hotter, and she took one of the seamen's straw hats and tied a red silk ribbon round it and shaded herself from the sun so that I could see only her chin and her long swan's neck and then the sun began to burn her there too, so that she must wind a soft scarf round her neck.

Tropic-money, Your Grace. If you've never crossed the tropic-line before, you must either give us money that we may drink your health or you must be ducked thrice into the sea from the yard-arm, and we wouldn't wish to duck a lady, so it would be kinder if you were to choose the first.

She laughing threw the seamen five guineas, and laughed again when the boy who had been sent up to catch the lark was ducked. His slender body flew past us three times and he dived through the water as sweetly as a dolphin and she cheered each time he dived.

By now we were come very close to Barbados which was to be our first sight of the New World. On the 25 November, we came into Bridgetown Harbour and anchored there at noon. All the guns in the ships and the harbour forts saluted His Grace. I shall never forget the scene as we were rowed ashore: the sun's rays bright upon the water, the smoke from the guns drifting into the sky and the water so blue as it never is at home and the hues of the Negroes' clothes that dazzle the eyes. All round the port of Bridgetown grow the bearded figs which give the island its name, having twisted roots that hang down from the branches like full beards. In the sun of noon those roots shimmer like cobwebs so that the island seems a lost realm from the pages of a romance.

When Their Graces stepped ashore to take a review of the forces of this place, they looked transformed from the sickly wheyfaces that had left Plymouth six weeks earlier. What miracles a sea voyage can accomplish if the weather be pleasant and if Cupid launch his fisgigs!

We dined that day with the Governor of the place upon shaddocks, guavas, pines (or pineapples as they now call them), mangrove-grapes and other fruits unknown in Europe (though the meats were worse than ours). Dr Sloane who was seated next to me said:

This is worth the fatigues of the journey, isn't it, Jeremiah? (He had a fancy to call me by my full name.)

He had no notion of how pleasant had been my fatigues.

As I lay upon my rattan bed in the Governor's house that night listening to the cries of the natives in the forest, I could not but wish that her pale body might be by my side and not shackled to her stertorous lord who had been drinking hard all the voyage and must have had three of the Governor's bottles of Madeira wine that night. So as in dreams we are carried to any place but that where we are sleeping, I was now transported to the little path at Churn where Emm and I had walked, but now in the dream I was walking with the Duchess, her clothing being dishevelled and her hair wild, and Mr Hignell the greasy old parson coming down from the church to reprove us for our lewd conduct and she beginning to cry. As he came closer to us I saw that the man was not Mr Hignell but Mr Pepys and he was crying out: You killed her, it was you.

I woke solitary to the cry of parrots, my body bedewed with sweat. And I wondered whether I would ever be free of Pepys. Did he dream of me, I speculated, as I dreamed of him?

Yet though I could not be with the Duchess at night, in the daytime we took many pleasant walks together while Kit was conversing (*scilicet* drinking) with the Governor. Dr Sloane came with us bearing a great satchel for his plants and while he was trotting off into the forest to gather the fruits of the martock tree or the custard-apple or the logwood for the laboratory, we would clasp hands or, if he were out of sight, our lips might touch, but only for an instant as even in the depths of the woods there were natives everywhere gathering wood to burn and fruit to eat. However far we might wander from the town, we could hear their laughter and chattering.

They are spying on us, she said.

No, no, these are their woods. This is where they take fuel and food.

I am sure they are spying. Did you see that woman there with the red kerchief on her head? I have seen her at the Governor's house.

That's a common manner of dress on the island. I have seen half a dozen red kerchiefs.

No, Kit is posting spies. He grows suspicious, though he says nothing.

And she called to Dr Sloane to say that she had walked far enough and we must go back.

It was the day we came into Nevis roads that the Duchess took to her bed.

Kit went ashore to be treated by the Governor, Colonel Hill, but she would not come. I inquired of one of her women whether she was sick. Nothing out of the common run, the woman said, indicating that it was a matter of the time of the month.

If only she could bear a child, said the woman (her name was Mrs Wright, though she was no kin of the captain of the *Assistance*, Mr Wright, a pompous fellow, not trustworthy), that would set her right. I was never ill after I dropped my first.

At which there came to me some premonition I could not perfectly express to myself. She would be distressed, I knew, for she was distressed each time Nature refused her dearest wish, yet I fancied her distress would be all the greater, since such sweet pleasures had preceded it but to no effect. Were women more likely, or less, to conceive if they had been amorous and the sun shining? I considered whether to ask Dr Sloane but feared lest I should put him on the scent. Besides, I doubted whether he was experienced in such matters.

It was not until four days later that she came out of her cabin. She was as pale as the moon and there was some wild look in her eye.

Good-day, I am very glad to see you.

She gave no answer but stood at the door of her cabin, swaying somewhat with the motion of the ship, shading her eyes against the sun.

How are you? Better I hope.

No answer again. Then she walked very slowly past me, she might have been walking in her sleep. After she had gone past me, she said – to no one, because there was no one there:

I must speak to the Captain. I will not have his woman on the ship.

But the Captain is not married and he has no woman with him, I said behind her.

He has a whore in his cabin and she must be taken off.

She walked on along the deck, I following her, until she met a seaman.

I must speak to the Captain.

He's on the *Assistance*, ma'am.

Then take me there.

Captain's orders are to sail in her wake till we come to Port Royal.

Will you bring my husband to me?

He's on the *Assistance*, too, ma'am.

Well, then, we must go alongside her.

I can't do that, ma'am.

Do as I say.

But there was no wind to bring the yacht up with the *Assistance*, although the lieutenant tried to please her. When he came to tell her so, she had gone back to her cabin.

Then an hour afterwards Mrs Wright, her woman, came out and beckoned me to her.

I have a message for you from Her Grace, but I hardly know how to give it.

How so?

Well, she says that when she came out on deck this morning, there was a man there who would not bow to her. So I says, what man is that? And she says, carelessly as you might say, I forget his name but he is tall and black. So I know she means you, and though it is but foolishness, I thought it best to tell you, for when these peevish fits are on her there's no knowing what she may do.

I did not bow?

So she says.

I don't know whether I did or not, we're too well acquainted to stand upon such ceremony.

I know that, Mrs Wright said and looked at me as much as to say that there was nothing of the matter she did not know.

Well, in future, my nose shall scrape the ground, Mrs Wright.

The next day, Mrs Wright told the lieutenant that Her Grace wished that whenever she left the yacht or boarded her again the whole crew should be mustered to greet her and in livery. The lieutenant said there must be some men elsewhere to sail the ship. Mrs Wright bore word back that Her Grace would have it that the whole ship's company should be standing by.

Thus those that were occupied in steering the ship or furling sails or navigating had to make themselves invisible, that the yacht might seem to be sailed by ghosts, while those that could be spared stood in a line with their buttons shining and their boots burnished as Her Grace came out to go to meet her husband on the *Assistance*.

By now we had come within sight of Jamaica, and a week before Christmas we sailed into Port Royal Harbour. She still had not spoken a word to me directly but passed by as though I were not there and if I were standing with Dr Sloane would put some question to him about the birds in the rigging or the state of the weather and if I should answer would repeat the question as though no one had spoken.

Yet when we came ashore (she was in the boat ahead of me), she stood up and waved to the Negroes who were walking on the beach and greeted the Lieutenant-Governor, though but few would recognise under that grave appellation old Sir Henry Morgan, the greatest pirate these islands have ever bred. He had been lately removed from the island council for some misdemeanour (though nothing to compare with the bloody deeds of his youth), and it was my master's intention to restore him, for the planters loved him, they being reformed pirates like he.

He stood there on the quay, a black Welshman who exhibited the signs of his intemperance and a thunderous look besides which bore witness to his notorious ill-temper. Yet the Duchess greeted him as sweetly as though he were the prettiest gallant she ever set eyes on.

Sir Henry, it is an honour to meet you. I have heard so many tales of your exploits.

Pack of lies, ma'am, pack of lies. These planters will prattle.

Well then, you must tell me the truth, must you not?

Hrrumph, be a great honour . . . The old man was much moved by her courtesy and his jaundiced cheeks blushed hot.

He dined with us that first night and many nights afterwards, and when I think of our time on the island – which was to be cut short by so tragic an event – it is of sitting out under the portico (for the house was made of brick as it might have been a house in Devonshire and was far too hot, while the Spanish houses were built low around a cool court) with the sound of the grasshoppers in the trees and the Negro attendants waving the great palm fans behind our chairs and the hot scent of the flowers while Sir Henry talked on in the mellifluous accents of his native Glamorganshire:

So we heard that the Spaniards had imprisoned several Englishmen in their dungeons, at Porto Bello you know, in Panama. We landed about three o'clock in the morning. They had three forts there, ma'am, the first of 'em gave us no trouble at all, dealt with the garrison in half an hour. But the second was a harder nut, too steep to climb. So I had these ladders made, broad as a Frenchman's arse, saving your presence, ma'am. Three or four men could climb them abreast. But we had to go across open ground to put them against the walls, and I didn't care to lose my best men before we had started. So I got together a dozen priests and nuns we had captured, told 'em they were going to meet their fellow countrymen, sent 'em to plant the ladders against the walls. But those Spanish devils shot 'em down without pity, so we sent another lot in before they had time to re-load. They shot a few of them too, but we got up the ladders and took the place.

And the garrison?

Well, they had to be punished for their cruelty to their own people, didn't they, ma'am? Yes, we had some sport with 'em.

And the Governor?

Oh we accounted for him too. There wasn't a Spaniard left in Porto Bello after we had done, not left standing, I mean. The women were damnably fine, madam, such eyes. But the men were too slow to tell us where they had hid their treasure, so we made the women do it.

Were the women quicker to tell then?

After we had finished with them, Your Grace.

Oh Sir Henry, I don't care to hear such things.

But she did. She sat motionless as the old villain unfolded his catalogue of pillage, rape and torture and all covered over with a cloak of patriotism:

So the President of Panama sent me a gold ring and told me not to give myself the labour of coming to Panama again. And thereafter the Spaniards began to accept our title to the island.

That is true, very true, Kit said somnolently, for he was drinking deeper than ever. You did that for old England.

I did so, sir, as a loyal Welshman. And we did it all with four hundred men against three thousand.

And the treasure, Sir Henry – Kit always wanted to know about the treasure, he was his mother's true son.

At Porto Bello itself, naught but small beer, enough to pay the garrison. But you recall the President paid us a hundred thousand pieces-of-eight to go away and three hundred Negroes into the bargain, though they were but poor specimens and I fancy they brought the swamp fever with them. Then at Lake Maracaibo . . .

But his proceedings at Lake Maracaibo were not to be related to us, or not that evening, for he began to cough and splutter and his face grew fiery red so that we expected an apoplexy and as though by some contagion Kit began to do the same so that I thought they would explode simultaneously.

Gentlemen, gentlemen, the Duchess cried. You must consult Dr Sloane together, for it seems you have the same disease.

But Dr Sloane had gone to bed half an hour earlier. When I asked him the next morning what ailed the Governor and the Lieutenant-Governor both, he said:

You can see with your own eyes, Jeremiah. It's intemperance, and nothing but intemperance, exacerbated by a sedentary life. If only we could persuade either of 'em to go riding or even to take a walk about the island, but they won't budge from their chairs. They both have a pain in the legs, there is an oedematous swelling and I suspect that his liver is not right.

Whose liver?

Both of 'em. The cases are entirely parallel. I don't know which of them will perish first. His Grace will take no medicine, he has a violent antipathy to clysters. Bleed me, bleed me, is all his cry, for he finds the bleeding eases the swelling in his veins, but it is not good to bleed a man without cause. I took five or six ounces from his arm this morning.

I marvelled silently that two such depraved rogues should have the conduct of the whole island's affairs and that one of them had won the island for the King, for without Sir Henry Morgan the Spaniards would still be snapping at our heels in every bay and inlet.

But if her husband would not exercise himself, the Duchess would wander all about the island quite without fear and with only Mrs Wright or Dr Sloane for escort, although the woods were full of runaway Negroes who lay in ambush to kill the whites who came within their reach. Me she could not abide to be by her. Thus I found myself pressed once more into Kit's employ, acting as his secretary in his discourses with the planters, a quarrelsome gang who had always a great catalogue of grievances against the Governor or the French or the Spanish, or all three at once.

Their great complaint was that our frigates were not numerous enough to protect the trade in slaves from the Spanish interlopers. Either the Spanish seized our African ships on the high seas, or they sent their agents to pay higher prices than the Jamaican planters could afford. The Royal African Company was contracted to furnish the island with Negroes at £17 a head, but the cry was that they sold the best Negroes to the Spaniards and left the sick and maimed for Jamaica. It was a wearisome business and the planters were a mean and grasping crew without either the refinements of civilisation or the boldness of the buccaneers.

Yet I made half a dozen friends among the better sort. We would club at Davies's chocolate-house in Port Royal (coffee not yet being grown on the island). And it was a pleasant morning's work to sit out under the canopy with a cup of chocolate, its bitterness being well sugared and with a spoonful of milk added, and to talk of plantations and factories and cargoes:

Lost two of my best Negroes in the mill last week. When the rollers are stuck, they will try to loosen the canes without telling the ox-boy to halt. Then another lost a hand in the ovens and will be good for nothing.

They complained of the Negroes, how they were lazy, deceitful and would run away into the woods rather than do an honest day's work. But there were always more Negroes to be had at the market on the Palisades (though they said no healthy one had come out of Africa these last ten years). Their greater anguish was upon the fate of their ships, for they all had some share in a ship that was carrying slaves to Jamaica or sugar and chocolate and tobacco to Liverpool and how bitterly they complained that no Englishman could imagine what risk they undertook to furnish him with his modern comforts, how every ship was at the mercy of storm and piracy and foreign enemies, not to speak of the disease that might render a cargo worthless, so that when the hold was opened half of 'em were dead and the others could not hope to work for six months, so that what with the expense of feeding them, and burying them it was a wonder, etc., etc.

Don't you think to insure them, I mean the cargo and the ships too?

Insure them, the planters laughed as though they were a chorus. Who would insure such perilous ventures in a place like this? We are not in Exchange Alley now.

Well, I said, greatly daring and not wholly truthful, I have a little experience of such matters and might be able to accommodate one or two serious gentlemen.

You? they said, and then more mildly, you? You mean you might . . . what per cent had you in mind?

Well, that would depend on the state of the nation, whether we be at peace or war, the season, the nature of the journey and the cargo. And being but in a small way of business, I could not insure the whole cargo but would need to confederate with others.

Mmm, the planter said, his greedy eyes alight with the fair prospect, I could pay seven per cent on a half-cargo to Boston that is to land next month.

Well, I said, let me make inquiry and I shall come back here two days hence. Good-day, gentlemen.

I took my leave of them and promenaded along the quay under the palm trees and let my eye roam over the calm blue sea. If my master that was a numbskull had remade his fortune in treasure-hunting, why should I not increase mine from insuring the treasure-hunters and the slaveship-owners? I had £2,200 in my chest in the strong-room at the King's House. By judicious assurance, I could quickly double it, so long as I never ventured too much at once and backed only sound bottoms.

My first venture was with that same merchant who had a ship bound for Boston. He paid me £70 to insure a ship worth £1,000 that docked safely a week later. Then I insured two sugar-ships for Bristol at the same rate which came in safe also. Being a beginner at the trade, I would not insure slaves, for I knew nothing of the diseases in the African ports. But I did know the importance of accurate intelligence and soon had agents in the other islands and on the American coast. I was often better acquainted with the state of the voyage than the ship's owner, so that when he thought the ship becalmed and overdue, and came to me for assurance, I knew the ship to be but two days' sailing from its destination. Thus does superior intelligence lead to profit. Within two months I had made £400. Indeed had I not also had to go to Kit's whistling, I could have made more.

My example had soon found imitators, so that when we met at the chocolate-house, there would be half a dozen of us bidding for the assurances, which comforted the shipowners, for in our rivalry they saw their salvation. What they did not know was that we had agreed amongst ourselves that none of us would take less than 7 per cent as *premio*.

There was a Jew from Portugal with eyes like a Negro's, one Samson Lucas, who was one of the first to join my mystery, a sly fellow but timid.

Jeremiah, my friend, I have insured a merchantman bound for Virginia, twelve hundred pounds at ten per cent, but it is a little too steep for me, for I stand in deep just now.

Samson, I said, I will take half of it off your hands for twelve per cent.

Thus I began to *re-insure*, which was a tidy business, for the rates were higher and the risks already weighed. But the cream of the business, its true quintessence, lay in the tardy trade, which worked thus.

A boastful owner with a *cigarro* between his lips and jewels upon his fat fingers will say: I have no need of assurance. My ships are sound. Why should I pay money to rogues of your sort?

But then he hears no word of his ship for weeks, then months, and Samson Lucas will say to him: I hear there are great storms off Bermuda (or in the Bay of Biscay or wherever the ship must go by).

Storms, you say?

The worst since I don't know when, the fortunate ships are hove to at St James, the unfortunate . . . well . . . And he spreads his long thin fingers like the scattered bones of so many seamen.

Humph, perhaps I should insure the *Peerless*.

Oh I fear it is too late for me, I couldn't contemplate it, but Jeremiah here, he would insure upon a colander.

Mm, I don't care for it – here I take up my part – it *is* tardy, but at fifteen per cent, I might . . .

Fifteen, that is robbery by daylight, sir.

It is a kindness, I hate myself for my indulgence.

Twelve, not a point more than twelve.

Very well then, as a friend I will oblige you, but don't tell your neighbours or they will know I have grown soft.

What he does not know is that Samson's man in Florida has had word from Jamestown that the *Peerless* is safely landed a fortnight ago. Nor does he know that the said S. Lucas will have a half-share of the *premio*, for there is honour among underwriters.

One afternoon, after we had conducted just such a pretty piece of business, Lucas said to me:

I think we must celebrate our success.

Quite so. Let us repair to Davies's.

Mr Davies does not stock the pleasure I was thinking of.

What? He has madeira as well as chocolate, doesn't he?

There's a pleasure sweeter than wine.

What do you mean?

Come to my house.

Somewhat bewildered, I followed Samson Lucas (he was a little neat man, anything but a Samson) along the promenade until the houses were few and the forest came down to the edge of the shore. His house was on a cleared ground, twenty yards from the sea, a little house with a roof made of palm leaves and a shaded porch. He sat me down upon an old cane chair that was half broken and brought out two pipes that he filled with a mixture from a lacquered bowl.

Mm, this is rare tobacco, I said, breathing in the rich and delicate fragrance.

I am glad you like it. It is to my own receipt.

What is your secret, Samson?

You call me by my name. You are the first Englishman to do so.

I didn't mean to –

No, no, it pleases me. I shall remember this day.

I shall remember this tobacco.

It is a mixture of the Jamaica leaf which is fine and the Virginia which is stronger, and thereto I add an ounce of poppy seed, for every two ounces of tobacco. The seed must be well crushed and the mixture fresh.

So I fell asleep on that afternoon as on many others that were to follow, and when I awoke it was already night and the moon shining on the waters and the lights of the ships shining out in the roads.

On waking that first time, I clapped my hands to my pockets fearing lest I had been robbed, then I became aware that Lucas was sitting in his chair watching me, or keeping watch on me.

You are safe here.

Oh, ah, I did not mean . . .

You are right to be watchful. The isle is full of thieves. I'll bring you a dish of tea, for your throat will be dry, I think.

Yes, yes, it is dry.

And I sipped the hot brew which had a taste like none I knew – there was mint in it and another herb I could not name. Samson Lucas talked of his life: how his family had come to the island when they might no longer stay in Portugal, how he married a half-Negro, whom they call *mulatto*. He loved her greatly, but she died of a fever and when she died he became estranged from the faith of his fathers.

Have you heard of the Prophet Muggleton? he asked.

Not only heard, I replied, in some surprise to hear that name so far from home, but at one time was well acquainted with him, and John Reeve too.

But Samson had heard only of Muggleton, for John Reeve was long dead and there was but one Witness surviving.

I heard his teaching from a trader who came here from Antigua, he said. It seemed a rational religion that an honest man could subscribe to.

So I told Samson about Reeve's belief that Heaven was but six miles up in the sky and that God was a man about five feet high. And he shook his head and said he had heard nothing of that and no such matter was written down in the books of the Prophet Muggleton which he had had sent from London and which he knew great parts of by heart, which was as well, because the books had now been eaten by termites.

So we talked on under the gentle shade of the palm trees with the birds chattering above us and the fishermen bringing up the nets which shone a bright silver from the shoals of fishes in them, so that you might imagine they had trawled through a treasure-ship.

And as I smoked my opium-pipe and watched its fumes rise up into the palm trees, I began to dream of the golden future that awaited my return. As yet I had no word from my Clapham agent, but it could not be long before the alderman or his heirs would be compelled to sell the estate and at the present rate of progress, my means should be ample enough. I might change the name; Gauden House did not sound elegant. Whom should I invite to walk along my peach avenue and take tea in my pavilions? Men of intellect and influence with the Court, chemists perhaps, great ladies, philosophers. I might even take pity on Mr Pepys and ask him to one of my entertainments. Yet perhaps he would be too infected by envy to come.

I was resolved also to explore the whole island. Now and then when I was released from Kit's audience chamber (in truth, but a small brick room such as a great man in England might use for his muniments), I would wander out of the town and there in the forest I would see her pale figure in the midst of a crowd of Negroes as though a ghost had come among them. They would beckon her into one of their straw huts where a sick person lay, and I heard afterwards that she laid her hand upon the affected part and the sick person, whether a child or an old woman, felt eased there. Then they would offer her a cup of palm wine or of rum which they had stolen from the sugar factory and she would take up the half-gourd they offered her and lift it to her lips with every show of solemnity, as though she were taking the Holy Sacrament (though at home she scarcely ever drank wine) and would thank the Negroes and they would clap their hands as if she had accomplished some marvellous feat. Then when she came out of the hut and continued on her walk, the people of the village would follow her chanting. Mr Baptiste the best of the Negro musicians composed a song in her honour which Dr Sloane took down the notes of. You must cry Alla, Alla when the bass is played and clap your hands.

They followed her through the woods, singing and clapping their hands, so that the humming-birds flew out of the wood, affrighted by the noise, and came past my head, making their own sweet hum as they went, just like a bumble-bee. As they came out of the gloom into the sunshine, their feathers seemed most transparent and delicately coloured, red and blue and green. Hur, hur, they went, like so many tiny wheels spinning.

Then the Duchess would send the people away and they would come back into the village and talk of her. I think they had never seen anyone so pale and attributed magical powers to her. She's so gracious and kind, they said, give thanks that she's our island's queen.

But with the traders and shopkeepers and the men of the Council she was haughty and insisted upon the most extreme ceremony. If something was omitted, she would speak sharply to the major-domo and if offended would walk out of the room, so that all the English on the island thought her proud and peevish and wished they had Lady Lynch back, who had sought to please them.

She continued cold to me, but she was warm towards Kit once more and would take his arm and accompany him to the quayside that was at the Palisades, where they brought the treasure in. It was as though her affections towards us were on a kind of seesaw: if one was up, the other must be down.

There was a little platform of figwood and cane built at the harbour with a canopy of canvas and there Their Graces would sit upon golden chairs (rattan painted gold by Mr Baptiste, the musician) and keep watch on the ingots of gold and silver and the plate and jewels and sacred ornaments that were being brought in from the hold of the ships, whether it be from Sir John Narborough's *Foresight* or the *Good Luck* or the *Boy Huzzar* (Capt. Mr William Phipps – no, now Sir William) or from one of the privateers that had a Commission from the Governor.

Oh this is like the time when we watched the football in Devonshire. I do like a dais.

Now we play with golden footballs, my love, we must not kick them so far.

So they ran on like foolish lovebirds. Together they would count the gewgaws brought up by the naked Negroes (naked so that they could hide nothing upon their persons, though I heard that they might sometimes swallow a jewel or conceal it in some less delicate orifice). And as the Negroes came up the gangplank, His Grace would call them over to inspect the articles more narrowly. And they would allot the ingots according to the per centums that had been agreed in England with the King and the Council, the King to have 5 per cent.

Here's one for His Majesty, and one for us, and two for the company. Now one for Sir John, and one for the Gentlemen Venturers, and a half for Sir Richard Haddock who has recovered his courage, and one for the King again and one for us.

So I took down the details and had the goods marked and sealed and sent up to the Treasure Chamber at Government House which was locked and guarded and set well away from the harbour where the Spanish or the Dutch might nibble at it. But though I had my head in the ledger and must keep my mind on my record so as not to omit anything, I could not but notice how gleeful they were, like children that share out toy marbles.

When the ship was empty and the night was coming down, they would rise from their golden thrones and make a promenade back towards Government House with the light open carriage trotting on before them in case they should become fatigued. The great moths flew quiet among the trees as they walked, she in her pale gown, he in his white shirt with ruffles and white silk breeches and hose, so that they too looked like moths in the quickening night.

But as they walked on before me, I could hear him cough and sputter in the twilight. For though he might savour fresh contentment in this second honeymoon, yet he drank as much as before, despite Dr Sloane's warnings. If there was a new Assembly chosen or a new ship landed (and the Captain to be dined), he would sit up too late and drink too freely, whereby in a short time he had a great pain in one of his legs. Moreover, the change from sherry (which he loved best but which could not then be had in Jamaica) to madeira wine made him worse. Dr Sloane warned him that if he did not alter his courses he would fall into his father the General's distemper, viz. the dropsy. But he paid no heed.

Then he went down to Old Harbour to see his father's friend Sir Francis Watson, and Major Peaks, and once more sat up too late and drank too freely. When he came back to town, he was very ill. His legs came out in yellowish weals which the doctors called erysipelas.

He was bled for it in his arm and Dr Sloane had a fomentation made of wormwood, sage, rosemary, rue and pimento leaves to which was added a bottle of wine – which I thought a paradox, for the surfeit of wine was his disease – but it did him no good, and now he complained of a pain in his belly. The doctor proposed clysters and suppositories, but he would hear of neither, and called for a new doctor, so Dr Trapham was sent for as one who understood the country. This stout pompous young man advised him to take a grain of bird pepper in a poached egg, for parrots (he said) always fly to bird pepper as to a natural remedy and it was very necessary for everyone to take it in this climate, though why it should benefit men as it benefits parrots he did not say. When Kit was at the height of his rage (which was extremely violent), the doctors feared that he would perish for want of food and great endeavour was made to force a poached egg, or now and then some chicken broth, down his throat.

But he survived and appeared to recover.

He's well, he's well, she cried to me the next morning. Isn't that news to marvel at, Jem? (It was the first time she had spoken to me or used my name for two months.)

Then she took me by the hand – her hand was so cold and small – and said:

Let us go for a walk, I have been at the sickbed two days.

I followed her into the garden behind the King's House where the lemons and pineapples and guavas and mangrove-grapes grew in rows as in an English orchard.

We must ride, Jem, ride deep into the forest. Fetch horses, fetch them quickly.

With some disinclination, for it was a hot morning, I left her gazing into the woods, while I went to the stable and had horses saddled. When I came back, she was sitting under a pine tree, looking down at the sea in a sort of trance.

Horses, she murmured wondrously, as though to say centaurs or sea-monsters: you have brought horses.

I thought her too frail to ride as far as the gates of the orchard, but when she was in the saddle she seemed stronger and went off down the sandy path at such a canter that I was put to it to match her pace.

On we went through the trees with the croaking of the tree-frogs, and the singing of the grasshoppers for our chorus.

Is not this glorious? she cried back to me, bumping along in her wake.

It seemed as though the island belonged to us alone and I had a fancy that if Kit did not recover we might resume our old relation.

Then the path became broader, and all at once we came out into a cleared space, and the soft sand became a heavy tarry road that smelled of burnt sugar so strongly that we could scarce breathe.

We stopped and gazed in amazement at the great wooden platform which carried three upright rollers that turned upon themselves slowly like a giant's whirligig. And around the platform were walking gangs of Negro slaves each holding sheaves of cane-stalks and feeding them to the whirligig which crushed them with a harsh noise. Next to it were long open sheds with round chimneys from which sugar-steam was smoking. Inside were huge copper kettles without lids, with slaves stirring them, the kettles each of different size the syrup being thicker in the smaller kettles, and beyond the kettles more slaves were pouring the liquid into clay moulds and then into hogsheads. The heat was so fierce that the Negroes went naked but none the less had sweat streaming down their bodies. I had to wipe my eyes constantly for the smoke rising from the kettles, and the noise of the cane-stalks being crushed was so loud that I could not make myself heard. That sweet sickly smell overcame my remaining senses so that I almost fainted. The Negroes sang, but it was a low, sad chant, not like the sharp cries of the overseer who was quick to reproach a slave who was slow to pour or to stoke the fiery ovens or to feed the Moloch with the green stalks.

The Duchess stood surveying the infernal scene, then led her horse away from the shouting and the heat and the stench of molasses.

Why must we make the world so vile?

That's how sugar must be made.

It is *vile*, she said.

I cannot help it, madam.

And I wondered that she should be so tender towards dolphins and Negro slaves and so cruel and capricious to her friends. But madness distracts us from our proper relations and makes strangers kin.

A week after came a ship from London that bore news of the birth of a Prince of Wales, and the next day old Sir Henry Morgan died. He lay in state at the King's House in Port Royal, then his body was brought to the Church of St Jaco de la Vega and a sermon preached, and afterwards he was buried nearby with great solemnity. Thus the greatest rogue and murderer of his time died in the odour of sanctity and will ever be remembered as the glorious founder of our Western empire, which in truth he was.

Dr Sloane lost no time in telling Kit that Sir Henry had not been so ill as he and yet had died of the dropsy and if Kit did not heed his prescriptions he would have the same end. This Kit did not wish to hear, and so he turned again to Dr Trapham who proposed a change of air.

We removed to Ligaunce in the mountains, but it rained there every day, so the Duke drank no less, for there was nothing else to do, and was no better. We came back down to St Jaco de la Vega in the hope of better weather, but the breeze failed from the sea, and the gnats and mosquitoes fed upon the weals on his legs.

But though he was not yet cured, he could no longer delay the thanksgiving for the birth of the Prince of Wales, for to omit such a ceremony would be a disloyalty that would be quickly reported back to his Sovereign. We ourselves were so much taken up with His Grace's illness that we had scarcely paused to reflect upon the momentous consequence of this birth. For now there was to be a Roman Catholic heir to the throne and the Protestant succession frustrated, and what James II had begun, James III might very well complete, namely, the reconversion of England to Romanism, which was not to be borne by a Protestant people.

The festival was set for the last day in September. There had been a storm the day before, but now the sun shone and the humming-birds went to and fro in the fragrant bushes and sometimes swooped over the long tables that were set out under the trees for all the persons of quality on the island with casks of wine at each table and sweetmeats piled high on them. And the Governor went from table to table and at every table he drank a royal health, voices echoing after him 'God save the King and Royal Family'. After each health, I gave the signal to the foot-guards who had their great pieces mounted in the orchard and they discharged a volley whereat the birds flew off the trees and the forts and the ships in the harbour discharged their guns, so that the whole island was full of merry noise.

I must drink a double health, Kit said, for the Prince of Wales a double health.

He began to go round the tables again.

Mr Baptiste, give us a catch.

And the Negro musicians that were assembled by the fountain began to play a melody upon their rude instruments that they had made themselves from driftwood and wire. It was an old Spanish air that they call Calypso, but they had artfully composed the words to celebrate the royal birth, so that each chorus ended God bless our lovely boy.

At each of the ten tables, Kit drank a second bumper. Then at the great table that was 250 feet in length and had 500 gentlemen at it, he drank a health in the middle and one at each end. Then he came to the ladies' table and he would have it that he must drink the health of each lady by name, if he could remember it, and if not he drank to the beauty of her eyes.

By the time he came back to his place, he could scarcely walk.

My legs, oh my legs, was all he could say. His face was flushed a yellow-purple and his eyes were inflamed as though they would burst with blood.

We took him, Dr Sloane and I, nay, half carried him to a little room that served him for his office and as he sat down, a great haemorrhage came from his mouth and would not be staunched so that it covered all the papers on his desk and flowed over on to the ground.

His speech became incoherent and distracted. My will, it must be done, oh it must be done, where is the gold, the gold must be in the box, oh Mother, do not let them – Then he spoke again of his mother and of some treasure that was to be protected from I know not who. And I remembered how Nan at the last had been much occupied with her jewels.

The Duchess could not be prevented from embracing him, half-fallen in his chair though he was, and pressing his swollen face to hers though the blood was still spurting from his gums, so that her pale gown of saffron silk was splashed with red.

Then we put him to bed where he lay in a violent delirium.

Too hot, ah too hot, he said.

I opened the window and let in the noise of the guns firing out in the harbour, and the sound of music in the town, and then the fireworks being discharged along the Palisades.

Now Kit seemed to think he was in a sea-battle with the Dutch. Or was it his father he was thinking of? I couldn't tell, his speech was so distracted.

Outside his room, the doctors were quarrelling.

More bird pepper, Dr Trapham said. Then, as soon as the delirium has passed, he must exercise his legs that the swelling in them may decrease.

I can't agree, said Dr Sloane, in such cases exercise will but incite the hydropic humours to flow downwards and make his legs swell again.

I have never known exercise to fail, exercise and a proper diet.

I fear there will be no improvement in his condition until the moon's aspect changes.

The moon? Dr Trapham gasped.

His Grace is much afflicted by the phases of the moon, Dr Sloane said.

The moon has nothing to do with the case. We're doctors of medicine, Dr Sloane, not ignorant astrologers.

I promise you, sir, that my diagnosis is based upon frequent observations in England.

Well, sir, in Jamaica we count such talk as mere idle superstition.

On 6 October Kit died, without ceremony, as though he wished to cause us no more trouble.

I went in to view his corpse. The colour had gone from his cheeks, and he looked much like his father, but smaller, much smaller.

There, you see, the moon's aspect had not changed.

If he had but exercised when his condition was improved, the second crisis would not have come.

Dr Trapham, will you assist me to preserve his body, for he must be carried back to England to be buried?

I fear that other business detains me on the west of the island.

But it is the Governor's body.

Well then, Dr Sloane, I will be plain with you. I don't care to work with a man who credits such nonsense.

I am happy to hear it, sir, for I would rather not co-operate with a Jamaica quack.

Then good-day to you, sir, said Dr Trapham.

And good-day to you, sir, returned Dr Sloane, whereat Trapham flounced off but could not find a carriage and must go down to Port Royal on the cart that brought up the casks.

Well then, Jeremiah, I must call upon your assistance.

I, I, I have no experience of such work, I stammered.

Don't fear, I will give you close direction, but first we must allow Her Grace to take leave of her lord. I'll fetch her.

As she came in, we withdrew to an outer room that she might express her grief in solitude, but she would not close the door and we watched her like spectators at a play as she threw herself upon his funeral bier (in truth a small lacquer commode where the Duke kept his fowling pieces and powder).

It was not till her pale form covered his little body and her lips were upon his that I saw she was still wearing the saffron dress she had worn at the celebration for the Prince of Wales, which was splashed with the blood from his gum-haemorrhage.

Oh my lord, oh my love, she moaned, what shall I do without you?

She must take off that dress, Dr Sloane whispered, or she'll be infected.

She will not, I said.

I hadn't thought she loved him so much.

This is for our benefit, Hans (I had never called him so before, but if I was to be his co-operator we must be intimates). She wishes us to report that she is much stricken.

You're a cynic, Jeremiah. She's mad.

Mad, yes, but it is a cunning madness and there is method in it.

Before the day was out, it was noised all round the island that the Duchess was distraught, disconsolate – and defenceless. She must be protected, she and her treasure, from the cut-throat Biscayans that thronged the harbour. Though they had hated her before, the Assembly – themselves being a piratical quarrelsome crew – rallied as one man to her defence. The militia abandoned all their other duties and ran to her aid, posting a guard on the King's House and the Treasure House night and day. And when she and her goods moved from the King's

House to Guanaboa for her health, for she was very weak, they had the whole regiment for escort. I saw them go off, the militia in their red coats on the little horses of the island, ducking under the palm trees as they rode alongside the four closed carriages that contained the duchess and her treasure, with the birds fluttering in their path, and the creak of the axles, for the carriages were heavy laden. Then the procession turned the corner and were gone, though we could still hear the noise of the axles.

Now, to work. Dr Sloane was brisk and cheerful at the prospect. I was less so.

Together we pulled Kit's nightshirt over his head and left his body naked on the commode. Already the flies were buzzing about the body.

We've no time to lose, Dr Sloane said.

I was still contemplating my old charge's swollen body and sadly shrunken cods (like empty gourds) and the shrivelled nut that had been his prick, but Dr Sloane had already sharpened his great surgeon's knife and was making a long incision, nearly two feet in length.

First the bowels.

In a minute he had delved into the stomach and brought out the tripes. Two snips and they were flopping into the strong cedar box he had had built for them.

Now the quicklime.

With a small trowel, I sprinkled a quantity of quicklime upon the oily tripes.

Meanwhile, Dr Sloane had taken out a little saw and was cutting a hole in the head of the corpse that he might remove the brain, for that too was to be put in the box with quicklime and taken down for burial at St Jaco de la Vega, for it could not be preserved long enough to be brought back to England.

I marvelled at how easily the brain came away from the head, like a sponge being prised out from a rock. How gross and vile were these substances that furnished the seat of our reason and the wellspring of our imagination (though in Kit's case only a trickle had ever flowed therefrom).

Close the box and seal it. That was the easy part.

Now Dr Sloane took the powder he had mixed earlier from cinnamon, myrrh and aloes together with an equal quantity of quicklime. Then he began to cut the skin, first down the arms and legs, then turned him over with my assistance (how stiff and heavy he was) and performed the same office on the back. When the skin had separated, he gashed all the muscles to the bone, like a butcher filleting a joint and together, using the Duchess's soup spoons, we filled the cavities with the powder. I thought he had mixed too much powder, but three-quarters of it was consumed.

Then he set to sewing up the cavities. This was work too delicate for me, for I am no seamster. And I could not but marvel at the dexterity with which all the limbs resumed their shape so that I could scarce see the seam. Already we had taken nearly two hours, but the business was far from done.

Now, the hot mixture.

This was a very different composition, being made of heated pitch, wax, rosin and tallow. When the ingredients were all melted into one another, we cut three old linen sheets into long pieces and dipped them in the hot mixture, then rolled them around the several limbs and filled the head and the stomach with the mixture.

I forgot to say that we were now wearing militiamen's gauntlets that we might not burn our hands.

You take the feet, Dr Sloane said, and when I give the word, we lift him together. One-two-*three*.

So we lifted him into his coffin, a stiff and dripping effigy, our nostrils full of the fragrance of the myrrh and the stink of the pitch. At first his arms would not go into the coffin, but together we pushed them in so hard that there came a loud cracking; we must have broken the bone.

More wax, quick. His cuticles are discoloured. We haven't much time.

So we poured in more wax till all but his nose was covered, so that he seemed to be floating in a black pond.

Then we let it stand till it was cold, which took the best part of a day, before we came to nail him up.

In the interim, that night, we took the cedar box that contained the bowels and the brains down to St Jaco de la Vega. It was a strange ride we had under the stars and the bearded fig trees brushing against the open carriage. Dr Sloane sat with the little box between his knees and discoursed of his patients (for like my old friend Mr Pierce he had none of that privacy that distinguished Hippocrates). At the church the parson was waiting for us and took us to the place where they had dug up the paving and there he conducted the burial rite as rapidly as though it was not lawful. Then we put a little cement over the poor fuddled brains and swollen tripes of my late master and put the stone back and went home.

So far so good, Dr Sloane said as we bade each other good-night. But the next day, as we began to hammer in the nails, several bubbles began to arise from the parts which lay uppermost, the hands and the face, so that his breath seemed to be disturbing the surface of the mixture. So we put in some fresh ingredients to quench the bubbles (which were gaseous emanations from the bloating of the body). Then we nailed him up again.

After it was closed, this coffin (of cedar) was placed for protection during the voyage in another coffin of lead, and the interstices filled with pitch.

There, that should do it, the doctor said, let's go and take a glass of wine.

The next day Dr Sloane called me back to the room where Kit lay.

I fear the joiners are bad workmen and the plumbers too.

The moment we came into the room, I could scarcely breathe for the extreme cadaverous smell.

We went out again and tied cloths dipped in vinegar round our faces, while the coffin-maker brought up another cedar coffin that he swore was snug. And we undid the lead coffin and then the inner one and took out the body again and put it in the new coffin and filled the interstices with the mixture again and caulked all the seams with waxed linen and then covered the whole with black cloth.

Do you still detect . . . ?

Yes, I think, but only a trace . . .

It will have to do. The lead will contain the mischief.

Once more we placed the cedar coffin inside the lead and nailed it down.

That was the last I saw of my master, yet after the trouble he had put us to I could not rid myself of the superstition that his unquiet spirit had escaped through the gaseous bubbles and was walking the island, hovering in the trees with the humming-birds and parrots or diving through the seas to rest on a bed of coral.

The disconsolate Princess came back from Guanaboa with her treasure and lived once more in the King's House with the guards all about her.

I must go to England, Dr Sloane, she said (me she again would not address by name). I have no place here.

Your Grace has a place in every Jamaican's heart.

They have been very kind. I have written to the Council. But I must go home, when the yacht is repaired.

It will be a month yet before Captain Monck is returned from Boston.

It was two months. And before he came we had more extraordinary news from England: Prince William of Orange was landed at Torbay. We knew it was true because it was proclaimed by the King himself. But what it meant, we knew not. Was William to become King or his wife the Princess Mary to be Queen (she had the better claim being King James's daughter), or both or neither? Were they perhaps King James's prisoners? Had they signed a treaty – or fought a battle? Was one of them dead, perhaps, or all of them?

In this delirious uncertainty we passed our time. Dr Sloane took notes of the parrots and the butterflies and the humming-birds, and we wandered along the beaches where the sand was of a curious whiteness, as though the sun had bleached it.

At length Captain Monck came back from Boston, the yacht being all fresh painted and varnished. Meanwhile Captain Wright had the frigate *Assistance* newly fitted up, and extra cabins built.

It was at darkest night, so as not to attract attention, that the sorrowing Duchess came aboard the *Assistance* with her treasure and her plate and 500 tons of furnishings (though much of that was to go in the thirteen merchantmen that were to come with us), and Dr Sloane and his collections which now took up six cabinets, and the servants and myself. Dr Sloane brought also some living animals to divert the Fellows of the Royal Society, viz. a large yellow snake seven feet long, an iguana or great lizard and a crocodile or alligator. He had the snake tamed by an Indian whom it would follow as a dog would follow its master, but after it was delivered to the doctor he kept it in a large earthen water-jar. He fed it on rats and the guts and garbage of fowl, etc., from the kitchen. The crocodile he put in a tub of sea-water towards the foc's'le and fed it with the same sort of food. The Duke's corpse was lodged in separate state in his yacht, with but Captain Monck and a dozen seamen for company.

Thus this convoy of the living and the dead, of men and women and wild beasts – surely never was there a stranger one since Noah put forth his Ark – set sail for England, knowing nothing of what we might find there. Nor did we dare come too close to any ship we might espy on the voyage, for we knew not if England or Holland be at war with France, or Spain or any other power. And as the dark form of the island slipped from our sight, with its sweet smell of molasses and its gaily coloured birds, we forgot the misery of Kit's last days and feared lest we were leaving a safe and pleasant home for wilder waters.

Yet there were pleasant days too on the homeward voyage as the doctor's iguana ran up and down the deck and we fed the snake and the crocodile from the kitchen garbage. We were glad to see the flying fish again and the dolphins. But none of us could put out of our mind that we knew nothing of what lay in wait for us in England.

Dr Sloane, we must know what the Captain intends. Bring him to me.

Thus we sat round the table in her cabin, the four of us. Captain Wright seemed uneasy. He was a ruddy fellow, yet with a skulking mien (I fancy he had something of a squint, which was no shame to him). He had showed great punctilio towards us, but little affection, although we had sailed with him for many weeks. He was a firm man for the House of Stuart and told us that each 30 January he would wear his colours half-mast in memory of the horrid murder of our blessed sovereign Charles I (I quote him *verbatim*, for he was solemn).

Well, said the Duchess, I must confess I'm partial to the Prince of Orange. He was my late lord's friend. We sent him venison and a pair of greyhounds when he came to London. I have his diamond ring still.

We don't know whether he is in London now, Dr Sloane said.

Perhaps they've made a treaty and he is returned to Holland. Or they may be at war.

I can't fight any ship whose captain holds his Commission from King James, from whom I received mine, the Captain said.

My husband had no cause to love King James, the Duchess said, he had scurvy treatment from him after he had beaten the Duke of Monmouth.

If we come to England and find the King gone to France, then it is my duty to make all speed to France and place myself and my ship at His Majesty's disposal.

Oh no, shrieked the Duchess, her face white as a ghost. You can't mean it, you can't be so cruel, Captain.

That is my duty, madam.

But I can't land in France with my husband yet unburied and all my things, and among a foreign people.

That is my duty, ma'am.

It is not so, Captain, I said. Your first duty is to protect Her Grace in her distress.

And that I will surely do, sir, as best I can, but I have my Commission from the King. This is his ship.

The great blockhead would not budge from this sentiment. We went on at him, but he was quite deaf. Then the Duchess, who had been silent, rose and said with piercing dignity:

Very well, Captain. You have your duty and I have mine. And you have your ship and we have ours. Dr Sloane, pray remove all my goods into the yacht. I shall sail home with my husband in his ship.

But, madam, the yacht will not carry it all.

Then take the lesser things into the *Generous Hannah* or one of the other merchantmen. And let us leave Captain Wright to his own devices.

So she swept out with all the disdain of a Cleopatra. I never loved her more than at that moment. I hadn't thought she had so much spirit in her.

So the command was given and the seamen began to bring up the chests from the hold and put them into a longboat with militiamen at each end, their muskets being cocked lest any privateer should come up with us at this time (we were but ten leagues from the Canaries where many a Biscayan would lay up). All afternoon long, the sweating seamen brought up the chests and let them down on ropes, very slowly that they might not be lost, into the longboat. Some pieces were too big for the chests and must be wrapped in cloth, and now and then the cloth would come loose and the silver or gold would wink at the sun. There was a great censer on silver chains with a figure of St James the Pilgrim atop it that took two men to carry and a large gold dish engraved with Neptune and dolphins and a great chalice. I am sure they were meant for the Church of St Jaco, but she said they were popish ornaments and belonged to her husband and were hers to dispose of.

So we all went into the yacht, and delivered ourselves to the command of her mysterious kinsman. But I must confess that I saw the *Assistance* sink below the horizon with a dire apprehension. For our little fleet with its few pop-guns was easy prey for any sea-rover who would scarce believe his luck when he found the treasures that were heaped in every corner of the yacht (we could scarce move for the chink of coin and the clanking of plate in the great chests). We took the animals with us but they did not live long. The snake escaped and got up to the top of the cabins where Her Grace's footmen lay and they being afraid to lie down in such company shot the snake dead. The iguana when running along the gunwale of the yacht was frightened by a seaman and leapt overboard and was drowned. And the alligator died a fortnight before we reached Plymouth.

My heart leapt when I was called on deck to see the Scilly Isles and the dangerous rocks of the Bishop and his clerk, and then Land's End and the Lizard.

But still we knew not whether there was peace or war, and with whom. So Dr Sloane and I went in a longboat at night and rowed nearer shore to look for a fishing vessel. We saw one such some way offshore, about two leagues, fishing, but when they saw us they did what they could to fly from us and we had the devil's trouble to come up with them.

What shall we say?

Say how does the King, I said.

But if they say he does very well, we're no further forward.

Then we shall have to think of something else.

We were some twenty yards apart and I could see the master's beard glistening by the light of his lantern.

How does the King? Dr Sloane called.

Which King do you mean? the man returned: King William is well at Whitehall, King James is in France. But beware, for the Channel is full of privateers and they have taken a dozen prizes already.

He went again to his fishing, and we went as quickly to the yacht to give the Captain notice to come into Plymouth as soon as he could, which we did that day.

But the strange thing was that as we came up to the Hoe, the first ship we saw was HMS *Assistance* (never was a ship worse named).

Captain Wright had reviewed his duty and had sworn eternal loyalty to King William.

It was raining hard as we came ashore, and I confess that I felt much aged. In my chest were nearly £5,000, but upon my shoulders lay the burden of the years. It had been but two years less four months since we had sailed from Plymouth, but time is a cruel worker. The dust rose from the floorboards to greet us at Clerkenwell. Dr Sloane took the attics to store his botanical collection where the specimens might be drier and flushed a nesting swallow. At night we had to chase bats out of the saloon. The butler swore he had greased the shutters, but the hinges were rusty and some would not turn. The men carried His Grace's coffin up to the library.

Do you smell somewhat of a . . .

Yes, Jeremiah, pray open the window. The Dean has sent word. We may bury him tomorrow.

It was a maimed rite with few to mourn. The King had sent a Dutchman, one Keppel, to stand for him. This mynheer seemed still at sea and may have fancied that it was the old General we were burying. The Duchess's family were all at Welbeck, where she went to restore her health after we had laid her husband to rest beside his parents. As the Dean mumbled his prayers for Kit, it was to Nan lying now six feet below me that my thoughts ran back, and as the earth rattled upon his coffin, in my fancy I was rattling the knocker with the Turk's head on it in giddy expectation.

There were Dutchmen everywhere. The great Catholics were all gone to France and those Protestants who came in with King James went out with him too, among them one Samuel Pepys, lately Secretary to the Admiralty. This time he fell never to rise again, but the ironical aspect was that I had nothing to do with his downfall (nor Will Symons either, for he was dead). Nor did I take much pleasure in it, my own ups and downs having left me scant-breathed for the sport. The affidavits we had procured, the witnesses we had sworn (to be candid, the lies we had rehearsed), all were crumbled into dust and nothingness. Thus it is that when we finally obtain that which we have so dearly prized, we find we have lost the power to enjoy it. The future which shone so brightly when it lay yet upon the horizon now looks shoddy at close quarters, and we turn our eyes backward to things past which seem to shimmer ever more gloriously as they go further off from us.

IX

The Coffee-House

But there were others where minds were keenly fixed upon the future. Some weeks before the *Assistance* had reached Plymouth, news of Kit's death had reached England. And as we were coming in to that port, Lord Bath was leaving the very same place for London carrying with him Kit's first will (*anno* 1675) together with the deed of six years later that confirmed his lion's share in the estate. *Simul,* down from Welbeck came the Duchess's mother with the second will (*anno* 1687) which left Lord Bath's share to the mysterious Thomas, known as Colonel Monck, and the other Monck cousins.

Both wills provided for a monument to the Moncks to be put up in the Abbey, at a cost of £5,000. Both provided for almshouses for twenty poor widows to be built in memory of Nan. Both supplied the Duchess with an annual widow's portion of £8,000, together with the use of New Hall during her life. But the second will was more to her profit, because the dreadful deed appended to the first gave over to Lord Bath all Kit's possessions should he remain childless, reserving for Kit himself only a life interest, while the second will gave her room to enlarge the Duke's personal estate, a third of which would fall to her. The deed was to be kept secret, but Lord Bath could not forbear to tell his daughter-in-law who felt compelled to tell Lady Clarges, who thought it her duty in respect and kindness to acquaint the Duchess with what was going forward.

Her lawyer Sir Thos. Stringer now confirmed the vile fact to her, that her devious lord had conspired with Lord Bath that the second will should be null and void. The secret deed (which she had not seen till then because he would not let her) had stated that the said deed and the first will could not be revoked save by another will that must be witnessed by six witnesses, three of whom were to be peers, and in the revoking of it the sum of sixpence must change hand. Now the second will had had only three witnesses, none of them peers, and there had been no sixpence to be seen.

Thus, Your Grace, it is a reasonable assumption that your late husband never intended the latter will to stand. Or at any rate the court might hold so.

Sixpence, for want of sixpence, I am to be defrauded, I and (hastily remembering) all his Monck cousins whom he held in such esteem. *Sixpence*.

These are, I fear, the conditions. They are fairly set out and witnessed. We cannot –

I shall fight this vile document body and soul to my dying breath. It shall not stand.

And fight it she did. The suit and its successors continue to this day. It is estimated to have employed more than 120 lawyers thus far, and to have consumed some £50,000 of the estate, although some claim that the expense was nearer £100,000.

All day long, she sat with Sir Thomas and his assistants. All night long, she read legal documents and charters. As I passed her door, with a chink of the candle's light showing beneath it, I could hear the rustling of parchment, and the low mutter of her voice whilst she read out the clauses and appendices to herself, as though saying them out loud were to confer increased authority on them.

. . . and the said charges and assigns to apply for the lifetime of Her Grace and to her *absolutely* . . .

Then as I went along the upper passage, I could hear Dr Sloane moving the pots and trays that held his dried plants and animals, for he was arranging a museum for the curious who wished to inspect his botanical treasures, though I wager many of them would rather inspect the other treasures that were locked away in the Treasury at the end of the passage with the two militiamen we had brought back from Jamaica standing sentinel at the door. Sometimes, very late I would see Her Grace in her pale gown go down the passage and make a sign to the dozy guards to open the door, and she would go in and converse with her jewels, being the dearest things in life to her, but I could not hear whether she spoke, for the doors were plated with brass.

It was a house of treasure and one that was alive with rustling and muttering but there was no human discourse to be had there. Dr Sloane went out each morning to call on his patients, for he had a growing practice out of doors. I for my part resolved to carry on my own trade, viz. that in which I had so prospered in in the West Indies. If I could enlarge my business only a little, I might at last set up a household of my own at Clapham, take a wife, and achieve that independent position in society which by misfortune and the malignity of others had hitherto escaped me.

I hastened to inquire of my agent at Clapham what intelligence he had of Alderman Gauden and his house, but I found only his sorrowing widow, for my man had been carried off by the smallpox while I was yet in the West Indies. The widow told me that Gauden had died soon after him at a ripe old age and the house had been sold the year before.

Sold?

Yes, to a Mr Hewer.

Hewer? Not Will Hewer that was a clerk in the Navy Office?

I don't know, sir, she said, he's a great India merchant. I've seen him in church, a jovial gentleman.

Red hair?

It would have been so once, she said. He presented his guest to me, Mr Pepys that was Secretary to the Navy. I hadn't thought he would be such a little man.

Could the world be so cruel? Even Pepys's boy had the advantage of me. Well, I would show them both. There were other houses, other peach avenues. We must press on.

Oh you must to the coffee-houses. There's no business done in taverns now. Garraway's is the place.

And indeed the stranger who told me this was the only fellow in the Crown that used to be thronged with merchants at mid-day. Truly London was much changed.

Mr Garraway's coffee-house was a bare room with sober merchants seated at tables and sawdust upon the floor. Were it not for the pipe-smoke and the aroma of coffee beans, you might fancy yourself in a Quaker chapel.

I hailed a waiter, whom they called Kidney (which I at first fancied was his surname but then found that all the waiters in the place were called so): Tell me, where may I find the shipping gentlemen.

Over there, sir. Who shall I say wishes to speak to them?

Don't trouble, I will make myself known to them.

As you please, sir, but they do like to have gentlemen introduced to them.

Well, I don't care for such solemnity, I will speak direct to them.

Waving Master Kidney aside, I went over to the table in the corner by the fire (which was not lit) and presented myself. They looked at me with as much interest as one might look at a sack of coal.

You're a merchant, sir? one of their number at length inquired, with the utmost languor.

I have done some underwriting, sir, in Jamaica.

Ah Jamaica, the languid gentleman sighed.

We have suffered such misfortunes with the colonial carrying trade, his neighbour said. No one will touch it, not for twenty per cent.

Ah the privateers, the languid gentleman sighed.

And the French. Better cleave to Norway firs.

Much better.

Or the Bordeaux trade.

But not Jamaica.

Certainly not Jamaica.

I coughed to make an interruption in this dirge: I did not mean that my interests are confined to that island. My intention is to underwrite any good risk. You gentlemen are brokers, I take it.

Office-keepers, sir. We prefer to be called office-keepers. Any rogue may call himself a broker, but *we* have to keep a place on the Exchange.

Well, however you may be called, I hope I may have the honour of doing business with you.

You must be introduced, you know, properly introduced. We have had such trouble with fellows walking in off the street and writing half a dozen lines and then disappearing into thin air.

Such trouble, said another of the brokers, a fat man who scarcely troubled to take the pipe out of his mouth.

Well, I am secretary to Her Grace the Duchess of Albemarle.

Aah.

It was gratifying to see the frowns fall away from their faces and a smiling welcome shine upon me.

It so happens, said the fat broker, removing his pipe from his mouth and knocking it out in the tray, that we have a ship bound for Africa that wants five hundred pounds, a very sound bottom, has done the run half a dozen times. We are offering twelve per cent, though to my mind it is only worth eight, but I like to oblige my frequent customers.

Fifteen, I said.

I beg your pardon, I didn't hear you.

Fifteen.

I thought you said fifteen.

I understand that is the going rate since the war broke out. You spoke of the French.

You're a hard man, sir. If I do too much business with you, I shall be in the almshouse by Michaelmas.

And he handed me over a long paper with lines written on it in various hands. I wrote £500 and signed my name, while he gave me his note for £75. As I did so, several of the company gasped, though they feigned to be coughing or sucking in the tobacco smoke.

You're a venturer, sir, said the man whose paper I had signed. I like that quality in a man. Welcome to our company. Do you take coffee, sir, or chocolate, or perhaps sherbet?

Chocolate, if you please. I gained a taste for it in the West Indies. My companion Dr Sloane recommends that it be taken with a little milk.

But they were not interested in Dr Sloane.

I trust the Duchess is recovered from her sad voyage. Do you think perchance that in the fullness of time she might take an interest in our trade?

She is yet in mourning, I said, and besides she has little head for business.

Quite so, quite so. I understand she is somewhat, ah, distracted by her loss.

Utterly mad, said another merchant, put out that he had not been quicker to offer me his paper.

As a March hare, said a third.

Gentlemen, I said, we may be barbarians in the colonies but it is our custom to speak more delicately of a lady. Her Grace is much saddened by her husband's death, and does not go out.

And the will, sir? What of that, what of the will, who shall win? I'm for Lord Bath.

That matter is yet *sub judice*.

But the whole town can talk of nothing else. Surely you must hold an opinion?

I am sorry to disappoint you, sir, but my lips are sealed.

Thus I gained a character for loyalty and discretion as well as for solid credit. Indeed, my success was greater than I had calculated, for on looking at Mr Groundsel's paper (such was the merchant's name), I saw that no other underwriter had subscribed for more than £100 and I deduced therefrom that assurances in London were broken up into smaller lines than in Jamaica, there being many more brokers to spread the risk between. Yet the inconvenience of rushing to and fro about the coffee-houses to rake together a hundred underwriters for a single voyage was so great that a broker would always welcome with open arms a warm man who would take on half the risk at one signature.

How gay the city looked to me as I walked back to Clerkenwell. The noise of hammers along Cheapside and the cries of the building men were as sweet to me as the call of nesting birds. The city was still arising from its ashes, and I too was a phoenix newly hatched from the ruins of my former life. Insurance was to be the watchword of the modern age. Every new-built office and lodging had its badge – the hand-in-hand, the phoenix or the sun, each advertising that it was stoutly protected against any renewal of the great conflagration. When I had made my name in sea assurance, I would turn to fire, being the next element of nature, and double my fortune there.

Thus I was singing to myself as I came up the steps of Her Grace's and near lost my footing as the sisters Wright came down them in a great hustle.

I will *not*, said one (I think it was Sarah).

It is only a fancy.

I will *not*, she has no right to ask it.

Don't fret, she'll forget it in a day or two.

What's your trouble, ladies? I asked, my *nonchalance* yet unruffled.

Her Grace has told us that we must not show her our backs . . .

We must leave her chamber backwards and curtseying to her, as though she were a queen . . .

I can't do it, I bruised myself so bad on that big commode.

It's the indignity, Jem, we'll not do it.

Well, I would humour her, she is much distracted, I said.

She says the gentlemen are to do the same, and three reverences when they come in to her.

I am sure she's but jesting.

I warrant you she's not. Try her yourself.

Very well, I will, I said, resolved not be put out by this nonsense.

I went up the great staircase to be met at the top by a footman in full livery whom I had not seen before.

Your business, sir? this fellow had the insolence to inquire.

I am Her Grace's secretary.

Her Highness has instructed me to admit no one without appointment.

I have a permanent appointment, I said and strode past him.

Angered now, I threw open the door to find her seated on a red velvet chair which had been placed on a platform at the end of the room as though she were giving audience.

She was wearing her saffron gown, the one that had been splashed with Kit's haemorrhage and she would not have cleaned.

You omit your reverence, sir, would you mock me?

May I speak to you plainly? It is nothing to me whether I bow half a dozen times to you or not at all, but your women are much put out and they are talking of quitting your service (not true, but I hoped to beat some sense into her).

There is insolence everywhere. I am at a loss to find a decent waiting-woman. It will be worse when I am married again, for then I shall require a proper household and this riff-raff will not do.

Married again?

It is unfitting for a person of my station to remain unmarried. I have told the Queen so. It will not be an easy match, for I will have none but a crowned head.

You told the Queen *that?*

Certainly. Who may I confide in if not in persons of my own rank?

She sat exceedingly upright in her chair, rigid as a chess piece, her hair as tangled as a bramble. At her side was a silver ewer with water in it. She was much given to washing her hands, the Wright sisters said.

After the fellow in the wig had shut the door behind me, I stood irresolute in the passage. No, more than irresolute, I was also much distressed. She was too frail a vessel for such great expectations to be embarked on her.

I climbed the stairs to Dr Sloane's room in the upper passage. He was in his collecting-chamber, arraying insects in a long glass case that stood by the window.

You remember this little fellow, Jeremiah? *Formica fusca minima antennis longissimis* I have christened him. This is the one that would eat everything: sugar-cane, dead cockroaches, even my humming-birds, so I hung them by a string from the ceiling and even then the ant found a way.

I contemplated the little brown ant with polite indifference, before beginning:

Dr Sloane, Her Grace is gone stark mad.

She is undergoing some degree of mental disturbance. That is true, but it is only to be expected after her bereavement. I have presented her a simple diet, without oatmeal or cheese, and a marmalade of quinces to settle her stomach, which is her weakest organ.

Marmalade will not recover her wits.

What would you have me do? Beseech her parents to confine her to Bedlam or to one of the private madhouses? Would you rather she were rattling her chains on common straw? No, my friend, time is the only healer in such psychical afflictions.

What afflictions?

It would appear to be a species of dementia, although I would not exclude the possibility of intermittent fits of acute mania. Dr Barwick is of the same opinion, although such diseases do not fall within his bailiwick. I have not yet had the opinion of Dr Sydenham.

Mania, dementia, these are all but words for madness. They tell us nothing.

It is true, said Dr Sloane, closing his long glass case and locking it with care, as though his ants would be the first things a thief would steal: It is true, I confess it plainly, that at present our knowledge of these diseases of the brain is but imperfect. We look forward to the day when we may prescribe medicine for mania and dementia as we now prescribe it for headaches and diarrhoea. But till then –

Marmalade.

We prescribe rest and quiet, nothing to disrupt the mind or the body.

And her fantasies, her command that we must bow three times to her and reverence her as though she were of the blood royal?

We must not agitate her. She must come to her senses of her own accord. This morning she appointed me her court physician. If I am to be of service to her, I must keep her trust, so I've sent to the heralds for them to draw up letters patent for my appointment, that she may sign them. A goldsmith on Clerkenwell Green is making up my badge of office with a red ribbon.

When she came out of her cabinet into the great chamber to dine, I bowed low three times. To my surprise, she smiled upon me.

Chamberlain, you are late. You must escort me.

I beg pardon, Your Highness.

And you have no chain of office. I cannot have a chamberlain without a chain. Dr Sloane knows of a goldsmith, he will attend to the matter.

So our little court in the kingdom of Clerkenwell took shape. The sisters Wright became Mistresses of the Robes and bruised their hips black and blue as they backed into chests and cupboards and tables. Dr Sloane became the Court Physician and daily prescribed her pills that he presented in a little gold box with her arms upon it (though the pills were nothing but sugar and camomile). And I was Court Chamberlain to Her Highness with a long white wand and a gold chain which I left in the porter's box when I went out that I might not be a laughing-stock on the Exchange.

My heart failed whenever I climbed the steps to that great gloomy house and entered into her dismal fairyland.

But if the fairy queen were to awake, would she fall in love with the first man her eye lighted upon? That was our dread, for she was but thirty-six years old and had not yet abandoned all hope of a child. Her old father had died that year and with his expiring breath he had prayed that she might marry again, and she was not disposed to disobey him in a matter where her will was the same as his.

She went out only to wait upon one or other of the Queens (I mean Queen Mary and Queen Catherine) or the Princess Anne, for she said there was no other decent society in England. The sisters Wright said it was as much trouble as to launch a galleon to prepare her for court. Her hair must be combed for upwards of an hour, then she must be bathed and painted and three or four gowns tried before she found one that was to her taste. Then off she would go down the steps, very stiff and stately, and into her father's old carriage. Dr Sloane would go out to visit his patients and I would go to the coffee-house, but all day we would be fearing lest some fortune-hunter at court might have ensnared her, for she was ignorant in the ways of the world, having been married *aet.* sixteen.

Yet it seemed she had a stronger protector than wisdom or experience, viz. her false sense of her own position.

There was none but *canaille* there, she would tell the sisters Wright as they undressed her: I am astonished that Her Majesty should tolerate such common people about her.

Then we would read in the *Gazette* that in truth she had been at a grand assembly full of great lords, ambassadors, etc. Undeterred, the fortune-hunters kept their noses on the scent and at last ran her to ground at Clerkenwell.

Mr Savile presents his compliments, ma'am, and begs to inquire whether he may have the honour of renewing the acquaintance which he made so pleasantly at Hampton Court last week.

He may not, for there was no such acquaintance. I know of no Mr Savile.

I believe he is Lord Halifax's brother, Your Highness.

If he wishes to offer his services as a gentleman-usher or a groom of the chambers, I shall have no objection.

I believe he wished to discourse with you on a somewhat different footing.

In that case, you had best make the matter plain by asking him to come in by the back entrance.

I thought it kinder to tell Mr Savile that Her Grace was not well and that in any case she did not entertain at home.

Mr Savile wrote, letter upon letter. She declared the letters ill-bred and ill-spelled, though she was the worst speller I ever met with, even amongst ladies. But she read them.

Lord Roos was worse. He sent her verses, which she read out to us in an affected high voice as though she were calling across an abyss:

> There's not a lily fairer blows
>   Nor cowslip in the dell,
> Than my Eliza, England's rose,
>   The Queen of Clerkenwell.

> Yet shall her doors be ever locked
>   Against her truest swain?
> However oft my way is block'd
>   I shall return again.

What an impertinent blockhead he is, she cried, though I could see she liked the verse. Eliza indeed, I shall Eliza him. Perhaps I ought to speak to him – but no, it would not be fitting.

At which we breathed a sigh of relief, for Lord Roos was known to have his ways with ladies – he was a pretty lad, though toothy, and her royal reserve might melt in his proximity.

The strangeness of our state was that we became accustomed to it. Behind the great doors of the house we acted in all respects as though we were at Court, while outside we carried on our business as any other citizen might do in workaday fashion. For my own part, I had never been so busy in my life. My correspondence with a dozen brokers, my search for intelligence from my fellow insurers and their agents, my deposits with the leading bankers of the city – all these matters consumed my waking hours, and when the boy gave me a letter in a fine envelope with a handsome seal upon it, I thought it must come from one of them.

Sir (the letter said)
If you would wait at the corner of Covent Garden by St Paul's Church at ten o'clock tonight, I shall have the honour of letting you know of a piece of business that might advantage us both.

Your most humble servant
Ralph Mt.
I shall be in a closed coach and I will show you a yellow glove at the
window of it.

At first I thought this to be a letter from my cousin Fluffy Ralph
come back to dun me in my days of prosperity, but then I remembered
that Fluffy Ralph was long dead.

But I was not one to turn away business, though the manner of its
approach were murky. So I determined to do as he said and see what
transpired.

It was a warm summer night, and the press of carriages about the
piazza was so great that I feared lest I might miss my man. It was a
quarter after ten by the church clock when a heavy coach that had
cloths draped over its doors, so that the arms were hidden, drove up
and came to a halt on the King Street corner.

For a minute or so, nothing. Then a hand in a yellow glove appeared
at the window and began to go to and fro, to and fro as regular as a
pendulum.

I went up to the coach and knocked on the window. The hand
disappeared. The door opened. The gloved hand beckoned me inside.
Trembling, I obeyed.

Inside, the hand dragged me down on the seat. I found myself
beside a short, fat, swarthy man, of coarse complexion (his skin was
as pock-fretted as the surface of Vesuvius). There was scarce room for
us both on the bench.

You know who I am, do you not?

Yes, I do know.

And I did. For this was no member of my own family (fool that
I was to think so) but Ralph Mountagu, Lord Mountagu, the most
notorious lecher and turncoat of his age. He had betrayed England
to France, then he had betrayed his trusting master King Charles,
in favour of Monmouth, then he had fled to France, then he had
come back and sworn eternal loyalty to King James, then he had
betrayed James for Monmouth again, then he had been the first to
come out for William and if he paid court to the Devil, he would
sooner or later betray him too. (He was a distant cousin of that

other Mountagu, Pepys's lord that was afterwards Earl of Sandwich.)

Well then, you know I am a widower.

Yes.

And you know my house burnt down, the one in Bloomsbury I mean, and I rebuilt it at great cost.

Yes, it is very splendid.

Well then, I need a wife. I mean to marry your mistress. They tell me you have influence with her.

You do not think . . .

What, that I'm too old for her? Let me tell you, sir, I have had some successes with women. The Comte de Grammont was good enough to say I had no equal in that pursuit. If you've got the knack, sir, you never lose it.

No, sir, I didn't mean that. It is only . . .

What?

Well, my mistress says she will have none but a crowned head. To give her hand to, I mean.

Tush, sir, do you think I don't know that *proviso*? It's the talk of the town. That's why I am consulting you, because I have a stratagem and I shall need your assistance.

A stratagem?

Yes, I mean to woo her in the character of the Emperor of China.

The Emperor of . . .

Yes, the device is nicely calculated. In the case of European royalty, she would have some acquaintance with their names, characters, quarterings, etc. But with the Emperor of China, she'll be as ignorant as I'll wager you are.

But you don't look . . .

Look like him? Sir, when you have seen my costume, you'll be totally persuaded yourself for all that you know to the contrary. And I shall bring gifts and be attended by a brilliant train. That is where I shall need your assistance.

Assistance?

First you must scatter the ground-bait: say, I hear the Emperor of China is in town, will see none but the King and Queen, and that privately. Then a little later, say, it is said he has expressed a wish to wait upon Your Highness, etc., then bring news of his attendants, his dress, his manners, all so that when you usher me into her presence she will know it could be none other than the Emperor himself.

No.

How do you mean, no?

I will not do it.

Will not?

No, it is a vile imposture upon a lady who is not in her right mind. You take advantage of her weakness.

There was a silence. My resistance had amazed him. I confess it amazed me too. The words spurted from my mouth, as it were, without my volition.

I forgot to say that you would be well rewarded. There would be a fee payable now and another thereafter upon the success of the courtship.

He spoke mildly as though I had presented only some trivial objection to the business in hand.

No, never. I could not do it.

You'll regret it, sir. I will even say, though I make no threat, that you will pay for it. I advise you to reconsider. My offer stands.

So does my refusal.

Well then we have no more to say to one another. You know where to find me, if your mind alters.

His gross little body trembled beside me as though he were finding some difficulty in restraining his anger, knowing that, despite our disagreement, he might later have need of my complaisance.

I tumbled out of his coach, glad to be away from this foul serpent of a man and to breathe the free air of Covent Garden.

How long was it after? Three weeks? It may be a month that I came upon one of the women washing the steps, as I was going out of a morning.

Well, this is very good, Tabby.

The Emperor wouldn't want to walk upon dirty steps, would he, sir? Them Chinese shoes is very dainty, ain't they?

What?

I ran back into the house and up the stairs to Dr Sloane's lodging.

He was putting his instruments in his bag before he went off to visit his patients.

Have you heard?

About what?

This monstrous deception that Lord Mountagu intends upon Her Grace.

Ah yes, the quack-emperor. I confess I'm somewhat disturbed by the project. I wish I'd been consulted at an earlier stage.

You *were* consulted, then?

Alas, too late.

How can it be too late? The Emperor is not yet come to call.

Too late to undeceive her without serious risk to her health. She is firmly persuaded that the Emperor is about to pay court to her. We can't tell her that it is in truth none but Ralph Mountagu.

Surely we can say that, alas, the Emperor is gone away, or changed his mind, or been taken ill?

But Mountagu will come whether we like it or no. I hear that he has spent a great deal on the China trade already.

How was she misled in the first place?

The sisters Wright were the conduit. They passed a series of messages from Lord Mountagu. By the time he consulted me, she was already persuaded.

He consulted *you?*

Yes, well, he said that in view of her delicate health he wished to gain my confidence, would retain my services throughout and not proceed without my co-operation.

So you had only to deny your co-operation and the vile scheme would be aborted?

Unfortunately the lady was already persuaded. You know how stubborn she is. I fear for her mind if she is told she has been gulled. In any case, she won't believe it, so I thought it my duty to accept his offer, strictly in Her Grace's interests.

So you are forwarding this wicked thing?

I have the oversight of it, yes. If at any stage I think that her interests would be better served if the marriage did not go forward, I shall say so plainly.

Have you taken a fee from Mountagu?

My arrangements with my patients must remain private. You may be sure that I will do what I can for the poor lady. And now I must be off, or my other patients will wonder where I am gone.

I followed him down the stairs, my head in a whirl of anger and confusion.

At the foot of the stairs, one of the Wright sisters came up to me with a bold look on her face.

Her Grace's compliments, sir, and would you be so good as to avoid the great chamber and its approach this afternoon, for she has a visitor who wishes to come in confidence and not be seen by the household.

Damn your impudence, I'll go in and speak to her now this minute.

You will not, sir, for she isn't dressed and the rest of the morning she will be at her toilet.

Without another word I rushed out of the house. My fury was so great that I was halfway down John Street before my reason asserted itself. It might be that my mistress was in her soul not as mad as she pretended, that she could at the last be disabused of her fantasies, or that Lord Mountagu's costume and his person in it would make so ludicrous an effect that she would burst out laughing. Thus it seemed to me that I must somehow be present at this absurd masque. Accordingly, I cut short my business in the City and returned to the house in the afternoon by a back way.

There was a little chamber behind the stairs where the porter kept brooms and poles for lighting the lamps and other such things. I squeezed myself into the narrow room that remained and prepared to wait. It was not much above an hour.

A knock at the great doors. The Wright sisters in their best gowns, clucking and simpering, fly across the hall.

The doors open. Through a chink, I can feel the rush of air and glimpse a piece of sky. There is a sound of bells tinkling, then the beating of a gong, very deep and solemn.

In comes a young Chinese boy in a green silk gown chased with dragons. He carries a little pagoda in miniature all wrought of gold. Behind him come two girls carrying blue-and-white bowls of China manufacture (though nowadays it is the Dutch who make them at Amsterdam or Delft). After them come two oriental slaves stripped to the waist, their skins black as pitch, bearing between them a japan cabinet, lacquered with scenes of Chinamen frolicking under willow trees and carrying home the hay over little bridges. Then another slave beating the gong. He also bears a head-dress of little golden bells, so that when he shakes his head, the bells ring. After him two attendants bearing golden palm trees twice as tall as they, so that they must dip them to bring them through the doors, and then more attendants yet bearing more trinkets that I failed to observe, for after *them* came – O shame, O treachery – Dr Hans Sloane. At least he was not wearing a Chinese dressing-gown. Far from standing by with a watchful eye, he was leading the Great Imposter into his mistress's private chamber.

There directly behind Sloane – I cannot bear to call such a man a doctor – came Mountagu, although it took a second, nay, a third glance to know him.

He wore a silk robe that reached to the ground, made of gold and silver filigree chased with figures of strange birds – half-stork, half-parrot – and monkeys and serpents. Upon his lip he wore a long moustache in the oriental mode. His eyebrows and eyes were painted too, so that they slanted away from his nose. On his head was a tall hat in the shape of an anthill, richly adorned. His fat hands were lost in the folds of his sleeves, and he bowed deeply as he came into the house, I think to propitiate our household gods, for there were no persons of note to bow to, though the sisters Wright were throwing him curtsey upon curtsey. With him came an overweening aroma of China spices – sandalwood and jasmine and I don't know what else, for his footmen swung silver censers about the hall, so that I had a trouble to breathe without sneezing. Then the procession took its way up the stairs, and I saw them no more, though I could still hear the bells tinkling and the gong sounding and the hall was yet full of the spices.

For some quarter of an hour by the hall clock, I was alone and ached in every limb, for I was pressed as tight in the broom cabinet as though I were in my coffin. Then came a clatter upon the stairs, and I perceived the boy who had led Mountagu's retinue lead them back down into the hall. But now they were no longer in solemn order but laughing and jesting as though they were off to drink, which in truth they were, for Mary and Sarah Wright came down after them with a great silver bowl of mulled wine (the scent of it filled my nostrils with longing). I could see from my spyhole that they had shed their pagodas and palm trees and the lacquered cabinet, all doubtless given to my lady.

Oh, this tar itches on my skin, like a plague of fleas, it is.

And that cabinet, weighed a ton, it did. I said we needed four men to carry it from Soho. They call it Coromandel lacquer, but with my own eyes I saw Mr Robinson painting it.

Although the imposture was an open book to me, yet the sound of their cockney voices amazed me.

His Lordship said he'd only pay for two bearers and we must black, for our skins were too pale else.

Well, the money is good, that I won't deny.

And maybe more to come later if all goes well. We're to bring more China-ware from the Lambeth factory tomorrow, for she says she hasn't got a complete set for drinking tea.

Well, here's to His Lordship and fair fortune to him.

I'll drink to that.

From my cramped crow's-nest I cursed their swilling and counted the minutes till they were gone. It seemed an eternity before they were summoned up the stairs again to accompany the Emperor to his coach.

I allowed another half-hour to elapse. All was quiet. I crept up the stairs. The footmen were gone and I stole into the great chamber, the door being ajar.

The Duchess was not seated upon her throne but rather lay across its step with a great tasselled oriental shawl about her shoulders. The room was transformed. On either side of the window the golden palm trees nodded. The golden bells depended from the chandelier. The doors of the great japan cabinet were thrown open and from them spilled gay-coloured bolts of silk and calico. The floor was matted with rich rugs that depicted hunting after deer and boar, warriors with bows and arrows and all the lascivious life of the oriental court.

She greeted me with a languorous waving of her arm, which was hung with Chinese bracelets.

Isn't all this marvellous? she said in a drowsy voice as though she had smoked a pipe of Samson Lucas's tobacco: The Emperor is very gracious. Our monarchs are mere barbarians by comparison, don't you think so?

Madam –

His English is quite perfected. As a boy, he had an English tutor, a parson of good family, from Leicestershire, I think.

Madam –

Do you know any prince at our Court who can speak a word of Chinese? Not one, I'll wager you. And he spoke some exquisite phrases in French too, he is well acquainted with King Louis.

Madam, that is not the Emperor.

Not the Emperor? What do you mean, you silly old man?

That is –

I won't listen.

I must tell you the truth.

I never heard such impudence. Thomas! Sarah!

She rose from her affected posture and with her foot began kicking at the gong which had been set down at the side of her chair.

The servants came rushing in, their cheeks still flushed from the wine.

Take this man away.

She went on kicking at the gong, although the servants were standing before her.

It was impossible to stay in such a household. She was now too mad for me to rescue her. With Dr Sloane suborned, what could I do against Mountagu? Even if I had succeeded in opening her eyes, another suitor would have deceived her soon enough. The only other course would be to lock her up in Bedlam with such as Mr Carcase, and what profit would there be in that? I pulled out my faithful chest from under my bed and counted my store. I was but £20 short of £10,000. I was an independent man.

I packed a change of linen into a small leather bag and took that and the chest downstairs. On the lower landing, I met Sarah Wright.

Beg pardon, Jem, but Her Grace says you're to quit the house today and not come back.

She was weeping, half fuddled with drink no doubt, but I gave her a kiss none the less.

Don't fret, Sarah, I was on my way out.

It was a relief to shake off the dust of Clerkenwell and set off on a new track. It would be best to find modest lodgings near the Exchange, for I had taken a great deal of business in the past month. The French had frightened off many of those who were usually to be found in Exchange Alley, and the brokers were desperate and would take names that in quiet times they would have disdained. An insurer of my quality who was not afeared to write £500 on a single ship (though it must be a sound one) was greeted with open arms.

The Duchess and Mountagu were married in September, that much was known, but nobody knew where or by whom. Was he still habited as the Emperor? Was she now dressed as a China-woman? Some who told the story of the courtship swore that she was, but others said she was now so mad that chains to restrain her were hidden under her bridal gown that the parson might not see.

Certain it was that nobody set eyes on her. She did not come to Court, but she must have been taken to Mountagu's house, for the Clerkenwell house was all shut up and was to be sold. Lord Roos had sent a verse to Lord Mountagu which he then retailed to the town, thinking it so witty:

> Insulting rival never boast
>   Thy conquest lately won,
> No wonder that her heart was lost,
>   Her senses first were gone.
>
> For one that's under Bedlam's laws
>   What glory can be had,
> For love of thee was not the cause:
>   It proves that she was mad.

I doubt whether Lord Mountagu paid much heed to this squib, for he was already fully occupied in his wife's lawsuit that he might double the fortune that was coming to him. Albemarle v. Bath became Mountagu v. Bath, and the lawyers grew fatter yet.

When I thought of such cruel rapacity, I wept for the world and for my late mistress who had been the plaything of fate since her childhood and was led astray by pride because she knew no better. She had had but one true desire in the world and that was to have a living child. This denied her, all else was mere caprice.

I had resolved to concentrate upon the Mediterranean and the Levantine trade, the voyages being short and the rates high in these stormy times, never less than 10 per cent and often 15 or 20 per cent.

For the shipowners grew ever more fearful of the French cruisers and privateers. Although we were now joined with the Dutch, our navies could seldom spare frigates for escort, and many a merchantman had to fret at anchor for a month or two until a convoy could be made up. Ships that had taken a cargo in February had to wait until May before Admiral Rooke could send twenty men-o'-war to keep them company. By then, there were 400 merchantmen. I had written lines on thirty-five of them myself for sums from £50 on the little *Anna* that was carrying dyes and Sheffield ware to Naples, to £600 on the *England's Glory* that was bound for Smyrna (indeed, the whole convoy was called the Smyrna Fleet, for that was its last port of call).

There were but two or three men in the City that had written more lines on the ships, and I was glad that the Grand Fleet was to sail with them to make assurance doubly sure.

It was a pleasant spring morning and I had no business on hand and so resolved to saunter down the Strand and take a turn by the river. The sun was so bright that I did not at first see the little old man just by the Water Gate that Mr Jones built (I can remember the very spot). He was somewhat plump, and seemed near-sighted, for he peered at the passers-by as though they were written down in print too small to read. There was something about the way he walked, a stumping pugnacious little gait he had, and I knew him instantly and thirty years of enmity dissolved in a lightning flash.

Mr Pepys! Sam.

He turned and peered at me.

You have the advantage of me, sir, I fear. My eyes are bad.

Jeremiah Mount, sir, your old acquaintance.

Jem, Jem, my dear friend (perhaps he had never known how hard I had tried to destroy him). You're much changed. But then we're all old men though Sir George was kind enough to say last week that he would not take me for a day beyond forty-five.

You live nearby?

He pointed to the windows of the building behind us.

Up there, he said. That's my lodging in retirement, though I hope that I may soon move to Clapham into the house of my old clerk Will Hewer who lodges here with me also. It's a fine house at Clapham. It belonged formerly to Alderman Gauden that once victualled the Navy but is now dead. But for the time being, I'm content enough here. I have my little library. Every Saturday some of the Fellows come to dine, we call ourselves the Saturday Academists. We talk of some learned matter and drink, rather too much, I fear. You must join us. I am quite retired now, I went out with King James. They tried to find fault with my stewardship, they locked me up twice and released me twice. That makes four times I've seen the inside of a prison cell for serving my King, but they never found a fault, Jem, not one, and so now they leave me in peace. My work is done and the new King knows it. But the other day he was heard to say when some piece of work was botched, 'This would never have happened in Mr Pepys's time.'

He chuckled and I saw that age had not diminished his faculty for self-congratulation.

Now you, sir, he said, what have you been doing with yourself? I have seen you but seldom since you were in the service of the Duchess of Albemarle.

He would bring up that humiliating recollection, and I could see how greatly he delighted in it.

Well, sir, I threw back, I am in a fair way of business as an insurer on the Exchange.

Marine or fire?

Marine.

Well, I hope you have nothing riding on the Smyrna Fleet.

I went white. I could scarcely stammer:

What, what do you mean?

Haven't you heard? It was all over Lloyds coffee-house this morning. I go to Lloyds once a week to keep up with the world. Admiral Rooke thought the French Fleet was safely in port, in Brest, I believe, and so he let the Grand Fleet go, but the Frenchies were waiting for him round the corner. That's all we know at present, but it sounds like a pickle. There were fellows in Lloyds looking to reinsure at twenty-five and thirty per cent. I always said that the fleet was too numerous, never does to put all your eggs in one basket, you know.

But I was in Garraway's yesterday and there was no word of it.

Oh you must go to Lloyds, they always have the latest intelligence. The Kidney there has the best agents.

I must – I could not finish the sentence but rushed from his presence without a word. By the time I reached Lloyds, the place was in an uproar. Some men were shouting, and battering their fists on the bar, others were sitting at the tables as pale as ghosts and as silent.

Mr Groundsel hailed me.

Ah there you are, I have a couple of ships need reinsuring and wondered whether you might oblige me.

From the Smyrna Fleet?

The same.

What's the rate?

Well – he looked as guilty as a thief just taken – I can offer forty.

Then the ship's as good as sunk.

Don't say so, Jem. We know only that –

But I brushed past him into the throng of desperate men, each trying to discharge the worst of his risks on to his fellow. If only I had been to Lloyds the day before, I could have gone part of the way to save myself.

Rooke did his best, but he was outnumbered. We learned a week later that a hundred of our merchantmen had been captured or destroyed (the Dutch lost more yet). The value lost with the cargo was above a million pounds.

Eighteen of the ships I had written insurance on were lost. Eight or nine would have been enough to bankrupt me, but eighteen! I too was utterly lost. I had not a friend living in the world. My last lover thought herself married to the Emperor of China. My deadly rival was living in happy retirement soon to remove to the house that ought to have been mine, surrounded by old friends and bathed in public esteem, while I was an outcast, disgraced, dejected, a futile encumbrance on the new age.

All my money was pledged at the bank. I had only a few shillings in my pocket that would pay the rent for another fortnight. I was without cash or credit. No one would lend me a penny, for it must go straight to my creditors. I gave up shaving. My linen was filthy, because the laundress would not wash any more until she was paid. I had already given up hope, and occupied the day wandering hollow-eyed through the streets of the City, rehearsing again and again the catalogue of my folly and cursing my rashness.

At length a terrible fatigue overcame my body and my spirit and I resolved to spend my last shilling upon poison, for I could not bear the thought of drowning. In my dreams, I heard the cries of the men drowning in the ships I had written lines for, while the Kidney at Lloyds called out every ship's name and her fate: *Mary Bell*, lost – *Bohemia*, captured – *Dandelion*, lost – *Maidstone*, in port Genoa – *Antelope*, captured – *Darling*, not known.

No, poison it must be. I searched my brains for my old chemical knowledge. I could not go into a druggist's and inquire out loud after a venom that was cheap and procured a quick and easeful death. Arsenic? Or belladonna? Or hemlock? Hemlock might be the best, Socrates had made no complaint about it. I would inspect the shelves of the druggist on Tower Hill to see what he had. But as I came to the door of the shop, I trembled and was unable to raise my hand, being as paralysed as though I had already taken the poison.

How now? Looking for the bell? Don't stand upon ceremony, come in, come in.

Someone slapped me on the back in hearty fashion and I wheeled round to come face to face with – my son.

It is you, isn't it? He stared into my haggard face, fearing that he was mistaken. My cousin that knew my mother when she was young, you're he, aren't you?

Yes, I said, that is I.

I thought it must be, because I remembered you had a powerful interest in maps and marine charts. You must see the new edition of the *Pilot*, the printing of it is so greatly improved.

I'm not looking for maps.

Not looking for maps? Then why –

I – but I couldn't say I was about to call next door to choose my poison (I had forgotten his shop was so near).

Well, come in anyway. My wife is here, and she will not forgive me if I don't bring you to her.

No, I cannot . . .

Cannot what? Aren't you well, you're so pale.

He looked closer at me and saw my state of destitution, smelled it too, I do not doubt.

Come in, come in.

So I went in with him and gazed with desolate apathy upon the charts and chronometers that were set out upon his tables and were presently inspected by a throng of prosperous gentlemen of the navigational fraternity.

No, Mr Harrison, I heard him say to a small brown man of a worried aspect, we've sold no more of your longitude book. I fear that the title was bad, but you would have the Latin.

But it's a work of supreme astronomical import, why, Mr Halley himself said . . .

I can't help that, sir, the public won't take it. Now then – he turned to me, anxious that I should shift out of his shop before I depressed the spirits of his customers – come along, sir, into the back.

It was a small back room with wooden panels in the shape of diamonds that was now in the mode. There was a crackling fire by which a fresh-faced young woman was seated at a tea-urn. She greeted me kindly and bade me sit down and take a glass of tea, for they had no dishes and slaked their thirst without ceremony.

As I sat in the little round wooden chair and felt the hot delicious brew flood through my veins, I was moved close to tears. This was the first kindness done to me in many a week. Thus coddled and mollified, I was unmanned and began to speak of my woes, but involuntarily, as though some advocate was speaking for me, but brokenly.

The Smyrna Fleet destroyed me, madam . . . I was prospering before that . . . if only they had not all sailed together . . . now I am bankrupt . . . nowhere to go.

But your home?

No home, madam. I was turned off . . . I was at my lady Albemarle's, but she is mad.

I hear she is married.

She is both, I fear . . . so I am a wanderer now.

Oh cousin, don't weep, I may call you cousin mayn't I?

You're kind to address me so . . . very kind . . . but I am not, or rather not only a cousin (why was I saying this? I can only blame the extremity of my state).

Not only my husband's cousin? But, she said, turning to him, you told me most explicitly, he was a cousin and of your own name too.

Of your own name certainly, and your husband's cousin, but more than a cousin.

As soon as I said this, I could have bitten my tongue out, but my frenzy drove me on. I could not go back, even though going forward was only to calamity.

How more than a cousin?

I looked at her more nearly. She was a pretty woman, but she had a modest look, as of someone who knew little of the world. I did not think she would like the truth when she heard it. But I could not hold myself back, my desperation was too strong.

It is a terrible secret, madam, I wish it may remain a secret.

Oh I love secrets, do tell it.

You won't care for this one.

I shall, I'm sure of it.

Well then, I said turning to Richard who had gone pale, detecting some serious portent in my manner where she had not, you remember I said I knew your mother very well in the old days?

You said you knew her.

Very well I knew her. We were . . .

No, I don't wish to hear this . . .

You were her lover, his wife said gaily. Well, a woman may have admirers before she is married, in these days at least.

No, my dear, Richard said, that is not what he means, or it is not all that he means.

Then she looked at me and saw, then looked at her husband for confirmation, but needed none, for she knew his lineaments by heart.

Oh, she said, oh, and then was silent, then rose and left the chamber.

So, he said, you've come here to extort something from me, what is it, money? What's your price?

I didn't mean to come here at all, I was passing by.

Do you think I'm an idiot?

I swear it, I said, my intention was to call upon the druggist next door.

To buy poison for your suicide, I suppose.

Well, yes, since you say so, I will confess that was my reason, though I had not meant to speak of it.

You expect me to believe that, sir? You're a foul knave. You come here with this hideous tale to threaten me and my poor wife, then you speak of killing yourself.

I have told you no tale, you have made your own deduction.

The tea and the fire were beginning to warm my limbs, as was the sensation of power, which because I had not sought it was all the sweeter. How like me he looked, how unlike me in everything else.

Are you seeking a place?

A place?

Yes, a place. I couldn't have you here, my customers would remark upon the likeness and there would be tattle.

You confess the likeness?

Don't provoke me. You know there is a likeness, else you wouldn't attempt this imposture.

You call me an imposter when I have claimed nothing.

He saw he had ventured too far and nothing would be gained this way.

Well then, he said, let us not quarrel.

I did not come here to tell you that I am your –

Hush.

I may not be, though if you remember Ralph, which of us would be the likelier?

Let us talk no more of the matter. I have a proposal. Ah my dear – his wife came back into the chamber, looking deathly white – I was just about to tell our, our friend that I have a place empty at the factory.

Factory? I inquired.

Down at Whitstable. We have a share in a modest but commodious factory for copperas. It is, I believe, the largest in Kent. You're acquainted with copperas?

Very well acquainted, I said. This is a marvellous coincidence. Some years ago, I pursued chemistry in the Duke of Buckingham's private laboratory. I had a great fondness for the manufacture of copperas.

Did you so? he said looking at me in disbelief. I could see him thinking: This is the worst day of my life, I have acquired a father who is homeless, penniless and the most deceitful liar in Christendom and who makes me, proprietor of a great stationer's on Tower Hill, into a common bastard, and now he pretends to be a chemist and a friend to the Duke of Buckingham.

Yes, it is a most ingenious process.

So it is. Then you'll feel quite at home there. I can't appoint you manager, for Mr Knewstub is an excellent fellow, but he'll be glad to have you as his assistant in the business.

Manager of a copperas workshop?

Assistant to the manager.

At Whitstable?

At Whitstable.

It's not the place I had dreamed of.

I dare say not, but it is a good place.

I may have it upon what condition?

You can guess the condition.

My silence about the matter I have not spoken of.

Just so. I send a carrier on Tuesdays who will take you.

I sat by the fire and said nothing. Then I lifted my head and saw his wife's eyes raised in pleading towards me.

What will you pay?

A hundred guineas a year.

I'll take three hundred.

But I pay Mr Knewstub three hundred.

Three hundred, you may think of it as my pension.

Very well then.

The contract was made, or so I thought. But then I saw that his wife was still vexed and her demeanour fearful.

Oh but my chuck, she said to her husband, if you should send down this, this gentleman bearing your name and, well, I see no resemblance except you both being dark-complexioned, but you said you thought he was like, though I think he is more like the late King, I mean King Charles.

Yes, my love, as ever you are in the right. It would be discommodious for you too, sir, would it not, to be thus identified with your, your Master?

Could he not bear some alias, only for the time being? she mewed. I was beginning to think her the worse of the two. At least she was none of my blood.

That is a masterstroke, my love. What shall we call him? Black perhaps, because he is so dark?

Or Long, because he is so tall?

They stood there debating how I should be called, as though I were a lapdog he had just given her, but my body was too weary, my heart too full of misery to complain.

I know, said my loving son, I remember my father saying that in Kent where he was born there were so many of our name and all with the same Christian name that they were called by the village where they lived. And you, sir, did you have such a nickname?

Why, sir, yes I did, it was Jeremiah Churn.

Then would you consent, purely as a favour to a lady, well, to your . . .

Don't say it, Richard, don't say it.

Very well, a favour to a lady, would you –

If you wish it.

I do wish it because my love wishes it. That is settled then, Mr Churn. God grant you a pleasant journey. Whitstable is a handsome port and is like to become very busy when the war is done.

The next day being a Tuesday, I took the carrier down to Whitstable, along that same Kent Road that I had first travelled solitary to meet Nan, then with Fluffy Ralph and then down again with Nan and the Lord General to bring in the King and then with the Lord General to go and fight the Dutch and back the other way in a coach with my leg bandaged, and now in a filthy old carrier's cart to go and grub for copperas. I shared the back of the cart with the empty bottles and jars that had held the inks and dyes and bleaches. The jars stank like the Devil's groin and they chinked against one another as we went over the rough cobbles and the cracks in the road.

X

The Shore

Home, said the carter's man, as we came down over the low hill to the sea's edge, a grey troubled sea like an old woman's hair.

No home to me.

That it soon will be, Whitstable is a kindly port, and he gave me a broken smile with what teeth he had yet in his mouth. To me the place seemed a poor huddle of seamen's hovels that cowered behind the sea wall for fear of the easterlies. He stopped to let the horses drink and I got down.

No, it's further on yet.

The road became a rough track of mud and shingle, much rutted by the passage of carts such as ours. We were beyond the town now. There was but a single cabin with a roof of rotting straw beside the strand. Then we passed under a low cliff. The rain came down in a fine drizzle or was it a sea-fret, I couldn't tell, my eyes were misted over.

Here we are then, the cop'ras houses.

Out of the drizzle, they came at us like sea monsters rearing out of the deep: half a dozen great black houses, their walls, roofs and gables all pitch-black. Though we were yet a hundred yards from them, the stench of sulphur was so vile I could scarcely breathe. From their chimneys came a smoke blacker than I had ever seen, so that the air above was one thick stygian cloud.

That's ours, the Mendfield House.

He pointed to the largest of the houses set back behind the others.

Brings up near twice as much cop'ras as the rest. Look at the size of the bed.

He showed me a low flint wall that enclosed a fair space, half an acre nearly. It might have been a parson's garden but that it was filled with goldstones shelving down from the cliff so that when the stones were dissolved the liquid might run down into the lead piping and into the house. The smell was the smell of Hell and these were the Phlegraean Fields besides which my little copperas bed at New Hall had been a pretty playground.

Come along, come along, shift those jars.

An angry warty little man in a dirty leather apron burst out of the black house like a wasp out of a bottle.

Knewstub's the name, cop'ras is my trade, busy is my motto, the little man said.

He seized my hand in a fierce grip.

Welcome aboard, Mr Churn. You'll find us a tight ship but a comradely ship. We make no distinction of rank here. Example: we all take a hand with the jars, wash 'em, fill 'em and seal 'em, all together.

Ah do we so?

I'd counsel you to take off your Sunday best. You'll find an apron and breeches in the store-house and mind you cover yourself from head to toe. This stuff burns like the Devil.

On a filthy table in the store-house I found shirt and breeches set out together with a foul leather apron. I could hardly see to put them on, the little window being as blackened as the rest of the place. My former garments I hung on a hook at the back of the store-house which seemed to serve as Knewstub's office, for there were papers heaped on a rickety desk and a barrel of beer beside it. The old clothes on the peg looked like a scarecrow and had a livelier air than I sensed in myself. All life seemed drained from me and I came out into the foul drizzle stumbling over the shingle like a dead man clambering up the shores of the Styx.

Now then, Mr Churn, we take turn and turn about at the boilers, for they are devilish hot and a man can only stand so much at a time. Then you go to raking the beds that the rain may wash the stones equally, then the same with the troughs, though they takes less stirring. Mr Richard tells me you have some experience with cop'ras.

Yes, in my laboratory, I did once . . .

Well then you'll know what a troublesome customer your cop'ras is. Water him too much and he turns to mud, water him not enough, and the stones just sits there winking at you saying we're too artful for you. Same with the boiling, boil him too hard, and you lose half of him, boil him too little and the iron won't take up the brimstone.

Yes, yes, I said with a knowing air.

Then this is a various house. Some just does the grapes – we call 'em the grapes here – and sends them up to London to be dissolved. But we do it all, the inking and the dye and the mordant – we have a fair trade in the mordant because of the cotton and wool-dyers hereabouts. They swear by Mendfield's house for keeping their dye fast through a dozen boilings. Then we sell part of the brimstone to the King's works, finest quality only, nothing but the best for our gunners. The best of the goldstones we keep back for the King too, for the pistol-flints, we are fair put to it there with the flints from Queenborough, but ours are the finer. We put the old women who rake them in to gleaning the best for the flints, there you see 'em at it now, though it's picky work in the drizzle.

Through the rain I could barely espy half a dozen women bent low over the shingle raking to and fro with a painful slow motion.

At that moment I could imagine no more miserable task on God's earth. Within half an hour I was to learn that the old women's lot was blessed in comparison of the boiler men.

Sweep slow and full, Mr Churn, else you'll plash yourself, slow and full.

We stood on a narrow perilous platform alongside the great lead boiler that was held upright by brick walls ten foot high. Knewstub put into my hand a long paddle made of lead, as tall as a man and twice as heavy. I could scarcely lift it off over the lip of the boiler and when I let it down into the boiler it nearly carried me with it.

You must walk with it, Mr Churn, keep pace, keep pace.

I began to walk round the boiler with the giant's paddle ever about to escape my grasp or pull me into the cauldron after it. After five minutes, my arms were mortified with fatigue.

Ten minutes with the paddle, Mr Churn, then five minutes with the bellows. This is a capricious devil, the furnace, though I say it myself, and it wants regular bellowsing.

After two more circuits of the boiler, I was ready to exchange my mode of serfdom and was about to go down the narrow steps to the furnace when Mr Knewstub yelled at me.

Take it out! Take it out, damn you.

I purposed to leave the paddle in the boiler for my return.

Well, you'll do no such purposing. I've lost two paddles already this month from idle men letting them slip into the broth, and they are costly articles.

Very well, I said, but I would be obliged if you did not speak to me so.

I shall speak as I please, this is a factory not a nunnery. Do you understand that, Churn?

Yes, Mr Knewstub, I said, putting a delicate accent upon the Mr.

Good, now then, to the bellows.

The bellows were great heavy boards bound with iron, and the leather between them as stiff as wood. Even if I had been fresh, it would have been a weary business to make them blow.

You seem short of puff, Churn. Let me show you.

He snatched the bellows from me and with a slow but steady compression made the fire blaze again. His forearms were thick as knotted ropes.

There, like that, you'll get the knack in a fortnight, but by God you're old for the work, I wonder what Mr Richard meant by sending you. We had plenty of likely Whitstable lads up for the work.

I mumbled some poor words about my good fortune in having the place, meaning not a word of it.

Think naught of it. We're always glad of willing hands.

Hands? I thought, but I was to be his deputy, was I not, but of that not a word and I was too fatigued to argue the point.

You'll lodge in town, at the World's End. It's a clean house and Mrs Splint is a civil landlady. And I shall see you at All Saints on the Lord's Day, ten o'clock sharp.

But –

You're not a Dissenter, I trust.

No, no. I was beyond any discourse on the matter.

Because we employ none but good churchmen, no atheistical fellows and I need scarce say none of *them*.

I bade him good-day and trudged back to the miserable hamlet – it

were flattery to call it a town. As I came on to the wasteland beyond
the cliff, the sky cleared, though it was still a grey and mournful
firmament above a grey and mournful sea, that same sea I had seen
the ships joggling on when I was a boy with Emm and then had seen
the Dutch masts riding upon when I was the General's man and still
had hopes of glory. But here I was as I began – destitute in an attic
(thank you, Mrs Splint, that will do very well, though I would prefer
a bigger jug, if you please).

I had unpacked my few wretched goods and washed and put on clean
garments. The shirt and breeches smelled horribly and I determined to
hang them out of the window which gave on to the yard.

Put those clothes away, came a cry from the yard. I looked down
and saw Mrs Splint feeding her chickens.

But, Mrs Splint, they stink and I don't want to pollute your
bedchamber.

And I don't want the world to know that I have cop'ras men lodging.
Nothing gets a house a worse name than to be associated with the
cop'ras.

So I took the filthy garments in and put them in the cupboard
and kept my other things upon the table that they might not be
dirtied.

I went down into the tavern where there were already a few old
fishermen gathered.

Ah you'll be from the cop'ras trade then, said the first. You can tell
a cop'ras man a mile off.

Smell him, you mean, said another.

Tom, don't be coarse. We must speak delicate.

I'm obliged to you, sir, I said, it's true I've come down here to survey
the works and assist as best I can.

You're a surveyor then, sir.

Oh a jack of all trades, I fear. I was once a stationer and then
secretary to General Monck and manager of his estates, before I was
injured in the Dutch war, the second one I mean. Then I was in Jamaica
with his son, the second Duke. I remember once Captain Morgan the
pirate you know who was the Lieutenant-Governor of the island saying
to me –

My tale made a great impression upon my hearers, and they poured drink down my throat, which was no discomfort for I was as dry as a salted herring.

You've had a most curious life, sir. You've seen sights that are not shown to many.

It's true I have had moments of consequence.

You must write your memoirs, Mr Churn. Any man who has seen such things ought to bequeath his memorials.

No, no, I fear it would make a tame recital.

I venture to contradict you, sir, said one of the men who seemed to have some learning, a boatbuilder by the name of Prosper Smith: If such a book were published, I should subscribe for it.

Then I would give you your money back.

We clinked glasses and became friends and shared a barrel of the local oysters with a loaf of bread fresh baked and the world took on a kinder hue even at the World's End.

As I went up the staircase to my miserable lodging, bending my head to avoid the beams, the thought still buzzed in my head like a bee grazing in high summer: *memoirs*.

The more I ruminated upon the question, the more plainly it came to me that no one of my acquaintance had nearer knowledge of the great events of the past forty years. None could speak with better insight, not only of affairs of State and military matters but of the intimate life of the Court and matters of the heart touching high persons. Of commerce too, of stationery and shipping and assurance, I was an adept such as no other chronicler could claim to be. I was also an impartial observer, for I did not enter upon any piece of business with a view to advancing myself to the highest place but merely to keep my head above water.

Yet no such person had written that which he was best fitted to write, viz. the story of his own life. No other clerk to the Council had kept a diary or a book of memorials, so far as I knew. I would be the first man to tell the world the aspect of great matters from the underside. Mine should be the worm's-eye view.

The next day, I went to the miserable shop that sold paper in lieu of a stationer proper and bought myself a ledger, quarto, bound in good Dutch leather. It is that which forms the first volume of these memorials and by good fortune I have found a match to it for the subsequent volumes, which together make a handsome set.

. I began writing in the ledger that night and every night thereafter, however tired I might be from the copperas work, which I became somewhat more attuned to as my muscles were exercised by the weight of the paddle and the stiffness of the bellows, though my back ached horribly from bending to rake the stones. Yet my thoughts remained so concentrated upon my toil that I scarce reflected upon the strangest circumstance of all, namely that I was now but five or six miles from the village where I was born and bred. If I climbed to the top of the low hills behind the miserable port, I could see in the distance the village of Churn with its queer spire sailing across the marshes.

Churn – my new surname. How odd it sounded, and yet for that disguise I now gave thanks, for else I had feared lest someone from over the hill should report it back to my friends that Jem was now a common labourer in the copperas works. But as I became accustomed to that labour, I must confess my thoughts did turn to the revolution in my affairs which had brought me back to my own country though in such a sorry state. And here I gave thanks again for that voyage upon which I was now launched. The composition of my memorials brought me an unexpected consolation, viz. that it distracted me from the miseries of my life and transformed them into scenes in a play. I had no histories or encyclopaedias to hand, and the parson was an ignorant man without a library, so that I may be in error about the date of such-and-such a battle and this or that Act of Parliament, and that shall be apologised for in a preface which I shall pen when the whole work is complete and made up into a book, which I trust shall not be till *anno* 1700, for I mean it to be the Chronicle of a Century as I saw it. But if there may be public error in these pages, there is also private truth. For on the recollection of my own experience my memory is exact and each moment comes alive to me again as I re-live it in my brown ledger.

After I had written my portion for that evening, which I reckoned should be 1,000 words that the work might be brought up to the present date before the year was out and compute to a grand sum of 100,000 words, though I fear I have already overshot my target and begin to wonder whether any bookseller will take the book – after I had done, as I say, I would descend into the World's End for a well-earned glass, having put on my old mulberry coat and my canary vest and a clean shirt.

It was a warm night in May when I came into the front room where the customers were wont to gather. I was a little amazed to find it empty, but I heard voices in the back room, which was more private and where men went when they wished to be apart from the common throng of topers.

There I heard a single voice that came to predominate over the others, though it was not loud. Indeed, it was low but seemed magnified into a melodious sound that made the walls hum. I knew the voice, how well I knew it.

No, the voice said, I do not open the gate of Heaven but to those that themselves do knock. If a man ask me to be saved, I shall tell him that it is not I that can do it but he must do it himself, he must let his faith strive together with the guilt of his sin and we shall see which shall be master.

But how then are we to be brought to the true religion?

You must come on your own two feet by using the motion of your own heart and soul.

You mean, by praying?

Oh, you may pray if you wish, but God takes no notice of your prayers.

No notice, sir? That is a cold doctrine.

It is the truth, my friend.

Will he not reward us if we do his bidding and so take notice of us that way?

That is Error – and here the Prophet's voice took on a sharper note – we are to do well not that God may take notice of it and so reward us, but because we do not want to displease that Law which is written in the Heart. This is fine ale, sir, excellent ale.

It is Kentish ale, the best there is, one of the fishermen said, but he spoke mechanically, for evidently his mind was confused by what the Prophet had said.

God takes no notice of us, you say?

I say so.

Does he not come to us upon our deathbed and forgive us our sins if we repent?

I wish that I could say that he did. It would be a consolation, but he does not.

So we are damned to Hell and there is no way out of the bottomless pit for any of us?

The bottomless pit is within a man, not without, and besides, the soul is a mortal thing, dying with the body, and so after death it sleeps until that day when we shall all be raised or damned. You said that Mrs Splint had some fresh cheese, from Canterbury, I believe?

Yes, yes, I will ask for some and for bread too.

One of the hearers came past me – it was Prosper Smith – and there was a puzzled gaze upon his face, yet he seemed also uplifted, as I had seen men and women so often uplifted before, women most especially, although in his doctrine there were none but males in Heaven.

To let him go past me, I had to come out into the middle of the passage where the Prophet could see me and I him.

He sat in the middle of the bench, upright, unbowed by age, his long red hair now turned to grey lichen, with his lips sucking on his old clay pipe but his face still commanding, his lineaments still as carved as an Indian's, his eye still as a hawk's. He must have been above eighty years of age.

So, Jeremiah, you are come here.

He spoke without amazement, though it was thirty years and more since we had met. He did not mean to say that the hand of Providence had brought us together, or any such thing as another preacher might have said. Here I was, there was no mystery in it. Yet him saying so seemed to make it a wonderful thing.

This gentleman when he was young got my letter to the Lord Mayor printed at his own charge. At that time he was a Ranter, were you not?

Of that company but not one of them.

The Prophet, like his God, paid no notice to me on this fine point.

But you heard the words that God spake to John Reeve, didn't you, and you believed that it was the voice of God and asked for John Reeve's blessing?

I did.

There were many such in those days, desperate atheistical ranters who proclaimed that God was in a table-chair or a stool, but they came to believe, most of them, that we were the two last Prophets and Witnesses of the Spirit. Ah, here's the cheese and do I perceive a mutton pie, there's nothing like Kentish mutton.

He put down his pipe and began to eat, in his slow ruminative fashion. At first the topers watched him as though his eating were some miraculous event. Then they began to talk among themselves about matters of the day – how one boat had lost its mast in the great wind, how some said Tomkinson's oysters were bad – and the Prophet joined in the conversation, quietly as a visitor must do. And I could see how amazed they were that a Prophet should be so curious as to material things and should not wish to be always preaching and proselytising.

When he had finished, he looked at me and said:

I want to know something of what's befallen you since we last met, but tonight I'm weary, we'll talk of it tomorrow. Let us walk upon the shore.

At these words, my whole body seemed filled with light and as though emptied of weight. Perhaps it was only that I was tired after long hours raking the beds, for the boilers were not lit that day. Perhaps it was that and the ale too. Perhaps it was that it was so long since any man had asked after me not for advantage, but I fell into a kind of swoon and toppled over upon the floor where I sat as though felled by a blow.

At any other time, they would have said I was drunk, but now there was a hush as though we were at prayer and some man said: Lord preserve us.

Let us hope that he may, the Prophet said, but we have no right to expect it.

He rose from his seat and pulled me to my feet and shook my hand. And even in these simple motions there was such grave majesty that the rest of them gasped as though he had performed some magical trick. And I too who had shaken off the shackles of superstition so many years before felt the old power flow from his fingers into mine.

Go in peace, the Prophet said.

And I stumbled up the stairs, and fell upon my bed in my mulberry coat and was asleep in a minute, a long sweet sleep, the sleep of a careless boy.

The next morning I rose refreshed and came downstairs expecting to be before the Prophet, but Mrs Splint told me it was nearly nine o'clock and he was already gone out.

I went out on to the shingles and at first could see nobody, but then an old woman coming up from the Swale to gather goldstones told me that she had seen an old man walking that way. I went up to where the shore became the bank of the river and the shingles were heaped high and there I saw him, an immense figure suffused with golden light, for it was a fine morning and the sun shone full upon him. So bright was the light that his hair seemed reddened once more and to me he was as he had once been in that tavern in the Minories (though to a stranger he might have looked like an old man stumbling upon the pebbles).

Good-morrow, Jeremiah, these pebbles make hard walking.

There's a path behind.

I like to be by the sea. Now let us sit down and you shall tell me your tale.

So we sat upon the high bank of shingles and I began to tell the history of my life since we had last met, which I did with some fluency, for I had spent the past year writing it in these journals and was now all but arrived at the present day. He asked me no questions concerning my narrative, but sat there motionless as though he had been carved of oak.

I feared the old man and did not wish to annoy him. Yet I wished also to seem not inconsiderable or petty in his eyes, for he had always esteemed me as a gentleman set apart from most of his disciples, and so – it was pure folly – I began to embroider my narrative:

On my coming back to England from Jamaica, I said, I continued my practice in assurance and became well known on Change as a man of business. But after some years I wearied of the town and meeting a kinsman on Tower Hill I took the position in his copperas factory that he offered me. The work is hard, but it is exceeding useful, for green vitriol is the source of ink and dye and also the mordant that keeps the dye fast –

But the Prophet was not much interested in the uses of vitriol. I could see that his mind was fixed elsewhere.

You have travelled far, Jeremiah.

So I have.

And have you met many of our faith in your wanderings?

I met a Mr Lucas in Jamaica, with whom I smoked a pipe or two. He was well acquainted with your teachings.

We have friends everywhere, but they are few and scattered. The expenses of travel in these times are very heavy.

They are so.

At my age, I cannot travel far but by coach. My legs will not tolerate much walking.

Just so.

Our loyal friends in the faith are honest people, but they are not rich, for they do not whore after the things of this world but content themselves with plain living. Those blaspheming hypocrites called Quakers are well furnished with money though they pretend to be poor. Now, Jeremiah, I ask you this plainly: you have strayed from the true faith, haven't you, since we last met?

Umm, I said.

You took service with that Antichrist who is now justly abhorred of all men?

It is true I was appointed Clerk to Cromwell's Council, and in that office I could not very well –

I will hear no more of it, the Prophet said with a grand sweep of his hand. The flesh is weak and ambition is a scarlet temptress. I perceive that you are an honest-hearted man at bottom.

I hope I may say I am.

I, Lodowick Muggleton, say you are an honest-hearted man and I will give you room to prove it.

How so?

I ask you a simple thing, a convenient matter, namely, that you should hire me a coach that I may travel about Kent upon God's work. Thus you may say that you have given wings to God's last true prophet that is alive upon this earth. Mr Powell in Bread Street will let me have his carriage for five pounds the month or seven pound ten shillings for two months.

I would willingly help you, but I have no money.

No money? Don't trifle with me. I saw you in your fine mulberry coat lording it in the tavern last night. Don't tell me you have no money.

It is an old coat, sir, I had it when I was with the Lord General, and I have spent all my wages in the tavern and owe Mrs Splint five shillings beside.

You're a canting hypocrite, Jeremiah. Didn't you tell me that you were a prosperous man of business in the marine insurance in London and you were in command of a great manufactory here?

It was all embellishment, sir.

So you lie to me first and then you deny me. You are a treacherous toad that puffeth yourself up and then shrivels into a nothing when asked of your charity to assist your loving friend in the Lord.

It is not denial, it is poverty.

I do not believe you. You are a mannikin, sir, a worthless mannikin.

Well then, I retorted, angered by his words, I do not believe you are God's Last Messenger and I would not pay for your coach even if I had the money which I have not.

WHAT?

The Prophet rose up, somewhat unsteady upon his legs but towering above me none the less, though I am a tall man.

Whoso lies to me and denies me lies to the Lord and denies the Lord. And seeing God hath chosen me his Last True Prophet and hath set me in his place here upon earth, to give judgement upon all lying hypocritical spirits who deny me as they would deny him, *therefore* (and here his voice rose to a mighty resonance that seemed to rebound upon the far shore of the river and return to us again), therefore I do pronounce Jeremiah Mount cursed and damned, soul and body, from the presence of God, elect men and angels, to eternity.

But –

I tell you, Jeremiah Mount, that your soul shall die two deaths: the first death is natural, the second death is eternal, and when God shall raise you again in the resurrection, which to the dead will not last above a quarter of an hour, you shall pass through the first death into the second where the worm of conscience shall never die nor the fire of Hell go out, in utter darkness, where there is weeping and gnashing of teeth for evermore. And you shall remember you were told so by the Last True Prophet and Witness of the Spirit, Lodowick Muggleton.

With these words the Prophet stepped down off the shingles and began to walk back to Whitstable at a stately pace leaning upon his stick. I sat upon the shingles and watched him go. When he was a hundred yards distant, he turned about and shouted at me again:

You're a mannikin, sir, a mannikin.

At least I think that is what he said, but his words were half-drowned by the noise of the tide upon the pebbles. Then he walked on and was lost to my sight behind the bank of shingles.

It is not every day that a man is cursed to all eternity in such a high style, and for a time I was breathless as though a horse had kicked me in the belly. But then, when he was out of sight, the old worm began to burrow within me, I mean the worm of doubt not of conscience. How did he know that there would be only a quarter of an hour to the dead between the first death and the second death? Might it not seem like forty minutes or an hour or two? And how could I be consumed by the fire of Hell and the worm not be consumed also? And how could the darkness be utter if the fire was so fierce? Then I saw what foolishness it was that he should call me mannikin when his God was but five foot high (how dwarfish he would have looked besides the Prophet) and his Heaven was six miles up in the sky, and I laughed and lay upon the shingle and threw pebbles into the sparkling water so that they danced upon it like swallows.

And it came to me then that liberty was the most precious thing to have. I did not mean freedom from prophets and preachers only, or from superstition, but freedom from all connection that may tether a man. It came to me also that a man prospers when he follows the promptings of his heart and not the calculations of his brain and that I had been most fortunate in the company of those who had followed that receipt, I mean Nan and Peter Llewelyn and Will Symons and Samson Lucas, for the wandering star shines brightest. And the

Epilogue

But here the manuscript breaks off and another hand has written in a more flowing script:

These books removed for safe keeping
R. M. Whitstable, 17 May, 1695

On turning the page, I found an ancient newspaper cutting pasted in, so faded as to be scarcely legible and looking to be of much the same date as the manuscript. What it said was:

> *A strange and tragical accident interrupted the visit to Whitstable of the proprietor of a copperas factory at that fair port. Mr Richard Mount of the Mendfield House had purposed to inspect the works with his wife and a party of ladies and gentlemen from London, when a mechanic employed to run the copperas into coolers by a gross mischance slipped in up to his breast. Every assistance was given by Mr Knewstub, the manager of the works, and his men, but in twenty-four hours a mortification ensued and two hours after the man died at the World's End, a tavern kept by Mrs Abigail Splint, where he lodged. His name was J. Churn.*

'How would Richard Mount have got hold of the memoirs?'

'Oh,' my fellow editor replied without hesitation, 'he would have been quick to go through Jem's things, to prepare himself for any revelations which might damage his social position, he had to destroy any incriminating material. He could have told Mrs Splint that he was anxious to make sure Mr Churn's possessions were sent on to his relatives.'

'Do you think she noticed the mysterious Mr Churn's resemblance to Richard? Did Knewstub?'

'They probably both did, but people were used to that kind of thing then. They'd hold their tongues to keep their job,' Doddy said.

'Anyway, RM's son and his grandson kept the Mendfield House for most of the following century, so it worked out all right for them. Jem was like Banquo, I suppose, met an untimely death.'

'". . . thou shalt get Kings though thou be none." Anyway, not so very untimely. By my calculations he was well into his sixties.'

'Did Richard read it all, do you think?'

'Yes, I imagine so, just to see what else he might find out about his father.'

'In that case,' I asked, 'why didn't he burn the memoirs after he had read them? I mean, they aren't exactly a credit to the family name.'

'No, I expect it was a kind of, well, piety,' Doddy suggested. 'Here was the last, the only record of his true parentage and it would have been somehow sacrilegious to get rid of it.'

I was not convinced by this and pressed on: 'And why did Jem fall in the cooler? He must have known those platforms and ladders pretty well by then. You don't normally hear of older workmen having the bad accidents. It's usually the younger men, the ones who are more impetuous in their movements.'

'Perhaps he was running to see his son,' Doddy hazarded.

'Or running away so as not to be seen by him.'

'To spare him embarrassment, you think?'

'Or not to be too much moved by seeing him again?'

'You think so?' Doddy said. 'I think you're giving Jem credit for too much delicacy.'

'Not me,' I said.

The archivist *extraordinaire* looked at me, grunted or smiled – perhaps both – and said he had to nip out to the bank before it closed.

After he had gone, an odd heaviness fell upon me. I felt almost paralysed and sat quite still for a minute or two, expecting the feeling to pass which it did but only to be succeeded by a clumsy restlessness. I stood up and began packing away the transcripts and the other papers and reference books we had been working on, but with a weird flurry as if there was some sort of closing time imminent. While I was shaking a pile of papers level on the table, my elbow knocked against the dumpy oak box and sent it crashing to the floor. I picked it up, put it back on the table, then began to put the original ledgers back in it. As I settled the last one in, there was a squeaky noise from the bottom of the box, quite faint and rather human, the kind of noise you might make when a child punches you in the stomach. I stood motionless for a few seconds. The noise seemed like a tiny protest. Then I took the ledgers out again, one by one, and felt the bottom of the box.

There was a bit of give in the bottom and another squeak, fainter still, when I pushed it down until there was no give left in it.

I put the box upside down and rapped it firmly on the bottom a couple of times. There was a slapping sound. Holding the box at an angle, I could see the delicately hinged flap that had come loose when the box had fallen. Prising it up with the tips of my fingers, I saw into the secret compartment.

How could we have been so stupid as not to realise that Jem would have been using one of his old captain's portable libraries for his own?

There were only two objects in the secret compartment: a dusty, roundish thing and a piece of paper. The round thing had a minimal fragrance when I held it in my hand. It was shrivelled and studded with tiny black twiggy bits. When I blew the dust off it and held it to my nose, the fragrance seemed more familiar. I pulled off one of the tiny twigs and bit it. Cloves. A pomander. The one Nan gave him after his first visit to the Three Spanish Gypsies. I put the pomander back in the box and took out a piece of paper: stained, torn at one corner, the brown ink so faded that I had to take it to the window to read it. There were two lines of writing on it: the first easily legible in a tidy clerk's hand: 'To John Capps of HMS *Lion* seven pounds ten shillings'. Then below it, in a hastier scrawl: 'paid to Mr Pepys'.

Notes

I   The Marsh

Jem is describing here the marshes of North Kent, between Canterbury and the Isle of Thanet, then as now a queer cut-off place with flint-and-ragstone churches rearing out of the low swampland, ancient, marooned, aloof, while half a mile away lorries roar by on their way to the Channel ports. Many of Jem's kinsmen grow apples there to this day. Mount is still a common name in the Canterbury telephone book. The weirdness of Romney Marsh – which lies to the south-east on the other side of the North Downs – is legendary and noted by Wells, Dickens and Kipling (the saying 'The world, according to the best geographers, is divided into Europe, Asia, Africa, America and Romney Marsh' is first found in *The Ingoldsby Legends*, 1840–7). But the marshes round Churn are stranger still. Something about the sea light perhaps.

Although Jem gives no date, these fears of Dutch competition and of actual invasion must date from the late 1640s, when Jem would have been about sixteen. He nowhere gives us his date of birth, and the Churn parish register for those years has long been lost. The First Dutch War did not break out until 1652. It was in the Second Dutch War (1665-7) that Jem played a remarkable if brief part.

The erotic works mentioned here as part of Jem's stock have mostly disappeared, apart from *Aretine's Postures*, and *The Night-Walker*, a bestseller of the day. *Waggoners Pilot* was the standard series of chart-books which preceded *The English Pilot* and, later, *Great Britain's Coasting Pilot*, of which we shall hear more. Waggoner was an Anglicisation of the Dutch surname *Waghenaer*. Many of the best early sea-charts were Dutch and accordingly pirated by unscrupulous English publishers, including Mount & Page.

II   The Shop

John Aubrey also quotes the verse about the Five Women-Barbers in his portrait of General Monck. Like many other chroniclers of the time, he is scornful of Nan's origins. Snobbery, a fruitful failing in a diarist, tends to handicap historians.

The Three Spanish Gypsies seems to have been one of the most successful mercer's shops of its day. Yet its proprietor Thomas Radford has disappeared into thin air. Even in his own time, nobody knew when he died or what happened to his fortune.

William Fisher, Jr, had been in business as a stationer on Postern Row, Tower Hill, since the late 1630s. It was this same business that Richard was to marry into and bequeath to his sons.

Postern Row was a row of houses that formerly stood in the middle of the present roadway on the north side of the Tower and had once ended at the Postern Gate of the old City wall. After the wall was demolished, Postern Row remained for another century and was itself demolished only in the nineteenth century when the road was widened as an approach to the new Tower Bridge. Apart from the premises in Postern Row, Richard Mount also owned a house at the back, in George Yard, where there was a toll bar (no doubt to compensate for the expense originally incurred in breaking through the wall), and the family collected the fees until 1766, when Parliament passed an Act to demolish the remainder of the wall and all the City gates. When becalmed in traffic beside the Tower, I like to think of Richard and his sons coming home from business in the evening and looking in at the tollbooth to inquire about the day's takings.

The menagerie in the Tower of London continued in existence from Edward I's time until 1834, when the last animals were moved to the new London Zoo.

The story of Jeremiah's first meetings with the Two Messengers is described in *The Acts of the Witness of the Spirit of Lodowick Muggleton* (II.5 and III.4). Apart from the meeting recorded here, other contacts must have occurred for years after Jem lost his faith, because there is even a reference to one in the *Calendar of State Papers: Charles II– 4, Oct. 28 1663*: '68. Jer. Mount to Mr Muggleton, of London. Private affairs. Sends letters to be forwarded.' Yet there is nothing of this connection even in the immortal edition of Pepys's Diary by R. C. Latham and W. Matthews, to which all Pepysians owe an unending debt. To this day, Jeremiah has succeeded in keeping dark his Muggletonian past. It was no way to get on in the Restoration Civil Service.

Mary Court married Ralph Mount in January 1654. Jem, unreliable in so much else, usually gets his dates right.

It may seem odd to us that General Monck should have been sent to command the fleet, knowing little or nothing of naval tactics or indeed of the sea. But life was less compartmented then, and Monck did beat the

Dutch in this the First Dutch war. The Second Dutch War a decade later, when Monck was Commander-in-Chief, did not go so well.

III   The Palace

The Cockpit, where Jem lodges in Peter Llewelyn's old rooms, stood roughly where the Cabinet Office now stands. Much the same business is carried on there today, but only a few fragments of the old buildings remain.

I do not understand why the French should have complained that the London smog was blighting their vines, when the prevailing wind was then as now in precisely the opposite direction.

On 16 December 1653, Oliver Cromwell was declared by the Instrument of Government to be 'Lord Protector for his life'. Among many other palaces and states, Hampton Court and Whitehall were vested in 'the present Lord Protector and the succeeding Lord Protectors'. Cromwell took up residence at Hampton Court in April 1654, with several squatters from Kingston still *in situ*. Parliament allotted him £54,000 a year for the upkeep of his estates, rising to £100,000 in the last year of his life. Furniture and works of art valued at £35,497 which had belonged to Charles I were put at his disposal. Three of his daughters, Betty, Mary and Frances, and their husbands all had lodgings in Hampton Court.

This first meeting between Jem and Sam must have taken place some time in 1655, because Pepys and Elizabeth were married in December that year.

IV   The Barge

Alan Broderick, a drunken crony of Clarendon's, told his master that Nan was an 'extreme good woman' and 'because it was (as she saith frankly) her old trade, she would save the king half in buying linen for his tables and beds' (*Clarendon State Papers iii.739*). Others were not so appreciative. Thurloe described Nan as 'an ugly common whore', and Pepys could not stand her. Her greed on behalf of her relatives was much remarked on, though such behaviour was the norm among those of nobler birth than Nan.

While sailing with Mountagu to fetch the King, Pepys had been put in charge of his patron's eldest son, Edward ('the child'), then aged twelve, who kept on disappearing during their visits to Delft and the Hague, partly because Pepys was trying to pick up a woman. He had no luck.

Edward Mountagu, Earl of Sandwich (1625-72) was the son of a Royalist but himself joined the Parliamentary side, fought at Marston

Moor and Naseby and then retired to his estates at Hinchingbrooke before returning to politics as a moderate friend and ally of Cromwell's in the 1650s. Tired of revolutionary instability, he went over to the King and brought him back from exile and was accordingly showered with honours. As an Admiral, he won a brilliant victory at Lowestoft in the Second Dutch War, then fell out of favour, but resumed his command in the Third Dutch War, though opposed to it, and died in the Battle of Sole Bay. Linguist, musician and artist, he shared many of Pepys's tastes, and traits – being talented, secretive, lecherous and ambitious – but they drifted apart before his death. His mother was Paulina, the daughter of John Pepys of Cottenham, usually described as Samuel's aunt, in fact, great-aunt, but by a slippage of the generations Sandwich was only eight years older than his first cousin once removed, the tailor's son, and on occasion Sam was not too subservient to shrink from giving 'my lord' unwelcome advice, such as that he must give up his mistress.

Sir John Robinson (1625-80) was Lieutenant of the Tower for nearly twenty years after the Restoration. He had been a colonel in the Civil War and Master of the Clothworkers' Company. Pepys shared Jem's opinion of him. His interminable views on the traffic problems of the City were a well-known conversational hazard of the day.

V   The Tower
Before the Civil War, the Palace had no less than three tennis courts. After the Restoration, one was converted into Monmouth's lodgings, another which had been converted under the Commonwealth into a garden belonging to Sandwich's apartments was converted back into a tennis court, much to his annoyance, by Captain Thomas Cooke, Master of the Tennis Court for nearly forty years. There is no record of his employing M. de la Tuile. Charles II was an extremely keen player. It is hard to tell quite how good he was; Pepys says: 'To see how the King's play was extolled without any cause at all was a loathsome sight though sometimes indeed he did play very well and deserved to be commended; but such open flattery is beastly.' The King liked to weigh himself before and after playing. After the game, he had sweated off 4½ pounds. Prince Rupert was also a keen player.

The Counter or Compter was the name given to the two prisons owned by the City and used for the punishment of civil offences, one in Great Wood Street, the other in Poultry. Both were destroyed in the Fire and rebuilt.

Alexander (d. 1672) and Dorothea (b. 1609) St Michel: he was the son of a minor nobleman of Anjou, disinherited for turning Protestant and so came to England. After being dismissed from Henrietta Maria's court, he went to Ireland where he married, in about 1639, Dorothea who was the widow of Thomas Fleetwood of Co. Cork. The children, Elizabeth and Balthazar – the erratic Balty – are said to have been born in Devon.

Prince Rupert (1619-82), son of the Elector Frederick and James I's daughter Elizabeth. Commanded the Royalist Navy (1648-52) and was an Admiral in the Second and Third Dutch Wars, as brilliant a naval commander as he had been as a cavalry leader in the Civil War. Also a keen entrepreneur and trader, engraver and scientific dabbler or 'projector', the pejorative term used by his critics.

Will Hewer (1642-1715) was Pepys's office-boy-cum-manservant, then moved with Pepys to the Admiralty in 1673, becoming Chief Clerk in 1674 and Judge Advocate-General in 1677. He was also briefly imprisoned by the incoming regime in 1679, used the same shorthand as his old master, and kept a diary (mostly lost). He made a huge fortune, no one is quite sure how. Bought what is now No. 12 Buckingham Street, then York Buildings, and shared it with Pepys. Also bought a country house in Clapham which he filled with Indian and Chinese curiosities and of which we are to hear more.

James Pierce was in fact the most celebrated naval surgeon of the day. He had been surgeon in the *Naseby* before the Restoration, rose to become Surgeon-General of the Fleet in the Second and Third Dutch Wars. Introduced hospital ships and the keeping of proper medical records. His report on the treatment of the sick and wounded is a landmark in military medicine. He was also surgeon to the Duke of York and other members of the royal household, hence his fund of gossip. His beautiful wife Elizabeth bore him nineteen children.

VI   The Laboratory

The stained-glass window of Catherine of Aragon and the wretched Prince Arthur, originally intended for Henry VII's chapel at Westminster, first found its way to Waltham Abbey, then at the Dissolution of the Monasteries was transferred to Beaulieu and buried underground to preserve it from destructive Puritans, and then transferred again to New Hall at the Restoration. In the eighteenth century, it was sold to a Mr Conyers for £50, who in turn sold it to the parishioners of St Margaret's, Westminster for 400 guineas. Today the window forms the East window of St Margaret's, Westminster. It is the most beautiful window in London and one of the strangest survivals. New Hall still stands, or a large part of it does, a low rambling palace outside Chelmsford. Since 1799, it has been the property of the canonesses of the Holy Sepulchre, which is a nice revenge on the atheist Bucks.

In most respects, the Duke of Buckingham, 'fiddler, chemist, buffoon', was, as Dryden says, everything by starts and nothing long, but his passion was at least sustained in two fields: women and chemistry, of the applied sort (he hoped to make some money out of the latter to pay for the former). He took out a patent for making mirrors, drinking glasses and coach glasses and imported Venetian workmen for his Lambeth factory.

The Chelmsford doctor's decoction of willow bark was in fact a primitive form of aspirin, quite common at the time although it took modern science another two centuries to manufacture an artificial compound (acetylsalicylic acid) with the same effects as were clearly spelled out by Culpeper. The word Aspirin is first found in 1899.

Throughout the Great Plague, it was frequently rumoured that evil men who knew they had the Plague would spend their last few days consorting with those they had grudges against. Many similar stories have been told during the Aids epidemic, but few actual cases proven, then or now.

Despite the glass case, the Lord Mayor of London, Sir John Laurence, was on the whole thought to have had a 'good Plague', as, of course, had Monck, Pepys, Evelyn and anyone else who stayed in London.

The ring was indeed left to Jem in Peter Llewelyn's will, though it was not there described.

The Great Fire shows Pepys at his best: quick, decisive, inventive. As soon as he saw that nobody was doing anything effective to combat it, he went straight to the King at Whitehall, got his permission to create firebreaks by demolishing buildings that lay in the Fire's path, then rushed back to the Lord Mayor whom he met in Canning Street 'like a man spent, with a handkerchief about his neck'. To the King's message, he cried like a fainting woman 'Lord, what can I do? I am spent. People will not obey me. I have been pulling down houses. But the fire overtakes us faster than we can do it.' It was not until the King and the Duke came down in person that afternoon that the orders began to be obeyed, by which time the fire was unstoppable. Even then, Pepys managed to save the Navy Office by getting dockyard hands from Woolwich and Deptford to blow up the houses round about.

Pepys was just as much taken by surprise as everyone else by the Dutch raid up the Medway. Although he had had reliable report on the Saturday of a Dutch fleet of eighty sail off Harwich and of gunfire heard to the north-east of London the night before, he spent an agreeable weekend, including a visit to his mistress Mrs Martin, and a boat-trip up the river. It was only on the Monday that he rushed down to Deptford to get the ships ready. When he returned to London and, on the Wednesday, heard that the Dutch had broken the chain, he decided to send his wife and father into the country immediately with £1,300 in gold in their night-bag. His clerk Gibson was sent off to Huntingdon with 1,000 guineas. Pepys himself wore an extremely cumbersome girdle containing £300 in gold. He also had £200 in silver coin, which was too bulky to carry. He thought of throwing it into the earth closet but worried about how to get it out again.

Commissioner Peter Pett (1610-72) succeeded his father as Navy Commissioner (superintendent of the dockyard) at Chatham. Since the family almost monopolised offices in the Thames yards, they had already come under attack for corruption and embezzlement, and it was natural that he should be made scapegoat for the disaster of the Medway. As Marvell put it in *Last Instructions to a Painter*:

> After this loss, to relish discontent,
> Some one must be accused by Parliament;
> All our miscarriages on Pett must fall;
> His name alone seems fit to answer all.

There then follows a bravura sequence of rhyming couplets, each detailing some fresh blunder and the last word of each being 'Pett'.

Yet afterwards Pett was merely sent to the Tower for a short time, then examined by the House of Commons, and finally, despite talk of impeachment, allowed to retire into private life – one of those examples of the capriciousness of retribution in public life that often surprise one's expectations.

VII   The Hospital

Nan died at the end of January 1670, two months after Elizabeth Pepys, three weeks after her husband and a month after her son's wedding. Elizabeth was buried in St Olave's, Hart Street, the Navy Office church. A poignant bust of her, showing the liquid eyes and goofy teeth, is skied on the north wall of the chancel. Nan was buried alongside her husband in the Henry VII Chapel, where her son and daughter-in-law later came to join her.

The Committee for Accounts, later called the Brooke House Committee from its meeting place, was nominated at the end of 1667 to inquire into the misconduct of the war and, more generally, the management of the Navy, but it did not get into its stride for another two years. Pepys's brilliant performance before the Committee in March 1668 was only an hors d'oeuvre to the hearings in January and February 1670 at which the King intervened to save Pepys and himself. After this, there were no more hearings, and the Committee lapsed when Parliament was adjourned. Richard Ollard's Life of Pepys disentangles the whole imbroglio beautifully.

The murder of the beadle in Whetstone Park presented the King with a difficult choice: either to let off both his beloved Monmouth and old Monck's son or to appease the righteous anger of public opinion. He chose the first, a politically damaging move which was held against him for some time.

New Bedlam was built more or less on the site presently occupied by Liverpool Street Station in fifteen months between April 1675 and July 1676, and continued to be London's leading lunatic asylum, until in 1815 the 122 remaining inmates were transferred by hackney coaches to the third Bethlehem Hospital across the river in St George's Fields at a cost of £18. By a coarse irony, in 1936 this third Bedlam became the Imperial War Museum after the patients moved out to Kent. Cibber's two stone figures, all that remains of the Moorfields Bedlam, still belong to the Bethlem Royal Hospital's Museum at Beckenham.

James Carcase was put in Bedlam for posing as a priest and other eccentric behaviour. He was one of the more popular patients with upper-class visitors, and his book, *Lucida Intervalla*, contains several poems addressed to them. *Lucida Intervalla*, published in a crudely printed edition in 1679, may well be the first book to have been published by a Bedlamite.

The Popish plot, though invented by Titus Oates and eagerly backed by republicans and malcontents such as Shaftesbury and Buckingham, clearly owed a great deal to the fertile imagination of John Scott, and the Dog and Dripping Pan (a real tavern) was probably the centre of operations for the whole business which is marvellously described by Sir Arthur Bryant in *The Years of Peril*, the second part of his great three-volume life of Pepys. We owe much to Pepys himself who became obsessed with Scott and put together two volumes of evidence against that nonpareil of seventeen-century conmen, calling it 'My Book of Mornamont' after an imaginary castle that Scott claimed to possess.

Theories of conception have varied so enormously in the pre-modern era that it sometimes seems as though every fancy which could come into a human brain had been proposed. One of my favourites is the belief practised by French aristocrats that if they bound up their left testicle before intercourse, they would be more likely to conceive a boy, the right side being the dominant or male side. The Duchess's theory was, as Will Symons claimed, common practice at the time, though we may doubt whether it was seriously believed or only a convenient fiction for getting an heir.

There is a fair case to be made for Kit's tactics against Monmouth. By strictly obeying orders and holding back till Monmouth came towards Devon, Kit allowed him to be picked off and defeated decisively. The trouble was that it was not Kit who did the picking off. He was thus blamed for the palpitations the rebellion had caused and given no credit for the victory – a fate often suffered by the first commander in any campaign.

VIII   The Island

Sir William Phipps (1651-95), the restorer of Kit's fortune, began life as a ship's carpenter and later became a merchant captain at Boston, Mass. After his treasure-seeking years, he returned to Massachusetts, where he led several naval expeditions against the French, though he failed to take Montreal. He eventually became Governor of Massachusetts, in which capacity he did nothing much to restrain the witchcraft mania then in full spate.

Richard Mount was bound apprentice to William Fisher on 10 January 1669 when he was barely fourteen years old. He married Sarah Fisher, his employer's daughter, in 1682. In 1684, the name of the business was changed to R. Mount, but it was probably still a partnership, as William Fisher was to live another seven years, though 'very infirm'. Richard began to print *Great Britain's Coasting Pilot* in the 1680s, and the firm continued to reissue the charts for another century or more. The Harwich chart, dedicated to Pepys at the zenith of his fame and power, was one of the earliest, dated 1686.

Hans Sloane (1660-1753) was born in County Down, studied medicine in Paris and Montpellier, was elected Fellow of the Royal Society in 1685 and its Secretary from 1693 to 1712, and later President from 1727 to 1741. He published the two volumes of his great *Natural History of Jamaica* – which is a travelogue as well as a botanical survey – in 1707 and 1725. He became an extremely fashionable physician, being consulted by Queen Anne and almost everyone else. Despite his generosity to poor patients, he grew rich enough to purchase the manor of Chelsea (hence Sloane Street and Hans Place). He bequeathed his collection to the nation. Under the guidance of Horace Walpole and others, this became the nucleus of the British Museum, whose first home, oddly enough, was to be Montague House, where both he and his collection had lodged sixty years earlier. He also founded the Chelsea Physick Garden, and the statue of him by Rysbrack, now much weathered, which used to be in the Physick Garden, now stands indoors in the hall of the present British Museum on the site of the old Montague House.

It may seem peculiar that Sir Henry Morgan should have achieved such respectable status in later life, being known to posterity as a pirate (Captain Morgan's Rum being only one echo of his fame), but the edge of empire was a rough and insecure place. The distinction between privateers, pirates and acknowledged servants of the Crown was blurred, and all assistance in holding territory and exacting tribute was gratefully welcomed. Morgan's terrible massacre at Lake Maracaibo was conducted under the official British auspices of the then governor of Jamaica, Sir Thomas Modyford.

The Muggletonians had a network of supporters across the Empire. Never very numerous and never attracting any socially important adherents, the religion was the only one of the Dissenting sects, apart from the Quakers, to survive the storms of the seventeenth century and to linger on into our own. Once shorn of the primitive materialism of John Reeve, Muggletonianism contained virtually no ritual and was not much encrusted by superstition and thus stood up quite well to the buffetings of nineteenth-century science. The last known Muggletonian, Philip Noakes, a farmer, of Matfield, Kent, died in 1979.

The Prince of Wales, later the Old Pretender, was born on 16 June 1688. Kit died on 6 October 1688. William of Orange landed at Torbay the following month. The Duchess and her party did not set sail until 15 March 1689. They landed at Plymouth on 30 May.

Pepys resigned the Secretaryship of the Admiralty on 20 February 1689, was imprisoned in the Gatehouse between May and July, resigned the Trinity House in August. He was again briefly imprisoned in the Gatehouse the following year before finally retiring into private life.

IX   *The Coffee-House*

Kit's will was the *cause célèbre* of the time, beginning shortly after his death and not being fully resolved until 1709, by which time Lord Bath was dead, Ralph Mountagu was dying and almost all of those who had originally hoped to benefit were dead, except the mad Duchess, who was by then entirely out of her wits.

Coffee was first introduced into England from Arabia and sold in Oxford at various establishments along the High Street in the early 1650s. By the late 1650s, the City was full of coffee-houses. Tea, cocoa, sherbet, and later pills and potions, were also sold. Doctors would call on coffee-houses at specified hours to see their patients. The first mention of Lloyd's coffee-house dates from the end of the 1680s, but marine broking and insurance were no doubt carried on at other coffee-houses, such as Jonathan's and Garraway's, well before that date. The present Stock Exchange is the lineal descendant of Jonathan's, just as the Shipping Exchange originated in the Baltic coffee-house. The remarkable thing about Lloyd's was that it remained a coffee-house throughout nearly a century of its progress towards becoming the world's greatest insurance market. In fact, it seems to have retained something of its old informal character up to the present day, which may help to explain its downfall as well as its long supremacy.

Half the fortune-hunters in the English nobility appear to have paid court to the Duchess in her widowhood. Ralph Mountagu's stratagem sounds incredible, but it is attested to not only by that usually reliable gossip Horace Walpole but by other sources such as Granger's *Biographical History*. The story was also appropriated by several dramatists of the period.

The so-called China trade was in full flood by the end of the seventeenth century, but as early as 1613 a 'cabinet of China worke' was given as a wedding present to Princess Elizabeth, James I's daughter. Gilt cabinets, embroidered cushions, lacquer chests, bedsteads and boxes were already being produced in English workshops, as well as the pseudo-Chinese pottery coming out of Delft and Nevers. London directors of the East India Company began to complain that genuine Indian fabrics being sent over were not suitable for the English market. Patterns had to be sent out to India to show Indian workmen how the English envisaged works 'in the China fashion'. The story took an extra twist when these articles, further cross-bred by the Indian weavers, were then in the eighteenth century exported as novelties to China itself. 'Japanesed' cabinets were made as far north as Scotland and as far west as New England. Blue-and-white chinoiserie jugs and plates were made at Lambeth and Bristol, Chinese tapestries and screens in Soho. The distinction between India, China and Japan was never clearly established in the minds of either customers or designers.

Throughout the war with France which followed the accession of William III and Mary II, British and Dutch merchantmen were constantly harried by French cruisers and privateers. But all previous losses were overshadowed by the disaster which overtook the Smyrna Fleet in May

1693. The 400 vessels had been waiting months for an escort and thought themselves well enough protected by Rooke's 20 men-of-war. But Tourville slipped out of Brest and joined up with the Toulon squadron just round the tip of Portugal and destroyed or captured nearly 200 merchantmen. Although the Dutch, still far ahead in the carrying trade, lost more, the damage to English merchants and underwriters was so shattering that a Bill was brought in to help the underwriters, who included Daniel Defoe, or Foe as he was called in this one of his many diverse ventures. The Bill passed the Commons, but the Lords, influenced by the pleas of the creditors, threw it out, and legislation to regulate insurance had to wait for the second shattering blow a generation later, the South Sea Bubble.

The Mr Harrison mentioned here is Edward Harrison whose *Idea Longitudinis* was one of the first books Richard Mount published; it has never been heard of since. Sixty years later, the firm also published the trail-blazing work of John Harrison (no relation, so far as we know): *The Principle of Mr Harrison's Time-Keeper* (1767). In the furious controversy over the best method of measuring one's easterly or westerly position at sea – a controversy which, through Dava Sobel's little book, has excited our own day almost as much as it excited eighteenth-century England – Mount & Page scored a double hit by publishing not only the most celebrated work by 'Longitude' Harrison but also the works of his unyielding rival, the Astronomer-Royal Sir Nevil Maskelyne, who for so long denied John Harrison the £20,000 price offered by the Longitude Act of 1714. Even if poor Edward Harrison had found the answer, he would have been too early for the prize.

It is not known when Richard Mount acquired his holding in the copperas house at Whitstable, but he must have been doing pretty well, for the Mendfield House was one of the larger establishments in what was a particularly thriving trade at the time. Richard and his heirs continued as proprietors of the Mendfield House until 1791, by which time copperas was about to be replaced by synthetic chemical dyes. Unlike Jem, the rest of the family knew when to sell, which is – a sad fact of life, I think – more important than knowing when to buy.

A plaque still marks the site of these grim early-industrial establishments on the Recreation Ground, Tankerton Road, Whitstable.

X   The Shore

Jem can hardly be blamed for believing that no other Clerk to the Council had kept a journal or a book of memorials. Pepys told only a couple of intimates of his Diary and only Will Hewer knew Shelton's system of shorthand which Pepys used. The Diary, with 'Journal' clearly printed on the spines, languished undeciphered on the shelves of Magdalene College, Cambridge, for more than a century before the successful publication of Evelyn's Diary spurred the dozy dons into action.

Richard Mount lived on until 1722 when he died, at the age of seventy, of a fall from his horse when he was riding over London Bridge. He, like his wife Sarah and her father William Fisher, was buried in St Katharine by the Tower, a church obliterated a hundred years later by the building of Telford's massive new dock. Frugal to the last (his motto was *Prudenter et constanter*), he desired that the £60 which might otherwise have been spent on his funeral be divided among his poorer relatives at Elmstead. Modest his funeral might have been, but there was a sermon preached at it by the celebrated Presbyterian minister John Newman, in which he described Richard as 'a hearty friend to the Societies of Reformation of Manners and Suppression of Vice' who did greatly 'lament the growing wickedness of the Time and Place in which he lived'. Was Richard thinking of his father in these lamentations? The sermon was afterwards printed together with 'Some short heads of advice left by the Deceased to his Children and found under his own hand'. The advice included a warning to 'be very cautious of being decoyed by the specious pretence of projectors or of trusting others too far in the management of any part of your Estate and have a care of adventuring in hazardous undertakings' – all of which was advice that might have been better addressed to Richard's father than to his sons, who turned out to be as prudent as he himself had been.

That eccentric rascal John Dunton, in his memoirs *The Life and Errors of John Dunton* (1705), describes my six-times-great-grandfather thus:

> Mr Mount is not only a moderate, but has a natural antipathy to excess; he hates hoarding either money or goods, and being a charitable man, values nothing but by the use of it, and has a great and tender love for truth. He deals chiefly in paper and sea books, and is a hearty friend to the present government. He was Master of the Stationers Company for three years, 1717–19, and gave the Clock to their Court room.

Such unmitigated virtue was unlikely to be forgiven. I don't know what has become of the clock.